WESTERN

Rugged men looking for love...

Nine Months To A Fortune
Elizabeth Bevarly

Hill Country Hero
Kit Hawthorne

MILLS & BOON

Elizabeth Bevarly is acknowledged as the author of this work
NINE MONTHS TO A FORTUNE
© 2024 by Harlequin Enterprises ULC   First Published 2024
Philippine Copyright 2024   First Australian Paperback Edition 2024
Australian Copyright 2024   ISBN 978 1 038 91778 2
New Zealand Copyright 2024

HILL COUNTRY HERO
© 2024 by Brandi Midkiff
Philippine Copyright 2024   First Published 2024
Australian Copyright 2024   First Australian Paperback Edition 2024
New Zealand Copyright 2024   ISBN 978 1 038 91778 2

® and ™ (apart from those relating to FSC®) are trademarks of Harlequin Enterprises
(Australia) Pty Limited or its corporate affiliates. Trademarks indicated with ® are
registered in Australia, New Zealand and in other countries.
Contact admin_legal@Harlequin.ca for details.

MIX
Paper | Supporting
responsible forestry
FSC® C001695
www.fsc.org

Published by
Harlequin Mills & Boon
An imprint of Harlequin Enterprises (Australia) Pty Limited
(ABN 47 001 180 918), a subsidiary of HarperCollins
Publishers Australia Pty Limited
(ABN 36 009 913 517)
Level 19, 201 Elizabeth Street
SYDNEY NSW 2000 AUSTRALIA

Cover art used by arrangement with Harlequin Books S.A.. All rights reserved.

Printed and bound in Australia by McPherson's Printing Group

Nine Months To A Fortune

Elizabeth Bevarly

MILLS & BOON

Elizabeth Bevarly is the *New York Times* and *USA TODAY* bestselling author of more than eighty books. She has called home such exotic places as Puerto Rico and New Jersey but now lives outside her hometown of Louisville, Kentucky, with her husband and cat. When she's not writing or reading, she enjoys cooking, tending her kitchen garden and feeding the local wildlife. Visit her at elizabethbevarly.com for news and lots of fun stuff.

Visit the Author Profile page
at millsandboon.com.au for more titles.

Dear Reader,

Zane Baston and Sabrina Fortune are learning what to expect when they're expecting, and it's not what they expected at all. First on the list? That they're expecting in the first place! Zane has just finished raising his four brothers, for crying out loud. And the last thing Sabrina has thought about in, oh...ever...is having kids.

But here they are, trying to figure out how to work this co-parenting thing. Cue the disagreements about names and nursery themes and gender-specific toys. It's gonna be a long gestation.

Eventually, though, they realize that when it comes to starting a family, the most important thing is, well, family. They'll do whatever it takes to ensure their twins (yes, twins!) have the best of everything there is.

I had so much fun writing about Zane and Sabrina and the fabulous Fortune family. I hope you have as much fun reading about them.

All the best,

Elizabeth

DEDICATION

For David. Again. And Eli. Again.
Because how could I write about family
without both of you being there with me?
Love you guys.

CHAPTER ONE

Sabrina Fortune was panicking. And pacing. But mostly panicking.

Eyes fixed on the phone timer that was slowly—too slowly—ticking down the seconds, she carefully placed one foot in front of the other to make her way across her bedroom. It should have been an easy trek, considering she still didn't have her new place completely furnished, and the only obstacles in the room were the bed, dresser and slipper chair she'd brought from her much smaller condo in Dallas when she'd joined her family here in Chatelaine Hills. And all of those were pretty minimalist style, so it was all barely there to begin with.

She really did need to buy some furniture to fill in the currently very sparsely furnished luxe log cabin she'd been calling home for almost a month. Ever since her mother, Wendy—after discovering she was a long-lost member of the famous Fortune family—bought a ranch in Chatelaine, Texas, and convinced her six children to join her in living on it. Sabrina had been the last to arrive in the tiny lakefront town and was still getting acclimated to her job as the ranch accountant. But her mother and siblings already had a million plans for the place, including, but not limited to, a dairy business, some sheep, a petting zoo, which— Sabrina hoped, since it would help her out with the fiber arts therapy camp she herself wanted to start—might even include some goats and alpacas and llamas, and…and…

And where was she?

Right. Panicking. And pacing so anxiously that her steps were becoming even more erratic than her thoughts. *Anxious* and *erratic* weren't words people normally used to describe her. Sabrina Windham—no, Sabrina *Fortune*, she corrected herself, since her mother had also convinced all of the Windham children to change their last names, too—was normally the most forthright, most do-right, most upright…most up*tight*, some had said, though naturally she didn't agree with that—and she didn't like feeling anxious and erratic now. But it wasn't exactly surprising in light of the news she'd received that morning. News she still couldn't quite believe. Hence the pacing and the timer and the frazzled nerves. When she bumped her hip against the edge of her bed's footboard *again*, she decided to leave the bedroom and move out into the hallway, where she would have better room to pace some more.

She studied the timer on her phone as she stepped through the door. Three minutes and thirty-eight seconds to go. The instructions for the home pregnancy test she'd picked up at a convenience store on her way home from the doctor this morning said she would have results in five to ten minutes, but not to wait any longer than that or she might get a false positive result. No way did she want to risk a false positive result. She didn't even want a true positive result. But she hadn't wanted to be hasty, either, and check right at five minutes, just in case that wasn't quite enough time and might give a false negative when what she really wanted was a true negative, so eight minutes seemed like a good compromise, and—

Breathe, Sabrina, breathe.

She closed her eyes and inhaled deeply through her mouth, then exhaled slowly through her nose. She'd read somewhere that that was what you were supposed to do when you were panicking. And boy was she panicking.

With measured steps, she walked past the two bedrooms on the other side of her own master suite, past the guest bath and the small den she was gradually turning into a home office. Then she turned to pace back again. She'd honestly been wondering what she was going to do with all this extra space, since the six guesthouses lining Lake Chatelaine that had come with the ranch—and which were now being occupied by Sabrina and her five siblings—were, in her opinion, way too big for one person. But it was looking like Mother Nature might have an idea—at least for Sabrina's own not-so-crowded house. Biting her lip, she looked at her phone again.

One minute and seventeen seconds to go.

She couldn't be pregnant, she told herself for perhaps the hundredth time in a matter of hours. Especially not *twelve weeks* pregnant. She didn't care what her gynecologist had told her that morning. There was simply no way Sabrina Fortune could have gotten knocked up. She'd only had sex one time in the last three years—which, okay, had been twelve weeks ago—and they'd used protection. Correctly, too, if memory served, though, admittedly, in the heat of the moment—and there had been *a lot* of heated moments that night—things, and condoms, could go awry. But she'd had irregular periods ever since getting her first when she was twelve. Just because she'd missed the last two, that didn't mean she was pregnant...

Twenty-two seconds to go.

She'd left the test in the master bathroom because she hadn't wanted to be tempted to watch the results as they materialized. They weren't going to materialize—at least not in the positive. Because she wasn't pregnant. She couldn't be.

Nine…eight…seven…six…

Hastily, Sabrina made her way back to the other end of the hall, into her bedroom and the en suite bath. Her phone's timer sounded just as she stepped over the threshold, a series of gentle beeps that erupted in her ears like the banging of a fireworks finale. The little plastic test tray was sitting on the edge of the sink where she'd left it, looking completely innocuous in the soft white light reflecting off the pale blue walls. At least, it looked innocuous until she drew close enough to see the results.

A perfect pink plus sign. Sabrina Fortune was indeed pregnant.

Strangely, upon seeing her own personal confirmation of what her doctor had already told her—and what she had been so determined to mire herself in denial about until she could prove it to herself—her anxiety evaporated, to be replaced by… Something else. She wasn't sure what. She only knew she wasn't panicking anymore. The sight of that little plus sign was just so…surreal. Everything suddenly seemed to shift, as if the floor beneath her tilted, and she tumbled into another world that looked like the one she was used to, but didn't feel like the same place at all. She might as well have been the only person who even existed in this strange new world.

Well, her and the life that was growing inside her.

Without thinking, she splayed her hand open over her belly, as if trying to find some kind of bodily proof, too, of what the test had just told her. But nothing felt different. She wondered how long it would be before anyone would be able to tell.

She shoved her phone into the pocket of the beige shirtwaist she'd donned that morning—since she'd planned to go to work after seeing her doctor—and ran restless fingers through her pale blond bangs.

Gingerly, she picked up the test tray, cradling it in her palm as if it were a sacred jewel. Then she went back down the hall to her home office to sit down at her desk. She pushed aside the handwritten figures from the ranch's previous accountant that she'd been trying to decipher yesterday—way back when she thought she was only seeing her gynecologist today to make sure this latest double-period-skipping wasn't something more concerning—and set the sliver of plastic at the center of her desk. Then she withdrew her phone again and snapped a quick photo. The little pink plus sign would fade soon, and the way she felt now, she might need evidence to convince herself later of what she still didn't quite want to believe.

She was pregnant. Twelve weeks. Almost to the day. She knew that, because it had been twelve weeks since she attended a glitzy fundraiser for a children's rodeo right here in Chatelaine, at the posh Chatelaine Hills Hotel and Resort. May 30. She'd never forget that date. Now it was September 2. How could it be more than three months since she met Zane Baston, the wealthy rancher with the dreamy green eyes who also lived right here in Chatelaine. Talk about tall, dark and handsome. Zane was all those things and then some. From the moment their gazes connected, something white hot had arced through the air between them, setting fire to a place inside her that had been cold for too long. As if they were two halves of a whole that had been separated for eons and were finally being pulled back together again. And, wow, had the two of them been pulled together that night. There were parts of Sabrina that were still sizzling, three months later. She'd never met a man like him.

And now that man was trying to pull a land grab of a small parcel of lakefront property that abutted the Fortune Ranch. A parcel of land Sabrina had already purchased and had big plans for but hadn't been able to claim yet because Zane Baston had some of his cronies at town hall doing everything they could to negate the sale so that he could claim the land for himself. Sabrina could scarcely believe her property nemesis was the same man she met that night three months ago. Except he thought he was dealing with Sabrina Fortune, she knew, and not the Sabrina Windham he'd met that night.

She closed her eyes again, but this time it was to envision what she'd written off twelve weeks ago as just one of those things, like the old song said. She'd never planned on seeing Zane again after that night, because she knew she'd be returning to Dallas in the morning. The only reason she'd come to the fundraiser in the first place was to check out the little town her mother had been raving about for months. Then again, now that she thought about it, being sure she'd never see Zane again might have been why she'd let things go too far that night.

She still couldn't believe they'd ended up in bed together. Sabrina was never that impetuous. Never that spontaneous. Of the six Fortune siblings, she'd always been The Cautious One. Especially after—

Well, suffice to say that for the last ten years, Sabrina had made it an extra fine point to live her life carefully. Thoughtfully. Deliberately. She seldom dated, and what few relationships—if she could even call them that— she had managed to develop over the years had all ended quickly when both she and her potential partner realized how hard it was for her to open herself up to an emotional commitment. She'd learned her lesson there.

Even so, she had to tell Zane he was going to be a father. He had the right to know. Then he could do with the knowledge what he would. Just how she was supposed to tell him, though?

She inhaled another deep breath and released it slowly. There was just one thing to do. The thing Sabrina had done her entire life when it came to times of turmoil. She was going to have to assemble her sisters.

"So I GUESS you're all wondering why I've called you here tonight," Sabrina said some hours later after pouring glasses of wine for her twin sister, Dahlia, and her older sister Jade.

She'd changed into her usual nightwear of pajama pants—these pinstriped in pink and pale yellow—and a tunic the color of buttercups. Her pale blond hair was bound at her nape in a loose ponytail, much like her sister Dahlia's, but that was about where the fraternal twins' similarities ended. Where they were both tall, Dahlia had curves that lanky Sabrina could only dream about, every last one of them evident in Dahlia's work-about-the-ranch blue jeans and white button-up shirt. Her blond hair was a shade lighter than Sabrina's, and her blue eyes were dark and expressive where Sabrina liked to think she kept her own thoughts to herself. Jade's hair was long, too, but was dark brown and fell loose around her shoulders. Her own style was more conservative as well, and hadn't changed much over the years, her blue jeans and T-shirt much like what she wore when they were in high school.

Really, all six of the Fortune siblings had features that ran the gamut. Some were dark, some fair, some were in between. Yet they somehow all managed to resemble both their mother, Wendy, and their father, Casper.

Jade and Dahlia accepted the wine from Sabrina gratefully, and each enjoyed a generous sip after giving her their thanks. Looked like they'd both had One of Those Days, too. But she'd also bet dollars to doughnuts those days were nothing compared to her own.

"You sound like you're going to accuse us of murder," Jade said from her seat on Sabrina's sofa.

Her living room, too, was still sparsely furnished, the delicate curves and pale colors of her furniture looking overwhelmed by the soaring beams and honey-gold logs of the living room. She was definitely going to have to do some furniture shopping soon.

"So who died?" Dahlia asked.

Sabrina sighed. "My sense of self."

"Well, that doesn't sound good," Dahlia replied.

"Have a sip of wine and tell us what's going on," Jade told her.

Sabrina looked down at her glass, into which she'd poured a generous serving of pomegranate juice. "It's not wine," she told them. "It's juice."

"Wow, you really have lost your sense of self," Dahlia said with a chuckle.

"Indeed," Jade concurred. "Explain yourself."

Sabrina smiled at her sisters in spite of the turmoil cartwheeling through her. Usually, these conclaves with her sisters weren't about anything too major. A lot of times, it was just girls having fun. Tonight, though, she needed help sorting things out. But how was she supposed to explain any of this to Dahlia and Jade when she didn't understand it herself?

In an effort to stall, she asked her sisters, "Hey, how's Hope doing? Have either of you spoken to her lately?"

Hope was a woman who Dahlia and their brother Ridge had discovered in his barn late one night last month with a baby in her arms, a wound on her head, and absolutely no memory of who she was or how she'd gotten there. Ridge had taken her in, along with baby Evie, but the last Sabrina had heard, they hadn't made any headway in discovering her identity or history. They didn't even know if her name was truly Hope.

"She's doing well physically," Dahlia said. "I talked to them yesterday. The doctor gave her and Evie both a clean bill of health and told Hope that her memory should return in time. Nothing seems to be jarring any recollections, though."

Sabrina couldn't imagine what it must be like to have no inkling of who you were. And to have a baby to care for on top of that. She was just happy Hope and Evie had found their way to a place where they'd be safe. Her youngest brother, Ridge, was just about the most decent human being Sabrina knew.

"But enough about Hope," Jade said. "What's happening with you? Why are we here?"

When Sabrina didn't reply right away, Dahlia and Jade grew visibly concerned.

"You okay, sis?" Dahlia asked.

Sabrina shook her head. "Not really. I'm…"

"What?" Jade demanded.

Just tell them, Sabrina instructed herself. "I'm… I'm pregnant."

She might as well have just told her sisters she had indeed murdered someone, so incredulous were their expressions.

"What?" Jade echoed, with even more concern this time.

"How?" Dahlia wanted to know. "I mean, I know *how*. But *who?*"

So Sabrina sat down and told them everything. How she'd succumbed so quickly to her attraction to Zane that night. How she wished she could put it down to something like too many glasses of wine or the magic of the evening or anything else. But she'd only had a couple of glasses, and the evening had been just like any other glitzy fund-raiser of the dozens she'd attended as an accountant for a Dallas nonprofit. There really had been nothing magical about that night.

Except for Zane. And his dreamy green eyes. Eyes that had been completely fixed on her face the minute she took her assigned seat across from him at the dinner table.

She bit back a sigh at the memories of the gorgeous man with amazing eyes and chiseled cheekbones who introduced himself with a laid-back, velvety *Hey, there, I'm Zane.* She'd nearly melted into a puddle under the table when he'd reached out a hand to shake hers. A jolt of something hot and electric had shot through her whole body, and she'd barely been able to remember her own name. When she hadn't given it to him right away, he'd picked up the place card above her dinner plate and turned it toward himself. *Sabrina Windham,* he'd purred in that luscious baritone—she hadn't yet changed her last name to Fortune. *I am very pleased to make your acquaintance.* The next thing she knew, they were sharing hot, moon-drenched kisses in the rose garden gazebo, And then... Oh, *and then.* Her body grew hot all over again just thinking about their night of uninhibited lovemaking back at his ranch...

"I've actually met Zane Baston a time or two," Jade said when Sabrina finished her account. "And you're right. He's pretty hot. Not so hot that I'd have a one-night stand with him..." she added meaningfully.

"We used a condom," Sabrina assured them. "I did mention we used a condom, right? Correctly, too."

Then again, it had gotten pretty intense pretty fast that night. Something else she'd confessed to her sisters. Amazing. That was what it had been. Every woman should have a night like that at least once in her life. But when Sabrina had opened her eyes the following morning, reality had come crashing back down around her. Without thinking, she'd dressed and collected her things while Zane was still asleep, then called for a rideshare, which had thankfully come quickly. She'd returned to the hotel, packed her bags, checked out and headed home, confident that she would never see Zane again. Even if, someplace deep inside her, she'd been wishing the whole time that there was some way she could stay in Chatelaine with him for— Well. For a while longer, at least.

"Which was maybe why I finally let Mom talk me into moving here to Chatelaine with the rest of you guys," she admitted to her sisters now.

"Oh, come on," Jade said. "You knew you'd miss us if you didn't. We've always been a close family, and Dad's death and Mom's learning about being a Fortune has only made us tighter."

This was certainly true. Her family had always been close. But they'd grown closer in the wake of their father's death from pancreatic cancer the previous year. It had happened so suddenly after all. Only weeks between his diagnosis and his funeral because, true to Casper Windham form, his workaholic tendencies had made him ignore his symptoms until it was too late. After that, family had come to mean more to the surviving Windhams—now Fortunes—than ever before.

"Truer words, big sister," Dahlia agreed. "In times of trouble, family stands strong, whether their name is Windham or Fortune or… Hey, are you going to give the baby Zane's last name, or will it be a Fortune, too?"

Sabrina uttered a helpless sound. "I have no idea. I haven't even told him yet. I haven't even seen him since moving to Chatelaine. I've been doing everything I can to avoid him because he and I are vying over that piece of land I need for the fiber arts grief camp I want to start."

"Oh, wow, I forgot about that," Jade said.

"Yeah, that does muddy things up a bit," Dahlia agreed.

"Especially since he doesn't realize it's the woman he met at the fundraiser who he's at odds with. That woman was named Sabrina Windham. He thinks he's trying to take the land from someone named Sabrina Fortune." She sighed. "But even without all that, I still have no idea how I feel about that night."

She was even less sure of how Zane would react when he saw her again. He hadn't exactly gone out of his way to contact her, either, after her return to Dallas. But Chatelaine was the very definition of small town. She was bound to see him eventually. He was bound to see her. And when he learned that she was pregnant, he'd put two and two together pretty quickly.

Then Sabrina remembered something else. She remembered how Zane told her that night about losing his parents when he was a teenager and raising his four younger brothers alone. Any man who would assume the care and feeding of four young boys when he wasn't that far from boyhood himself was a man who would always do the right thing. Once Zane found out he was going to become a father, he'd want to be a part of that child's life. The two of them could very well be connected forever.

"You have to tell him, Sabrina," Jade said. "He has a right to know he's going to be a father."

Dahlia nodded in agreement. "It'll be okay. Life is full of surprises. Stuff happens. It's a lesson everyone needs to learn."

"This is true," Jade said. "God knows all of us have had to learn it over the last year."

Everything her sisters said was what Sabrina had been telling herself all afternoon. Especially the part about life lessons. It felt like a lifetime had passed since their father's death and Wendy's discovery that the mother she'd always known wasn't actually her mother and that she had a dying grandfather who was leaving her an honest-to-God castle here in Chatelaine. She had wanted desperately to leave their hometown of Cactus Grove after her husband's death, and neither Sabrina nor her siblings had really felt any major ties to the place. Their father hadn't always been an easy man to love, having held his business closer than he had his family. It hadn't taken long for them to capitulate to their mother's wishes for both the name change and the move because Wendy had always done her best by all of them.

"I still can't believe Sabrina met Zane here in Chatelaine before we even moved here," Dahlia said.

"I know, right?" Jade replied. "What are the odds? We barely knew Chatelaine existed until we got here."

"Well, Sabrina knew," Dahlia said with a sly smile. "She had the greatest sex of her life here after all."

"Very funny," Sabrina retorted.

"Hey, your words, sis, not mine."

Actually, Sabrina had told them it was the most *amazing* sex. Though why she had let that little nugget slip, she had no idea. Pregnancy hormones, she told herself now. She'd heard they could make a woman feel a little, um, different.

"Anyway," Dahlia continued, "it's kind of unreal that Sabrina would have a one-night stand in some out-of-the-way town and wind up preggers."

"Hey," Sabrina retorted, "at least I didn't wake up in Vegas with no memory of the night before married to my nemesis since kindergarten. Unlike *some* people."

"Yeah, but I'm not The Cautious One," Dahlia reminded her. She smiled. "Besides. Waking up next to Rawlston that morning ended up turning out pretty well for me."

"I'm just surprised Sabrina had a one-night stand at all," Jade interjected. "Not after what happened with Pres—"

Here she halted, her expression indicating how sorry she was to have said what she did. Not the part about the one-night stand, but the words that came after that were way too close to broaching a subject no one in the family ever talked about. Sabrina's marriage to Preston Stallard. One that had ended before it could even begin. One she simply did not allow anyone—including herself—to talk about. Because it was just too painful.

"Anyway," Sabrina said, throwing each of her sisters a warning look, "what happened happened, and now I have to figure out what to do next."

"You haven't heard a word from Zane since that night?" Jade asked.

"Not as Sabrina Windham," Sabrina said. "And all the stuff with the land grab is going through our attorneys and Realtors."

She had been both relieved and disappointed not to hear from Zane after their night together. Then again, she hadn't contacted him, either. Maybe they'd both realized the morning after that it was just one of those things. For all Sabrina knew, that kind of thing happened to Zane all the time. She was probably just one of dozens of women he'd spent the night with this year alone.

"He needs to know," Dahlia said, echoing her earlier statement. "You have to tell him. Then he can make his own decision about what he wants to do."

"What is it *you* want to do, Sabrina?" Jade asked pointedly.

Surprisingly, it was the first time since realizing she was pregnant that she gave that some thought. She'd never really considered having children. First because she was too young. She and Preston had told themselves they had plenty of time. Then, after his death, she'd been certain there would never be anyone special in her life again to think about having children with. But she was thirty-two years old now. This baby might be her only chance to become a mother. Did she *want* to be a mother? Was she in a position to provide for a child? Was she ready to set aside her own wants and needs to put another human being first? Would she even be a good mom?

She was surprised to realize that all of those questions had the same answer. *Yes*.

She looked at her sisters and found them gazing back at her with much expectation.

So she told them, "I'm keeping the baby. And I'll find Zane tomorrow and tell him he's going to be a father. Then he and I can go from there." She smiled at each of her sisters in turn and added, "Also, I think the two of you are going to be the coolest aunties ever."

CHAPTER TWO

ZANE BASTON WAS sitting in the middle of the floor in his home office doing his best to figure out how to fit the peg of tent pole A into the hole of tent pole B—no easy feat when he hadn't even located tent pole B—when he heard the doorbell ring downstairs.

It was odd for anyone to come calling at the house now that three of his younger brothers were living on their respective college campuses, and the fourth was headed that way soon. So Zane ignored the summons. It was probably someone who'd likewise ignored the No Soliciting sign on the driveway gate he never bothered to close, and he knew his housekeeper, Astrid, would take care of whoever it was. Nobody ever wanted to mess with a Nordic Valkyrie old enough to be their grandma but sturdy enough to kick their butts to Asgard and back. And he really did need to find the pieces to the tent—and figure out how to assemble them all—before he left on his trip at the end of the month.

It had been his dream when he was a teenager to travel around the world for a year after he graduated from college. But within months of his receiving his degree, he and his brothers lost their parents when the elder Bastons' private plane went down. At twenty-three, Zane took on the role of raising his four little brothers, who hadn't even been teenagers when their parents died. Now three of those little boys had left the nest for college, and the fourth had one foot out the door. Before leaving, though, they'd pooled money from part-time jobs and trust funds so they could make Zane's trip happen—their way of saying thanks for all the sacrifices he'd made for them. For the better part of the year ahead, Zane was going to be able to visit all the places he'd only fantasized about before.

Boom. Dream come true. One item ticked off his bucket list.

It was a trip he would have been over the moon about ten years ago, when nothing had seemed more thrilling or important to him than seeing the world. But he kind of had mixed feelings about it now. A decade brought a lot of changes to a man's life. But his brothers had insisted that since the last of them was off to college, Zane *had* to go. Not only had they already worked out the logistics for the care of the ranch with his foreman, Mateo—who was also delighted Zane was going to finally be able to enjoy his dream trip of a lifetime—but the four boys had also pooled *a lot* of their financial resources to make sure he could. So, in a matter of weeks, Zane was off on the first leg.

Sydney, Australia, ready or not, here I come.

He was even wearing one of those half-flipped-up hats that his youngest brother, Cody, had found somewhere online and insisted Zane take with him. An Akubra hat, he'd called it. Zane just hoped they really wore these things Down Under. For now, though, he was only wearing it around the house and only to appease the kid.

"Mr. Baston?"

He looked up to see Astrid standing in the doorway of the office whose Spanish Colonial decor hadn't changed one whit since his parents' deaths. Dark wood paneling rose halfway up the creamy walls, interrupted by bookcases filled with family memorabilia and knickknacks, potted cacti and, oh, yeah, books. The big, ornate mahogany desk was complemented by a pair of coffee-colored leather chairs, and a massive wool rug patterned in Mexican geometrics spanned the floor. Zane had always loved playing in here when he was a boy while his father did the ranch paperwork. He could still feel the scratch of the old rug under his knees as he pushed his Hot Wheels along the pattern, pretending the jagged lines were roads. Hell, here he was still, sitting on the same rug.

Then again, his folks hadn't really changed any part of Night Heron Ranch at all from when his grandparents owned it. And his grandparents probably hadn't changed anything much from when his great-grandparents first settled here in the early 1900s. The big adobe Spanish Colonial with the terra-cotta tile roof looked, inside and out, like something from a fabulous forties film about the taming of the Wild West. He loved this place with all his heart. It had been perfect for growing a family, and it felt strangely empty already now that the last of his brothers was on his way out.

As he always did whenever Astrid called him *Mr. Baston*, he replied, "You can call me Zane, Astrid. Everyone does."

And as she had always done when she replied, she reiterated, "Mr. Baston, there's a woman downstairs who says she needs to speak to you. I told her you were busy and asked her to make an appointment for later, but she insists she needs to speak to you today, about something very important."

Okay, that was weird. Whatever business Zane had to conduct off the ranch, he conducted in Chatelaine proper over a cup of coffee and a cattleman's breakfast at the Cowgirl Café. And he'd made it a practice a long time ago to never bring women home with him since the house had always been full of impressionable kids. In fact, he'd only brought one woman here to the ranch—and only one time—but that was because all the boys were away that weekend, and the woman in question had been like none he'd ever met before. He still grew warm inside thinking about her and the way they'd come together that night. But she'd disappeared without a trace before he woke up the next morning, never to be seen again.

"She said to tell you her name is Sabrina Windham," Astrid told him.

Until today.

A tidal wave of heat tsunamied through Zane's belly just hearing her name again. He hadn't seen Sabrina for months. Not since that incredible night at the end of May.

Wow. Speak of the devil. With a blue dress on. Because he was still haunted by the vision of her that night at the fundraiser, when he'd glanced away from a conversation about freemartins that was going on way too long to see the most incredible woman he'd ever seen sitting down on the other side of his table. As if she'd felt his gaze on her, she'd looked right at him, and for one indescribable moment, the whole world seemed to slip away. The next thing he knew, they were talking like they'd known each other for years. After dinner, there had been dancing, so dance they did. Right out onto a terrace adjacent to the ballroom, across the terrace to the garden, down the garden path to a secluded passage of roses that had smelled heavenly, straight to a gazebo where Zane had kissed her. And kissed her. And kissed her. Then he was inviting her back to his ranch for a nightcap, and she was saying yes, and then they were at his ranch, ignoring the nightcap because he started kissing her again the minute they got through the door, and then they were in his bedroom, and then…

Oh, man. And *then*.

"Uh, go ahead and show her up," he told Astrid.

He'd never thought he'd see Sabrina again. They hadn't

exchanged phone numbers that night, so he'd had no way to contact her after the fact. He'd tried to find her online, but what few social media accounts he'd found for her had all been set to private. He'd thought about trying to message her on one of them anyway, but the fact that she took off literally under cover of darkness without even saying goodbye or leaving a note had been a pretty good indication she hadn't wanted to see him again. As much as he'd hated to do it, he'd chalked up their time together as just one of those things. Hell, he'd had one-night hookups in the past that had been easy enough to move past. Why should Sabrina Windham be any different?

But Sabrina Windham *had* been different. As much as he'd tried to forget her, he still found himself thinking about her from time to time. How gorgeous she'd been dressed in that sleek sapphire dress the same color as her eyes. How silky her hair had been, sifting through his fingers when he tugged free the comb holding it in place. How soft her skin had been when he'd pulled her naked body against his. That sweet, arousing little sound she made when he touched the heated, damp core of her. How he'd come apart at the seams when the two of them climaxed together. How…uh…um…

Anyway, he did still think about that night occasionally. But, hey, it had only been a few months. He knew he'd get over her eventually. Probably.

But what the hell was she doing here?

As if in answer to his unspoken question, she appeared in the doorway where Astrid had stood a moment ago, looking even more beautiful than he remembered. She was wearing blue again, but this dress was the pale blue of a summer sky. Her hair was up again, too, however today, it was neatly wound into a tidy topknot, with not a single strand out of place. She was clinging to a small purse slung over her shoulder, so tightly that she might as well have been carrying the nuclear launch codes in it.

"Hi," she said, so softly he almost didn't hear her. She smiled in a way that was at once anxious and arousing. With a bit more fortitude, she added, "Remember me?"

He smiled back. "Hell, yes, I remember you."

Without thinking, he took a few steps across the room, then stopped when he realized the reason he was doing it was to kiss her. As if that were the most natural thing in the world for him to do, even after not seeing her for months. Even after spending only a single night together, one that ended with her leaving without saying goodbye. One where, for a little while, at least, it had felt as if the two of them belonged together.

Her eyes widened a bit when he started to move toward her, but she didn't look like she wanted to retreat. He marveled again that an entire season had come and gone since he last saw her. At the moment, it felt like no time had passed at all. As if that very morning, he'd awakened beside her in the hazy light of a new day and kissed her hello, then shared breakfast with her before setting about his day, with no reason to think he wouldn't see her again when it was time to go home that evening.

Why would he feel like that? He hadn't awakened beside her in his bed the morning after they made love, and he hadn't kissed her hello that day. Hell, he hadn't even kissed her goodbye.

What was she doing here?

"It's good to see you," he said.

Yeah, it was a cliché, but it was true. It was good to see Sabrina again. Surprisingly good. A ribbon of warmth wound through him as she took a few steps forward as well. But she stopped when a good five feet still separated them.

"It's good to see you, too," she told him. She looked at some point just above him. "Interesting headgear for a Texas rancher."

He was confused for a moment, then remembered the Akubra hat. "A gift from my youngest brother, Cody," he said.

She smiled. "And how are your brothers?" she asked. "There are four of them, right? And the youngest one is off to college soon, if I remember correctly."

He was delighted that she did in fact remember correctly. "Yeah, Cody starts classes next week. Something for which I am extremely grateful, because he'd been threatening to drop out of high school for months and run off with his girlfriend to join the rodeo. The twins are both in San Antonio, since although they wanted to be separated, they didn't want to be separated, if you get my drift."

Sabrina laughed. "As a twin myself, I totally do."

Zane laughed, too. "That's right. I forgot you have a twin sister." He made a face. "Sorry, don't remember her name."

"Dahlia."

"Right. Like the flower."

"My sister Jade is also a twin, to my brother Nash. Fraternal, all of us."

"So are my brothers," Zane said with a smile. "Anyway, Shane is at Trinity, and Levi is at Texas A&M–San Antonio. And the oldest, Wyatt, is a junior at Baylor."

"Aren't you the oldest brother?" she asked with a smile.

Zane smiled back. "Yeah, I guess technically I am. But I've felt more like their parent since our folks have been gone." He remembered telling her the night of the fundraiser about raising his brothers. What he didn't remember was why he'd told her, since he didn't normally share that right off the bat with women. Something about Sabrina, though, had made him more forthcoming than usual.

She shook her head. "Four college tuitions at once. That can't be easy."

Zane waved a hand. "Nah, it's all good. My parents put college funds in place for all of us as soon as we were born. Then all four of my brothers ended up with full-ride or near full-ride scholarships. Smart as whips, all of them, and way more involved in the community than I was at their age." He smiled a little sheepishly. "They ended up pooling their college funds and the money they made from part-time jobs they got in high school to fund my trip."

Sabrina looked confused. "What trip?"

Oh, yeah. He hadn't told her that part the night of the fundraiser. They'd sorta gotten sidetracked by, um, other stuff.

"I'm leaving at the end of the month to spend a year traveling around the world. It was supposed to happen after I graduated from college—I spent years as a teenager planning it—but I had to cancel after our parents' deaths. Now that my brothers are all heading off on their own, they wanted to treat me to say thanks for the last ten years."

Now Sabrina looked a little panicky. Why would she look panicky? He was the one who was about to leave everything that was familiar for a year to go thousands of miles away.

"Wow," she finally said. A little panicky. "That's amazingly generous of them."

He shrugged. "When they told me about the trip, they said it wasn't near enough to pay me back for everything I'd done for them."

Although she still looked anxious about something, she smiled. "Those boys were raised right."

"Yeah, well, joke's on them, 'cause I got more out of

raising them than they got out of being raised. They're all headed back to their respective campuses in a couple days, so we had our official send-off last night. Shane and Levi chipped in on this tent I need to figure out, and Wyatt gave me a compass because he's so sure I'll get lost somewhere along the way. Such a comedian, that one."

Gingerly, he removed the hat, then tossed it toward a nearby rack, where it landed perfectly between a leather bridle that needed repair and his favorite Stetson. Then he looked at Sabrina again.

"But yeah. Cody got me the hat because the trip starts in Sydney."

She nodded. "And you're leaving at the end of this month?"

He nodded back. "Yep."

"And you're going to be gone for a year?" Why did she look so worried when she asked that?

"Leaving the thirtieth," he told her. "Though I won't arrive in Sydney until October second. International date-line and all that."

"Guess when you're going to be gone a whole year, a couple days is just a drop in the bucket."

He nodded and realized he had no idea what to say in response. So he blurted out the question that had come to mind the second Astrid mentioned her name.

"Sabrina, what are you doing here?"

Now she was back to looking panicked.

"I mean, don't get me wrong," he hurried to add. "It really is good to see you, but…" He expelled a restless sound and reminded her, "The last time we saw each other…the only time we saw each other—" he made himself clarify "—you kind of left without warning, and it's not like you tried to get in touch afterward."

"I know," she said. "And I'm sorry about that, Zane. I

truly am. I just… That night—" She halted, inhaled a deep breath and tried again. "I've never done anything like that before. Ever. I'm just not the type of person who can meet someone and hop into bed with them. I'm usually super careful and wary and…" She shifted her weight restlessly from one foot to the other and back again. "There are six kids in my family, and I've always been called 'The Cautious One.' Even when we were little kids, I looked before I leaped. No tree climbing, no eating dirt, no little white lies, no wandering off. I was way too careful. About everything."

Zane found this surprising. He'd immediately formed an impression of Sabrina as breezy and lighthearted, without a care in the world. No way could he see her as *cautious*.

She tried again. "After what happened between us, I didn't know what to do. That night was just so…"

He grinned at that. "Yeah, it was."

She chuckled, but the sound was nervous and, he had to admit, a little cautious.

"That night was wonderful," she assured him. "But afterward…" She blew out another errant breath. "I didn't know where we could go from there. My life was in Dallas then, yours was here. There was no reason to think our paths would ever cross again."

"So then…why are they crossing now?"

The gaze that had been so focused on his darted away. "I live in Chatelaine now," she told him.

The warmth that had been spiraling through him since her appearance pooled in the center of his chest and exploded. "Since when?"

"For about a month."

Now the heat dropped right to the pit of his belly. And not in a good way. She'd been here for a month but was only now contacting him? Why the delay? And what made her come now?

"And what's brought you to Chatelaine, Sabrina Windham?" he asked. Since it clearly hadn't been him, no matter how much he wished it had been. Had it been him, she would have come knocking at his door long before today.

"Actually, I'm not Sabrina Windham anymore," she replied, skirting the question. "I just told your housekeeper that so you'd recognize me. My name last name is Fortune now."

Zane's eyebrows shot up to his hairline. Naturally, he'd heard about how a whole new branch of the famous Fortune family had moved to Chatelaine earlier this year to join the ones who already lived here—everyone in town had heard. He'd even met a couple of them in passing. But he'd so been busy with ranch work and getting Cody off to college, he hadn't paid the newcomers much mind. He certainly hadn't heard about a Sabrina For—

Oh, crap. Yes, he had. His Realtor and lawyer were currently wrangling with hers over a piece of land they both wanted. *That* must be why she'd come to the house today.

Then another thought struck him. If Sabrina had gone from being a Windham to being a Fortune, that must mean—

"You got *married*?" he exclaimed.

Now she looked panicked again, even more so than before. "No!" she quickly assured him. "God, no. I'm not married. I'm never getting married again."

"Married *again*?"

Before he could ask her to elaborate on that, she hurried on. "Long story, but my mom found out she was a Fortune after my dad's death last year, and she changed her name to embrace her new family. She asked all of us kids to change our names, too, since we're also official Fortunes.

So now I'm Sabrina Fortune. *Single* Sabrina Fortune," she said adamantly.

Zane was surprised by the depth of the relief that wound through him to realize she was still unattached. He'd think about why later. He'd think about the *married again* part later, too. Not to mention the land-wrangling. But first things first.

"I mean, in my heart, I'll always be at least a bit of a Windham," Sabrina said. "Not all of us kids were super eager to do the name change. Especially since a new name doesn't change who you are."

"If the name is Fortune," Zane said, "and it's here in Texas, it totally changes who you are."

"Really?"

He grinned. "Oh, yeah. Might as well be European royalty."

Sabrina laughed. "Oh, right. Princess Sabrina, that's me."

"I don't know," he murmured. "You sure looked like a princess that night at the fundraiser."

Her cheeks stained with pink, and she glanced down at the floor. But she said nothing.

Quietly, he added, "Not to mention I kinda felt like Cinderella ran back to the pumpkin patch when I woke up alone the next morning."

She had the decency to look embarrassed by that. She opened her mouth to say something, but he held up a hand to stop her.

"You don't owe me an apology," he said. "We didn't make any promises to each other that night."

She looked like she wanted to object, but she backtracked, "If the name change makes my mother happy, and since all my brothers and sisters are on board with it…"

She shrugged. "I love my family. Doesn't matter what our name is."

"Family is numero uno in these parts," Zane agreed.

"I don't know what I'd do without mine," she said. "But I didn't come here to tell you about my family."

Here it comes, Zane thought. She was going to give him an earful him about the land they both wanted. But instead of lighting into him, she took a few more steps forward, opening her purse as she drew nearer. She withdrew her phone, punched in her code, did some scrolling, enlarged a photo she found in her collection and silently thrust it toward him. Her expression when she looked at him now was a mix of a million different emotions, none of which he could quite identify.

Warily, he took the phone from her and looked at the photo she'd chosen. It was of a small plastic tray, one of those medical testing kinds like a person used for a home diagnosis. One opening showing a very clear pink plus sign. He'd never seen a home pregnancy test in person, but this was sure what he figured they looked like. Either that, or Sabrina had some kind of contagious something or other, and she was telling him he had it now, too. Heat swelled in his belly again. One way or another, he knew, his life was about to change.

With even more trepidation than before, he asked softly, "What exactly am I looking at, Sabrina?"

"I was afraid the result would disappear after I took the test, so I snapped a photo. I knew I'd need to keep convincing myself after the fact."

His heart hammered hard in his chest. "Convince yourself of what?"

She inhaled an even deeper breath than before and released it even more slowly. "I'm pregnant, Zane. And you…

you're the father. That's why I'm here. To tell you that. Because you deserve to know."

It took a few seconds for that to sink in. Because time just sorta stopped for a bit. His heart rate doubled, the heat in his belly spread to every pore in his body and his breath quickened.

Yep, he'd been right. His life was definitely about to change.

CHAPTER THREE

IF SABRINA COULD have chosen any superpower in the world at that moment, she would have chosen the ability to read minds. Because she could no more tell what Zane was thinking after her announcement than she could have made the Earth move in the opposite direction like Superman.

He was even more handsome than she recalled. The night of the fundraiser, he'd been dressed in a dark suit and crisp white shirt with a bolo tie, his dark hair cut short and his cheeks cleanly shaven. His hair was longer now, ruggedly tousled, and he looked as if he'd skipped a few days with the razor. He was dressed now in battered jeans and a faded blue work shirt, an outfit that made him seem earthy and affable. His green eyes, though, were exactly as she remembered, thickly lashed and the color of sage, as clear and deep as an ocean.

His gaze kept ricocheting from the phone in his hand to her face, as if he couldn't quite work out what he was looking at. Sabrina sympathized. She'd spent pretty much the entire day after taking the test doing exactly the same thing. She knew she had the advantage of a day and a half to accustom herself to her condition. Zane had barely had a second and a half. She understood it was going to take some time for him to figure out what he was feeling.

Except that it…didn't. Because he suddenly smiled as if he'd just won a billion-dollar lottery. Then he let out a whoop of delight and crossed what little distance separated them to pull Sabrina into a hug. Her breath caught as he swept her off her feet and spun her around a few times before setting her back on the floor. He didn't release her, though, only kept his arms roped loosely around her waist. Which she told herself should feel intrusive. But it didn't. It actually felt kind of nice. The expression on his face now, though, was clearly ecstatic. She'd never seen a human being look so happy.

"I'm going to be a *father*?" he asked.

The question was clearly rhetorical, since she'd already told him she was pregnant.

"A real, live, honest-to-God father?" he repeated.

Sabrina couldn't find her voice for some reason—probably because she was still trying to identify that ripple of unidentifiable something curling through her—so she only nodded. His reaction was just so surprising. She'd been afraid that, at best, he would have been stoic and pragmatic and accepting. And that, at worst, he'd be angry and contrary and tell her she was on her own. The last thing she had thought he would be was delighted.

He seemed to understand her confusion because his smile gentled. But he still didn't release her. And, strangely, Sabrina didn't mind that at all.

"You thought I'd be mad," he said.

She nodded again. "Kind of. Even more so now that you've told me you're about to go on a dream trip around the world for a year. And you can still go," she hurried to reassure him. "You don't have to put your life on hold or anything. I'm the one who's pregnant. This baby is completely my responsibility."

"The hell it is," he replied, immediately contradicting her. "It's only half your responsibility. The other half is mine."

She didn't realize how much she'd been stressing over

that until she felt the relief ease through her. She had steeled herself to hear Zane renounce all obligation to their child. Not that she would have accepted that—she would have at least filed for some kind of financial support. But to hear him so readily accept half the burden of everything that was to come was more than a little heartening.

But then, why was she surprised? This was a man who, when he was still almost a kid himself, had taken on the responsibility of raising four boys half his age. And he'd clearly done so with great success. She'd seen for herself what a good guy Zane was, even if she'd only spent a matter of hours with him. Of course he was a good guy. She wouldn't have fallen for him so quickly that night— or spent the night with him—if he hadn't been. Even so, he was adjusting to the news of his impending fatherhood awfully quickly…

He gave her one last hug then, with clear reluctance, released her and settled his hands on his hips. But he didn't move away. And he didn't stop beaming.

"Look, Sabrina, I realize that in spite of the fact that we somehow managed to create life together, you and I really don't know each other that well. I understand why you might think I'd be put off by finding out you're pregnant, out of the blue, especially when we took precautions to avoid that."

"We're three-percenters," she said. "That's what the doctor told me. That condoms used correctly still fail three percent of the time."

"Yeah, well, I'd rather be a one-percenter," he said with a grin, "but I still don't mind being this particular statistic."

Sabrina didn't mind that, either, now that she was more used to the idea. Still, it was good to know she and Zane were of one mind on the matter.

He shrugged. "Truth is, I've pretty much been a father

for the last ten years. And as scary as the thought of raising my brothers was in the beginning, over time, I got into the rhythm of it, even if it meant spending every second of my free time ferrying them around to football practice and clarinet lessons…gay-straight alliance meetings, chess club, drama club, film club…"

Here, his face lit up with another one of those heart-stopping, brilliant smiles, the kind she'd seen from him so often that night they spent together—as if he just couldn't believe how much he was loving the moment he was in. Something inside Sabrina went warm and gooey seeing it, the same way it had that night. And, as also had been the case that night, she wanted nothing more than to lean in and kiss him.

Had to be the pregnancy hormones, she told herself. She'd replayed that night in her mind a million times since it happened, and she'd come to the conclusion months ago that it had just been one of those strange nights where the stars aligned in a way to make both of them feel extraordinary and respond to the events—and each other—in ways they never would normally. And whatever that phenomenon was would never happen again. She'd come to that conclusion months ago, too.

"Now that the boys are all off to college," he continued, "I'm pretty much going through the whole empty nest thing people go through when they're suddenly alone after raising a family. But where those folks are in their fifties and sixties and looking toward a retirement where they can do all the fun stuff together that they've put off doing to raise a family, I won't be retiring for decades." He sighed. "And to be honest, a life that doesn't involve raising those boys doesn't feel like much of a life to me."

She tried to sound encouraging when she said, "I would think you'd be looking forward to some peace and quiet."

He shook his head. "I'm a family man, Sabrina, plain and simple. I realized that a long time ago. But my family's all out there embarking on their own lives now, and I've had no idea how I'm going to fill in all those gaps. Now that I know I'm about to become a real father…"

That beaming smile returned. Sabrina did her best not to swoon.

"Well, now. I suddenly have something to look forward to again. And I get to be the father to a baby! I missed out on all that with my brothers. By the time my oldest, Wyatt, was born, I was twelve and didn't want any part of babies. I wouldn't even babysit when my parents asked. I missed out on all the boys' firsts. First words, first steps, first solid food."

My oldest, Wyatt, Sabrina repeated to herself. She knew Zane had meant his oldest brother. But the way he talked, he sounded as if he were speaking of his oldest child. Though she supposed, in a way, he was. For all intents and purposes, for much of his siblings' lives, he'd been their father.

"After I became the boys' guardian," he continued, "that was the first time I really got to know any of them. And I found myself wishing I'd been around more for their early years. This time, for our baby, I'll be there from the beginning."

Our baby. Up until now, Sabrina hadn't been thinking about the life growing inside her in those terms. Mostly because she truly hadn't thought Zane would be all that enthusiastic about taking on the responsibility. Now that she realized he was already thinking in terms of *our baby…*

Well, actually, now that she thought about it, that was kind of scary. Just how much input did he want to have in this child's life? She'd been thinking she would be the primary decision maker for…oh, everything. From naming the child to picking out preschools to touring colleges when the time came. But Zane was right—he was equally responsible for her baby. *Their baby*, she hastily corrected herself. She just wasn't sure she wanted him to be. Her life really was going to be connected to his, for at least the next eighteen years. This man she barely knew would be invading the life of her and her child for the foreseeable future. And that…

Yeah. That was kind of scary.

It didn't help that he continued. "I didn't know what I was going to do with myself now that the boys are all off on their own. I haven't even had much interest in going on this trip, if you want the truth. But I didn't want to let my brothers down. They all worked so hard and invested so much. I'm sure I can at least get some of their money back, though."

"Wait, y-you're not going to take your trip of a lifetime?" she stammered. "The one you had to postpone for ten years? The one you were so looking forward to?"

"Yeah, that trip. It's not as appealing now as it was when I was a kid. The closer it's gotten to time to leave, the less I've wanted to go. It just doesn't feel right, leaving the country for a whole year when the boys are still in college. I've kept thinking what if something happens and they need me? I could be on the other side of the planet. This trip…" He shrugged. "It just isn't as important to me as it was ten years ago. And it's certainly not once in a lifetime, like I thought it was then. I only thought that because I was young and figured I needed to do it before I got too old. But back then, 'too old' was, like, thirty."

He chuckled. But his levity didn't spill over onto Sabrina. She really was just beginning to realize how much impact Zane's impending fatherhood was going to have on her motherhood. She'd been working under the impression that he would stay in the periphery while she raised her child. But it was *their* child. She was going to have to include him in at least a few things. More than a few, if his reaction was any indication.

Then again, just how much thought had she actually put into this? It hadn't even been two full days since she found out she was going to be a mother. Even so, considering the circumstances, why wouldn't she think she would be the primary caregiver?

Very cautiously, she said, "Zane, just how involved are you planning to be in this baby's life?"

She might as well have just asked him if he wanted to drink hemlock, so stunned did he appear to be.

"What are you talking about?" he said. "We're going to co-parent, aren't we?"

He wanted to *co-parent*? she repeated incredulously to herself. Like split everything fifty-fifty? Which meant she would only see her child half of its life?

"Are we?" she asked with no small trepidation.

He looked even more confused. "Yeah... I mean, we're both the baby's parents. I want to be there for everything."

That didn't sound like *co-parenting* to Sabrina. That sounded like *parenting*. Parenting with a virtual stranger, at that. Which didn't seem like a good idea.

Wow, this conversation had gone right off the rails. Or maybe it had never even been on the rails. 'Cause it for sure wasn't going the way she'd planned.

"I wasn't exactly considering co-parenting this baby with you," she said honestly.

His dark brows knitted downward. "What exactly were you considering?"

She shook her head. "I'm not sure," she admitted. "I just came over today to let you know I was pregnant and that you're the father. I didn't expect..."

"What?" he said, his voice edged with challenge.

"I didn't expect you to want to be involved. Not to the point of actual parenting."

"Well, you were wrong," he said bluntly. "Why wouldn't I want to be involved in parenting my own child?"

"Because you just got your life back after raising four boys you'd never planned to raise," she reminded him. "And because—" She stopped herself before saying the last, because it sounded insulting even to her ears.

"Because what?" Zane demanded.

"Because you're trying to pull a land grab on a piece of property I need myself, and that's going to make things between us a bit sticky."

She waited for him to start fuming, to say something that would only ignite further the legal dispute that was simmering between them.

"I thought I was dealing with someone else until you told me you changed your name," he said. "And then you told me about the baby, and everything else in my head went south."

"Yeah, well, now you remember," she pointed out. "And now you understand it's going to be a thing between us."

He thought about that for a minute, then, said, "That's just business, Sabrina. It has nothing to do with us. Or our child."

"Oh, excuse me, but it has everything to do with us! And, by extension, our child."

He nodded, but the gesture was edged with something antagonistic. "Well, at least you're agreeing that it's *our* child. Like I said, the land thing is just business."

She'd been kind of hoping that once he realized she was the one he was trying to swindle, he would back off from his claim to the land. Obviously not. She knew all about *just business*. She was Casper Windham's daughter after all. Whenever her father had had to miss one of his children's major events—which had been often—it had been because of *just business*. Those nights when she'd come home from school excited to tell him about something that had happened and his chair had been empty at the dinner table because he had to work late had been just business. As had been those holidays when he was likewise absent from what should have been a fun event with the whole family. *Sabrina, you have to understand. It's just business.*

Maybe co-parenting with Zane wouldn't be such a big deal after all, she thought bitterly. Because if he was as *just business* as her father had been, she wouldn't be seeing much of him. And neither would their child.

What he said next only cemented that. "And you know what? There's no reason we can't approach co-parenting the same way. Like a business. You and I are both good at that. We'll just develop a successful model for co-parenting and follow it."

His comment about her being good at business, too, made her wince, mostly because she couldn't disagree with him. In a lot of ways, she was her father's daughter. She'd gone into business instead of pursuing her love of textile art because she'd sought his approval and known it would please him. How was she so sure she could put her child first when Casper had never been able to do that? Maybe she had a lot more to think about than she realized before she and Zane could come to any kind of consensus.

"I have to go," she said suddenly. "I just remembered someplace I'm supposed to be."

He looked more surprised by the statement than she had been to utter it. "But—"

"Really, Zane, I have to leave. We'll talk more later, 'kay?"

And then, without awaiting a reply, she spun on her

heel and fled. She threw a quick thank-you to his house-keeper as she flew by, then raced out the door and sprinted to her car. From her rearview mirror, she saw Zane coming down the front steps, gesturing for her to come back. Sabrina didn't care. She wasn't going back. Not until she thought a lot more about his position in the life of her child—*their* child, she amended reluctantly. Bottom line? She needed to figure out how she felt about his presence in their child's life.

And, more to the point, how she felt about his presence in hers.

SABRINA HAD NO idea where she was going after turning out of the long drive leading to Zane's house. At some point, she realized she was headed toward Chatelaine proper, so she just kept going in that direction. She hadn't eaten anything since that morning, and it was after lunch now. She might only be twelve-going-on-thirteen-weeks pregnant, but she was ravenous. The little person inside her must have some appetite. And as much as she was craving a cup of coffee—already she was having headaches from caffeine withdrawal after her decision to give it up for the duration of her pregnancy—a cup of herbal tea might be good for calming her frayed nerves.

As she approached the Daily Grind, she saw her sister Dahlia's car in the lot and immediately turned into it, too, to park a few spaces down. The bell over the coffee shop door rang cheerfully as she entered, and she quickly scanned the room for a familiar face. There was Sylvie, the wise-cracking waitress who had always been able to make Sabrina smile when she came in for her weekly macchiato. And, of course, there was Beau Weatherly, who all the Fortunes had learned pretty quick was Chatelaine's equivalent to Yoda or Dumbledore. Word around town said

the sixtysomething retired ranch investor had an answer
for just about any question a person could ask and insight
into just about anything a person could need guidance on.
He even had a sign on his table next to his iced coffee and
scone that read Free Life Advice. Sabrina would have run
to him right now for just that if he hadn't had a line waiting.

Finally, her gaze fell on not just Dahlia, but her sister
Jade, too. They were seated at a wide round table in the
back with three other women. She recognized two of them
as two-thirds of the Perry triplets, Tabitha and Lily, whom
she'd met shortly after her arrival in Chatelaine. Thanks
to the third woman's resemblance to the other two Sabrina was going to go out on a limb and guess she was the
third sister. Haley, she recalled. She knew all three women
were involved with some of her newly acquired Fortune
cousins, but she wasn't clear exactly who was married or
engaged to whom—or if there even were marriages and
engagements. Sabrina's newly discovered family was nothing if not large and prolific. Dahlia had formed a friendship with all three triplets, but her twin had always made
friends more easily than Sabrina had. Jade looked pretty
chummy with the sisters as well, though, so maybe it was
time Sabrina stepped up and made their acquaintance, too.

As she made her way over to the table, Jade looked up
and smiled, then waved hello and gestured her over. The
other women all turned their attention to Sabrina as well,
each smiling warmly in welcome.

"There's the little mama," Dahlia said as Sabrina moved
to sit in an empty chair beside her.

When Sabrina snapped her head up to glare at her sister, Dahlia's smile faltered a little. "Just how many people
have you told?" she asked her sister.

"Oops," Dahlia said, her smile turning sheepish. "But
you never said not to tell anyone," she added.

True enough. And Sabrina knew her twin had fallen more easily into small-town life than she had herself, a big part of which was sharing any little bit of news one might have come across. Even so, she wasn't sure how ready she was to broadcast her condition. She'd told her siblings and her mother—and don't think Wendy wasn't delighted by the prospect of becoming a grammy—but since Sabrina didn't know many other people in Chatelaine except for Zane, she hadn't given much thought to telling anyone.

Not that it wouldn't become obvious before long. It might just be her imagination, but when she was showering that morning, she'd studied her belly and thought it already looked a little more rounded than usual. Still, she'd at least like to be comfortable with the knowledge herself before telling other people about it.

"Don't worry," Lily said. "Nothing stays secret in Chatelaine for long. We all would've known soon, anyway."

Sabrina didn't doubt it. Especially after the way Zane had just reacted. He was probably on his phone right now, texting the news to everyone he knew.

"At least she didn't tell them who the father is," Jade said in their sister's defense.

Tabitha's phone pinged on the table near her coffee cup, and she picked it up, reading the text that had appeared on the screen. "Zane Baston," she said matter-of-factly.

Sabrina's mouth dropped open in shock. "How do you know?"

"I just got a text from Lupe Cruz, who cuts my hair. Her husband's sister is a cattle hand on Night Heron Ranch."

Damn. Zane really was telling everyone he could think of.

The other triplets' phones pinged in quick succession, and each looked at their respective screens.

"Yep," Haley said. "Just heard from Blanche, my neighbor. Her brother, Evan, used to coach intramural flag football with Zane when his boys were in middle school with Zane's brothers."

"Mine is from Erin Margolis," Lily said. "She's married to Petey Margolis, whose mother was one of Zane's mother's closest friends when she was alive."

Unbelievable, Sabrina thought. The Chatelaine telegraph must be working overtime today.

All three women quickly texted responses—probably words to the effect of We already know, what took YOU so long?—then set their phones back on the table and looked at Sabrina.

"Zane's pretty dreamy," Haley said. "Great genes. You could do worse for your baby daddy."

"And he's such a nice guy," Lily added. "He's done so great with his brothers."

"Yeah, he'll be an awesome dad," Tabitha stated. "How did you two meet, anyway? You've only been in town a month."

Well, at least Dahlia had left out the part about it being a one-night stand. Not that there was anything wrong with one-night stands. Not unless you'd always been The Cautious One.

Before Sabrina could formulate an answer to that question, the bell over the coffee shop door rang again. Automatically, she turned to look at the new customer and saw a tall, handsome man with sandy blond hair searching the room in much the way she had upon entering, as if he were looking for someone specific. He had a slender manila envelope tucked under one arm and a hopeful expression on his face. When his gaze lit on their table, that expression turned even more buoyant, and he took a step in their direction, letting the door close behind him. But he hesitated after a couple more steps, as if uncertain about what his reception would be, before continuing to make his way across the shop.

When Dahlia saw Sabrina's gaze fixed on something behind her, she turned in her seat to see what she was looking at. Immediately, her jaw dropped, and she poked Sabrina in the side as she always had when they were kids and she needed to get her attention *fast*.

"Oh, my God," she whispered urgently. "It's *him*."

"Him who?" Sabrina whispered back. Dahlia really did seem to know everyone in Chatelaine already.

Her twin leaned in closer and lowered her voice even more. She threw a quick glance at the triplets, who were all still talking about Zane being such an amazing family man that they had yet to notice whoever this was coming toward them. "Heath Blackwood," Dahlia told her. "Rawlston and I met him right after he arrived in town. He was literally still pulling his suitcase behind himself. He was looking for the triplets. He's pretty sure he's their long-lost brother. And he just might be. The triplets have always suspected they're actually quadruplets. He told Rawlston and me that he'd discovered all kinds of genealogical info online that linked the four of them. He made us promise not to say anything to anybody, in case he's wrong—"

Oh, sure, Sabrina thought, Dahlia could keep *that* a secret for a total stranger.

"—but Haley and Tabitha and Lily never mentioned meeting him, so I guess their paths just haven't crossed yet."

Heath Blackwood came to a stop at their table, finally grabbing all the women's attention. Especially Jade's, Sabrina couldn't help noticing. Her older sister actually kind of lit up at his arrival, even though Jade had never really been the lighting-up kind. He lifted the hand not holding the envelope to give his Stetson a polite tip. Then, as if just remembering his manners not to wear a hat indoors, he took it off completely.

"Excuse me, ladies, I don't mean to interrupt y'all's conversation, but I'm looking for—"

His gaze moved from the triplets to Dahlia, and he smiled when he recognized her.

"Well, hello there, Dahlia. It's good to see you again."

"You, too, Mr. Blackwood. I hope you've been enjoying your stay in Chatelaine." Before he could reply, Dahlia opened her hand toward the three women on the other side of the table. "May I introduce you to the Perry triplets?" She pointed at them each in turn as she said, "Lily, Tabitha, Haley, I'd like you to meet Heath Blackwood."

All three of the women smiled and greeted him warmly, but they also threw Dahlia a variety of curious looks.

Until Heath said, "Ladies, it's nice to meet you." He held up the manila envelope and added, "I believe the four of us are related. According to the information I have in here—" he gave the envelope a little shake "—I'm your brother."

Now the triplets' mouths dropped open in astonishment. Then, one after the other, they gasped. And then shot each other looks. And then smiled with delight.

Before they could say anything, though, Heath began speaking again. "I'm sorry it's taken me so long to talk to y'all. I just wasn't sure if it was the right thing to do. My family past is a bit murky." He nodded toward the manila envelope again. "But I've always been curious and finally checked one of those genealogy sites online and spit in the tube and sent it off. A few weeks ago, I got the results. They linked me to three women—each one of you—and said you were my sisters."

There was more gaping from the triplets. More gasps. More smiles.

"Oh, my God," Haley said. "We all took those tests, too, because we were hoping you might turn up! And you did!"

"It's true then?" Tabitha said. "The nice old lady from the GreatStore was right about there being four babies? We really are quadruplets instead of triplets?"

"But how did we get separated from our long-lost brother?" Lily asked.

"And how come we were never able to find a registry of your birth along with our own?" Tabitha added.

Heath looked more than a little confused by his sisters' reactions. He opened his mouth to say something, but they continued to speak, cutting him off, going on about the doctor who delivered them insisting there were only three babies, but Doris at the GreatStore insisting there were four she cared for after their parents' deaths when they were babies, one of whom was a boy.

"Ladies, hold up," Heath finally interjected. "I'm not a quadruplet. I'm not even your full brother. I'm your half brother. We have the same father. And I'm only older by two months."

Now the sisters were the ones to look confused.

"So that means our father had an affair?" Lily asked in clear shock.

"That doesn't make any sense," Haley added. "We always heard our parents were completely devoted to each other. Just what was going on thirty years ago?"

"I don't know," Heath admitted. "But I've already made up my mind that I'm moving here to Chatelaine to get to know what's left of my family. Maybe between the four of us, we can figure out the mystery. Starting with this…"

The sisters smiled in unison.

"We have a lot to talk about," Lily told him.

The other triplets nodded their agreement. Heath looked relieved.

"I was hoping you'd say that," he replied.

"Dinner at my place tonight," Haley said. "All of us together the way family should be. Just let us get the check, and we're outta here."

"Don't worry about it," Dahlia told them. "This one's on me."

"Me, too," Sabrina volunteered.

"But you didn't even have anything," Lily objected.

Sabrina smiled, their excitement and good cheer infectious. "Consider it a family-warming gift," she told them.

Dahlia nodded. "Yeah. Like a housewarming gift, only for a new family instead of a new home."

All four of the siblings grinned at that.

"New family," Tabitha echoed. "I like the sound of that."

"Me, too," Heath agreed.

Instinctively, Sabrina opened her hand lightly over the new life growing in her belly. *New family*, she repeated to herself. She liked the sound of it, too. She just hoped her own new family turned out to be as happy as the triplets-plus-one were promising to be.

She and her own sisters watched the newfound family make its way to the exit.

"How wild," Jade said. "It's like something from a soap opera. I'm amazed they were able to find each other."

"But they're together now," Sabrina said. "That's what's important. Family should always be together. In good times and in bad."

She told herself she wasn't being hypocritical when she said it. Just because she and Zane had produced a baby didn't make them family. Family was a lot more than genes and DNA. Biological parents was what she and Zane were. Nothing more. He had his family, she had hers, and their baby would be a part of both. Not a bad deal, really, having two families.

She just hoped the baby growing inside her felt that way, too.

ZANE'S BROTHERS HAD all been out yesterday afternoon when Sabrina stopped by, making their final rounds about Chatelaine to tell their friends goodbye before heading off for their fall semesters. But he'd known they would all be home for dinner at the house tonight, so he'd saved the news of his impending fatherhood for that. He waited until they'd all finished the last of Astrid's famous lingonberry-cardamom cake—the boys' unanimous favorite, saved only for special occasions like this—to spring the news on them. As they passed their crumb-laden plates down to their youngest brother, Cody, who was assigned to kitchen duty this week, Zane told them to wait before leaving the table, because he had something to tell them.

They all gazed at him curiously, if not a little anxiously. The last time he'd told them he had news for them all at this table, it had been to reveal how he'd broken up with a girlfriend they'd all come to like a lot. Before that, it had been to tell them about the death of their golden retriever, Noodles. And the time before that, it had been their parents' deaths. Safe to say there hadn't been many happy announcements made at dinner in the Baston family.

Well, that was about to change. From now on, Zane vowed, there would be nothing but good news to pass along to his brothers.

"What happened now?" Wyatt asked. He looked too grave and earnest for his twenty-one years, his blue eyes intent behind his tortoiseshell glasses, his overly long auburn hair pushed back from his forehead.

"It's nothing bad," Zane hurried to assure them all. "Just something important y'all need to know about."

The twins, Shane and Levi, were nineteen years old and the closest in resemblance to Zane with their green eyes and dark hair. Even though they still looked a lot different from each other in every other aspect, they released an identical sigh of relief.

"So you're not going to tell us Gumbo had to go live on a farm in west Texas?" Levi asked.

Gumbo was the Australian shepherd they'd adopted after losing Noodles. He'd tried to tell them that classic fib about their late pet simply moving to another part of the state, but when you lived on a three-thousand-acre ranch, it was hard to convince a bunch of kids that their beloved dog was happier with more space to run around in.

"Gumbo is fine," Zane told them. "And so are Dumpling and Cornbread," he quickly added, verifying he had seen the semiferal cats who kept the barn free of vermin just that afternoon.

Though why the boys had always been so fixed on food names for their various pets, Zane would never know. If given the opportunity to name the baby he was about to tell them about, the poor kid would probably end up being Biscuit or Pork Chop.

"Then what's up?" Cody, the youngest at eighteen and the fairest of them all with his sandy hair and hazel eyes, asked.

As much as Zane had practiced in his head all afternoon how he wanted to tell the boys his news, he was still at a loss. He'd always prided himself on setting a good example for his brothers when it came to things like drinking and smoking and partying. The first he hadn't done much of in the first place, the second he'd never done at all and the third he'd curbed significantly after becoming their guardian. The girlfriend he'd broken up with three years ago had almost become his fiancée, which was the only reason the boys had met her in the first place. She'd been the only woman who hadn't taken off the minute she found out about his responsibility to four orphaned boys. He'd truly thought she was the one. Until he overheard her talking to a man he later found out was her husband about how much money they were going to make once she "married" him.

Yeah, that had been fun.

Anyway, how was he supposed to tell four impressionable young men, who were away from his influence altogether now that they were in college, that he'd had a one-night stand that resulted in an unplanned pregnancy? Even if he and Sabrina had taken precautions, that was pretty much a *Do as I say, not as I do* scenario, and Zane had always tried his best to avoid those.

He cleared his throat. "Okay, so it's kind of a goodnews, bad-news situation," he began. "So I'll start with the bad."

"You said it wasn't bad," Shane reminded him.

Damn. Already caught in a lie. Those kids were too smart for their own good.

"Okay, it's not *that* bad," he amended. "But I'm going to have to postpone my trip around the world."

"What?" the boys cried in unison before they began barking out individual objections one after another.

Zane lifted a hand to quiet them. "I said postpone, not cancel," he reiterated. "I'll still go around the world someday. Just…not for a while yet."

His brothers began to protest again, so Zane lifted his other hand to quiet them. "There's a good reason for it," he promised.

"It better be good," Wyatt told him. "You've been looking forward to this since before Mom and Dad died."

"I know," he said. "And y'all sacrificed a lot personally for me, and I can't thank you enough for that. But here's the thing, guys." Zane smiled, letting his absolute happiness about what he was to tell them shine through. "I found out yesterday that I'm going to be a father. And you're all going to be uncles."

For a moment, none of the boys said a word. Then, as one, they whooped and hollered almost as much as Zane had when Sabrina told him the news.

"What are you talkin' about?" Shane said with a laugh.

"How did this happen?" Wyatt added, chuckling.

"Who's the mother?" Levi wanted to know.

"When's the baby gonna be here?" Cody demanded.

Oh, boy, Zane thought. He truly hadn't thought about all the questions he was going to have to answer. Instead of going in order, he went with easiest first.

"What I'm talking about is a new member of our family. By the time you guys come home for spring break next year, Baby Baston will be here. And how it happened is exactly the way all of us learned about in sixth grade health class."

The boys were still looking at him expectantly. Zane hoped if he stopped here, they'd forget about the *who*.

"And the baby mama?" Wyatt asked.

Zane sighed. He should've known better.

"She's a very nice lady I met at a fundraiser a while back," he told them. "She and I hit it off, one thing led to another and…" He scrunched up his shoulders and let them drop. "Neither one of us planned for this to happen, obviously. And we used protection," he added pointedly. "We were just part of that small percentage where it fails. Which should be a lesson to all y'all," he added firmly.

But all the boys did was smile goofily at him.

"Anyway, it did happen," Zane continued, "and now we're going to try to make the best of it. That's why I have to postpone the trip. So I can be here to help with anything she needs during the pregnancy and birth and whatever comes after that."

"What's her name?" Levi asked.

"Sabrina," he answered simply. His brothers waited

for a last name, but before they could push it, he hurried on. "You don't know her. She was living in Dallas when we met."

Too late, he realized his mistake in saying even that much.

"You haven't been to Dallas in years," Cody said. "And you've dated a few women since then. Just how long have you known your baby mama?"

Damn. Busted again.

"All right, fine. She and I had a little one-night fling when she was visiting Chatelaine a few months ago. We took precautions," he told them again. "Which should be a lesson to all of you," he added again. "Don't mess around." There. Teachable moment taught.

All four boys only laughed. "Oh, no you don't," Wyatt said. "You're not going to turn this around on us. You're gonna be a daddy!"

His brothers went back to their whooping and hollering and calling each other Uncle Whatever. Then they started throwing out names, starting with characters from their favorite games—Geralt! Shepherd! Tom Nook!—to their favorite books—Septimus! Montmorency! Percy!

Then Cody said, "Wait, what if it's a girl?"

His brothers—and Zane, for that matter—looked at him as if he'd grown a third eye.

"It's not going to be a girl," Wyatt told him with much conviction. "Bastons are never girls. Dad was an only child, but Grampa had brothers. Great-grampa had brothers." He looked at Zane. "Has there ever been a girl Baston in this family that didn't marry into it?"

"Not that I ever heard," Zane told them.

Which was just as well, since having raised four boys, Zane wasn't sure he would have the first clue how to raise a baby girl.

After a lot more back and forth debate over what to name the kid—whether it ended up being a boy *or* a girl—all his brothers did finally agree on one thing: that whatever bedroom was assigned to the baby here at the house, that room would *not* be any of theirs. Which was fine with Zane. His parents' room had been vacant since their deaths. It hadn't even been used for a guest room. But his folks would definitely be smiling down from Heaven when they saw their first grandbaby occupying that room after them.

"Better get yourself used to unicorns and fairies," Wyatt said for good measure, clearly not convinced that the baby being a girl was out of the question.

"Very funny," Zane retorted. "I'm just glad we still have some of y'all's hand-me-downs around here somewhere. Those cowboy pajamas and Tonka trucks are going to come in handy pretty quick."

"Well, we're sorry you're going to have to put off the trip," Cody said, "but at least it's for a good reason."

"The best," Zane agreed. "And I made some calls today, and I was able to get ninety-nine percent of the trip refunded, either in cash or travel vouchers. So anytime I want to go in the future, I can. Who knows? Maybe Sabrina and I can take the trip together for a late honeymoon."

All four of his brothers' eyes nearly bugged out of their heads. Only when Zane saw their expressions did he realize he had spoken aloud a thought that he had vaguely entertained—and quickly discarded—after Sabrina's abrupt departure yesterday afternoon. A million thoughts had cartwheeled through his head as he considered every possible aspect of their situation, one of which had been a marriage of convenience for the sake of the child. Why not? Those kind of marriages had been around for millennia and were still a time-honored tradition in a lot of places. And, hell, people got hitched for worse reasons.

The idea had only hung around for a minute or two, though. Now that Sabrina lived here in Chatelaine, it wouldn't be that difficult for the two of them to co-parent their child from their respective homes. They could work out the logistics and arrangements with an attorney before the baby's arrival. Fifty-fifty time, he'd figured. A week at her place, a week at his. Or two weeks apiece. Even trading off every other month could be manageable, because they could still do stuff with their child in between times. They had plenty of time to work it out, he'd decided. Marriage didn't really have to be an option, even for the sake of convenience.

Did it?

"Wait, what? Honeymoon? You two are getting *married*?" Wyatt asked before Zane had a chance to explain any of that.

Cody, of course, had to take it one step further. "Big brother, are you in love with this Sabrina?"

Of course he wasn't in love with Sabrina. That was ridiculous. He barely knew her. Besides, he'd sworn off love a long time ago. Romantic love didn't exist as far as he was concerned. At least not for him. He'd seen it faked too many times to believe it was real.

"My feelings for Sabrina are…complicated," he finally told his brothers. "There. That's a word you young people use, right? And no, I'm not saying Sabrina and I will be getting married. I'm not saying anything until she and I get to talk about this some more."

"Then why do you sound *a lot* like you wanna marry her?" Levi asked.

"Yeah," Shane agreed. "You sure seemed confident when you said the trip could be your honeymoon."

"That was just—" Zane expelled a restless sound. Dammit, he hated it when his brothers got all know-it-all on him. And not just because, too often, they were right. "I was just weighing all my options. And I really don't think that's one of them." He hurried to hammer that home when he saw Cody about to object, too. Once that kid got an idea about something, he never let it go.

"Look," he told his brothers, "Sabrina and I still have a lot to talk about where the baby is concerned. But I wanted y'all to hear about it from me first. Word's already spreading like wildfire around town."

Which, in hindsight, he should have known would happen even though he'd only told two people—his foreman, Mateo, and Millie Santiago, Chatelaine's sole travel agent. But he'd sworn both to secrecy. Which, okay, had been a stupid thing to ask for in a small town like Chatelaine.

Wow. Hindsight really was twenty-twenty.

"But Sabrina and I will work it all out," he assured his brothers.

And they would, he assured himself, too. Just as soon as they figured out how the hell to do that.

CHAPTER FOUR

It was just past nine when Sabrina heard a knock at her front door. She was freshly showered and wearing her pajamas—pale lilac cotton this time with a matching T-shirt—and had just brewed a cup of chamomile tea. To say she was surprised was an understatement. The only people she'd had at her house since moving in were members of her family. Certainly everyone in Chatelaine knew the Fortunes had bought the old Madison property, but considering how many houses were on the place, there was little chance anyone would know which of the log homes belonged to which Fortune sibling short of driving past each one looking for their respective cars.

She checked the app for her doorbell camera before going to answer and was even more surprised when she saw Zane standing under the porch light, his Stetson in one hand and what looked like a small box in the other. Looked like the driving by to identify the cars thing had occurred to him, too. She knew she should have parked in the garage.

The two of them hadn't exactly ended things on great terms earlier in the week, what with her fleeing his house without even saying goodbye—the second time she'd done that, she couldn't help thinking. She'd kind of hoped she could avoid him for a bit longer before having to see him again.

Apparently that wish hadn't been granted.

With a resigned sigh, she left her tea on the kitchen counter, tucked a few errant strands of hair into the messy bun she'd slung atop her head before her shower and made her way to the door. By the time she turned the knob and opened it, Zane was halfway down the front steps, having evidently given up on her answering. He spun around at the click of the dead bolt, however, and smiled at her with more than a little relief.

"Hey," he said softly by way of a greeting.

"Hello," she replied just as quietly.

"I'm sorry to stop by so late," he told her. "But I haven't gotten a wink of sleep the last couple nights, and tonight wasn't going to be any different. I don't think I'll be sleeping again until the two of us get a few things settled."

She nodded. "Yeah, I get that. My brain has been pretty noisy the last few days, too." She opened the door wider. "Come on in. It's not that late."

His clear relief turned to gratitude as he climbed the steps again. But he hesitated a moment at the threshold, as if he still wasn't sure of his welcome. So Sabrina pushed the door open more and took a few steps backward, giving him a wide berth.

Not quite wide enough, though, not to notice how good he smelled, a mix of leather and sandalwood. He'd showered, too, before coming over. His hair was even still a little damp, she noted, curling a little at his nape. It was all she could do not to reach out and run her fingers over it to flatten it out. He'd obviously changed into fresh clothes, too, dark jeans and western-style shirt the color of a pine forest.

He truly was one of the most handsome men she had ever seen. Haley Perry was right. She could have done a lot worse, gene-pool-wise, for her baby's father.

"I was just fixing some tea," she said as she closed the door behind him. "Would you like some? Or a cup of coffee?"

He was shaking his head before she even finished the question. "Thanks, I'm good." He extended the box toward her. "But I brought you some cookies Astrid made this afternoon. She calls them havreflarns."

Sabrina chuckled at the name. It was a funny-sounding dessert coming from a woman who looked like she could tear a kraken in half with her bare hands.

She opened the box long enough to see what looked like a dozen very thin oatmeal cookies. And, unable to resist, she lifted one out to sample it, too. Definitely oatmeal cookies, but super crispy oatmeal cookies. She was about to put the lid back on the box, but grabbed one more cookie to join what was left of the first in her other hand before doing so. When she looked up at Zane, he was grinning.

"Yeah, they're a fave around our house."

"I'm eating for two," she reminded him.

His grin broadened. "Did I say anything?"

No, he didn't. And she had to admit she kinda loved him for that.

"Tell Astrid I said thank you," she said.

"I will."

She nodded toward the living room. "Come on in."

Sabrina had started a fire in the big stone fireplace before making her tea, and it had caught nicely by the time they entered. The tawny log walls glowed like satin in the firelight, and shadows danced merrily on the vaulted ceiling. As he followed her inside, she was aware that the only other light in the room was the buttery glow from a single torchère in the corner, making the space look even cozier in spite of its sparse furnishings. She crossed the wide, Navajo-print rug to take a seat on a sofa the color of cream, pushing herself into a far corner to give Zane plenty of room in case he wanted to sit there, too.

Instead, he folded himself into the matching chair beside it. Still close, but far enough way that she knew he was deliberately giving her some space. She kind of loved him for that, too. She nibbled her first cookie nervously before realizing her appetite had disappeared, so she placed both on top of the box she'd laid on the coffee table. Zane set his Stetson on the table, too, then leaned back in the chair and looked at Sabrina intently.

"So," he said. But he didn't elaborate.

"So," she echoed.

For a moment, the room descended into silence broken only by the crackle of the fire, Sabrina and Zane gazing at each other as if neither had the first clue what they were doing there.

Finally, Zane said, "We're going to have a baby."

Sabrina nodded. "Yes, we are."

"That, um, that's kind of a big deal."

"It is."

"I'm sorry if I said something the other day that—" he sighed heavily "—that didn't sit right with you. You took me by surprise when you left in such a hurry. I guess I might have overreacted a little."

"No, it wasn't that," Sabrina told him. "I think I just hadn't put enough thought into it myself before breaking the news to you. I was thinking in terms of what *I* was going to do about the baby. Not what *we* were going to do. It truly hadn't occurred to me that you might want to be as deeply involved as I'm obviously going to be. And I don't want you to take that the wrong way," she said quickly. "It's not that I thought you'd be coldhearted and disinterested. It was that I just didn't consider you in the equation. I was too busy panicking for myself. That's why I took off."

He studied her in silence for a moment. "I guess I get that," he said. "I can't imagine what it must be like for a woman to realize she suddenly has someone else to think about for the rest of her life. And I know a lot of guys don't step up to the plate for that." He leaned forward in his seat. "But, Sabrina, I'm not one of those guys. I *want* to have to think about someone else for the rest of my life. Maybe I won't be growing this baby inside myself and pushing it out later, but I want to be just as involved as you are with everything else that I can be."

"And I get that," she told him. "But…it's complicated, Zane."

"It only seems complicated now because it's so new," he assured her. "And because you and I need to get to know each other better. I think if we talk through it, and we give it some time, we'll figure out it's not nearly as convoluted as it seems right now."

She knew what he said made sense. But what he said also meant the two of them needed to spend more time together. Which, yes, also was logical. But there was a part of Sabrina that kind of liked knowing so little about Zane. Not knowing him made it easier for her to mold him into whatever she wanted him to be. And what she wanted him to be was a man who would keep his distance. She'd spent the last ten years avoiding entanglements because she hadn't wanted to experience the grief and heartbreak that came with loving and losing someone again.

Not that she thought she would fall in love with Zane. She'd pretty much come to the conclusion that she would never fall in love again. Not a single man she'd dated since Preston's death had come close to being important to her. In fact, no one she'd dated had lasted more than a few months. Not because any of them had been off-putting in any way. On the contrary, it had taken a lot for a man to interest her enough to date him in the first place. But that was just the point. None of those infinitely likable, attractive men had done anything for her. Ergo, she just wasn't going to love anyone the way she'd loved her husband.

But even after seeing Zane only briefly the other day, knowing he was half-responsible for the life growing inside her, she was already coming to…have feelings for him. Just what those feelings were, though, she had no idea. And she didn't know where they were coming from, either. Was she drawn to him because he was Zane Baston, good guy? Or was it because he was Zane Baston, baby daddy? And who knew if those feelings—whatever they were—would last any longer than her pregnancy?

"That night of the fundraiser," he began again when she didn't respond, "you and I talked about a lot of things. The work you were doing for your nonprofit, my plans to expand Night Heron Ranch, the books and movies we loved when we were kids, where to find the best Tex-Mex in the state…"

Sabrina managed a chuckle for that. "I still say Austin."

"And I still say Amarillo."

"Agree to disagree," she said with a smile.

"If memory serves, we agreed to disagree about a lot of things that night. I still can't believe you don't like George Strait."

"I never said I didn't like him," she replied. "I just said I was more of a Miranda Lambert girl."

He shook his head hopelessly. "And you like the Astros more than the Rangers."

She shrugged. "One of my friends from college is married to an Astro," she explained.

He sighed melodramatically. "At least you like the Dallas Cowboys."

Sabrina wrinkled her nose a bit. "Actually, I only said that to make you happy after the Astros-Rangers thing. I'm really not much of a football fan at all."

He feigned shock. "Are you sure you were born in Texas?"

She laughed lightly. "Ask me about my chicken-fried steak addiction."

Zane's smile went supernova. Sabrina tried not to melt. "Well, alright then," he said. "Now we can talk about co-parenting this kid."

The way he was looking at her now was a lot like the way he looked at her that night at the fundraiser, when they first started to realize that something—something flirty and warm and appealing—was happening between them. If things kept going the way they did then, that something would soon turn into sensuous and hot and arousing. And although Sabrina didn't have a moon-drenched rose garden outside for them to dance to for stolen kisses, the golden firelit living room was becoming every bit as romantic, every bit as tempting. Zane was tempting in that moment, too. Because those thoughts of moonlight and kisses were starting to take over thoughts about…oh, everything else.

He seemed to realize the avenue her ruminations were wandering, because his smile suddenly fell, and his gaze turned smoky and hot, as if he were now thinking about the way that night had ended up, too. Without thinking, she pulled her legs up in front of herself, wrapping her arms tightly around her knees. Though whether she'd completed the gesture to keep Zane at bay or to keep herself from acting on her impulses, she honestly didn't know.

Pregnancy hormones, she tried to tell herself again. But something told her it was an entirely different set of hormones at play just then.

"I, um, I'm just not, ah, not sure where to begin," she stammered.

And she wasn't just talking about the baby now, she realized. Suddenly, it seemed like she and Zane should be making plans and rules for themselves, too.

She blew out an unsteady breath. "Every time I start thinking about the two of us trying to bring this child up together-but-not-together, my brain just freezes."

The word *freezes* had the desired effect on both of them. Zane's thoughts about the two of them seemed to cool along with her own when she brought up the topic of the baby again.

"What if we don't have the same vision for child-rearing?" she continued. "What if my idea of boundaries and rules is completely different from yours? And if they have to live one way at my place and a different way at yours, that's just going to confuse the poor kid." She grimaced. "That's no way to raise a well-adjusted little human."

"We have six months to work that out," he said. "And for the things we don't agree on, we'll just compromise and stick to whatever arrangement we come up with."

"It's not just that," she told him. "It's the whole splitting locations. Our child is going to be shuttling from one house to another for their entire childhood and adolescence. That's not a good way to establish a sense of permanence."

"Kids of divorce live that way all the time, Sabrina," Zane pointed out. "And they turn out just fine."

"But most kids of divorce have one primary parent and one primary residence that serves as an anchor of sorts. Our child, if we co-parent, won't have a primary at all. It will all be fifty-fifty. I worry they won't be able to bond well with either of us."

Zane looked at her for a moment in silence. Then he blew out a long, ponderous breath. "Okay, then, how would you feel about a marriage of convenience?"

Sabrina was sure she misheard. *"What?"* she asked.

"A marriage of convenience," he repeated. "You and I get married and live together and raise the child at Night

Heron Ranch. You could have your own room," he added quickly when her disagreement with the suggestion must have shown on her face. "But we'd both be in one place for our child twenty-four-seven."

Putting aside, for the moment, the fact that the thought of marrying anyone, for any reason, was the most disagreeable thing she could imagine, she asked, "Why Night Heron Ranch? Why couldn't we live here?"

His eyebrows shot up to his hairline. "You mean you'd actually consider it?"

"Of course not!" she told him. "I'm just saying you're being awfully presumptuous to think we should live at your place, just because you're the man."

"It's not just because I'm the man. It's because I have a working ranch I need to be present every day to work on. You work at your ranch office. You can live anywhere in town."

"Oh, sure. Spoken like a self-entitled man who's had his way from the day he was born just because he's, you know, a man."

Instead of arguing with her, Zane bit back another smile. "Is this our first newlywed spat?" he asked. "'Cause this feels like a newlywed spat to me. You're just trying to pick a fight to push the envelope and see what you can get away with in this marriage."

Sabrina did her best to look peeved. Then she smiled, too. "No, it's not a newlywed spat. For one thing, we're not newlyweds. Nor will we be," she added adamantly. "Because we're *not* getting married. Especially not for the sake of convenience."

Sabrina had sworn since losing her husband that she would only ever marry again for love. And since it had become clear over the last ten years that love wasn't going to happen for her again, neither was marriage.

Zane's relief that she had turned down his proposal was almost palpable. His gaze dropped to her lap, and, very softly, he said, "But we still need to figure out how we're both going to be present in this little buckaroo's life without joining ours."

As had been the case all week, every time Sabrina thought about the baby, she opened a hand protectively over her belly. "Yeah, we do," she said just as quietly.

"It'll be okay, Sabrina," he promised her. "If we don't approach this from a marriage-of-convenience stance, maybe we could go back to looking at it like a business arrangement. You and I are both savvy businesspeople. There's no reason why we can't run our family the same way we would a business."

There it was again. Him thinking they could raise a child the same way they could run a corporation. What was that old saying about women always marrying their fathers? Good thing Sabrina wasn't marrying Zane.

She spoke carefully as she said, "Okay, supposing we do approach this co-parenting thing the same way we would if we were starting a new venture together."

He nodded once. "Alright. Let's think about that."

"First thing we need to start a business is a solid plan."

"Sounds good."

"We can bypass naming the company until the time comes, and we'll work on the mission statement as we go."

Zane nodded. "Both of those are pretty self-explanatory, anyway."

"Right. And we don't really have to go into products and services or a market analysis."

"Agreed."

"Financials?" she asked.

"I think we're both good there."

She pointed a finger knowingly. "Budget," she said. "We need to figure out a budget for monthly expenses."

"Since you're the accountant, I'll leave that to you."

"I'll work one out tomorrow."

"Okay, so what's left?" Zane asked. "'Cause this business isn't really sounding like much of a business to me at this point."

"Yeah, co-parenting doesn't really seem to lend itself to incorporation, does it? Though I guess we could use some aspects of a business model. Make up some spreadsheets for feeding times and flow charts for visitations. What do you think?"

He made a face at that. "When you put it like that, not much. Maybe my only parenting experience is with my brothers and never involved babies, but I can tell you one thing. You can't flow chart or spreadsheet any of it."

She sighed. Point made. "So then the business approach to co-parenting doesn't sound like a very good one, either."

They really did have a lot to muddle through. She just hoped it wasn't more than they could cover in six months. She expelled a restless sound but Zane smiled reassuringly.

"Look, Sabrina, I know neither of us planned this thing, but it is starting to feel kind of weirdly right, you know? Like it happened for a reason or something. I'm not much of a believer in fate, but I do feel like this baby will be a good thing. For both of us."

She smiled. "Once we figure it all out. Which I'm sure we'll do. Any day now."

Zane smiled back. "Next week's pretty open for me. How about you?"

"I have an appointment for an ultrasound on Wednesday," she told him. "I don't suppose there's any chance you'd like to come with me, is there?"

His smile went supernova. "You mean get to meet my kid in all his, uh, sound waves? Count me in!"

It was the first time either of them had used a specific pronoun to refer to the baby. "What makes you think it's a he?"

"It's gotta be," Zane told her with complete confidence. "There hasn't been a girl born in the Baston line for as many generations back as I can remember."

"There's a first time for everything," Sabrina reminded him.

"Not for this," Zane told her. "We're having a son, Sabrina. Mark my words. You can count on that as sure as you can count on bluebonnets in the spring."

ZANE STOOD WITH his back turned in the sonogram room at Sabrina's doctor's office while she made herself comfortable on the padded table. He knew he probably looked ridiculous to the ultrasound technician—they'd already had to correct the receptionist and one nurse that they weren't a couple, just, you know, having a baby together. He listened while Sabrina patiently explained it to the tech, too. The tech who replied with yet another platitude about *Hey, that's cool, lots of people are doing that these days*, when, in fact, Zane couldn't think of a single other couple in Chatelaine—or anywhere else for that matter—who'd just woken up one morning and thought, *This is a good day to plan an unplanned pregnancy with someone I've only known a matter of hours*. Yeah, times had changed since previous generations, but they hadn't changed that much.

"You can turn around now," he heard Sabrina say.

When he did, he saw her lying with her shirt pushed up just under her breasts, a paper blanket covering her lower half and her torso completely exposed. Maybe he was only imagining things, but it looked to him like she was already showing a little bit. There was an elegant curve to her belly that hinted at the fact that there was something going on down there besides the digestion of the breakfast they'd shared together at the Cowgirl Café that morning. He found himself wondering how long it would be before they could feel the little guy moving around in there.

He took a step toward her, then hesitated. Just how close was he supposed to be for this thing?

"You won't be able to see anything from there," the tech told him. "Come on over."

She didn't have to tell him twice. He moved to stand immediately beside the table, his eyes darting from Sabrina's face to the black sonogram screen, then back to Sabrina's face again. Her expression was a mix of excitement and anxiety, the same things he was feeling himself.

"Deep breath," she told him, before taking one herself. Zane did likewise, and, together, they released it. Yeah. That helped.

"Alrighty," the tech said as she fired up her equipment. "Let's see what we've got going on in there."

The badge she had clipped to her lanyard said her name was Patsy Barnard. She was old enough to be somebody's grandmother, but she had a bright stripe of rainbow colors streaking through her white hair from her forehead to the tip of the loose braid at her nape. Her reading glasses were as speckled as a bag of Skittles, and she was wearing hot pink lipstick paired with lime green fingernails. Zane figured they were in good hands with Patsy.

"Now, the gel is gonna be a little cold when it hits your tummy," she told Sabrina, "but it'll warm up fast."

"Thanks for the warning," Sabrina told her.

Even so, she squealed a bit at first contact. Zane chuckled, they shared one more smile, then both turned their heads to watch the screen. At first, it was just black with some gray blobs floating around. Patsy said she was going to check out not just the baby, but the placenta and Sabrina's uterus and fallopian tubes, to make sure everything looked the way it was supposed to. She told them that in addition to making sure the baby was indeed thirteen weeks at this point—which Sabrina and Zane could've told her the exact moment of conception—she would look for any sign of problems and even measure the baby to see how big it currently was.

"And there it is," she said.

All Zane saw was a bunch of gray squiggly lines with a few blotches of white moving around them. Thankfully, Patsy pointed to one of those blotches of white and said, "There's y'all's baby. Almost two and half inches. 'Bout the size of a peach."

"Peach," Sabrina repeated softly. "That's our baby, Peach, Zane."

He smiled. So they already had a nickname. It fit. He liked it. And it was a food name, so his brothers would love it, too. He felt Sabrina's hand weave itself with his, her fingers curling tight with his own. When he looked down from the screen, she was looking at him, her eyes damp with tears. But she said nothing more. Which he totally got. There were no words for what he was feeling, either.

Patsy was about to say something else, but stopped, her mouth still open. She moved the wand around on Sabrina's belly some more, then paused.

"Let's turn on the sound to see if we can hear a heartbeat," she said.

When she did, all Zane heard was some scratchy, bloopy sounds. But then, when he focused more intently, he heard it. The *lub-dub, lub-dub, lub-dub* of their baby's heartbeat.

"Wow, that's really fast," he said. "Is a baby's heartbeat supposed to be that fast?"

He and Sabrina both turned to look at Patsy. Who was now, he couldn't help noticing, grinning from ear to ear.

Immediately, however, she reined in her smile and cleared her throat. "Yanno," she said, "lemme just see if I can get Dr. Brewer in here now instead of after we're finished."

Before either of them could say another word, the tech was off of her stool and out the door, the ultrasound wand still sitting on Sabrina's midsection. Zane looked at Sabrina. Sabrina looked at Zane. An unmistakable frisson of fear arced between them.

"Why would she need the doctor?" Sabrina asked.

"And why in such a hurry, before we're even done with the ultrasound?" Zane replied. "I mean, she was smiling there for a minute, so surely there's nothing wrong, right?"

Sabrina nodded. But she didn't look anywhere near convinced. He wasn't convinced, either. Especially when several long minutes passed before Patsy and Dr. Brewer returned. The tech was still smiling, though, something that quelled Zane's fears a little. Dr. Brewer was looking noncommittal, but she didn't look worried, so there was at least that.

"Let's just have a look-see at this ultrasound, shall we?" the doctor said.

She looked to be in her fifties, with chin-length salt-and-pepper hair and no-nonsense black readers perched on the bridge of her nose. Her own lanyard, in addition to holding her ID, was decorated with assorted enamel pins of women's reproductive parts and a button that said, "May the forceps be with you," so it was hard for Zane to stay worried.

Sabrina, however, still sounded concerned when she asked, "Is everything okay?"

Neither of the other women replied right away. Instead,

Dr. Brewer took a moment to study the screen and listen to the sound of what still sounded to Zane like a much-too-fast heartbeat.

"Is the heartbeat supposed to be that fast, Dr. Brewer?" he asked.

Dr. Brewer looked at Zane, then Sabrina. Then she smiled brightly. "It's not that the heartbeat is particularly fast," she said. "It's that you're hearing two of them."

Zane didn't understand. Did ultrasounds normally echo like that? Was the equipment malfunctioning? When he glanced down at Sabrina, she looked as confused as he was.

"Is this thing working right?" he asked, pointing at the ultrasound machine.

Dr. Brewer nodded. "Oh, yes," she told him. "It's working perfectly. And so are you, Sabrina," she added with a smile for her charge. "Everything looks and sounds exactly as it should in there. You are right at thirteen weeks along." She pointed to a white area on the sonogram screen. "This is your baby, who Patsy tells me you're calling Peach."

Sabrina nodded, but said nothing.

"But Peach isn't alone in there," Dr. Brewer said. She moved her hand to another white patch immediately to Peach's left. "This is your other baby."

When neither Sabrina nor Zane said anything in reply, Dr. Brewer grinned nearly as big as Patsy had. "You're having twins, Sabrina."

Sabrina's eyes went wide, and Zane's mouth dropped open.

Twins? he repeated incredulously to himself. That meant two, right? He remembered he had twin brothers. And that, yep, there were two of them. The word *twins* definitely referred to *two*. Sabrina was also one of two sets of twins in her own family. So there it was—three whole examples of how *twins* ran in both their families, and twins definitely meant *two*. For some reason, though, the implication of what Dr. Brewer just told them couldn't quite gel in his brain.

"Twins?" Sabrina asked.

"That's right," the doctor told her.

Even after hearing the word from Sabrina, Zane couldn't quite grasp the idea of two babies growing inside her. Two babies that were half her and half him. Two babies. Two *babies*. *Two* babies.

Oh, yeah, there it was. The realization of exactly what this meant. It stabbed him in the middle of his brain with all the force of two storks zooming out of the cabbage patch.

"Wow." Sabrina stared at the screen, her expression bordering on incoherent. "I thought…or maybe I just wondered… I mean I never suspected… Okay, yeah, I'm a twin… And my brother and sister are, you know…" She didn't finish the sentence, as if she were afraid to say the word again. "And Zane's brothers are…too, but I thought that the odds of having even more…was just… Holy cow!"

"Yes, indeed," Dr. Brewer said with another smile.

"Y'all want to know their sex?" Patsy asked. "Boys? Girls? One of each? 'Cause we can probably find that out, too, if you want."

Zane looked at Sabrina. Sabrina looked at Zane. As one, they smiled and said, "Yes."

Patsy took her seat on the stool again, picked up the sonogram wand from Sabrina's belly, then started maneuvering it around to get a better look. Sabrina's and Zane's attention, however, remained totally fixed on each other.

"Twins," Sabrina murmured again, pushing the word out of her mouth as if she were just learning it.

"Yeah," he said thickly. "How about that?"

Patsy interrupted by crying out, "It's two girls!"

"Congratulations to you both," Dr. Brewer told them. "I have two daughters myself. Daughters are wonderful."

Daughters? Zane repeated to himself. His brain couldn't process that word any better than it had *twins*. The Baston line was about to welcome its first girls? He was going to have *daughters*? *Two* of them?

Wow. Gosh. Huh. How about that?

"Peach's sister is a bit smaller," Patsy told them, "but still perfectly within normal size. About as big as a plum."

"Peach and Plum," he heard Sabrina repeat with quiet wonder. "We're having a Peach and a Plum, Zane."

Peach and Plum, he repeated to himself. Sisters. Twin sisters. Two twin sisters.

"Zane?" he heard Sabrina say again. But his name seemed to be coming from the bottom of an ocean a million miles away. "Are you okay?"

He nodded but wasn't sure he trusted himself to be able to form any words that made sense.

"You don't look so good," she added.

"He'll be fine," Dr. Brewer said. "I've seen that look before. You just need to take him home and fix him a pot of strong coffee."

"Or pour him a stiff bourbon," Patsy added.

Or both, Zane thought. Yeah, both sounded good.

Vaguely, he heard Sabrina's doctor giving her instructions on how Sabrina should care for herself and the twins growing inside her. Then he heard Patsy say something about how she would print two sets of images from the sonogram of the twins for her and Zane to show around until they had the official newborn photos six months, or even less, from now. He obediently turned his back again when Sabrina asked him to so that she could get dressed, then back again when she told him she was ready. Well, that made one of them. Then, somehow, the two of them made it out to the reception desk where Sabrina settled the insurance info and scheduled her next appointment, and out to the parking lot where Zane had parked his truck.

It registered on some level that he was sitting in the driver's seat and needed to start the engine and get them to wherever they were supposed to be going. Problem was, he didn't know where they were supposed to be going. In more ways than one.

"You want me to drive?" he heard Sabrina ask from the bottom of that faraway ocean again.

He shook his head. "Just give me a minute."

"Okay."

Twins. Girls. Zane was about to become the father of two daughters.

"Twins," he said aloud.

"Yes," Sabrina confirmed unnecessarily.

"Two girls."

"Yep. You okay with that?"

Zane gave himself a minute to think about how to answer that question. But he immediately realized he didn't need any time at all. He was okay. He was more than okay. He was about to become a father. A real life, honest-to-God father. Of not just one, but two kids. Girls. Which, yeah, came as a surprise, but was still…

Wow. The idea of having daughters was suddenly really, really cool. Maybe he hadn't expected it, but the idea of two little girls running around a house that had only known little boys until now seemed like it was going to be a lot of fun. Once he figured out how to handle two little girls.

"I'm more than okay," he told Sabrina, turning to her with a smile. "And how are you?"

She grinned back. "It's going to take some getting used to, but… I'm more than okay, too."

He shook his head once, to clear it of what little fuzziness remained. Then he turned the key in the ignition and started the truck.

"We should go somewhere to celebrate," he said. "Have a glass of champagne or something."

"Except that it's only nine thirty in the morning," she pointed out.

Right. Probably not going to find much champagne around Chatelaine this time of day.

"And I can't, because I'm pregnant," she added. "With twins."

Twins!

"Then we'll go to the Daily Grind and celebrate with coffee," he said.

"Except that I'm cutting back on caffeine."

"Did I say coffee? I meant herbal tea."

"Do you like herbal tea?"

"I hate it," he admitted. "But if you're cutting back on stuff for the sake of the baby's health, then I'll cut back in solidarity with you."

She smiled. "You don't have to do that."

"I know. But I want to. We're in this together, Sabrina. I mean it. Whatever I have to do to prove to you that we can do this fifty-fifty, I will. Even if it means drinking… What kind of herbal tea do you like?"

"Raspberry hibiscus."

Well, that sounded terrible.

"Even if it means drinking raspberry hibiscus tea," he told her. For the next six months. Dammit.

"Thanks, Zane."

He forced another smile. With any luck, the Daily Grind would be out of raspberry hibiscus tea. He threw the truck into gear and headed for the parking lot exit. It hit him as he stepped on the accelerator, though, that the two of them were embarking on a journey that would ultimately take them a lot farther than the Daily Grind. Just where they ended up, though...

Well, now. He kinda couldn't wait to find out.

CHAPTER FIVE

"WHAT BAD LUCK that they're out of raspberry hibiscus tea," Sabrina said as she and Zane took a seat at the back of the Daily Grind. "But what good luck that they had my second fave—ginger pomegranate."

"Yeah, that was lucky, all right," Zane replied.

Somehow, though, he didn't sound as happy to Sabrina about the development as she was. He reached for the sugar caddy and withdrew what looked like a dozen packets.

"It's actually kind of naturally sweet," she told him. "And all that sugar isn't really good for you."

He eyed her warily. "Are you telling me you're cutting back on sugar for the baby, too?"

She nodded. "I'm trying to cut it out completely. I gave the rest of the havreflarns to my mom."

Zane looked as happy about that as Sabrina had been. But, hey, sometimes you had to sacrifice for the greater good.

She lifted her unsweetened, but still sort of naturally sweet tea to her mouth to blow on it. "My mom said to tell you and Astrid thanks, by the way."

Zane nodded as, with clear reluctance, he returned the sugar packets to their caddy.

"And it's for the sake of the *babies*," she said. "Plural. We're having twins, remember?"

Even as she uttered the words, she still couldn't quite believe it. She had just gotten used to the idea of having *a* baby, and now she had to start all over again, getting used to the idea of having *two* babies. Two girls. Two. Twins. In case she hadn't mentioned that.

"The first girl Bastons in the family tree," Zane said.

Sabrina laughed lightly. "Look at you, bucking the family traditions and setting trends and bringing equality to the line."

He chuckled, too. "Yeah, but after raising a passel of boys, I don't have the first clue what I'm supposed to do with daughters."

"You raise girls the same way you raise boys, Zane. With love, respect and understanding."

He didn't look anywhere near convinced. Sabrina didn't blame him. Even if two babies didn't exactly constitute a passel, compared to the number of children she'd been planning on raising—namely, zero—it was a lot.

"It'll be fine," she tried to reassure him. Even if she hadn't quite reassured herself of that yet.

"I know," he said. "I do know that. It's just…" He inhaled a breath and released it slowly. "It's just a lot to take in."

She nodded. And they still hadn't worked out the specifics of their co-parenting. She knew they still had almost six months to make plans, but those months were going to fly by. February twenty-first. That was the projected due date for the twins if they went full term. But it was likely that they'd arrive early. Thirty-two to thirty-eight weeks instead of the usual forty. That was what Dr. Brewer had told her. Sabrina would follow every instruction to keep those babies in their protective womb as long as she could, but, when it came down to it, it wasn't entirely up to her. As her doctor had also told her, babies were gonna do what *they* wanted to do. And not just while they were in the womb, either.

Her head started to swim, and the room began to spin. She set her tea on the table, closed her eyes and leaned back in her chair to make it stop.

"You okay?" Zane asked.

She nodded.

"Can I get you anything?"

She shook her head.

"Maybe you should get something to eat. It's been a couple hours since breakfast. And you barely touched that. No wonder you look like you're about to faint."

"Thanks, Mom," she said.

He chuckled again. "That's *Dad* to you," he corrected her.

When she opened her eyes, she saw him looking at her with concern, in spite of his laughter.

"Seriously, maybe you need to eat," he told her. "All I saw were pastries at the counter. Do they have anything here that *isn't* sweet?"

"I doubt it."

"All right then. I'm taking you out for brunch."

"Zane, you don't have to do tha—"

"Oh, yes, I do. You're having Peach and Plum with a cattleman, Sabrina," he reminded her. As if she needed reminding of that, looking at the big Stetson sitting on the chair between them. "A cattleman whose baby girls are gonna grow up big and strong. So their mama is gonna need protein. Lots of it." He grinned. "Now finish up that tea you've been pretending to enjoy, and let's get outta here."

ZANE'S IDEA OF going out for brunch, Sabrina discovered shortly after leaving the Daily Grind, actually meant going to his place for brunch. But she had to admit that the dish his housekeeper prepared for them on the fly, something

made of eggs, bacon, tomatoes and chives, had been delicious. And so had the fried sausages she put on the side.
Not to mention the smoked salmon and goat cheese on
crispbread.

Scandinavians must like protein as much as cattlemen,
she couldn't help thinking. Maybe she should come to
Zane's house for brunch every morning. Or just spend the
night beforehand so she didn't have to drive uncaffeinated,
seeing as how that was super dangerous.

Then again, the ideas that were suddenly running
through her head at the thought of spending the night here
were even more dangerous. Because now all she could
think about was that one night she did spend here with
Zane. The one where they generated so much heat and so
much passion and so much…oh, just *so much*…that they'd
created a life together. *Two* lives.

Wow, was it getting hot in here? Damn those pregnancy
hormones, anyway.

Before her thoughts could get away from her, Sabrina
turned her attention back to the matter at hand. But the
matter at hand mostly seemed to be how the two of them
were now lingering in awkward silence at Zane's big dining room table over cups of the cloudberry tea Astrid had
prepared for them from her own private stash. The housekeeper had been hovering over them like two children
since Sabrina's arrival, so Zane had told her not to worry
about cleaning up after them, that he would be fine clearing their plates and tidying up the kitchen himself.

"Now that was a proper meal," he said, finally breaking the silence as he leaned back in the big chair at the
head of a gigantic table that was surrounded by a dozen
other armless chairs like it. His was obviously the Head of
the Household throne. His father had doubtless sat in that

chair, too. And his grandfather. As well as his great-grand-father. And however many greats had come before them.

Like the rest of the house, the dining room was furnished in what Sabrina could only liken to a wealthy Spanish settlers' decor—most of it probably original to the house, too, she couldn't help thinking. Bare wood beams striped the ceiling that soared above them, and an enormous wrought-iron chandelier dangled over the table. The dark wood floor was spanned by wool rugs of varying sizes—from massive to less massive—decorated with complementary Native American designs, and all the furniture was big and dark and masculine, with lots of angles and sharp edges. They were going to have to do some serious toddler-proofing of his whole house before Peach and Plum were old enough to walk.

She tried to imagine two little girls sitting at the table opposite her, giggling over whatever they had most recently found funny. For some reason, they were fraternal twins in her mind's eye, one blond like her, the other brunette like Zane, but both having eyes that were a mix of her blue and his green. Mostly, though, she thought about how they would be swallowed up by the absolute bigness and unbridled masculinity of this house. Not that her log house was particularly small or feminine. But she'd done her best since moving in to soften and cozy it up as much as she could. It was a lot easier for her to imagine two little girls living in her house, with its smaller scale and curvy furniture, than she was seeing them here. How odd it was going to be for them to travel between two such contrary environments.

In how many other ways did she and Zane differ? she wondered. In what ways were the two of them going to clash when it came to raising their children? As much as they had talked about how they were going to be co-parenting, they still hadn't set up many guidelines for how they were going to go about it.

Where even now they should have been talking about their plans for the babies, they had instead spent the entirety of their meal talking about a million other things—Zane's family's history with Night Heron Ranch, Sabrina's hectic move to Chatelaine, the latest town gossip. It was painfully obvious that they were steadfastly avoiding the one subject they should have been focused on and instead ended their brunch talking about how many plans the Fortunes had for their newly acquired ranch. Which Sabrina couldn't help thinking made an obvious segue for something else they needed to talk about—her reasons for acquiring that adjacent plot of land she and Zane were at odds over.

"And then there's my textile camp," she said pointedly. "That's what I'm planning to put on that little piece of land I recently bought."

He eyed her knowingly. "But there are still some questions about the provenance of that land. It's not for certain that the sale to you was entirely legal. It's very possible it still belongs to my great-grandfather. And if that's the case, it's going to be out of play for you."

"It's mine," Sabrina told him. "Bought and paid for. My Realtor looked into the provenance, too, and said the sale your great-grandfather made was entirely legal, so the heirs were within their rights to sell it to me."

"But you still haven't closed," he reminded her. "Because there are still some potential provenance questions. And I'm going to need that property to water my cattle now that the pond on Night Heron Ranch is drying up."

"Ponds can be revived," she told him. "I read about it online. There are a lot of ways to do it. Have you looked into that?"

Because she had after Zane told her about his reasons for wanting the land, too, before leaving her house that night last week. Naturally, she didn't want his cattle to go without water. But even he had said that night that it was going to be inconvenient to drive his cattle that far from their usual grazing fields just to get them water every day. Ponds could be revitalized for relatively little cost and trouble. There was no reason he absolutely *had* to have that land.

"I have looked into it," he assured her. "And it's possible. But it's also time-consuming. And I think, in the long run, access to the lake from that bit of land is going to be the better alternative. Besides, you can put a textile camp anywhere."

"Not really. There aren't any small properties available besides that lakefront bit that's only a stone's throw from my house. That lakefront bit that I own."

"Not yet, you don't," he said. "Why do you need a textile camp anyway? Just what is a textile camp to begin with?"

"Exactly what it sounds like," she told him. "A camp for people to make things out of different kinds of fabrics and yarns. And to even learn to weave and spin textiles themselves." She shrugged. "I've loved to knit and crochet since I was a little girl, and I'm pretty handy with a sewing needle. My sister Dahlia is raising sheep on the Fortune ranch, so it makes sense for me to piggyback off of that. I'm going to try to convince her to add goats and maybe even alpacas at some point, too. Or see if Jade can have those in her petting zoo. The fibers from those animals are gorgeous. And I've always found working with textiles to be very therapeutic."

She hesitated, dropping her gaze to the table, then looked back up at him. "Especially when it comes to dealing with grief. That's what I'd like for this camp to be.

A grief therapy camp for people who are trying to work through the loss of a loved one."

Zane studied her in thoughtful silence for a moment. Then, clearly choosing his words carefully, he said, "That first day, when you came here to tell me about the baby... *babies,*" he quickly corrected himself, looking less panicky than he had since the sonogram, "you mentioned you were married before."

Heat detonated in the pit of Sabrina's belly. "I did? I don't remember that."

"Yeah, when you told me you'd changed your name to Fortune, and I thought you'd gotten married. You said you were never getting married again."

Oh, that's right. She remembered now. In the heat of the moment, she hadn't realized what she'd revealed. She'd never told anyone outside her family about her youthful marriage. She hadn't even told her family about it until she'd had to—after Preston's death, when she'd been so grief-stricken that she'd alarmed her parents and siblings to the point where they practically had to stage an intervention. Her father had been so angry about her relationship with a man who opposed him on every level and who he had been sure could only be interested in his daughter in order to get his hands on the Windham fortune, that Sabrina had been forced to see Preston in secret. She'd hidden their entire relationship, never mind the fact that they married.

"My husband's name was Preston," she told Zane without preamble. "We met and fell in love in high school. And he...he died. He died less than a year after we got married."

Zane said nothing for a moment. Then, very quietly, he told her, "I'm sorry, Sabrina. I didn't know."

"Of course you didn't. Hardly anyone does. I didn't even

tell my sisters—who I tell *everything* to—that Preston and I got married. Not until after he passed away."

"Do you want to talk about it?"

She didn't. She hadn't talked about it to anyone for more than a decade. But for some reason, she felt like Zane had the right to know. And maybe sharing this with him would open up avenues to the two of them sharing other things. Things that would help them get to know each other better and maybe pave the way to talk about other important things. Things like how to parent two children neither of them had anticipated.

"My father didn't approve of the relationship," she began. "When Preston and I were still in high school, it was fine. Dad figured he was just my first boyfriend, young love and all that, someone I would naturally break up with in time and move on to someone else, the way teenagers often do."

"But you didn't break up," Zane guessed.

She shook her head. "We just got closer. And when Preston chose a biology major in college with a concentration on ecology and interned for an environmental watchdog agency that had my father's plastics company listed as public enemy number one in Texas… Well. Lead balloon and all that. Not to mention the fact that Preston was never going to make a fortune in life with his chosen profession, so that just convinced my father that he was only after the Windham money."

She smiled sadly and looked past Zane, out the window to where Night Heron Ranch sprawled off to the horizon. "Which is actually kind of funny when you think about it," she said softly. "Why would he want to put my father out of business if all he was after was my father's money? Anyway—" she hurried on, still not looking at Zane "—he died ten months after we married. An undiagnosed heart condition that was probably congenital." With much understatement, she concluded, "It hurt. A lot. I never want to go through that again. Not that I will, since I'm never going to fall in love again. The end."

When she met Zane's gaze again, it was to find him studying her in inscrutable silence, as if he were carefully weighing everything she'd just told him. His sea green eyes were deep and mesmerizing, and it was all Sabrina could do not to drown in them.

Finally, he said, "No offense, but I kinda sympathize with your father on the only-after-your-money thing." He lifted a hand when he saw her open her mouth to protest. "Not that that was the case with your husband," he said, to clarify. "I don't doubt he loved you as much as you loved him. I'm just talking from personal experience myself. I can see how a father would want to protect his daughter from that."

"What do you mean?" she asked.

"I mean I've had my fair share of gold diggers in the past," he told her. "Women who I eventually discovered were only interested in landing a rich husband."

"I think you're selling yourself short," Sabrina told him. "You have a lot more to offer a woman than money."

Oh, boy, was that an understatement. Any man with gorgeous eyes like his, eyes that even now were smoky with wanting, and a sensuous mouth like his, a mouth that promised pleasures like no other, and corded, muscular arms like his, arms that could hold a woman with both gentleness and a passion that—

Um, anyway. He had a lot more to offer a woman than money.

He grinned at her comment, but it wasn't exactly a happy one. "Well, thank you for saying that, but too many women just see dollar signs when they look for a mate. Or maybe I just don't have the best judgment when it comes to women. Present company excluded, of course."

She smiled, too. "Thank *you* for saying that."

"But even at that, money wasn't enough for some women once they realized I was responsible for the care and feeding of my brothers. Guess they figured money goes fast when you have all those mouths to feed. Joke was on them, though. My parents set up trust funds for all five of us. We're all trust fund babies."

Sabrina chuckled. "Yeah, same here."

"Anyway, there were a handful of women who—" here he halted, as if he were trying to pick his words carefully "—okay, one in particular," he finally continued, "who got past the extra mouths and said it didn't matter. That the fact that I had stepped up to the plate to take care of my family made her love me even more. The boys loved her, too, after they met her. Which was a huge deal, since I never introduced any of my other girlfriends unless it got serious, and it almost never did." He exhaled roughly and a shadow crossed his face. "What I didn't realize with this particular girlfriend was that she was just better than the others at hiding the fact that what she really loved was the Baston bank account. The day I went to her place to surprise her with a ring and a proposal, I overheard her through an open window on her phone. She had it on speaker and was talking to someone I later found out was her husband about how much money the two of them were going to pocket after she 'married' me and finagled a joint bank account."

Sabrina winced. She knew these things happened. She just wished *these things* hadn't happened to Zane.

"I'm sorry you went through that," she told him. "Clearly we both have excellent reasons for not wanting to get married."

He nodded. "We do."

She couldn't help smiling at the way he phrased his response. Once he realized what he'd done, he smiled, too.

"Okay, we *don't*," he amended. "But I'm still confident we can raise our children successfully, even without the gold bands and the piece of paper filed at the courthouse."

Sabrina hoped he was right. But she still couldn't ignore the fact that neither of them seemed to be in any hurry about how they were going to go about that. Why did they keep bringing up the fact that they needed to make a plan, then proceed to completely ignore the fact that they needed to make a plan?

She sighed. It was going to be a long gestation.

ZANE AND SABRINA didn't see each other for the next four days, since both had to do some catching up in other areas of their lives in the wake of all the sudden twin madness. And he had to admit, he was kind of grateful for the separation. Although they still had a lot of figuring out to do in the coming months—both individually and as co-parents—he reckoned they could both use some time to do the individual part before tackling the co-parent part again. Maybe the reason the two of them were having so much trouble talking about their expectations from each other was because they hadn't had time to think about their expectations of themselves. Co-parenting, he was already beginning to realize, was hard.

He was working in the barn when he was surprised by the arrival of his brother Cody, who was supposed to be a couple hundred miles away in Houston. He'd driven off with a Rice University sticker on the bumper of his car almost a week ago, wearing the blue-and-gray Rice T-shirt Zane had given him at his high school graduation. Classes started there five days ago. Cody was supposed to be neck deep in syllabi by now. Even more concerning, his youngest brother, who was just about the most happy-go-lucky kid Zane had ever known, looked super worried about something.

"What are you doing here?" he asked. "Is everything okay at school?"

Cody shook his head. "Not really, no."

"What's wrong?"

The kid looked even more worried. "I hate it, Zane."

"You've barely been there a week."

Zane told himself not to panic. It was understandable that his little brother wouldn't acclimate right away. Being away from home was a huge adjustment, and Houston was a massive city compared to tiny Chatelaine. Hell, Zane himself had been homesick for a month when he first left home to go to Baylor. Cody would get past it. He just needed time.

"And I miss Hannah," his brother added.

And there it was. Zane told himself he shouldn't be surprised to hear Cody say that. He and his girlfriend had started dating when they were sophomores in high school and had been thick as thieves ever since, planning for their future together as only two teenagers could—completely oblivious to the realities of life. Hannah wasn't going to college—she'd turned her part-time job as a housekeeper into a full-time one at the Chatelaine Hills Hotel and Resort after graduation. They both loved horses, and they'd both talked about pursuing careers in rodeo work, because hey, being a rodeo cowboy and barrel racer were both such lucrative, steady careers that would make them rich and famous in no time. It had taken Zane nearly the entirety of Cody's senior year to talk him out of it and convince him to act on Rice's acceptance letter and generous financial package.

He'd assured his youngest brother that he and Hannah

both had plenty of time to pursue rodeo work later if they still wanted to, confident that both kids would come to their senses after they'd had a few years to mature.

"Cody, we've talked about this," Zane reminded him. "College is such an amazing opportunity. It can open any door in life you want to open. If you end up deciding the rodeo is where you want to be, fine. But that can wait a few years while you explore other options."

Cody was shaking his head before Zane even finished talking. "I don't want other options, Zane," he said. "I want to join the rodeo. Hannah does, too."

Zane wanted to tell him it didn't matter what he wanted, that what their parents had wanted was for all five of the Baston boys to get a college education.

"You have to go to college," he insisted. "You need to get your tail back up to Houston right now. Otherwise, I'll hog-tie you and drive you back myself."

"Hannah and I are in love," he insisted. "I came back today because I can't bear to be apart from her."

Zane knew he had to choose his next words carefully. "It's great that you two are in love," he finally said. "Because love, real love, can get you through anything. Even four years of college."

He could tell Cody wanted to argue. He could practically feel the frustration radiating off his brother. He just hoped the kid's head won out over his heart.

Finally, Cody's shoulders slumped, and the challenge Zane had been fearing evaporated. "I hate it at school," he said softly.

"I get it," Zane told him. "I hated college at first, too. But then I loved it. Just give it time. You'll see." With much reluctance, he added, "And if you want to come back to visit Hannah on the weekends sometimes...*some-*

times," he said with emphasis, "your room at the house is always there."

Cody nodded and mumbled, "Okay."

Somehow, though, Zane knew it was going to be a while before anything with his youngest brother was okay. He told himself again that Cody just needed time. The same way he and Sabrina did. Time could take care of a lot of problems, could straighten out a lot of things. All they needed—all of them—was a little more of that. And then everything—for all of them—would be okay.

CHAPTER SIX

SABRINA HADN'T VISITED her brother Ridge at his house since she first arrived in Chatelaine, and she was surprised at how far along he'd gotten with the place. Last time she was here, he still had some boxes to unpack, and all the furniture had been scattered helter-skelter until he could figure out how he wanted things done. He'd served her coffee in his travel mug and cookies straight out of the box. But now...

"Wow, this place has come a long way," she said as he closed the front door behind her. "It looks downright cozy in here."

And it really did. What could have been a masculine gray, brown and beige color palette was both brightened and softened by the addition of colorful accent touches, especially a vase of wildflowers sitting on one of the end tables. No way was Ridge responsible for those.

"I wish I could take the credit," he told her. He was dressed for an evening out on the town, nice jeans and a chocolate-colored polo that matched his dark hair and eyes. "But the truth is Hope has helped out a lot."

Sabrina made a quick survey to see if his mysterious houseguest was within earshot. Even seeing that she wasn't, she lowered her voice as she asked her brother, "How's she doing, anyway? You two have been kind of scarce lately."

"She and Evie are both fine, but I gotta admit neither of

us still has any idea what her story is. Is she married? Is she running away from something? Or *someone*? Like the baby's father? I've scoured the internet looking for news about a missing woman and her baby, but there hasn't been anything. It's…worrying."

Sabrina nodded. The whole family was concerned. Even in the short time since she'd appeared in Chatelaine, all the Fortunes were becoming attached to Hope and her baby and were growing more apprehensive each day with what her past might hold.

"But yeah, sorry about the being-scarce part," Ridge added. "There's been a lot to do around here. It's been great having Hope's help putting it all together."

"Oh, I only helped, did I?"

Ridge had the decency to look sheepish as he turned to greet the woman with dark blond hair flecked with red in the light, who was striding into the living room cradling a baby against her shoulder. Her amber eyes were lit with teasing at Ridge's comment. Even so, Sabrina could detect an air of distance in her, as if Hope was still wary around the man who'd discovered her. Not that Sabrina blamed her. She couldn't imagine not knowing the facts of one's own life. Of course Hope would be wary around them.

"Okay, she's pretty much responsible for how nice the place looks," Ridge told his big sister. To Hope, he added, "Did you manage to get some sleep?"

"A little," she said. "Enough to get me through the evening, anyway."

Sabrina had come over tonight because Ridge had asked her to babysit so that he and Hope could get a little time to themselves, away from the demands of an infant. She had jumped at the chance both because she hadn't seen Hope or Evie for a while, but also to get in a little baby practice for herself. Sabrina had never really been around kids much in spite of working for a children's charity when she lived in Dallas, and she for sure had never been around babies before. She figured tonight would give her a little intro into what she and Zane had coming.

While Sabrina had only met Hope a handful of times, it was clear as she strode across the living room that the woman had come a long way, too, in the weeks since she'd shown up on the ranch. The superficial injury to her head that she'd had that night Ridge and Dahlia found her in his barn had healed, and she didn't look as haunted as she had during those first days. Her eyes were no longer shadowed by strain, and her hair was caught at her nape in a tidy braid. Blue-eyed Evie strongly resembled her mother, right down to the highlights in the downy hair sticking up on her head and the star-shaped birthmark mother and daughter both had on their necks. She was dressed in a daisy-spattered sleeper and looked like she'd doubled in size since the last time Sabrina had seen her.

"Holy moly, what are you guys feeding this baby?" she asked with a chuckle as she went to greet her charge for the night.

"Right?" Ridge said. "Babies are amazing. Sometimes she seems like she's bigger in the morning than she was when we put her to bed the night before. Evie's changed even faster than this house has."

"But there's still plenty to do around here," Hope said. "A lot left to unpack. It'll be Christmas before this place is in shape."

"Yeah, if we ever even *find* the Christmas stuff," he grumbled good-naturedly.

Sabrina smiled down at Evie, and when the baby smiled back, a ribbon of delight unwound inside her. "She smiled at me!" she cried as she looked up at Ridge and Hope again. "She likes me!"

"Of course she likes you," Hope told her. "You're a big sweetheart. You're going to be a great mom, Sabrina."

Sabrina wished that statement would make her happy, too, but instead, a curl of anxiety coiled up tight inside her. Some of that was her concern that she didn't know the first thing about mothering, but some of it was twisted up with Zane, too. Talk about not knowing what she was doing.

She hadn't seen him for days, but it felt more like months had passed since their brunch at his ranch. And not a single one of those days had gone by without her thinking about him. A lot. There were times when she could almost convince herself that everything between the two of them would work out fine—eventually. But there were other times when she wondered if they would ever be able to free the knots in their relationship.

"I hope you're right," she said. "I feel so clueless."

And not just about the baby. But if she started telling Ridge and Hope about everything that was going on with her and Zane, they'd never get out the front door to enjoy their evening.

"You'll learn as you go, just like every other new parent," Hope assured her. "Really. It'll be fine."

As if to punctuate that, Evie lifted a pudgy little hand to wrap her fingers around one of Sabrina's, then cooed in a way that made her feel as if Hope was right, and that everything would be fine. *Eventually.*

"So how have you been, Hope?" Sabrina asked. "Have you been able to remember anything about your past?"

She shook her head sadly. "No, but I've been having some weird dreams."

"Like what?"

"It's of two people. I can't see their faces—it's all a blur—but I can tell they're an older couple. And in the dreams, I seem to know them."

"Well, that's encouraging. Do they say anything?"

Another head shake, then Hope told her, "They both reach out for me, and at first, that's really comforting, and it makes me feel happy in the dream. But then I suddenly realize that they're angry about something. Are they angry at me? Angry about something I've done or said? Are they people from my past? Or is it all just a bizarre dream that doesn't mean anything? I don't have any idea."

"Well, it sounds to me like your brain is trying to work things out," Sabrina said gently. "That's something."

"I suppose."

"But tonight, we're not going to worry about any of that," Ridge interjected. "We're just going to have a nice dinner at the LC Club, then take a walk along the lakefront, maybe stop for ice cream at some point, and just relax."

Hope smiled. "Relaxing. What a concept!"

"Evie, listen to them," Sabrina cooed to the baby. "Talking like you're a lot of trouble. I don't believe them for a minute. You're just the sweetest, cutest, bestest baby in the whole wide world."

At least until mine come along, she added to herself. *They're going to give you a run for your money in the sweet and cute and best department. Right, Peach and Plum?* she added to the twins growing inside her. *You're going to be sweet, aren't you? Right?*

As if they heard her inner dialogue loud and clear, Hope and Ridge both chuckled.

"Yeah, babies are a breeze, Sabrina," Ridge said with a mischievous smile. "Just you wait. You'll have nothing but time on your hands after those little bundles arrive."

"Yeah," Hope agreed. "And you'll feel so well rested. All the time. Really. You will."

Sabrina eyed them both warily. They didn't seem like they were being quite honest. Hmm…

"Hey, would you guys mind if I invited Zane over tonight for a little bit?" she asked them. "Just so, you know, he could get some hands-on baby experience, too?"

Now her companions' smiles turned knowing. "Oh, so he can get some *baby experience*," Ridge echoed.

"Yeah, it could have nothing to do with those dreamy blue eyes of his, could it?"

"Of course not," Sabrina was quick to deny. Zane had green eyes after all. But a frisson of heat shot through her all the same. "I just think he'd welcome the chance to spend a little time with Evie, too, that's all."

"Gotcha," Ridge said. Still smiling his smug-brother smile.

"Of course we don't mind," Hope said. "Zane seems like a good guy."

"Thanks," Sabrina told them. "You guys have fun tonight. Don't worry about a thing. Zane and I will have a nice relaxing night here with Evie."

WHEN SABRINA HAD invited Zane to come over to her brother's house where she was babysitting a literal baby, Zane had envisioned the two of them having a fun night with the little bundle of joy. Tummy time on the floor, like he'd been reading about, with him on one side of Evie and Sabrina on the other, while they watched the baby coo and laugh and reach for squishy toys. Or holding her in his lap while he read her one of those cute little board books he'd seen at Remi's Reads the other day. And, okay, bought a couple, too. Or maybe doing that *Open your mouth, here comes the choo-choo train* feedings where he chugged a spoonful of strained prunes into the little girl's mouth.

What he *hadn't* anticipated was thirty straight minutes of crying for no reason that he or Sabrina could find a cause for.

"Here, let me try, again," he said when Sabrina's gentle bobbing up and down of her body and soft words didn't calm the baby down.

She happily turned Evie over to him, and Zane began walking in slow circles around the room, murmuring nonsense words into the baby's ears. For a moment, her crying did ease up some—maybe because there was a new voice in her ear. But after a moment, she went right back to howling again.

"I don't understand what we're doing wrong," Sabrina told him. "She's been fed. Her diaper's fine. She doesn't seem to be hurt. Is she maybe scared of something? Scared of us?"

"She wasn't scared of us earlier," Zane pointed out.

In fact, she'd seemed to like them both at first. Little Evie had been fascinated by Zane's Stetson when he came in, and she'd laughed when he took it off, as if she hadn't expected that to happen and was delighted by the surprise. He and Sabrina had both held her and sat with her on their laps, talking to her and having her respond with her little baby *oohs* and *aahs* and gurgles and spit. Which Zane hadn't even minded on account of it was cute spit.

Then, out of nowhere, she'd just started crying. Even screaming at times. A lot.

"Maybe she just misses her mommy," Sabrina said.

Her expression suddenly changed, and she moved to the chair where she'd left her purse. She withdrew her phone from the side pocket and started scrolling. "Hang on," she added. "I still have a voicemail from Hope with some pointers."

She pressed Play, nudged up the volume and Hope's voice sounded even louder than the baby's crying. It took a few seconds for the sound to register with Evie, but when it did, her crying stopped. Immediately. Sabrina turned down

the sound to a more normal volume, and Hope's voice listing mundane facts about feeding time, favorite book, favorite song, where to find clean jammies, etcetera droned
from the speaker. She might as well have been telling Evie
that Santa Claus was coming to town, so happy did the
baby become by the simple sound of her mother's voice.

"Unbelievable," Zane said as he continued to study the
baby and gently rock her. "All she wanted was to know
her mommy is still around."

"I guess that's pretty important when Mommy is your
entire world."

Now he snapped up his head to look at Sabrina. "Wow.
I never thought about it like that. From the babies' points
of view, we're going to be *everything*. They're not going to
be aware of anything but us for a while. That kind of adds
a whole 'nother level of pressure, doesn't it?"

He could tell by Sabrina's responding expression that
she hadn't thought about that until now, either. *Great. They
could panic together.*

"If we're not careful with the twins," she said, "we could
turn them into serial killers."

He chuckled at that. "Or we could turn them into the
people who will bring world peace."

"Yeah, I like that better," she told him.

Hope's recording came to an end, and the baby started
to fret once more. So Zane told Sabrina to hit the play button again. When she did, Evie went back to happy, even
smiling, at the sound of her mother's voice. They continued
to hit replay for another ten minutes, until Evie opened her
mouth in the biggest yawn Zane had ever seen.

"I think somebody's finally starting to get sleepy," he
said softly.

"Here, let me take her," Sabrina said. "Hope mentioned
her favorite song is 'You Are My Sunshine.' It's guaran-

teed to put her out like a light. I know my voice isn't like Hope's, but maybe it will be close enough."

Zane knew that about the song. On account of he'd just heard Hope say it in her recording a dozen times. But Sabrina was right. The baby was more likely to be lulled by a woman's voice singing her a lullaby than a man's. He handed the baby back to her—feeling oddly bereft once the little bundle was out of his grasp—then followed her to the baby's nursery upstairs.

Which, he couldn't help noticing upon arrival, was almost better furnished than his own bedroom. It was cozier, too. And far more welcoming. Hell, Zane was halfway ready to crawl into the crib and grab a few z's himself.

"Dang," he said. "Hope and Ridge went all out for Evie, didn't they?"

Sabrina nodded. "And they did it fast. It's adorable, isn't it?"

A soft white-and-beige background held pops of green, all of it inspiring a feeling of calmness and serenity. There were stuffed animals everywhere he looked—probably courtesy of Ridge, since Hope and Evie, Zane knew, thanks to all the gossip in town, had shown up in Chatelaine with literally just the clothes on their backs. It was the perfect room for a growing baby. Sabrina had told him how her little brother had taken mother and child under his wing, but Zane had had no idea the extent that had happened. Looked to him like Ridge was planning for something of an extended stay for the two.

"You know," he told Sabrina as she made her way toward a rocking chair in the corner, "you and I probably ought to start thinking about putting together a room in our houses, too, for the twins. I mean, I know we still have five or six months before they're here, but I guess it's never too early to start planning."

She sat down with Evie cradled in her lap and started rocking to soothe the baby's fretting. "I've thought about that, too," she said, "but I just haven't had much time to really do anything concrete. You're right, though. If we put it off too long, our babies are going to be sleeping in milk crates. There aren't a lot of baby outlets in Chatelaine, though. Or, you know, even one baby outlet in Chatelaine. I know the GreatStore probably has stuff, but I'd really like to compare different places."

"Maybe we can make a trip to Corpus Christi next week," he offered. "Surely they have a lot of baby places there."

She smiled. "I'd like that."

She looked like she was going to say more, but Evie began to fuss again, so she turned her attention to the baby. Zane switched off the overhead light, leaving the room bathed in the soft glow of a moon-shaped night-light near the crib, just enough light to see where everything was, but not enough to disturb sleep. Sabrina began to hum the melody to the song Hope had said was Evie's favorite, then she started to sing, her voice as soft and gentle as a well-loved blankie. Evie quieted immediately, making those dainty little cooing sounds Zane had found so delightful when he first heard them.

He really didn't have any experience with babies. Nada. None of his friends had procreated yet, and his family members were all either too young to have any or too far-flung to share their offspring. Evie was so little. And according to Sabrina, she was already around four months old. Just how small were Peach and Plum going to be when they were born? Especially since he'd heard twins often arrived early. How was he supposed to handle two tiny little human beings who were completely vulnerable? His daughters would be dependent on him for everything for years. He would be their first line of protection from all the bad things in the world.

Nobody knows, dear, how much I love you...

As he listened to Sabrina sing to the baby, something inside Zane swelled almost too big for him to hold it. Something fierce and enormous and scary. It was all he could do to rein it in before it overwhelmed him completely.

He knew in that moment that he would do whatever he had to do to make sure his girls stayed safe and healthy and happy. And not just his daughters—their mother, too. He wasn't sure what all this...*stuff* was that was mushrooming inside him, but he knew it wasn't going to go away. He knew it was only going to get stronger. And he knew it was going to take some time before he figured it all out. But yeah—it was never going to go away. That much he did know.

By now, Evie had nodded off, and Sabrina was standing slowly and carefully to carry her to her crib. She settled the baby gently onto the mattress, switched on the baby monitor hanging on the side, then turned to look at Zane. She covered her mouth with her index finger, then tiptoed melodramatically to the door where he was standing. But the smile she'd been wearing faltered some when she drew close enough to get a good look at him.

"What's wrong?" she whispered.

"Nothing," he told her just as softly. "Nothing is wrong."

"You look like someone just told you the world is ending."

He shook his head. "No, not at all. Just the opposite, actually. I think I just realized the world is only now about to begin. A new world, anyway. One unlike anything I've ever known before."

She studied him in silence for a moment, then nodded.

"I think I know what you mean," she said. "Everything is going to be different once Peach and Plum arrive."

He wanted to tell her everything was different *now*. But if he said that, she'd want to know what he meant. And truth was, Zane honestly didn't know. He wasn't sure what to think at the moment. All he knew to do right now was feel. And what he felt...

What he felt was indescribable.

So he only replied, "Yeah. It will be. So you and I better get on the stick and make some of those plans we keep talking about but never talk about."

"Later this week," she promised. "Whatever day you have free. Let's go to Corpus Christi. It's time you and I finally started making our nests for the two little chicks who will be hatching before long."

CHAPTER SEVEN

"ZANE, EVERYTHING DOESN'T have to be pink and lavender."

It was the third time Sabrina had made the comment, since this was the third store she and Zane had visited since coming to Corpus Christi after making their decision to shop for the nurseries in their respective homes. Chatelaine wasn't teeming with home improvement stores any more than it was baby boutiques, and they'd been looking for paint and such, too.

Corpus Christi, on the other hand, had a lot of specialty shops and boutiques dedicated specifically to child-related environments ranging from indoor to outdoor, with every theme under the sun. She just wished Zane would stop gravitating toward the same theme over and over again. They'd started in the paint store, where he'd gone straight to the pastels—specifically, the traditionally girly pastels. At the baby furniture store, he'd wandered toward all things white and frilly, specifically a couple of cribs with pink and lavender canopies. Now they were at one of those everything-a-baby-could-need superstores, and he had his gaze trained on a stuffed unicorn with a skimpily clad fairy on its back.

"In fact," she added, "I'd prefer if we just avoided gender specific colors entirely." It was the third time she'd told him that, too. This time, though, she backed it up with solid research. "Baby nurseries need a variety of different colors, regardless of whether that baby is a boy or a girl.

Colors that are bright and gender neutral and provide a great contrast to each other, since brightness and contrast are what you want when a baby's vision is developing."

"Says who?" Zane wanted to know.

"Says all the baby books and blogs I've been reading," she told him.

All three of them. That she'd quickly scanned last night in preparation for this shopping excursion. Not that she mentioned that part to Zane.

"Besides, not every girl loves pink and lavender," she said. Again. He started to reach for the fairy-riding unicorn. "And not all of them love unicorns and fairies."

He pulled his hand back. Then he hooked both hands on his hips in challenge. "Yeah, well, after raising four boys, you'll forgive me if I'm a little excited about having some girls in the family," he told her. "Maybe I want to go a little overboard with the girly stuff."

Okay, she could see that. But having worked for too long in a male-dominated world—and having never exactly been a girly-girl herself—Sabrina still balked at introducing someone else's ideas of what they specified as girl-or boy-centered items. Sheesh. Every store they'd visited had actually had departments devoted to gender.

"Let's just stick to the basics until we know what's going to spark Peach's and Plum's interests," she said. "Bright, contrasting colors. And animals. Kids of all kinds love animals."

In spite of their little disagreement, Zane smiled. "You really want that Noah's ark quilt we saw when we came in, don't you?"

Okay, yeah, she did. It was the cutest thing she'd ever seen. But that wasn't why she'd brought up animals. She just appreciated excellent craftsmanship when she saw it, that was all.

"I just think it will go great with the four different colors I'm going to paint the nursery at my house—each one bright and contrasting." Okay, kind of bright, she amended. A little. Okay, fine, they were all in the pastel family. She just liked softer colors. So sue her. But they *were* all gender neutral. And they *did* contrast. "And now I'm thinking about hiring an artist to paint a cute mural of an island full of animals on one of the walls in there. What are you thinking for the nursery at your house?"

Judging by his expression, he either hadn't given any thought to that at all, or he knew she was going to dislike the ideas he had been entertaining.

"You were going with unicorns and fairies, weren't you?"

"No." He denied it in a way that told her that had been exactly his plan. That was only reinforced when he added, "I mean, I do live on a ranch, Sabrina. And unicorns are horses. Sorta."

"Well, there you go," she told him, pretending she had no idea he'd been going for the gender stereotype. "Horses. Ranch. Why not put a ranch theme in there? With horses?" *That* aren't *unicorns*, she added to herself.

He frowned. "Right. A ranch theme for a baby nursery. I'll just line the walls with creekstone, hang some mounted longhorns over cribs made out of fence posts and barbwire, and throw a big ole cowhide rug on the floor. Decorate with a few saddles and branding irons, and it'll be the perfect room for my baby girls."

She knew he was being hyperbolic on purpose, but she said, "Hey, they might want to take over their father's ranch business when they're old enough, you never know. That would go a long way toward preparing them."

He glared at her.

"I'm just saying you could do some cute little baby cows and ponies and maybe some chicks and ducklings and—"

"I don't raise poultry, Sabrina," he bit out.

"Yeah, but Peach and Plum won't know that."

He dropped his hands from his hips but did at least move away from the unicorn. "You know what? Wyatt's an art major. I think I'll just consult with him on this."

Well, that was certainly promising. Sabrina perked up even more. If his brother was an artist, then maybe…

"Would he possibly be up for a commission to paint a mural in his nieces' nursery at my place?" she asked.

Zane laughed. "Hell, he'd probably pay you to let him do it. Those boys are already fighting over who's going to be the coolest uncle."

Sabrina laughed. "They'll have to get in line. My brothers are having the same argument."

Zane sighed heavily. "A ranch theme might work," he conceded. "Wyatt could probably do something really nice with that. But no chicks or ducklings or anything else. Just cows and horses."

She was going to throw in a bid for lambs, too, since Dahlia was raising sheep, but she didn't push her luck. However, she made a mental note to bring it up later, when he was in a better mood.

Instead, she only suggested, "Let's see if they have anything here that might jump-start that on your end of things." Because she was for sure getting those Noah's ark quilts.

Funnily, the shop did have some cute accessories for a ranch nursery. Zane bought two baby quilts spattered with cartoon cowgirls, some sheets decorated with horseshoes and two little armoires that opened with what looked like minuscule barn doors.

"There," he said when they finally made it to the check-out counter. "Let's see what Wyatt can do with those."

Hopefully find a rug and some prints that would tie it all together, Sabrina thought. Not that she didn't have her own work cut out for her since yes, she'd only found a few things that would work with the Noah's ark quilts. But at least she had the rug, one with two entwined giraffes that was also just about the cutest thing she'd ever seen. And if she could pay Uncle Wyatt to paint a couple of murals in the girls' room, she wouldn't need more than a few prints for the other walls.

They paid and arranged for delivery of their purchases for the following afternoon, then Zane looked at his watch. "Wow. This took a lot longer than I thought it would. It's almost dinnertime. Are you hungry?"

Was she hungry? Sabrina echoed to herself. She was pregnant with twins. *Of course* she was hungry. She didn't think she was going to stop being hungry until after they were born.

"I could definitely eat," she told him as they made their way out of the store and into the balmy evening.

The sun was dipping low above the buildings, but the pedestrian traffic on the sidewalk was still brisk. Zane looked one way up the street, then down the other, then back at Sabrina. A couple walking by brushed him softly, so he took a step closer to her to move outside the throng of passersby.

"I've only been to Corpus Christi a few times," he told her, "so I'm not all that familiar with the restaurant scene. How about you?"

She shook her head. "I don't think I've been here since I was a little girl. My folks used to bring us here for vacation sometimes. Well, Mom mostly. Dad would stay for a day or two, then fly home because he had business to attend to."

"I'm sure we can find something. What are you in the mood for?" Zane asked.

Mexican, Sabrina decided immediately. No, Mediterranean. No, wait, Indian. Maybe Italian? Or Chinese? But then, good ole fried chicken and corn on the cob sounded good, too. Maybe all of the above...?

Wow, their daughters already had really eclectic tastes in cuisine.

"Um, I'm open for anything?" she said with much understatement. Zane would probably be way better at narrowing things down than she was, since he currently only had one stomach inside his body. "What sounds good to you?"

"Steak," he answered immediately. "Steak always sounds good to me. I'm gonna go out on a limb, though, and guess that red meat isn't great for someone who's pregnant."

Sabrina shook her head sadly. "I'm supposed to cut back on red meat consumption. But we can go someplace that has steak and other stuff."

Zane shook his head, too. "Nah. I'm in this with you. If you can't have a big ole bloody steak, then I'm not having one, either."

"Zane, you really don't have to make the same sacrifices I am for this pregnancy. Especially since, you know, cattle. Beef. It's kind of your thing."

"Yes, I do have to make the same sacrifices," he replied. "But after those girls are born, you're coming to Night Heron Ranch, and I'm going to grill you the best steak you've ever had."

She smiled. "It's a date." When she realized how badly she'd misspoken, she quickly corrected herself. "I mean, that sounds like fun. Thanks."

Too late, though. Even with the correction, she was

definitely thinking about dates with Zane. And not just the one that had ended with the twins' conception, the memory of which sent a sizzle of heat shimmying down her spine. But also the potential for other dates with him in the future. Which she shouldn't be thinking about at all, because dates meant there would be more to their relationship than co-parenting, and there totally would *not* be more to their relationship than co-parenting, sizzling spine notwithstanding.

She could tell by his expression that Zane had noticed her slip, too, and that his thoughts now were mirroring her own. At least the ones about remembering their first date together. His eyes darkened as his gaze fixed on hers for a moment, then he dropped it lower to focus on her mouth. His lips parted fractionally, and he seemed to lean in a little. Without even realizing she was doing it, Sabrina leaned in, too. Closer and closer they drew to each other, until she could feel his heat joining with her own. Then someone hurrying by them bumped Zane's shoulder and uttered a quick apology before moving on. It was enough to bring them both back to the present, and they pulled apart, each suddenly becoming way more interested in the comings and goings of Corpus Christi than they were in each other.

"Um…so…" Sabrina stammered, not even sure what she intended to say.

"Yeah…so…" Zane agreed just as vaguely.

She reminded herself they'd been talking about dinner and was about to ask him again what he was in the mood for. Then she realized what a loaded question that would be in light of the last few moments and tried again.

"We passed a restaurant up the street near where we parked," she said. "It looked like one of those places that serves a lot of different things. I wouldn't think it would be that busy on a weeknight."

Zane nodded, but still looked as confused by their sudden shifts in mood as Sabrina was. Even so, "Sounds perfect," he said.

AND IT WAS. Sabrina ordered a few things from the appetizer menu to cover as many of her cravings as she could, and Zane, after reluctantly reading the descriptions of the steaks, opted for pork chops, which Sabrina decided not to tell him were technically considered red meat, too, despite the "other white meat" ad campaign, since he'd been so good about sacrificing so many other things.

He really was going to be a good father, she thought. Not just because he already had experience with it via his brothers, but because he was just such a decent human being. Someone who understood the big picture, that it wasn't always about one person, and that you sometimes had to make sacrifices in order to secure the well-being of others. Sabrina was already understanding that that, really, was what good parenting came down to. Her life wasn't just hers anymore. She had others to think about now. Because two little babies, who would become two little kids then grow into two adolescents, would be vulnerable. They would need someone not to just care for them and make sure they were clothed and fed and educated, but someone to watch out for them, too. Someone to have their backs. Someone who would always—always—put them first.

And it wasn't just their babies, Sabrina knew, that Zane would do all those things for. He would do them for her, too. Somehow she knew that to the depth of her soul. Probably because she realized she felt the same way about him. He was the father of her children. Of course she would do whatever she had to do to keep him safe and healthy and happy.

And she made herself admit that, on some level, she

would do all those things because Zane was becoming important to her for other reasons, too. Reasons that had nothing to do with the twins and everything to do with her. And with him. And with them. She just wasn't quite ready yet to explore why, exactly, that was. There were just too many feelings tying together inside her lately that she wasn't sure yet where to begin unknotting them.

They took their time as they ate, talking about even more things they hadn't yet considered when it came to the babies. They needed to start interviewing pediatricians. Looking into day care—or decide if they would even send their babies to day care. It was entirely possible that between the two of them and their families, they already had that covered. Sabrina knew she could take the girls to work with her, but she wasn't sure how difficult it might be to juggle her responsibilities for Fortune Ranch with not one but two infant schedules. Once they were old enough to be out and about, Zane said, they could tag along with him for some of his ranch chores. He even offered to talk to Astrid about taking on some childcare duties in exchange for a hefty salary raise.

And schooling. Would Chatelaine's sole preschool be a good fit for the girls? And what about the town's only elementary, middle and high schools? They were going to need to look into those, too, and especially tour the preschool if they wanted to get on the waiting list there. Chatelaine seemed to be bursting with babies lately, what with all the newcomers to town and weddings and procreation going on as a result.

They spent so much time talking over dinner that neither realized just how late it was getting until they looked up to find they were the only diners left in the place. Zane asked for the bill, apologized to their server for overstaying when she brought it, then laughed in Sabrina's face when she told him she wanted to pay her share.

"Next time's on me then," she told him as he signed the receipt.

"We'll talk about that next time," he told her.

Next time, she repeated to herself. The handful of times she'd dated since her husband's death, the words *next time* hadn't come up a whole lot. She just hadn't felt much chemistry with those men. Which, she supposed, was another reason things had happened so quickly with Zane that night. The chemistry she'd felt with him had been nothing short of... Well, whatever branch of chemistry was most explosive. The thought that there would be a string of *next times* with him now made her remember what happened on the sidewalk earlier in light of her similar thoughts. And that sent a thrill of something hot and electric zinging through her like a live wire.

She tried to tell herself the only reason for any *next times* with Zane in the foreseeable future would be because the two of them were co-parenting the babies growing inside her. There was no reason for hot and electric. No reason for zinging. No reason for live wires. Unfortunately, she couldn't quite convince herself of that.

"We better get going if we want to be back in Chatelaine before bedtime," Zane told her.

She looked at her watch. It was already *past* her bedtime. Pregnancy had sapped her in a way she didn't know was possible. She used to be such a night owl. But she couldn't remember the last time she'd gone to bed after ten. Doubtless, she would be taking a nap on the way home.

Unfortunately, getting some shut-eye on the drive home didn't happen because they saw the entry ramp onto the interstate was barricaded by a police car. When Zane checked his phone to find out why, it was to discover that all eastbound lanes were blocked until morning thanks to an overturned semi that had spilled its entire load of soybean oil all over the road.

"Well, that's not good," he said unnecessarily.

"What about alternate routes?" Sabrina asked. "There's got to be more than one way from Corpus Christi to Chatelaine."

"There is," he told her. "But too much of it is two-lane country roads that I'm not familiar with at all. And I learned my lesson as a teenager that back roads in Texas in the middle of the night can be more than a little dangerous." He met her gaze levelly. "When you're a kid and don't know any better, you feel immortal enough not to care. But we're not kids, and we have more than ourselves to think about now." His gaze dropped to her lap. "I'm not willing to take any risks with the precious cargo you're carrying."

"I appreciate that, Zane," she said. "And I agree. But that does leave us with a bit of a problem. We can't sleep in your truck."

He chuckled. "No worries. We'll just get a couple hotel rooms for the night."

Except that that was a problem, too, they soon found out, thanks to a major tech convention that was going on all week. Zane and Sabrina both spent the next thirty minutes parked and scrolling through their phones to find accommodations. But every hotel they checked was booked solid. Until finally, they found one a half-hour outside the city proper.

"Here's one," she said. "But yikes. It's called the Rendezvous Motel. Not sure I like the sound of that. That sounds like the kind of place that books rooms by the hour."

Zane brought up a travel site to check it out. "It's actually got decent reviews. It's an old place from the fifties, but it sounds like it's clean and family friendly."

"They only have one room left," Sabrina said. Even so, she tapped the *Reserve now* button before it was gone, too. She put down her phone. "But it's a double," she told him. "So we should be okay."

Sabrina didn't relax, though, until they arrived at the Rendezvous Motel and saw that it was adorable, a relic of the mid-twentieth-century motor lodge culture that had been lovingly restored to its original, well, adorableness. Lots of turquoise paint. And potted cacti. Not to mention a ton of pink and green neon.

But only one bed, they discovered when they checked in to claim their room. The desk clerk—who looked original to the place, too, with her puff of white hair and beaded-flower cardigan and cat-eye glasses—told them they were *super* lucky to find it, since the previous reservation for it had been canceled less than an hour before Sabrina booked it. And good thing there was only two of them, otherwise someone would be sleeping on the floor, since they were all out of cots, too.

"There's only one bed?" Sabrina asked in reply to the clerk's comment. "But the listing said it was a double room."

"Right. Double room. One double bed."

"No, double room means two beds."

The desk clerk was clearly surprised by this. "Since when?"

"Since always."

"Huh. Gonna have to look into that. Anyway, payment up front. Please and thank you. Sign here."

Sabrina looked helplessly at Zane, who shrugged his concurrence with her confusion as he handed the clerk his credit card. What were they supposed to do? his expression said. There was nowhere else for them to stay, and there would be no driving home tonight.

The receptionist at least had a couple of essential toiletries kits to give them, so they could brush their teeth and such, and there was breakfast provided in the morning, she told them. Then Zane and Sabrina were left to their own devices—and a room with only one bed.

One *full-size* bed that seemed way tinier than the queen she had at home. The whole room was tiny—if charmingly furnished like something out of a road trip movie starring Doris Day and Rock Hudson—right down to the bathroom that was hardly big enough for a person to turn around.

"I'll sleep in the tub," Zane told her.

"Are you kidding?" she said. "A toddler couldn't sleep comfortably in that tub."

"Then I'll sleep on the floor."

She expelled an errant sound. "Look, we can both sleep in the bed," she said. "We're adults. And, hey, we've shared a bed before."

Of course, look how that had turned out. They'd created life not once but twice the last time they shared a bed. Still, there was little chance of that happening again, was there?

Then she remembered their near-kiss on the sidewalk a matter of hours ago, and all the heat and sizzle that had accompanied it. Heat and sizzle that were still shimmering just beneath the surface and trying to bubble their way back to the top.

"It'll be fine," she told him. Almost convincingly, too.

It *would* be find, she assured herself more forcefully. She was half-asleep already. It had been a long day. They could just brush their teeth, fall into bed and they'd be out like a light in no time. By tomorrow morning, with any luck, the highway would no longer be a menace, and they could zip right back to Chatelaine. At worst, they could take the side roads in full daylight and make it home just the same.

A good night's sleep. That was what they both needed. And there was absolutely no reason to think that wasn't what the two of them would get.

ZANE WOKE SLOWLY, not sure at first where he was, because in some dusty corner of his brain, he was pretty sure he wasn't in his own bed. That bed was king-size, with plenty of room for a man to spread out—and he did like to spread out when he slept—while this one was small and crowded. Crowded because he was pretty sure he wasn't alone. That was another dead giveaway that this wasn't his bed, because he hadn't woken up with another person since... Well, he'd been about to think since that night with Sabrina, but she'd left before dawn, so he'd been alone that morning, too.

This morning, though, he felt a warm, soft body pressed affectionately against his own. In fact, this body was entwined with his, from the slender leg looped over his own from behind him to the graceful arm draped possessively around his waist to the silky head tucked into the crook of his neck.

This had to be a dream. A really good one, too. One he didn't quite want to end. So he snuggled more intently into his pillow and—what the hell, it was his dream—reached behind himself to drape his arm over the body behind his. When he did, he heard a soft sigh, then felt his companion push herself more intimately against him. Then he felt the hand at his waist move up over his chest, splaying open over his heart. Which, it went without saying, began to beat more rapidly. Instinctively, eyes still closed—since he was dreaming after all—he turned to his other side to face his imaginary partner, only to have her curl up even closer to him. Her mouth went to his neck, and she brushed her lips against the sensitive skin there before dragging a few kisses along the line of his jaw and back again.

Zane responded by turning his head so that his mouth covered hers, kissing her once, twice, three times, before skimming his hand down her back to cover her fanny. In turn, she deepened their kiss and pulled him closer, crowding herself into the cradle of his thighs. He sprang to life at the contact, moving his body again so that she was flat on her back beneath him. For long moments, he and his dream woman vied for possession of the kiss, until she sighed against his neck and murmured, *"Oh, Zane"* in a voice that sounded really, really familiar. That was when it finally dawned on him that, well, maybe he wasn't dreaming after all.

He opened his eyes at the same time Sabrina did, and both of them immediately stopped what they were doing. Which left her with her fingers twined intimately in his hair, him affectionately cupping her, ah, derriere, and both of them gazing at each other in complete disbelief and mortification.

"I was dreaming," she said vehemently.

"So was I," he assured her just as quickly.

She nibbled her lower lip. Zane tried not to help her. "I mean… I *thought* I was dreaming," she said.

"Same here."

It took another minute—another minute where Zane just wanted to stay in bed like this forever—before it occurred to either of them to disengage. And then they did so with all the speed and propulsion of an Indy 500 racer. Zane moved to one side of the bed and slung his feet over to the floor while Sabrina fled to the other side and did likewise. A long moment passed before either of them spoke again, and when they did, it was to speak at the same time.

"That shouldn't have happened."

"That was a major mistake."

Zane knew both of those things were true. The problem was, he couldn't deny how much he wanted *that* to happen again or how *that* hadn't felt like a mistake at all. In fact, it kind of felt like he and Sabrina had just been picking up where they left off the night they were together. As if the last few months never happened, and this was how that night should have ended—in the dawn of a new day, one where they were wrapped in each other's arms. A day the two of them then spent together. Doing the kind of things people did after they'd just had the most spectacular night of their life and wanted to make sure it happened again. And again.

"I am so sorry," Sabrina said.

"I am, too," Zane told her. Even though he kind of wasn't.

"It won't happen again," she added.

He nodded. Then when he remembered her back was to him so she couldn't see it, he told her, "No, it won't."

"Pregnancy hormones," she said. "I've discovered they can do weird things to the brain."

"Right."

"So that's what happened. Pregnancy hormones."

Which maybe explained her actions, but not his. And which meant they had another five or six months of this unless they steered clear of each other. Though that would be a bit difficult when they were going to have to spend so much time together preparing for their babies' births.

There was another long moment of silence, then, very softly, Sabrina said, "We should probably head down to the motel dining room for some breakfast and then make our way back to Chatelaine."

In a matter of minutes, they were seated at a table, but the awkwardness between them showed no sign of abating anytime soon. Remembering his promise of solidarity with Sabrina, Zane opted to eat the same thing for breakfast that Sabrina did—plain Greek yogurt with fruit and a muffin on the side. *Oh, boy. Yummy.* At least there was coffee. Decaf. Yay. But after a few swallows of that, he pretty much managed to fool his brain into thinking it was real coffee and at least felt coherent enough to try to make conversation. Just, you know, not about what had happened that morning.

"We should still be able to beat the delivery truck back to Chatelaine," he told Sabrina. Who was looking at everything in the dining room except him, he couldn't help noticing.

"It's fine if we're not," she said. "I can text Dahlia or Jade and ask if one of them can wait at my house for me. They both live close by enough to be there in minutes."

"And Astrid's at my place," Zane said.

And that was pretty much the extent of his dialogue, at least until he had a couple more cups of fake coffee in him. And even then, he had no idea what to say. He told himself it was because his brain was too smart to fall for the no-it's-really-caffeinated lie. But it was more because the memory of their steamy morning embrace was crowding out every other thought that tried to enter his brain. And every time it did, he got hot and bothered all over again. When he looked at Sabrina, it was to see her still driving her gaze over everything except him. Her cheeks were stained pink, though, and he wondered if maybe she was having as much trouble forgetting about this morning as he was.

And if she was, what were they going to do about it?

"So then I guess we're good," she said.

"I guess we are."

Wow, if this was any example of how their conversation was going to go for the rest of the day, it would be a long, boring drive back to Chatelaine. But maybe that was a good thing. After this morning, they needed boring. Boring was safe. Unremarkable. And led to absolutely nothing. All they had to do now was figure out how to keep things lackluster for the next few months.

He looked at Sabrina. She looked back at him. And just like that, little explosions went off all over his body. Oh, boy. It wasn't just going to be a long drive back to Chatelaine. It was going to be a long five or six months.

CHAPTER EIGHT

SABRINA COULDN'T REMEMBER the last time she and her family sat down to have breakfast together. Not since coming to Chatelaine, for sure. So when Wendy invited them all over to her place a few days after Sabrina's tumultuous morning wake-up with Zane, she welcomed the chance to see everyone. Especially her sisters, whom she was hoping to steal away for a bit to share what happened with Zane and ask them if she could keep blaming pregnancy hormones for her increasing attraction to the father of her children. Or if maybe, possibly, there could be something more going on with her and Zane than that.

Her mom had done a lot with the ranch's main house since moving in, making the place feel warm and cozy in spite of its large size. Sabrina and her siblings all knew their mother was still acclimating to living by herself after their father's death. Although Wendy's marriage to Casper had been rocky at times, it had lasted thirty-three years and produced six children. It couldn't be easy to go from a crowded house full of family in the place where you grew up to living in a big mansion alone in a new place. They'd all done their best to drop by for visits or get Wendy out of the house and into Chatelaine proper when they could. But they knew she still felt lonely sometimes. A couple of Sabrina's siblings had even tried setting their mother up with one of the handful of eligible bachelors her age that they'd met since moving to town, but Wendy had shot down all their efforts. It was good, though, to see her gathering her family around her again this way.

"All right," Wendy said when all of her children were seated in the dining room. "I want us to go around the table, and I want to hear what each and every one of you has been up to. Sabrina first."

Dangit. Sabrina knew she should have sat farther away from her mother than immediately to her right. This could be tricky. How did one tell one's mother that one almost had another one-night stand with one's previous one-night stand?

Thankfully, Wendy clarified. "How are my granddaughters doing in there?"

Her mom was over the moon at the prospect of welcoming not just her first, but her second grandchild into the family. She called Sabrina almost daily to chat about how to take care of herself and what to expect when expecting twins, since she'd gone through it twice herself, and no two pregnancies were the same, and, by the way, while they were on the subject, was there any news Sabrina wanted to tell her mother about how she and her baby daddy were getting along?

"You mean since we spoke on the phone yesterday?" Sabrina asked with a smile. "I imagine they've gained a couple millimeters or two in length and probably at least a tenth of an ounce in weight."

Her mother made a face at her. "Oh, you. Have you felt the twins moving around yet?"

Sabrina shook her head wistfully. "Not yet. Soon I hope."

Wendy directed her attention to her youngest son, on Sabrina's other side. "And, Ridge, how are Hope and Evie doing?"

"As well as can be expected," he replied. "She's still

having those dreams about the older couple, and their faces are a little less cloudy than they were at first, but she still doesn't recognize them or even know if they're real people or just, you know, dreams."

One by one, Wendy went around the table asking her children how everything was going in their respective lives, and one by one, they all told her. Sabrina learned that Jade's high school reunion was coming up next month, that Nash was genuinely enjoying being foreman of the Fortune ranch, that her brother Arlo was thinking about investing in yet another ranch he wanted to turn around and that Dahlia's herd of sheep was coming along nicely. Which, oh, goody, meant more wool for Sabrina to use at her textile camp—provided Dahlia could spare any this early in her venture—once Zane finally realized that revitalizing his own pond was a much better option for his ranch than trying to steal land she already owned.

The family had finished breakfast, and Sabrina and her siblings were cleaning up the aftermath when, out of nowhere, the sound of cell phone notifications from pockets and purses interrupted their animated conversations.

"Must be one of those county-wide alerts about something," Arlo said, pulling his own phone from his back pocket. His expression changed, though, when he read what was on the screen. "What the heck? Not this again."

The other Fortunes all pulled out their own phones to see what their notifications were about since, presumably, they all received the same one.

"It's from the mystery wedding person again," Dahlia said.

A month ago, all the Fortunes, Wendy and her children alike, had received save-the-date cards for a wedding to take place in January. There was just one problem—none of them knew who had sent the invitations, and none of them knew anyone who was planning on getting married, in January or any other month. Especially anyone in Chatelaine, which was where the wedding would be taking place. Now all of them were receiving a text from an unidentified number Sabrina could only assume was the same person who sent the invites.

"Anybody have this number in their contacts list?" she asked them all. "'Cause it's sure not in mine."

All of her siblings and her mother said no.

"But it must be the same person who sent us the save-the-dates, right?" Jade asked.

It was safe to assume that, yes. But it didn't make the text any less baffling.

Dear Wedding Guests, it read. Which dress and suit do you like best? A, B or C? What followed was a string of photographs of different styles of wedding garb varying from western to formal to what Sabrina could only liken to "down home."

"It was weird when we got the invites last month," Ridge said, "and it's even weirder getting texts now."

"Right?" Jade agreed. "Whoever is doing this must know us all. Who could it be?"

"Obviously someone who has all our numbers," Arlo said.

"So who has all our numbers?" Dahlia asked.

The family members all exchanged curious looks. None had an answer.

"It must be someone from Cactus Grove," Sabrina said. "We haven't been in Chatelaine long enough for someone to have collected *all* our numbers."

"Unless Mom's been handing them out," Dahlia said with a meaningful look at their mother.

Wendy held up her hands in mock surrender. "Don't

look at me. I never give out your all's contact information without asking your permission first."

Which Sabrina figured was true. Her mother was an absolute tigress when it came to protecting her children.

"Wonder who else they texted?" Jade asked.

"Looks like just the seven of us," Nash replied after a tap on his phone. "Unless they blind cc'ed a bunch of other people. But I'm not sure how you'd do that without making the text an SMS, and this one doesn't appear to be that."

"Let's take another approach," Dahlia said. "Who do we know that likes dresses like these?" She scrolled through each of the photos on her phone, back and forth and back again.

"Or who do we know who likes suits like these?" Arlo added, doing the same kind of scrolling himself.

"Ask me," Ridge said, "I wouldn't be caught dead in the monkey suit."

"Yeah," Nash agreed. "I hate having to put on one of those things when I have to go to some big to-do."

"Besides, Nash is more of the square-dancing type," Arlo quipped, holding up the western-wear photo.

"That's not what men wear to square dance," Wendy chastened. "I actually kind of like that one. I like the tuxedo, too, though. And the last one."

"I like C best," Ridge said. "Only not in that awful pale blue."

"I like the blue," Wendy objected.

"Mom's just being polite," Ridge said. "In case the sender works for the NSA and is listening in on our conversation. Blind ccs and all that."

Wendy playfully swatted her youngest, and they all laughed. "I just can't decide which one I like best is all."

"I like C best, too," Sabrina said, agreeing with her youngest brother. "The dress especially."

"You don't think it's too plain?" Dahlia asked.

"It's perfect," Jade agreed. "I can see Dolly Parton in the first one, though, so there's that. Dolly can do no wrong."

"B is too formal, though," Dahlia said. "Pretty, but too conventional. People should do their own thing for their weddings and not succumb to tradition."

"Spoken like someone who married on the fly in Vegas," Sabrina said with a grin. She still couldn't quite stop needling her sister about the circumstances of her wedding, since it sounded like something from a rom-com.

This time it was Dahlia who did the swatting.

"Stop!" Sabrina said, laughing.

Dahlia gave her twin one last thwack, then she laughed, too.

"Maybe it is the NSA," Ridge said, laughing along with his sisters. "It would explain how they got all our numbers."

"I guess we'll solve the mystery of who this is from at the wedding in January," Dahlia said, "and which outfits they end up choosing."

"But why is it such a big mystery?" Sabrina wondered aloud. "Usually people can't wait to tell everyone they're getting married."

"We'll just have to wait for an actual invitation," Jade said. "First one who gets one, let the rest of us know."

IT WAS WITH no small amount of trepidation that Sabrina pulled her car to a stop in front of Zane's house the Friday following the weird wedding text breakfast with her family. She didn't know why she was so nervous. It was only dinner. Okay, admittedly *with his entire big family*, whom she had yet to meet, but still just a meal. He was going to be dining with her and her entire big family at her place next week, too, so that all of Peach's and Plum's clans on both their parents' sides could get to know each other before their arrival. Co-parenting meant co-familying, too, she and Zane had decided.

The minute she opened her car door, she heard sounds of raucous joy coming from inside the house. It was a beautiful, balmy evening, so the windows were open wide, and the large great room, she recalled, faced the front. When she looked in that direction, she could see bodies darting about and hear music playing, something twangy and folksy and fun. She inhaled a deep breath, reminded herself that everything was going to be just fine, then began to make her way toward the front door.

Astrid was opening it before Sabrina even made it to the porch, the housekeeper's smile warm and welcoming. "Miss Fortune," she said. "It is so nice to see you again."

"Please call me Sabrina, Astrid," she replied. "Something tells me we're going to be seeing a lot of each other before too long."

"I look forward to that, Miss Fortune," Astrid said. "It will be nice to have the sound of children's laughter in the house."

Okay, they could work on the *Miss Fortune* thing later, Sabrina thought as she made her way into the house proper.

The festivity grew louder as she walked deeper inside. And when she arrived at the great room, it was to discover there were even more people present than just Zane and his brothers, including some young women who were clearly *not* brothers, presumably girlfriends of some of the boys. Everyone seemed to notice her entrance at once, because they all stopped talking and looked her way. Not even in those anxiety dreams about being naked in public had Sabrina felt more on display.

She glanced down to make sure she had in fact remembered to put on clothes before she left. Yep, she'd even correctly buttoned her lavender, untucked blouse—the one that hid the unfastened fly of her jeans—and she had her flat gold sandals on the right feet. Okay, maybe she hadn't done the best job with her braid, but the escaped tendrils she could feel framing her face were fashionable. She was almost sure of it. Then she looked back up at the crowd. They all broke out in smiles and laughter again, and ran over to make her acquaintance.

"All right, all right, don't overwhelm her," Zane said as his family descended. "You don't want to scare her off before she's even learned which one of you is which."

With clear reluctance, the crowd of young people reined themselves in. Barely. Zane looked gorgeous, as always, tonight wearing dark jeans and a plaid western shirt in every color of green that made his eyes even brighter than usual. He'd gotten a haircut in the days since she'd seen him, something she had mixed feelings about. On one hand, the shorter style also showcased his eyes and chiseled features. On the other, she kind of liked him rakishly scruffy-looking.

He gazed at her nervously for a minute, as if he wasn't sure how to greet her. Then, softly, he said, "Hey, thanks for coming," leaned in to give her a quick kiss on the cheek, then settled his arm loosely around her waist. There was nothing untoward in either gesture. Both were clearly light and affectionate. Before she realized what she was doing, Sabrina was leaning into him, too, and wrapping her arm around his waist as well.

And wow, there went the spine-sizzling heat again, just with those two simple gestures. She was beginning to wonder if there would ever come a time when she didn't feel hot and bothered around Zane.

She pushed the thought away, smiled as amiably as she

could and lifted her other hand in greeting. "Hello," she said to the room at large. "I'm Sabrina."

The boys all began to talk at once, so Zane lifted his hand to stop them. "I'll make the introductions," he said over all their voices, loudly enough—and with enough big brother authority—that they all piped down.

He pointed at the brother standing closest to him and said, "This is Cody, my youngest. And mouthiest," he added with a grin.

"Hey, I'm not the mouthiest," Cody objected playfully. "I'm the most verbally gifted."

The others howled at that.

"And this is his girlfriend, Hannah." Zane indicated the cute, petite redhead beside him.

Although he'd introduced both kids warmly, there was something in his voice that made her think his relationship with them at the moment was a tad cool. Then she remembered how, the day she'd come here to tell him about her pregnancy, Zane mentioned having to talk Cody out of running away to join the rodeo with his girlfriend. He was probably still worried about the possibility. Then again, when she and Preston had been their age, they'd been chomping at the bit to get out from under their parents' thumbs and live their own life together, too. Zane might very well have a reason to be concerned.

"This is Wyatt, my oldest younger brother," Zane continued, gesturing toward the next boy in line. "And his girlfriend Lakshmi," he added for the dark-haired, dark-eyed girl beside him.

Wyatt extended a hand in an assertive, *I'm-the-oldest-brother-okay-except-for-Zane* fashion, and Sabrina shook it. "Really glad you could come tonight, Sabrina," he said. "We've all been looking forward to meeting you."

The others murmured their agreement and, Sabrina

couldn't help noticing, seemed to be steering their gazes to her abdomen, where their future nieces were currently residing. She did her best not to chuckle.

"This is Shane, one of the twins," Zane continued down the line. "And his boyfriend Esteban."

Shane nodded and Esteban smiled as both said their hellos to her.

"And this is Levi, the other twin," Zane said as he gestured at the last boy in the group.

"No, Shane is the other twin," Levi countered. "I came first. He's the backup."

Sabrina laughed at that. She was going to have to use it on Dahlia at some point, since Dahlia was a whole twenty-two minutes younger than her.

"My girlfriend, Chloe, couldn't make it," Levi continued. "She's doing a study-abroad in Japan this semester. But she'll be back by Christmas vacation, so you can meet her then."

Sabrina would be seven months pregnant at Christmastime. Peach and Plum would probably be more like Pumpkin and Watermelon by then. And Sabrina would be as big as the Alamo. Oh, boy. She couldn't wait.

She marveled at Zane's family. They all seemed so... young. She found herself wondering what her daughters would be like as teenagers and college students, then stopped herself. *Don't wish it away*, she cautioned herself. Once those girls were born, time, she was certain, would zip by faster than the speed of light.

"It's nice to meet all of you," she told them. "And have faces to put to names for the girls' uncles."

She almost added *and aunts, too*, but didn't want to presume. They all were really young, and people did come and go in life. Then she glanced at Cody and Hannah, at the way they were gazing at each other. Oh, that was a familiar look, she couldn't help thinking. She used to look at Preston like that. Young love was a powerful force. Something told her that *Aunt Hannah* would indeed eventually be a part of the girls' lives.

Then she looked at Zane and wondered how she looked at him lately. What she'd felt for her husband way back when had been so immediate, so intense. The way feelings so often were when one was a teenager. What she felt for Zane, though... Well, certainly there had been an immediacy and intensity between them when they met. Doubtless because he'd made her feel like a teenager that night. Since seeing him again, though, things had felt a lot less... Well. Her feelings were deeper and more complicated than the lightheartedness and lightheadedness that came with youth. What she was feeling for him was fuller somehow. More dimensional. More adult. More everything, really. She just wished she knew what to do about it.

"Come on," he told the group. "Astrid said dinner would be served at seven sharp, and you know how she is."

Shane looked at his watch as he took Esteban's hand. "We only have thirty seconds," he told his companions. "We better hurry."

Zane reached for Sabrina's hand, too, and she twined her fingers with his as if it were the most natural thing in the world to do. And somehow, she knew that feeling wasn't entirely due to the fact that the two of them would be co-parenting their daughters.

Dinner was, not surprisingly, delicious. Who knew a Valkyrie who made havreflarns and cloudberry tea could also create the best chicken enchilada casserole and jalapeño corn bread Sabrina had ever tasted? One thing she didn't have to worry about where the twins were concerned was whether or not they'd be properly fed during the time they spent at their father's place. Sabrina only wondered if maybe she could stay over with them sometimes.

There it was again. A stray wish to take up residence here at Zane's ranch. Just what was her brain trying to tell her these days?

The dinner conversation was all over the map, with Zane's family talking about everything from childhood vacations to family pets to failed school projects. Eventually, though, the discussion veered to focus on Zane. Including, inescapably, Zane's former girlfriends.

"So, Sabrina," Wyatt said over the remnants of dessert, "did Zane ever tell you about the girlfriend he had who quoted poetry every time she talked?"

The other brothers laughed.

"And not even her own poetry," Wyatt added. "It was all stuff from hundreds of years ago."

"Including *The Canterbury Tales*," Shane said. "In Middle English."

"It was when I was in college," Zane told Sabrina. "She was an English major. A really serious one."

Sabrina chuckled. College years really could be blunder years.

"Or the one who got busted for growing weed and mushrooms on the campus quad," Levi added, "and then tried to pass them off as requirements for one of her labs."

"Also college," Zane assured her. "She was a biology major."

"Oh, don't forget when he used the dating app!" Cody added.

"No," Zane said decisively. "We are not going to talk about the dating app. I was only on it for two weeks."

His brothers all snickered.

"And in two weeks," Shane said, "you had, what? Five first dates that ended really badly?"

"Or didn't even get started," Levi stated. "There was the woman who, as soon as the server brought the bread basket, starting tearing it up and putting it in her purse to feed her pet rat that she'd brought along."

"Which was a health code violation," Zane said. "So I had every right to leave after prepaying the bill."

"And the one who, halfway through dinner," Cody added, "whipped out her multilevel marketing campaign and gave a thirty-minute spiel loud enough to lasso in the whole restaurant."

Zane laughed a little anxiously and threw Sabrina a nervous look. "Well, at least it was for a product that could have some potential use."

"Oh, I'm sure lots of people at Chez Whatever It Was were chomping at the bit to buy sex toys that night."

Sabrina wished she could laugh along with the rest of his family, but she wasn't finding all the talk of Zane's past, ah, *romantic encounters*, particularly funny. And not just because they were clearly making him uncomfortable, too.

"And don't forget the Elvis impersonator!" Wyatt added with a laugh.

Zane seemed to sense her apprehension, because he lifted a hand and told his brothers to knock it off. "That app stuff was years ago," he added. "And all it ended up doing was cementing my conviction that romantic love doesn't exist."

Sabrina told herself she should be happy to hear him say that, since she no longer believed romantic love existed, either. For some reason, though, his assertion was accompanied by a sick feeling in the pit of her stomach.

Indigestion, she told herself. She'd started having episodes of that as her pregnancy moved along. What she was feeling had nothing to do with anything Zane said. She'd just overdone it on the enchilada casserole.

But the brothers weren't quite ready to let their roasting of their big brother go and went on to describe a litany of other less-than-stellar experiences Zane had had with women over the years, going all the way back to high school. And even if none of those encounters had been particularly, ah, productive, they kind of flew in the face of his assurances to Sabrina that he hadn't been involved with very many women. No, maybe he hadn't been in many serious relationships, but he certainly had more experience with the opposite sex than Sabrina did. And why that bothered her, she had no idea. It just kind of skirted dishonesty on his part somehow. She found herself wondering if there were other things he hadn't exactly been honest about, either.

"Wow, Zane," she said when the levity was dying down. She tried to inject a lightness into her voice that she was nowhere close to feeling as she added, "You've dated a lot more women than you let on."

"No. I haven't," he tried to reassure her. He shot his brothers a good, long glare. "These guys are exaggerating. Hard."

But she couldn't help noticing he hadn't said they weren't telling the truth.

"Okay, I have *dated* my fair share of women," he said, backpedaling. "But dating didn't mean I was involved with any of them."

"This is true," Levi said when he seemed to realize Sabrina was taking their ribbing of Zane way more seriously than they intended. "He never brought any of those women home to meet us. We only know about them because they came up during the talk about red flags when we were all old enough to start dating."

The other brothers all nodded earnestly.

She wished she could believe that. But after an evening

filled with so many, ah, revelations, not all of which had been exactly good, it wasn't doing much to help the nausea rolling in her stomach. She did her best to smile one of her no-hard-feelings smiles in an effort to pretend it didn't matter. Fortunately, she must have been at least a little convincing, because the conversation started up again, this time with much better stories about Zane.

How he let Wyatt beat him at chess when he was teaching him how to play.

How patient he was with Cody when he couldn't figure out a ring knot.

How he came to every opening night Levi had in drama club and sat front row, center stage, even when the play was the student-written *FOMO and Juul-iet*, which, yes, he admitted was every bit as terrible as it sounded.

And finally, how accepting and loving he was when Shane was terrified to come out and tell his big, brash cattleman brother he was gay.

That was when Sabrina realized maybe she was being too hard on Zane and that, yes, he was as good a guy as she had realized from the moment they met. This house really did feel a lot different when it was full of his family than it had when she was here visiting him alone. She understood now why he had been so happy when she told him she was pregnant. Houses like this had been built at a time and in a place where families were big and rowdy and boisterous. Just like Zane's. He really was going to be a wonderful father, she thought, regardless of how they worked out the co-parenting thing.

Which they *were* going to work out. Any day now.

CHAPTER NINE

ZANE AND CODY had just started rinsing the dishes to put in the dishwasher when he realized his brother hadn't said a word since dinner. Which was funny, considering he'd been the most vociferous of all of them when it came to razzing his big brother earlier. It was the main reason, actually, that he'd asked his youngest sibling to help him clean up instead of one of the older boys. He'd felt more comfortable leaving Sabrina to get to know the rest of his family because the rabble-rouser was in here with him instead. The other boys had matured quite a bit since heading off to college, but Cody still had a lot of growing up to do. It was just another reason he was adamant that the kid get his degree. And on that note...

"So how's school been since our last talk?" he asked matter-of-factly. "Settling in a little better?"

Cody didn't answer at first. He seemed way more concerned about making sure the glassware was lined up on the top rack with perfect precision. Zane noted a movement at the kitchen door behind his brother and saw Sabrina, who was carrying a stray plate they must have left behind. She seemed to sense the stilted mood in the kitchen, however, because the smile on her face fell, and she closed her mouth over whatever she had planned to say. Zane threw her a grateful look but didn't indicate she should leave. In fact, he was kind of glad to have her here, even if it was just for moral support. Not to mention she just looked really pretty this evening.

Cody hadn't noticed her arrival. When he finally looked up at Zane, it was with an expression of consternation. "It sucks," he grumbled. "I hate it. I don't want to go to college, Zane. I wanna rodeo."

Instead of jumping down his brother's throat about that—*again*—Zane tried to be understanding. "I know you do. But you have plenty of time for that, and college—"

"College won't teach me anything I need to know," Cody interrupted. "It'll just waste time. Time I could be using honing my skills. I'm a good cowboy," he insisted when Zane tried to interrupt. "And Hannah blue-ribboned in three events at the Barrel Blast last summer. She and I are both ready for rodeo *now*."

Helplessly, Zane looked at Sabrina. She smiled her encouragement but said nothing. This was clearly between him and Cody.

"It's not that easy, Cody," Zane said.

"Yes, it is," his brother countered.

"You're too young. Both of you are. You have no idea what the world out there holds. In a few years, you'll both be in a better position to figure out what you want. What's really important."

Cody growled a sound of frustration. "We already know what we want, Zane!" he shouted. "We know what's important! You're the one who refuses to see it!"

"Cody, you're too young to realize how—"

"I'm eighteen!"

"Exactly."

"I'm old enough to vote, to be sent to war, to serve on a jury, to get a credit card, to buy a house… I can do damn near anything I want to."

Zane hated that he couldn't argue with any of that. Even so, Cody was still too young to be making big decisions.

"And you know what else I can do now that I'm eighteen?" he asked, his voice filled with challenge. "I can refuse to go to college. I can get married to the woman I love. And you know what, Zane? Hannah and I might just do that. We don't need your permission. We don't even have to tell you about it. We can just run off and elope. And then join the rodeo. With or without your consent."

As if to illustrate that that was exactly what he and Hannah were going to do, Cody jutted up his chin, guided the upper rack into the dishwasher and closed the door. Then, very calmly, he turned to walk out of the kitchen. He paused when he saw Sabrina, but only for a second. Then he strode right past her.

As he did, he said, "See if you can talk some sense into him, Sabrina. Tell him I'm right."

And then he was gone, back out to join his brothers. And his would-be fiancée. A bolt of something hot and unpleasant shot through Zane's brain at the very idea of him and Hannah running off to get married and his not being able to do a thing to stop it.

"Do you believe that?" he said after his brother was gone.

"Which part?" Sabrina asked. "About him not wanting to go to college? Yes, I believe that. College isn't for everyone."

"It is for my family. Like I told you before, my parents set up college funds for all of us. They were adamant that we all get degrees. Didn't matter what in. Just that we got a college education. If they were in this kitchen right now and heard what Cody just said, they'd be telling him the same thing I did."

And they would have. Of that, Zane was absolutely certain.

"That doesn't necessarily mean they'd be right," Sabrina

told him softly. "And really, Cody wasn't wrong about the other stuff, either."

She might as well have just smacked him across the face with a wet fish. "How do you figure that?"

"Eighteen is the legal age to do all the things he mentioned," she said. "Plus a million more. The US government thinks it's perfectly okay to let Cody make big decisions at his age. A lot of eighteen-year-olds have taken on way more responsibility than Cody has, and they're doing just fine."

"A lot of kids his age aren't my little brother."

"No, they're not," she agreed. "But you're not your little brother, either, Zane."

Ouch.

She took a few more steps into the kitchen and set the stray plate in the sink with the others he and Cody hadn't finished loading. Then she turned to look at him full on. Only inches separated them now, and he realized he'd done her wrong by saying she only looked pretty tonight. Truth was, Sabrina was the most beautiful woman he'd ever seen. Her lavender shirt somehow made her eyes look bluer, and her pale blond bangs were wisps of silk falling over her forehead. She smelled nice, too, something floral and spicy and downright irresistible. It was all he could do not to lean in for more.

"I wasn't much older than Cody when I married Preston," she said. "But we might as well have married when we were eighteen. Both of us knew we were ready. And yes, maybe it didn't turn out so well for us, but that had nothing to do with our maturity level."

He sobered at that. Okay, yeah. Maybe there were a lot of young people out there who learned hard lessons earlier than other people did. Sabrina had learned one of the worst after losing her husband when she was so young.

"We knew our parents would react the same way you're reacting to Cody right now," she went on, "and even if they'd forbidden us to get married, we would have done it, anyway. We would have turned our backs on both our families and gone our own way without them. Is that what you want to have happen to Cody? To forbid him from following his heart and losing him?"

"Of course not. But he's—"

"He's going to do what he wants to do, Zane. You telling him he can't is just going to make him more determined. And if you keep it up, it's just going to ensure that he never speaks to you again."

Zane felt so helpless. He'd spent the last ten years being the final word for all four of his brothers. The older ones had always heeded his decisions. But then, they'd all agreed with those decisions. They'd all wanted to go to college. But Cody had always been such a handful. So high-spirited and willful. So...so...

"He is so young, Sabrina," Zane said quietly. "He has no idea what the real world is like."

"Maybe. Maybe not. He might know a lot more than you think. But that's just it, Zane. It's up to him to find out. It's not up to you to protect him for the rest of his life."

She was right. He knew she was right. But that didn't make it any easier for him to accept. Still, maybe he and Cody needed to sit down and have a longer talk about what he really wanted, and what all that involved. More to the point, maybe Zane should listen to his little brother. Then maybe they could find some kind of common ground.

Maybe.

"Is this the way you're gonna be with Peach and Plum?" he asked Sabrina.

She laughed and relaxed a little. She untangled the arms she'd crossed as she'd spoken about her marriage, settling one on the kitchen counter and the other on her hip. "Probably not," she admitted. "I'll probably be as fierce a protector of them as you are of your brothers. But I hope that at least part of me will be able to see that they're their own person and that it's only up to me to do my best to educate and guide them and hope they make good decisions once they're on their own."

"And if they don't make good decisions?"

She lifted one shoulder and let it drop. Then she raised the hand on her hip to cup his cheek gently in her palm. Warmth spread from Zane's face to every other part of his body at the contact.

"Then I'll be there to catch them when they fall," she said softly. "Just like you will be."

Zane covered her hand with his and smiled. Then he removed it and pressed her palm to his lips, giving it a quick kiss before moving both their hands back between them. But he didn't let go.

"I guess that's really what parenting comes down to in the long run, isn't it?" he said. "Being there for your kids not just when they succeed, but when they fail, too."

She nodded. "Probably something you and I should do for each other, too," she said. "Have each other's backs, I mean."

He gave her fingers a gentle squeeze then, reluctantly, let her hand go. "This isn't going to be easy, is it?" he asked. "This parenting stuff."

Sabrina sighed. "I'm guessing no. But I'm also guessing it will have rewards that make up for that."

Zane nodded. Not sure anything else needed to be said on that score, he turned his attention to the still-not-cleaned-up kitchen and shook his head. "Hopefully there will also be rewards when they stiff you on the cleanups they promised they'd help with."

She chuckled. "Let him visit with his brothers and girl-friend. They're only home for the weekend. I'll help you clean up."

Zane nodded. "Thanks. Probably best to leave Cody be for now, anyway. Pushing him any more could just make things worse."

"And I need to get used to cleaning up after more than just me," she said as she joined him at the sink.

He laughed, too. "Oh, cleaning up after the Baston bunch will definitely help you out on that score."

CLEANING UP AFTER a large family was more time-con-suming than Sabrina would have guessed. In fact, by the time she and Zane returned to the dining room to rejoin his family and their various significant others, every last one of them had disappeared.

"Okay, that wasn't exactly a quick cleanup," she said, "but it's way too early for any of them to have turned in for the night."

Zane seemed just as puzzled. He looked as if he was going to reply when his gaze lit on something at the center of the table. She watched as he approached, then picked up a pad of paper, holding it up for her to see that there was a note scrawled on it. For a minute, she feared maybe Cody and Hannah really had run off to elope, taking the rest of the dinner guests with them as witnesses. But judging by the smile on Zane's face as he read over the missive, that wasn't the case at all.

"They've all gone into Chatelaine for trivia night at Remi's Reads," he said when he looked up. "Remi's does it every few months. It's a pretty big deal. Chatelaine Bar and Grill donates pizza. The LC Club donates a grand prize of dinner for two. There's gift cards and other stuff from some of the other restaurants." He nodded toward the note again. "My brothers also say they're all going to grab a bite to eat afterward. Guess enchilada casserole and dessert, not to mention free pizza, just isn't enough when you're a growing boy or girl. And they say that they're doing all this so that us *lovebirds*—" he pointed at the note "—their word, not mine, can have some time alone. You and I have been directed to go to the library."

Sabrina grinned. "And what are we supposed to find there?"

"No telling. Probably should check it out, though, to make sure it's nothing that needs care or feeding. Wouldn't be the first time one of those boys smuggled in a stray something or other and stayed mum until it was too late for me to do anything about it. That's how we wound up with six barn cats at one point."

"Then by all means, lead the way."

The library was upstairs and down the hall from Zane's office, Sabrina discovered, and it was just as rustic and masculine as the rest of the house. There was a fireplace, though, where someone—gosh, no telling who—had lit a small, cozy fire. Someone else had placed an ice bucket holding a bottle of something with two slender flutes before it, and a cozy-looking throw had been spread out like a picnic blanket. And yet another someone had set up the sound system to play music that was soft and sexy and full of saxophones.

"Gee, this isn't obvious at all, is it?" Zane said in a deadpan voice.

"This is exactly what a college student would consider a romantic scenario," Sabrina replied. "It's straight out of Hollywood."

Of course, it wasn't just college students and Hollywood who would think that. She thought it was pretty romantic, too. Shame about the wine, though.

As if reading her mind, Zane crossed to the ice bucket to withdraw the bottle from the ice. Then he smiled again. "Sparkling apple juice," he said. He squinted at some numbers around the neck. "Bottled this year, no less. An excellent vintage, even if it is a screw top."

"Best not let it go to waste then," Sabrina agreed.

She joined him at the fireplace, and he poured each of them a glass. Then he looked around the room again. "Hmm. That sofa over there—" he gestured to a love seat that had been awkwardly shoved to one side "—is supposed to be right here in front of the fireplace where people can sit to enjoy it. Looks like someone—" no telling who "—decided to do some rearranging."

"The blanket is fine," Sabrina told him.

"You sure?"

She nodded. "It will be good to stretch out my legs."

He set their glasses on the hearth, then folded himself, legs crossed pretzel fashion, onto the blanket. Then he held up his hand toward Sabrina, who took it and managed to situate herself beside him. She realized pretty quickly, though, that yes, she could indeed stretch out her legs, but she had nothing to lean against as she did. Zane seemed to realize her dilemma, because he moved closer and positioned himself so that she could lean back against him. Then, just to be sure she didn't tip over, he put his arm around her. She gratefully leaned into him, accepted the glass of juice he held out to her and listened to the soft crackle of the fire. And she tried very, very hard not to think about how good she felt in that moment.

Pregnancy hormones, she tried to tell herself again. But, really, she was beginning not to believe herself when she said that. She hadn't been pregnant when she met Zane that night at the fundraiser. And the way she was feeling right now was a lot like the way she'd felt that night.

For a few minutes, neither seemed to know what to say. Then Zane asked, "So…how have you been feeling lately? Good?"

She nodded. "The nausea I was feeling before I saw the doctor has pretty much gone away. I get tired a lot, though. Sometimes so tired that I have to lie down for a little while or even take a nap. But the doctor said that's normal. Good, actually, because it means the babies are growing well."

"Have you felt them move yet?"

She shook her head. "Still too soon according to the reading I've been doing. But I'm hopeful it won't be too long. Especially since there are two of them in there."

"You'll tell me when that happens, right?"

She turned her head to look at him. How could he think she would keep that from him? "You'll know the second I do."

He smiled. "Thanks."

Due to their position on the floor, their faces were so close. Mere inches separated Zane's mouth from hers. His eyes, those gorgeous green eyes she'd nearly drowned in the night she met him, were clear and bright and happy, and she felt herself going deep under, the same way she had then.

"So," she said in an effort to keep herself from succumbing, "it was nice of Astrid to stay late tonight to fix dinner."

She told herself to move away, to figure out how to be comfortable without the toasty warm feeling of having Zane beside her, because just changing the subject did nothing to keep her from melting into this man.

"She was happy to do it," he said softly. "She misses the boys, too, and loves to be around when they're home. I think she's going to be hovering over Peach and Plum, too, whenever they come to visit. I saw some booties-in-progress in her knitting basket the other day. She never had kids herself, so she's getting her Amma on with the twins."

"Amma?" Sabrina asked, still way more focused on Zane's amazing eyes—they had a tiny circle of gold around the pupil that was mesmerizing—than what they were talking about. What were they talking about, anyway?

"That's a Viking word for grandmother," Zane said, the words tumbling into her ears on a warm breath. "Or so Astrid said. In a not-so-subtle hint."

Sabrina smiled. "My mother is still trying to decide what she wants her grandbabies to call her. Though last time we talked, she was leaning toward Glamma."

He chuckled lightly.

"That or Queenie."

Now he laughed outright. "I wish my folks could be around to meet their granddaughters. Your mom would have to fight my mom for Queenie."

"Your folks will be around, Zane," she said with quiet certainty. "Every time you look at your daughters, your mom and dad both will be right there."

For another long moment, neither said a word. Then, very slowly, Zane started to lower his head toward hers. Without even thinking about what she was doing, Sabrina tipped her head back, too. Then he was covering her mouth with his, brushing his lips lightly over hers, sending heat splashing through her belly and to all points beyond. When he pulled away, she curled her hand around his nape and pulled him back. This time she was the one to kiss him, in the same sweet, gentle way he had her.

Then the song that had been playing so quietly in the background segued into another, and both Zane and Sabrina smiled.

"You remember this song?" he asked.

She nodded. "Oh, yes. This is the song we danced to that night at the fundraiser."

"And if memory serves, we didn't get to finish it."

They hadn't, actually. Because Zane had danced her out of the hotel ballroom and into the fair, fine night outside, across the patio and onto the hotel grounds, all the way to the secluded gazebo where they shared their first kiss. And then their second. And their third. And there probably would have been a fourth, fifth and sixth if Zane hadn't asked her if she wanted to blow off the rest of the fundraiser and go home with him instead. And, of course, if Sabrina hadn't eagerly said yes.

He brushed his lips over hers once more. "So you wanna finish it now?"

She grinned. "I'd love to."

He stood and extended a hand toward her, pulling her up alongside him after she accepted it. Then he roped an arm around her waist and took her hand in his. She'd forgotten what a good dancer he was and remembered how she'd wanted to ask him where he learned that night of the fundraiser, before the two of them got sidetracked.

So she asked him now, "Where did you learn to dance?"

He chuckled and groaned at the same time. "My mother made me take cotillion classes when I was in middle school," he told her. "She was so sure they'd come in handy when I started dating, and then I'd be all set for my wedding day."

She tried to imagine an adolescent Zane in a ballroom full of other kids, all of them awkward and uncertain. But she couldn't. She'd bet he was every bit as confident and suave as he was now. Every girl in his class had probably wanted him for her partner.

"I hated it," he told her. "But believe it or not, I honestly think it made me a better rider. Gave me better balance in the saddle. I made all the boys do cotillion, too. Told them it was what Mom would have wanted. And she would have. If Cody does well in rodeo, he can thank me for making him go to those lessons."

Sabrina smiled inwardly that Zane already seemed to be coming around to his little brother wanting to buck the Baston trend of college. It showed how much he'd listened to Cody tonight. That was a good quality in a parent-to-be.

It was a good quality in a partner, too, she thought before she could stop herself.

"Where did you learn to dance?" he asked Sabrina.

By now, he'd guided her all the way around the library and was starting another circle. "Believe it or not, as a college PE credit. They only offered ballroom dancing for one semester because so few students enrolled, but I jumped on it. I was terrible at every sport you can name, but I always loved dancing."

"Well, hopefully our daughters will get your grace and my athleticism."

Our daughters. She was pretty sure that was the first time either of them had said those words out loud in that way. Until now, it had always been *the twins* or *the babies*, or *my twins* or *my babies,* or the nicknames Peach and Plum. She didn't think they'd ever even said *our* twins or *our* babies. But now Zane had said *our daughters* as if it were the most natural thing in the world.

Their gazes connected, as if he had just realizd the same thing, and they were suddenly clicking…or something…in a way they hadn't until now. A way that was more familiar. More intimate. And somehow, in that moment, Sabrina knew they weren't going to finish this dance tonight, either.

As if reading her mind, when Zane danced her toward the library entrance this time, he kept going out into the hall. And then farther, past a half dozen rooms, until he arrived at the one she remembered as being his. He guided her through the door, nudging it closed behind him, and kissed her again. The way he had that night at the fundraiser, in the gazebo. A kiss that had made heat seep into every cell of her body and ignite flames everywhere he touched her.

It had the same effect tonight. But there was more tonight, too. Tonight, his kiss made her feel as if nothing in her life would ever go wrong again. As if she were exactly where she was supposed to be in the world. Deep down in her heart it felt as if the two of them had been leading up to this moment from the second they met and were just finishing something they started months ago.

Oh, yes, Sabrina thought when he pulled away to gaze into her eyes. Everything was just as it was supposed to be.

She wanted Zane. The way she'd had him that night at the fundraiser, stretched out beside her, nestled on top of her, moving behind her. She wanted his hands stroking every inch of her body, wanted to touch every part of his in return. He seemed to want that, too, because he cupped a hand over her nape and bent his head to hers again, covering her mouth with his.

He moved his hand from her back to her front, to free the first few buttons on her shirt. So Sabrina freed a few of his, too. The silky skin she found underneath was roped with muscle and sinew and grew hotter everywhere her fingers fell. As she touched him with one hand, she lifted her other to thread her fingers through his silky, brown hair, cupping the back of his head to pull him closer still. She returned his kisses with equal ardor, and with each brush of her lips over his, her desire for him—her need for him—grew stronger.

He just felt so good. All of him felt so good. He surrounded her somehow, and everything else faded to nothing. In that moment, Zane was everything. He filled every corner of her brain, every chamber of her heart, every breath of her spirit. The thought of that should have over-whelmed her. Somehow, though, it just seemed to fit so perfectly.

When he pulled his mouth from hers, she reluctantly let him go. He didn't go far, though. His face hovered just over hers, his green eyes seeming darker somehow, his lips curved into a tempting little smile.

"Are you sure about this?" he murmured as he lifted a hand to wrap an errant wisp of her hair around his finger.

She nodded. "More than sure. It feels like this has been a long time coming. Like we've wasted so much time tip-toeing around it."

"It does kind of feel like the natural order of things, doesn't it? Like that night four months ago was just a pre-lude to all this. You and me, right here, right now."

He was right. It felt like no time at all had passed since they'd last been in this room together. Like this was her second chance with him. Her chance to get it right. To wake up beside Zane in the morning instead of escaping under cover of darkness. She smiled. All roads led to Chatelaine. She didn't know why it had taken her so long to see that.

Zane released the strand of hair he'd twisted around his finger and kissed her again, reaching around to free the tie that held what little of her braid that remained in place. He pulled back as the pale blond tresses tumbled free around her shoulders, then buried his fist under the silky mass to curl his fingers around her nape and pull her forward. Nuzzling her throat, he dragged his open mouth lightly up and down the side of her neck, nosing aside the collar of her shirt to kiss her collarbone, too.

As he did, he freed a few more buttons on her shirt and

tucked his hand inside, discovering the champagne-colored lace of her bra. He grazed his thumb along the lower line of the garment, skimming his fingers over her sensitive flesh and then lower, over each elegant rib he found. Little bonfires erupted everywhere he touched her. What he was doing felt wonderful, but she wanted—she *needed*—more.

As if she'd spoken that need out loud, he dragged his lips back up along her throat, over her ear, jaw and chin, then finally covered her mouth again. Sabrina opened to receive him, and he tasted her deeply and thoroughly.

As he did, he dropped his hands to her waist again and began to move her backward, toward his bed. Impatiently, the two of them tugged down the covers, then returned to their embrace. Zane pressed his big body into hers, urging them both down onto the mattress until Sabrina lay on her back, her head cushioned by the palm of his hand. He positioned his own body alongside her, draping a leg over hers until his thigh was pressed into that most intimate part of her. She gasped at the contact, and he took advantage of her response to kiss her passionately again.

A tremor of anticipation shook her as he crowded himself more insistently against her and unfastened the remaining buttons of her shirt. Deftly, he unhooked the front closure of her bra until she felt a whisper of warm air caressing her naked torso. He trailed a line of butterfly kisses down her neck, along her shoulder and collarbone, between her breasts and finally, finally over one tender peak. He opened his mouth wide over her nipple and sucked deeply, the erotic pressure of his lips and tongue almost more than she could bear.

Oh. That felt…delicious. She wove her fingers through his silky hair to urge him closer still, silently begging for more. So Zane gave her more. He licked the undersides of her breasts with long, lingering strokes, taunted the stiff peaks with the tip of his tongue. With every taste, he pushed a hand lower, completely unzipping her jeans to dip his fingers inside, skimming along the waistband of her panties.

Sabrina was so focused on enjoying the pleasure she was feeling that she didn't pay attention to where his seemingly aimless wandering was taking him. Not until he pushed his hand beneath the silky fabric of her panties and buried his fingers in the damp, delicate folds of flesh between her legs. At that, she cried out, clenching her hands more tightly in his hair.

He paused his caresses at her response, as if awaiting a signal from her whether he should stop or continue. When her gaze found his, though, he was giving her a predatory little smile that told her he was enjoying himself as much as she was. She gave him a single, silent nod that she was having a good time, too, then she felt the fingers pressed against her moving again. Slowly, gently, two of them scissoring that most sensitive part of her before dipping inside to penetrate her. Her eyes fluttered closed at the contact, and her breathing grew shallow. Zane moved his fingers again, backward, forward, left, right, drawing erotic circles before thrusting his fingers inside again, more deeply.

"Oh, Zane…" she whispered. "Oh, that feels so… Oh…"

She heard his rough chuckle but couldn't quite bring herself to open her eyes. She remembered now what an attentive lover he'd been that night. He'd taken his time with her, touching her in ways she'd never been touched before, making her feel as if it was her first time all over again. And although this wasn't their first time, it did feel new. Like a new beginning for both of them. A do-over of sorts. And wow, was he doing it over well.

Vaguely, Sabrina registered the removal of her jeans, panties and sandals. She sensed Zane removing his clothing, too, then drawing near again. But there was nothing vague about her response when, instead of returning his fingers to the damp, pulsing core of her, his mouth went there instead. Her eyes snapped open wide, her fingers tangled in the sheets and she cried out again at the waves crashing through her when he flicked his tongue against her. All she could do after that was feel. Feel and marvel at the tremors and emotions wheeling through her, until they shattered into a billion shards of joy.

She called his name at her completion and pulled him up and into her arms. Clutching his shoulders, she clung to him for long moments. Before she could say anything, though—not that she had any idea what to say, since her brain had turned to pudding—he nestled himself between her legs and coaxed them wider still. She opened to him completely, wrapped her fingers around his long, rigid shaft and guided him to where they both wanted him to be.

He entered her with agonizing slowness, allowing her to acclimate her body to his. Sabrina drew her knees up toward herself, pressing the heels of her feet into the bed. Farther and farther Zane pushed himself, until he was buried as deep as he could be. He seemed to be everywhere inside her, filling places she hadn't realized were empty, heating parts of her she hadn't realized had cooled. For a moment, he stilled himself braced atop her, his gaze locked with hers. Then he withdrew and drove himself forward again. And she knew in that moment that Zane would never, ever leave those places inside her that he had claimed.

After that, she gave up thinking at all, because his movements became more rapid, more insistent. Again and again, he buried himself inside her, deeper and faster and harder. She bucked her hips upward to meet every thrust, wrapped her legs and arms tightly around him, until their damp, heated bodies seemed to fuse. Just when she was certain the two of them had indeed become one, his pumping ceased, his body went rigid atop hers, and he spilled himself inside her.

He turned their bodies so that she was atop him and kissed her again. First passionately, then gradually with more tenderness, a gentle denouement to their fierce climax. She dropped her hand to his chest and opened it over his heart, only to find it still beating as rapidly and raggedly as her own. It took a few moments for both of them to find their way back to the here and now. And when they did, all they could do was turn to look at the other and smile. Somehow, she knew they were both thinking the same thing. That this time, they weren't going to screw it up. They were going to do everything right. Because this time, they had more than themselves to think about.

That, she also knew, was why this time was even more amazing than the first. And she couldn't wait until they could do it again.

CHAPTER TEN

ZANE WAS ALMOST afraid to open his eyes the morning after his second night with Sabrina. He didn't want to awaken and discover that she had taken off again without saying goodbye. So instead, he slowly moved his hand across the top of the mattress until it connected with warm, soft, naked flesh. Immediately, he opened his eyes. There, in the soft early dawn light tumbling through his bedroom window, was Sabrina. Still asleep on her side facing him, her arm stretched toward him, her knuckles just shy of skimming his chest.

The euphoria that curled through him at seeing her there was almost more than he could stand. He covered her hand with his and lifted it to his mouth, then, one by one, kissed each of her fingertips. She stirred and smiled sleepily, then opened her eyes, too. He was afraid she might panic when she realized where she was and remembered what they had done last night. Instead, she lifted her other hand to push a few errant strands of blond from her eyes and smiled some more.

"Good morning," she murmured.

Oh, it was definitely that. "Good morning."

"What time is it?"

The right time, he wanted to reply. The perfect time. He glanced at the clock, then back at a delightfully sleep-rumpled Sabrina. "Not even seven," he said. "Sleep some more if you want. Night Heron Ranch is a pretty lazy place on Saturdays. And the boys probably won't be up till almost noon."

She winced at that. "They must have seen my car still here when they came home last night. And they must have seen that your bedroom door was closed."

"Yeah." Zane grinned. "And they must have realized that their plan last night worked exactly the way they wanted it to."

She winced again, but it was followed by a smile.

"They're big boys now, Sabrina," he reminded her. "They know what goes on between two consenting adults who are—" He stopped himself before revealing too much. Just how exactly *did* he feel about Sabrina, anyway? "Who are having a baby together," he finally finished saying.

She didn't seem to notice his hesitation. Instead, she scooched herself closer to him and opened her hand over the center of his chest. Beneath it, his heart started pounding wildly, just from a simple touch. He wanted to make love to her again. And then again after that. In fact, he wanted to spend the entire day in bed with her. Would there ever come a time when he'd had his fill of Sabrina Fortune?

"Last night was amazing," he told her.

She nodded. "Yeah, it was. Even better than the first time."

He wondered why that was. Seemed like the first time two people came together would always be the best. Especially a one-night stand—all the steamy excitement and taboo naughtiness of two virtual strangers coming together in the most intimate way possible. But she was right. Knowing more about her, spending time with her, sharing something besides sex with her, all of that had brought something more to the experience. Had made it even more intimate. Was it going to be even better next time? Then better the time after that?

And why was he suddenly looking forward to a lot of *next times* with Sabrina? It had been ages since he'd wanted a woman as much as he wanted her. Hell, he didn't think he'd ever wanted a woman as much as he did her. But especially since swearing off romance and love and all those things a person couldn't trust, he really hadn't looked forward to spending so much time with a woman. Now, though…

Well, now he was beginning to wonder if he'd been a bit hasty in dismissing all the love and romance stuff.

"We should do it again," she said, smiling.

Well, okay then. He bent his head to hers for a kiss.

"I mean when your brothers aren't right up the hall," she said with a chuckle.

He kissed her, anyway. Just a brief, chaste one, since anything else would have definitely led to what she didn't want to do in a full house, but it was still enough to get his motor revving.

"But we should definitely do it again," she repeated when he pulled away.

"The boys are all going to be driving or flying back to their respective schools tomorrow," he said. "And Astrid's off on Sundays. Got any plans for tomorrow night?"

She cupped her hand over his cheek. "Only to spend it with you."

"It's a date then," he said.

She smiled. "Our first."

Oh, wow, she was right. They'd technically known each other for months, had made love twice and they still hadn't been on a proper date, just the two of them.

"We really didn't go about this in the right order, did we?" he said.

She shook her head. "But we're getting there, anyway."

They were getting somewhere, that was for sure. And

they both seemed to be on the same path toward approaching it. Just where exactly *it* was, though… That remained to be seen. But at this moment, it felt pretty damned good.

"Come on," he said. "Let's get dressed and go downstairs. I'll fix you and our daughters a big ranch breakfast."

They had finished eating and were working on their second cups of decaf—Astrid had stocked up after Zane told her about Sabrina's prenatal sacrifice—when his phone pinged with a text about something he hadn't thought about for weeks. A text from his attorney that simply said, All done. You're good to go. Zane should have been delighted by the message. Instead, his heart sank, and a hole opened up in the pit of his stomach. Talk about bad timing.

"What's wrong?" Sabrina asked from her seat beside him.

He glanced up quickly. "What? Oh, nothing's wrong. Just some business I've had going on has been settled, that's all."

"On a Saturday?" she asked. "I didn't realize you were such a workaholic."

"I'm not," he assured her. "I thought it was going to be a while yet, before this was tied up." He forced a smile he was nowhere close to feeling. "Guess someone's doing business over a round of golf or something."

She didn't look anywhere near convinced. "You don't look like a man who's happy to have some business taken care of. You look like a kid who just found out there's no Santa Claus."

He laughed, but even he could hear the distress in the sound. "That's crazy. Santa Claus is totally real."

She didn't return his laugh. Didn't even chuckle. She did smile, but it didn't look any more genuine than the one he tried to force.

"Okay, so anyway," he interjected, "how do you want to spend the weekend? Before our first date tomorrow night?"

Her anxious expression cleared—some—and she opened her mouth to reply. But her phone started ringing somewhere in the room. She looked over at where she'd left her purse the evening before. The tightness in his chest clenched harder. He wanted to tell her not to answer it, since he was pretty sure he knew what that call was about. She seemed to sense his fear, because instead of ignoring her phone, she strode slowly over to withdraw it from the side pocket of her purse. He found some relief in the fact that the phone stopped ringing before she could get it out.

That relief evaporated, however, when he heard her say, "That's weird. It was my Realtor."

He was hoping she'd say something about calling back later, since, hey, Sabrina wasn't a workaholic, either, so why would she want to do business on a weekend? Instead, she pressed the button to return the call just as an alert dinged to let her know there was a voicemail.

"Hi, Dasha, it's Sabrina," she said when the recipient picked up on the other end. "Sorry I missed your call. I couldn't get to my phone in time. What's up? I didn't play the voicemail yet."

Naturally Zane couldn't hear what Sabrina's Realtor was telling her over the phone. But he didn't have to. He knew exactly what she was telling her. That the parcel of lakefront land she'd been so sure was hers, the property she was supposed to be closing on in less than a month, upon which she wanted to build a grief camp for people coping with the loss of a loved one, had just been deemed a possession of the Baston family. Turned out that the sale his great-grandfather had completed with the previous owner had never been legal in the first place, and now it had been rightfully returned to the person who should have inherited it by now—Zane Baston. Not necessarily because of any legal loopholes, but because the old boy network of Chatelaine, Texas, of which the Bastons of Chatelaine had been members since the town's founding, had worked the way it always did, favoring one of its members instead of the upstart new kid in town.

Never before had Zane felt more terrible about getting exactly what he wanted.

"Uh-huh," Sabrina was saying into her phone on the other side of the room.

She had her back to him, though, so he had no way to register her feelings. Not that he really needed to discern those. He was pretty sure he knew exactly what she was feeling.

"I see," she said. Evenly. Coolly. Like someone plotting murder. "And there's nothing we can do?" She listened some more then said, "No, I appreciate what you did, Dasha, I really do. I know how these things go, though. God knows the business world is full of stuff like this. And my father was an absolute master of the corporate double-cross."

At this, she finally did turn around to look at Zane. And if looks could kill, he would have been dismembered on the spot, and his body parts set on fire. With a flamethrower.

"Listen, I'll have to call you back," she said to Dasha. "I'm not at home right now, but I will be in a matter of minutes. Maybe we can regroup and figure out something else." Very pointedly, she asked her Realtor, "Do you know a good attorney? One who's an absolute shark?" After a second, she replied, "Great. Text me her number."

Then she was disconnecting. And glaring at Zane some more. He wished he knew what to say to defuse the situation. Unfortunately, the bomb had already detonated, so it was moot.

"How dare you?" she said evenly. "That land was mine. I was supposed to close next month."

"Sabrina, I—"

"That camp was my dream, Zane. And you knew it."

"I know, but—"

"How *could* you?"

He waited to see if she would actually pause long enough for him to respond to her charges, and when she did, he pointed out, "You can put your camp anywhere, Sabrina. And your family's ranch is a couple thousand acres at least. Plenty of room. I need that access to the lake to keep my animals alive."

"You can revive your pond," she reminded him. "It isn't that hard. I need access to the lake, too, because water has healing properties, and I was going to build an area for meditation and contemplation on the water."

"Your family's ranch abuts the lake. Use some of that."

"I can't. That part of the ranch is where our houses are. My siblings support my vision for the grief camp, but I don't think they'd like having it right outside their window with all the activity it's going to generate. And I don't blame them. And anyway," she said, hurrying on when he was going to object again, "that's beside the point. The point is that you went behind my back and used some shady business tactics to steal that land from me. And you've been lying to me for weeks."

Actually, it was his attorney who did the shady business tactics, he wanted to say. Problem was, he'd done it with Zane's blessing. But that was before he realized it was Sabrina he was competing with. He'd thought it was some faceless Fortune newcomer to town who'd never made any kind of contribution to Chatelaine and felt like they could just take whatever they wanted. Then again, he hadn't exactly backed off once he *did* discover it was Sabrina who'd snapped up the land he wanted, had he? No, it had been business as usual. He'd just felt kind of bad about doing it, where before he wouldn't have felt anything at all.

"I need that land, Sabrina," he told her. It was the only leg he had to stand on.

"You lied to me," she said again. "And you stole from me. And all the while you were acting like you cared about me."

"I do care about you."

Hell, he more than cared about her. He just hadn't quite figured out what, exactly, that *more* was.

"If you cared about me, you would have been honest with me. And you wouldn't have taken something you knew is important to me."

A door opened upstairs, and Zane heard Cody's voice calling out to his brothers, asking who wanted waffles, because he was going to make some. Sabrina heard him, too. With one final scowl for Zane, she stuffed her phone back into her purse and slung it over her shoulder.

"Any other business you and I have will be going through our lawyers," she told him. "And that includes where Peach and Plum are concerned. Don't ever contact me or speak to me again."

"Oh, Sabrina, no," he said. "No. We can work this out. We just need to talk about it. Tomorrow night, after the boys are gone."

As if to illustrate how very much she meant what she just said, she turned her back on him again and made her way out of the dining room. Zane followed her, doing his best to convince her that he hadn't done anything wrong, that she just needed to see his side of things to understand that it was just business, and that they could work this out. *Please*. But she only hastened her step, wrenched open the front door and passed through it. She thumbed the fob for her car to unlock it, climbed inside and locked the doors behind herself. Then, without giving him another glance, she threw the vehicle in gear and drove away. And all Zane could do was stand there, left in the literal dust kicked up by her car, and wonder how in the hell he was going to fix things this time.

HE AWOKE THE next morning to a head full of confusion and fear. He'd spent the entire day after Sabrina stormed off veering between panicking about the fracture in their relationship and pretending for his brothers that there was absolutely nothing wrong. He told them the reason for her absence was that she had just had some family stuff to see to, and she was sorry she couldn't be there to send the boys back off to school. Then he'd told himself he might very well have screwed up so badly this time that there was no way to fix it.

There had to be a way to fix it. Unfortunately, he'd spent so much of the night tossing and turning and fearful and fretful that he couldn't seem to piece together a coherent thought.

Desperate times called for desperate measures, he finally decided. There was only one person in Chatelaine he could turn to at a time like this. Fortunately, he knew exactly where to find the guy. Beau Weatherly had been handing out his Free Life Advice for years at the coffee shop, and from what Zane had heard, he'd never steered anyone wrong with his guidance. Hell, the guy knew pretty much everything about everything. Living a life as long and full as his gave a person the kind of insight Zane could only hope he acquired someday. Beau would surely know what to do to help him out, too.

He looked at the clock on the nightstand. It was almost 8:00. Beau was at the Daily Grind every morning between

7:00 and 8:30 a.m. to dish out his pearls of wisdom. Zane was going to have to hurry.

But when he made it into Chatelaine, he was dismayed to see a host of cars parked at the Daily Grind. He jumped out of his truck and raced into the coffee shop, then was relieved to see Beau still sitting at his table. His iced coffee was almost empty, and all that was left of his scone was crumbs. There was no line to talk to him, though, and the woman who was with him now was standing up and shaking his hand. Before Beau could get up, too, Zane hurried to his table and sat down in the chair the woman had left empty only seconds before.

Beau would stay long enough to talk to him, Zane knew. He'd lost his wife five years ago after nursing her through a long illness, and he'd dealt with his grief by being a friend to everyone in Chatelaine. His Free Life Advice table was the culmination of that. The guy's insights were both generous and priceless.

"Morning, Zane," Beau said. "Figured I'd be seeing you at some point. Kinda thought it would be before now, though."

Zane dipped his head in greeting but said nothing. His brain was too full of thoughts zipping around and not landing anywhere. He had no idea where to start explaining things to the other man, especially with only— He glanced at his watch. Hell. There was only six minutes left of the life guru's time. He looked at Beau Weatherly again, at his kind dark eyes and the way his thick, silvering dark hair fell carelessly forward on his head. Zane hoped he held up as well as this guy when he was in his sixties.

"I gather this has something to do with Sabrina Fortune," Beau said. "Been hearing a lot of chatter about you two."

Zane nodded again. But he still said nothing. It was like

every word he knew was suddenly foreign to him. Beau studied him expectantly for some minutes more, but he didn't say anything, either. Finally, he picked up his iced coffee and drained what little was left. Then he wadded up the scone crumbs in his napkin. He was giving Zane time to sort his thoughts. Problem was, Zane couldn't light on a single thought long enough to voice it.

"You know, silence can be very noisy," Beau finally told him. "What I'm hearing from yours is that you already know the answer to your predicament. Just do what's in your heart, not your stubborn head. You have a good heart, Zane. It's already trying to tell you what you need to do. You should listen."

And with that, Beau picked up the Stetson sitting on the table beside him and stood. Then he collected the remnants of his breakfast to toss on his way out and left. Zane watched, open-mouthed as the older man sauntered toward the exit, frankly kind of shocked by what Beau had just said.

Or, rather, didn't say. This was the *great life advice* he'd wanted and needed? That he already knew the answer to his problem? Beau was supposed to guide him through the steps on how to fix his problems with Sabrina. Tell him everything he needed to do to make things between the two of them okay. Like maybe how Zane needed to apologize for misleading her about the land, even if he hadn't done it intentionally. And get him to admit that he could have been wrong to do that. Then Beau could have helped him see that it would have been better to have considered her feelings on the matter and understand just how important her grief camp was to her. Like maybe, you know, communicate with her. See if there was some way they could reach a compromise.

And maybe, just maybe, how he should tell her he was

pretty sure he'd fallen in love with her over the past few weeks. And how he couldn't imagine living without her.

Oh. Okay. So maybe Beau was right. Maybe Zane already did know the answer. But it created a whole new problem. How were he and Sabrina supposed to communicate their feelings and compromise on a piece of land when she was convinced he was a liar and a creep?

First things first, Zane thought. Apologize to Sabrina. Somehow. And acknowledge—oh, boy, this wasn't going to be easy—that he was...wrong. There. He said it. In his head, anyway. Now he just had to figure out how to get the words out of his mouth. Most of all, though, he had to tell her how much he loved her. How he wanted to spend the rest of his life with her. With her and their daughters. Like a real family.

No. Not *like* a family. *As* a family. A real, honest-to-God family. That was what he wanted with Sabrina. He would say—and do—whatever it took to make her believe that.

And he hoped like hell that, at least on some level, she felt the same way about him, too.

CHAPTER ELEVEN

SABRINA WAS PORING over columns of numbers at the Fortune Family Ranch offices a few days after telling Zane to figuratively jump in the lake he'd stolen from her when she started feeling sick. Nothing major, really, just a little nausea that she told herself was due to the leftover gazpacho she'd had for lunch, even though she'd barely touched it because it had been too spicy for her liking. This in spite of the fact that she'd made it herself the night before, and she hadn't been able to get it spicy enough then. Last night, the growing babies inside her had loved the extra kick. Today, evidently, not so much. She popped an antacid and went back to the numbers on the spreadsheet she'd opened on her desktop and tried to ignore how fuzzy they suddenly seemed. But she couldn't quite help dropping a hand to splay it open over her belly.

She was starting to show now, even if only she—and, okay, Zane, during that night they spent together—were able to see it. To the outside world, she looked like her usual self. She was still wearing her regular clothes, just not pulling the zippers up all the way on her skirts and pants, and she was opting for the oversize shirts she normally saved for weekends relaxing at home, letting them hang untucked. It was fashionable, she assured herself. It was.

Her phone pinged with an alert, but she didn't bother picking it up. She was sure it was a text from Zane. Again.

He'd been texting and calling for days, apologizing and telling her they needed to talk. That he could explain. That they could work things out. Yes, she knew all along that the two of them had been at odds over that land. But she'd thought after all they talked about, when he finally understood how much it meant to her, he'd back off. Instead, he'd dug in more deeply. How could she work things out with someone who had so blatantly lied to her? Lied to her while romancing her? While making her fall in love with him?

Because Sabrina had fallen in love with Zane. She knew that. It was why his deception and betrayal hurt so badly. That morning at his house, after spending her second night with him, she'd awakened feeling so…wonderful. So complete. So happy. As if nothing in her life could ever go wrong again. And even if somehow it did, then she would have Zane there to help her through it.

The way they'd had breakfast together that morning, as if it were something they did every day… She'd been thinking it would be something they did do every day after that. First together, then with their daughters. That morning, she'd just felt like her entire life had moved around a corner and found nothing but perfection on the other side.

Perfection. Ha. Never had she found herself in such a mess. There was no way she and Zane could work through this. But there was no way she could erase him from her life.

Another pain shot through her belly, and she told herself again it was nothing but too spicy of a lunch. Until the discomfort grew worse over the next thirty minutes. And then even worse after that. Maybe if she got up and moved around a little bit, it would level off. Pushing her chair away from the desk, she rose to standing. Then immediately had to grip the edge of the desk to steady herself. Woo. She was lightheaded, too. Must have risen too fast. Once the dizziness passed, she released her grip and took a step away from the desk.

Okay, good. She didn't fall. Carefully, she placed one foot in front of the other to make her way across her office to the door. It should have been an easy trek, considering the room was only about ten feet by eight feet due to it originally being a child's bedroom in the house the first owners had built back in the fifties. The Fortunes had thought it would be perfect for the ranch offices, with just enough rooms to give each sibling their own workspace. But even after walking the small distance between her desk and the hallway, Sabrina was nearly worn out, and she was having trouble catching her breath.

She gripped the doorjamb on each side and looked down the hall of what she couldn't help thinking was an impossibly small house for a family by today's standards. With measured steps, and still pressing her hand against one wall for balance, she walked past Dahlia's office, past her brother Arlo's, past Jade's and Ridge's offices, all the way to her brother Nash's—the largest office, since he was their ranch foreman. Then she turned to pace back again. Okay, that was better. Her head was starting to clear, and her breathing was returning to normal.

Until she started feeling stabbing pains in her lower torso that felt like someone was dragging a knife through her midsection. That was when she started to panic.

Opening her hand over her womb again, she managed to make her way to her desk, where she'd left her phone. Somehow, she was able to punch in Dahlia's number, and when her sister answered, she could describe the episode she was having. Vaguely, she heard her twin say she was on her way over. Then she dropped her phone as she crumpled to the floor. And then…then everything went black.

ZANE WAS BUSY inspecting the fence line of his ranch before inclement weather starting setting in—it would take
a while to cover the entire circumference of five square
miles of ranch—when he heard his phone ringing in his
back pocket. Damn. He had a foot of barbed wire wrapped
around one gloved hand, and the other was steadying a
fence post. No way could he answer, as desperately as he
wanted to. What if it was Sabrina? Finally?

Then again, it was highly unlikely that she would be
calling him. He must have texted her a hundred times over
the last few days and left nearly that many messages. She'd
completely ignored him. He told himself to give her time
and space, that with a little more of both, she'd eventually
come around. Maybe not to forgiving him just yet, but to
at least talking to him. And once they talked, maybe she'd
finally be able to forgive him. And then hopefully the two
of them could work things out.

Whoever was trying to get ahold of him now was doubtless one of those "spam likely" calls. He wasn't even concerned when his phone pinged to alert him that the number
left a voicemail. His car warranty was up-to-date, he hadn't
applied for any loans that he might be eligible to receive
an even larger amount for, his taxes were all paid and he
didn't know a single member of the Nigerian royal family.

But when the phone rang two more times, followed by
two more voicemail notifications and then a half dozen
text alerts sounded after that, he hastily finished his fence
patching job and tugged his phone out of his pocket. Maybe
Sabrina needed him after all. The calls and texts came
from two different numbers, however, neither of which
was Sabrina's. And neither of which he recognized, though
both had Texas area codes. What got his attention, though,
were two words in each of the texts that appeared on his
home screen: Sabrina and hospital. That was when he

stripped off his gloves and unlocked his phone to read the texts in full.

Each was from one of Sabrina's sisters, and all of them were frantic. He was hurrying toward his buckskin quarter horse, Hawkeye, before he even finished reading them. The gist of it was that Dahlia had found Sabrina unconscious in her office after her sister called her complaining of abdominal pain, and now all three Fortune women were on their way to the ER at County General Hospital. Panic-stricken, Zane launched himself onto Hawkeye and raced him with all the speed of a Thoroughbred back to the barn. He left the horse with Mateo to cool him off, hurriedly explaining that Sabrina was in the hospital, then he ran out again. He was barely thinking as he jumped into his truck and raced off to County General, his head too full of what-ifs to make sense of anything but his fear.

He found Dahlia and Jade in the ER on the edge of their seats, both looking as haggard and worried as he felt. When they saw him enter, they both jumped up and began talking at once, so furiously that Zane could hardly understand a word.

"Stop," he said, holding up a hand. "I'm not following either one of you."

Both exchanged a quick look, then Jade deferred to Dahlia, who began to explain again.

"Sabrina called me about an hour ago to tell me she was having abdominal pains, and she passed out in the middle of the conversation. She was able to say she was at the ranch office, though, so I drove over there and found her unconscious in front of her desk. She woke up shortly after that, but was still really lightheaded. Jade and I both had to help her walk into the ER when we got here." She gestured toward a door on the other side of the room. "They took her in back in a wheelchair and she's been there ever since."

Jade nodded. "We were able to sit with her for a little bit, but then they took her off to run some tests. They didn't want to do an X-ray because of the twins, so they're doing an MRI. Also another ultrasound to make sure the babies are okay. And maybe some other stuff."

Zane wasn't crazy about the fact that Sabrina had called her sister instead of him, though he guessed he understood, all things considered. But when it came to their babies, he kinda hoped she would put all their issues aside. Still, he was here now, and he sure as hell wasn't leaving this time until he saw her. He just hoped and prayed she and their babies were all okay.

"Did they say how long it was going to take?" he asked the sisters.

They both shook their heads.

Jade said, "I've never known a hospital to be particularly speedy, though."

Neither had Zane.

"There's a coffee shop around the corner if you want something to eat while we're waiting."

Right. Like he could stomach anything at the moment.

"Nah, I'll just wait with you two if you don't mind."

Now both nodded. Sabrina had canceled the dinner he was supposed to attend to formally meet her family, but he had no idea what kind of explanation she'd given them for doing it. Her sisters weren't exactly being warm and fuzzy, though—not that a situation like this called for that—so he sensed they at least knew he was the one who'd screwed up. Still, maybe Sabrina hadn't told them about the specifics of their argument. Or, if she had, her sisters knew something like that had no place in what could potentially be a life-or-death situation.

No, Zane immediately censured himself. Whatever was

going on with Sabrina and the babies, it was *not* life or death. He wasn't about to put that kind of thinking out into the world and invite God knew what back in. Sabrina was going to be fine. So were Peach and Plum. Her doctor was going to figure out what was wrong—which was nothing major, he assured himself again—and then treat it, and everything would be back to normal. He and Sabrina could talk through their differences and fix whatever was wrong between them, too. *Healing*. That was what this day was going to bring. For everything.

What felt like days later, the ER doctor finally came out to talk to them. It heartened Zane that he recognized her from high school—Sofia López had been a few years ahead of him but had been inarguably the smartest kid at Chatelaine High. He'd heard she came back to her hometown to practice and was super relieved to know someone like her had been caring for Sabrina. He was even more grateful to see that she was smiling as she approached them. Her dark hair was cropped short, and her oversize glasses were the same purple color as her scrubs.

"Hello, I'm Dr. López." She introduced herself to Dahlia and Jade when she stopped in front of them. She smiled at Zane. "We went to school together, yes?"

He nodded. "Zane Baston."

"Right. Good to see you." Then she cut to the chase. "Sabrina is going to be fine. The pain she was feeling in her lower abdomen was, believe it or not, indigestion. It had nothing to do with the twins she's carrying. They're dancing around in there like they're listening to Selena singing 'Bidi Bidi Bom Bom.' So no worries on that."

"What caused her to faint?" Zane asked gruffly.

At this, Dr. López tsked. "The fainting came after *some-*one—someone who's pregnant with twins and should know better—said she skipped breakfast this morning because she had a very important business call, and then only ate half a bowl of soup for lunch. Sabrina also said she hasn't been sleeping well the past few nights and has been stressing over some things in her personal life. It was a perfect storm for something like this to happen."

Not sleeping well, Zane echoed to himself. Stressing over personal things. Yeah, well, that made two of them.

"I think this was a wake-up call for her, though," the doctor continued. "She's promised she's going to take it easier and pay more attention to her eating and sleeping habits." Now she looked at Zane. "She also said she'd like to talk to you. Presuming you're the…let me think how she put it…" She feigned deep thought, then said, "I remember now. The tall, dark-haired, good-looking, stubborn, unreasonable, insufferable, but still kind of okay guy, even if he can't understand the most basic things about how relationships are supposed to work." She grinned. "Or something like that. Anyway, she's in room 217."

Zane started grinning at the word *stubborn*. Sounded like Sabrina was finally coming around. *Stubborn, unreasonable* and *insufferable* were way better than some of the things she'd called him last time they were together.

Dahlia looked like she wanted to object that Sabrina had asked for Zane before her sisters, but Jade put a hand on her shoulder and squeezed gently. "I think Zane seeing Sabrina first is a good idea," she said. "Don't you, Dahlia? Don't you think it's good that Sabrina wants to talk to Zane before she talks to us?"

It took a minute, but Dahlia's expression gradually changed from displeased to begrudging contentment. "Why, yes," she agreed. "Yes, Jade, I think that's very good. Go ahead, Zane. We'll just grab a bite at the café and talk to Sabrina in a bit."

Zane offered them both a grateful smile in return, murmured his thanks to the doctor, then headed off to find room 217.

SABRINA HAD FINISHED her dinner of yummy hospital food—chicken potpie, creamed spinach, fried green tomatoes, biscuit with butter and chocolate cake, all of which she figured were going to send her straight to the cardiac ward if she had to stay here more than one night—when she looked up to see Zane standing at the entrance to her room. Damn. Right when she was lifting the last bite of that chocolate cake to her mouth, too, after assuring him she was cutting out sweets while she was pregnant. As subtly as she could, she lowered the forkful of cake back onto her place. Then, as *un*subtly as she could, she glared at him.

"I'm not speaking to you," she said.

Even if, she had to admit, it was really nice to see him. She'd been terrified when she woke up on her office floor with Dahlia trying to rouse her. The panic in her sister's eyes had just made it worse. All the way to the hospital, all Sabrina had been able to think about were her daughters and Zane. Telling herself over and over again that the babies were going to be fine, and berating herself for cutting ties with their father over something the two of them could surely work through if they just tried communicating. As much as she'd appreciated Dahlia being with her, and then Jade when her other sister arrived at the hospital the same time they did, the person Sabrina had really wanted to be with was Zane.

She was still angry with him. But she was still in love with him, too. And one of those emotions, she had come to realize, was definitely stronger than the other.

"Sure sounds like you're speaking to me," he replied, biting back a smile.

"Only long enough to tell you I'm not speaking to you."

"So you spoke."

This time he didn't even try to hide his grin. But it was one filled with relief, as if he were thanking every star in the universe that she and the babies were okay. And that she was talking to him instead of throwing things at him.

He nodded toward the cake she'd tried to hide. "So much for cutting back on sugar."

Instead of feeling guilty, she shot him a look of triumph. "Dr. López said it's fine. That the occasional sweet is part of a balanced diet, not to mention a fun treat, as long as I don't overdo it. You're just trying to be a big bossy know-it-all."

Instead of looking offended, he just grinned wider. "Hey, I don't mind at all. That means I can go back to enjoying Astrid's havreflarns again." This time he nodded toward the coffee cup that she'd also been gifted with for dinner. "What's Dr. López say about caffeine?"

It had been excellent enough to find out that she and the babies were perfectly fine. The chocolate cake thing had just been, well, icing. But the good news had just kept coming today. "Caffeine is also fine in moderation," she informed him.

She might as well have just told Zane he won another billion dollar lottery. "Oh, thank God," he said.

"What? I thought you loved the ginger pomegranate tea at the Daily Grind."

"Oh, yeah," he said with the kind of enthusiasm that was clearly... What was that word? Oh, yeah. *Fake.* "Yeah, that ginger pomegranate tea was awesome. But, you know, coffee is even more awesome."

She couldn't disagree. As much as she liked herbal tea, it really didn't do anything to promote coherency. And she liked coherency even better. Her dinner coffee, though, wasn't why she was feeling so coherent now. That was due to the still-too-fresh-in-her-memory horror she'd experienced that afternoon, fearing she was about to lose everything.

"I'm sorry I haven't answered any of your texts or calls," she said without preamble.

"I'm sorry I lied to you," Zane replied just as resolutely.

"Then why did you?"

He expelled a soft sigh. "Because I honestly kind of forgot all about the land thing once you told me about the pregnancy thing."

"How could you forget it when I kept bringing it up?"

"Because it wasn't me handling the transaction. It was my attorney. And he's more about getting things accomplished than he is about telling me what he's doing."

"But you knew he was trying to get the land for you," she said.

"I did."

"And you knew he was going to resort to nefarious means to get it."

"I did not," he replied.

"Oh, come on, Zane. You said you were being honest."

"I am, Sabrina, I swear."

He took a few steps into the room, then hesitated, as if he still wasn't sure of his reception. Sabrina wasn't too sure of his reception yet, either. But she did kind of wish he would move a little closer.

"Look," he began, sounding almost as tired as she was, "back when I thought I was dealing with a stranger who wanted that land, I told my attorney to do whatever it took to get it for me. But I meant whatever was *ethical*. I had no idea he'd skirt the issue to make it happen. And hell, for all I knew, there really was a problem with the provenance, and the land really did still belong to my family.

I have to talk to him—*we* have to talk to him," he quickly said, clarifying. "And even more important, we have to talk to each other."

She studied him in silence. A few weeks ago, she wouldn't have believed him. But back then, she hadn't really known him. Now, though... She let her anger go. Sabrina knew Zane was a good person. She knew he was decent. But more than that, she knew she loved him. And she wouldn't be able to do that if he was the kind of man who could woo a woman from one side and steal what he knew was important to her from the other.

He took a few more steps into the room, then stopped, looking like he still wasn't sure of his reception. And although Sabrina would have preferred receiving him just about anywhere but the hospital—and wearing just about anything but an ugly blue hospital gown—she was so happy to see him in that moment that she really didn't care much about anything else. He was right. They did need to talk. A lot. So she lowered the side rail on her bed between her and him, scooted over as much as she could, patting the mattress beside her. She didn't have to ask twice. Zane made his way across the room and perched on the edge.

He looked wonderful, she couldn't help thinking, all scruffy and unshaven, his blue work shirt and jeans streaked with dirt, as if he'd rushed to the hospital from whatever he'd been doing on the ranch without giving a thought to his appearance. His eyes, though, those gorgeous green eyes, were shadowed and exhausted-looking, as if, like her, he hadn't been getting much sleep.

"We should probably talk about what happened the last time we were together," he said softly.

She shook her head. "No. I don't want to talk about that. It was stupid, and it's in the past, and it's not important anymore. It's not the thing that matters most."

He looked relieved, but not quite convinced that it wasn't important anymore. "Well, what is important now?" he asked. "What does matter most?"

She reached for his hand and twined her fingers with his. Then she moved both to her belly and splayed them open over it and each other. "This," she said. "This is what matters. The babies we created and will be guiding through life, together." She smiled. "At least until they're grown-ups. Then we'll have to pretend we're letting them guide themselves. But we'll always be there with them, Zane. For them. And we need to focus on that."

He pressed his hand gently against her tummy, then turned it so that his palm was pressed against hers. Then he laced their fingers together and closed his hand over hers.

"I think we need to focus on us, too," he told her.

And the way he said it made something inside Sabrina melt into a mass of…so many things. Relief. Happiness. Devotion. Love. She really did love this man. Loved him in a way she'd never loved anyone else. With Preston, her love had always been young and innocent and unsophisticated. First love. Young love. Love two people shared for each other and no one else.

But with Zane, it was so much different.

Sabrina had learned so much in the past decade, about life and herself. She'd experienced the gamut of emotions, both good and bad, and come out on the other side with a much better understanding of just what it meant to love and understand someone else and commit your whole heart to that person. And not just Zane, but Peach and Plum, too. The four of them were irrevocably intertwined. Whatever she had to do, whatever sacrifices and concessions she had to make, she would. Because she knew Zane would do the same for her. They could fix whatever was wrong between them. She knew they could. And it would only make them stronger in the long run, and able to handle everything else that was going to come at them after their daughters were born.

She got that now. All the antagonism between them, all the frustration, all the misunderstanding... It had all been a part of learning about each other. And teaching each other, too. Because on some level, somewhere deep inside themselves, they'd realized they were going to be together, in one way or another, forever. Their hearts had realized that, even if their heads hadn't yet. It had become so clear to her today, when she'd feared she was going to lose it all. But she didn't know how to tell Zane that now.

"I think we need to focus on us," he said again, "because *us*, you and me, is just as important as *them*, those babies we're going to be raising."

Tears pricked her eyes at the look on his face and the gentleness of his tone. But she still had no idea what to tell him. That was okay, though. Because Zane seemed to know exactly what to say.

"You know what I think?" he asked her. "About why you and I were never able to talk about co-parenting and how we always started but got sidetracked by something else?"

She shook her head. "No. Why?"

"I think the reason we always stopped talking about it almost as soon as we started is because, somehow, even without realizing it consciously, we both knew that we'd never be co-parenting at all."

She should have been alarmed by that. But the way he was looking at her now was anything but alarming. Rather, it made all the fears and worries that were lingering inside her start to slowly wash away.

"We won't be co-parenting?" she asked.

He shook his head. "Nope. I think we both knew it wasn't our thing. I think instead we realized that what we were going to be doing was *parenting*. The way two people do when they love their offspring as much as they love each other and want to do what's best for the family they're creating together."

She expelled a soft sound as more tears pricked her eyes. "And do you love me, Zane?"

He nodded. "With all my heart."

"Then say it."

He smiled. "I love you, Sabrina Windham Fortune. With all my heart. And I don't want to lose you. I want to spend the rest of my life with you."

Wow. All she'd asked for was three little words. What she'd gotten in return was a life plan. One that she realized mirrored her own.

"I love you, too, Zane Baston. With all my heart. With all three hearts beating inside me right now."

She wasn't sure, but his eyes seemed to go a little damp at that. "Well, then, what say these four hearts join together to make one family?"

She squeezed his hand tight. "I think it's a good plan," she told him. Then, with mock seriousness, she added, "Just don't think this lets you off the hook. We still have a lot to talk about."

"We do," he agreed, his smile growing broader. "And the sooner we say what we need to say, the better."

Oh, Sabrina didn't know. She figured they'd said the most important stuff just now. Anything else they had to say would just be communication and compromise. But then, that was what being a family was all about, wasn't it? Well, those and love and respect. Mostly love, though. That was the part she liked best.

Funny, how she'd come to Chatelaine because of her Fortune family only to find a whole new one waiting here for her.

"I love you, Zane."

"I love you, Sabrina."

Together, they looked down at the little mound hidden under her hospital gown.

"We love you, too, Peach and Plum," she told their daughters.

Zane laughed. "And we can't wait to meet you."

EPILOGUE

SABRINA DIDN'T THINK she'd ever seen more spectacular sunsets than the ones in east Texas. The sky above her was awash with pinks and golds and lavenders, colors that stretched and shimmered in their lake reflections. There must have been something about the curvature of the Earth here that just made the end of the day more beautiful. Or maybe it was just that the sunsets were happening in Texas, where everything was bigger and broader and better. Bigger and broader, too, was Sabrina, who had well and truly started to show in her sixteenth week of pregnancy. She'd even sprung for a few wardrobe pieces to accommodate the changes to her body that the two little girls growing inside her had brought. She loved her new maternity dress dotted with tiny bluebonnets. So much that she'd even tied a blue ribbon around the bottom of her loose braid to match them.

As for the better part...

She looked at the man beside her. Well, now. Zane was more than better. And he was going to be the best father in the world.

"You sure you're not marrying me for my land?" he asked, smiling.

"You mean *my* land," she countered.

"*Our* land," he corrected them both.

The land they were standing on right now, watching as the sun dipped low over the horizon. They'd be filing the paperwork for that later in the week, with no help from any

old boys' networks or shark lawyers. Even though they'd
set their wedding date for next summer so that their daughters could be there, too, they'd bought this parcel together
and were making plans for it as a united front.

"Yeah, our land," she said. "And no, I'm not marrying
you for that. I'm marrying you because I love you and can't
live without you. Oh, and also because you're the father
of my children."

"Well, that's gonna be handy," Zane said, "because I
love you, too, and can't live without you, either. You or
those little ones growing inside you."

He moved behind her, wrapping his arms around her
waist to splay his hands open over her softly burgeoning
belly. Automatically, she covered his hands with hers. A
bright blue sapphire on her left ring finger glittered in the
twilight when she did. Zane had bought it for her because
he said it reminded him of that devil-in-the-blue-dress
gown she'd been wearing the night they met.

"How y'all doing in there, Peach and Plum?" he asked
their daughters as he skimmed his hand tenderly over her
baby bump. "Got enough room to move around?"

Sabrina laughed. "If they don't, they'll just make more.
And then more. Will you still love me when I'm as big as
Lake Chatelaine?"

He dipped his head to hers and brushed his lips over
her cheek. "To distraction," he promised.

For a long moment, they only stared out at the lake
and the sunset, each lost in their own thoughts. Finally,
Sabrina said, "I'm thinking I'll put the Serenity Shelter
right here where we're standing. Especially now that I've
seen how breathtaking the sunset looks from here. What
do you think?"

"Serenity Shelter," he repeated. "Is that what you're
planning to call that part of the camp?"

She nodded. "I think it fits."

"I think you're right. And yes, this would be the perfect spot. Where are you going to put the rest of it?"

Since she already knew down to the square foot how she wanted the grief camp laid out, she told Zane exactly where she wanted to situate the textile lab, the education station, the loom room and a small pen to house some of Dahlia's sheep for a one-day-a-week loan, or even some of some of the animals from Jade's petting zoo she was hoping her sisters would agree to. Children and adults both liked petting zoos, and it had been scientifically proven that exposure to animals could help soothe a person's anxiety and grief. It was yet another way to help people through a tough time.

Speaking of which, this was as good a time as any to tell Zane about her other decision.

"And, Zane?" she said. "I'd like to name the camp Preston's Promise, after my late husband."

He met her gaze with a sad smile. "I like it," he told her. "It's the perfect way to honor his memory."

"Thanks."

She spoke for another minute about some of her other plans for the place, then asked Zane about his own.

"I was thinking we could put up a hedgerow over there," he said, gesturing to their left, "to separate the camp from the watering grounds. Something that will grow fast and dense. Arizona Cypress might be a good solution."

She grinned. "When did you become a gardener?"

He grinned back. "I've been doing some reading."

They both had. Sharing land for two entirely different purposes wasn't going to be nearly as hard as she'd thought. This parcel wasn't huge, but it was big enough for both of them. They really should have thought about a compromise to begin with. But they'd kind of had other things on their minds there at the start. Bringing babies into the world had required the greatest compromise of all, so everything else had flown through the window for a bit. Of course, now that their new family would be living at Zane's house—Sabrina would be moving in next month—the compromises were becoming a bit less overwhelming.

She sighed as she watched the sun disappear over the horizon. The sky was now smudged with the blues and purples of dusk. Zane suggested they return to her house before it got too dark to see what they were doing, especially since they'd ridden to the lakefront on his horse Hawkeye. They could come back here anytime, he reminded her, since they were co-owners.

Co-owners of a lake, she reflected. Much better than being co-parents to their daughters. They'd be parenting their girls together. With all the love a mother and father could give their children.

Life was good, she thought. And it was only going to get better from here.

* * * * *

Don't miss the stories in this mini series!

THE FORTUNES OF TEXAS: FORTUNE'S SECRET CHILD

Follow the lives and loves of a complex family with a rich history and deep ties in the Lone Star State.

Nine Months To A Fortune
ELIZABETH BEVARLY
August 2024

Fortune's Faux Engagement
CARRIE NICHOLS
September 2024

A Fortune Thanksgiving
MICHELLE LINDO-RICE
October 2024

MILLS & BOON

Hill Country Hero
Kit Hawthorne

MILLS & BOON

Kit Hawthorne makes her home in south central Texas on her husband's ancestral farm, which has been in the family for seven generations. When not writing, she can be found reading, drawing, sewing, quilting, reupholstering furniture, playing Irish penny whistle, refinishing old wood, cooking huge amounts of food for the pressure canner, or wrangling various dogs, cats, horses and people.

Visit the Author Profile page
at millsandboon.com.au for more titles.

Dear Reader,

The late David McCullough once said, "History is who we are and why we are the way we are." Javi Mendoza and Annalisa Cavazos would agree with that. Annalisa is passionate about Texas history, especially the Texas Revolution. Javi cares more about recent history—like how the town con man cheated his family, ruining their small business and destroying their hopes of a new home. Those two timelines have fallout lasting right up to the present day—and they're about to collide.

Javi and Annalisa also have history together. Annalisa has loved Javi all her life, but he's never seen her as anything more than a good friend. Now she's determined to give up her hopeless crush and stop waiting around for what she can't have. Right on cue, Javi moves back to Limestone Springs and into Annalisa's life.

Will Annalisa follow through on her resolution? Will Javi restore his family's fortunes? And what ever happened to the lost silver that was taken secretly across the Rio Grande to aid in the Texan war effort over a century ago?

I hope you enjoy Javi and Annalisa's story.

Kit

DEDICATION

To David and Holly Martin,
whose stories, music, wisdom and friendship
have enriched my life for decades.

ACKNOWLEDGMENTS

For this book, I owe a debt of thanks to all those
who shared their knowledge about classic
cars, particularly David Martin, Greg Midkiff and
David Tucker. Thanks to Ann Logan for introducing
me to Ed Cappleman of Cappleman Cars and the
Oil City A's, and to Ed for graciously answering my
questions and showing me around his gorgeous
showroom and garage. Thanks also to my critique
partners—Willa Blair, Cheryl Crouch, Laura Glueck,
Mary Johnson, Janalyn Knight, Nellie Krauss and
David Martin—for their friendship, encouragement
and unfailing good sense and taste, and to my
editor, Johanna Raisanen, for her professional
insight and expertise.

CHAPTER ONE

THEY'D SCHEDULED THE bonfire for a cool September evening right on the verge of fall—a fitting time of year, Annalisa thought, for something so momentous. She'd always loved fall. The gentle melancholy of cooler, shorter days brought relief from the brutal heat and glare of a Texas summer, along with the hope that other things could change for the better, as well. Most people thought of spring as the season of fresh starts, but for Annalisa that season was fall—and a fresh start was what she desperately needed.

Eliana gave her an encouraging smile as she poured a glass of blackberry mead and held it out. "You're doing the right thing," she said.

Annalisa took the glass and stared out over the twilit pasture of her friend's ancestral ranch. "I know I am. It's just hard to do it."

"Of course it's hard. But I'll be here to help you every step of the way. And then it'll be done, over, finished, and you'll never have to go through it again."

The bonfire had been Eliana's idea to begin with. She'd said that Annalisa needed a ceremony to provide closure, and she was probably right. Annalisa had realized for a while now that her lifelong crush on Javier Mendoza was a lost cause, but she couldn't find a way to move past it on her own.

Oh, she'd dated other men through the years, with varying degrees of seriousness. But whenever a relationship ended, her mind and heart always went back to Javi. It was maddening, the hold he still had on her after all this time. She'd barely even seen him in person over the past two years, ever since he'd moved away from their hometown in the Texas Hill Country to work in the oil fields in the western part of the state. But out of sight was definitely not out of mind.

All her life, it seemed, Annalisa had been waiting for Javi. Waiting for him to call her, to text her, to break up with whatever girl he was dating at the moment. Waiting for him to move back home where he belonged. Waiting for him to open his eyes and see her as something more than the friend he could always count on.

Well, not anymore. It was high time Annalisa faced the truth—that Javi was never going to feel for her what she felt for him. Time to let go of the hope that had been fettering her and sabotaging her romantic relationships for years. Time to stop waiting and get on with her life.

She drew her legs beneath her on the sturdy outdoor chair. A nice blaze was already crackling away in the firepit, but the heat hadn't reached her yet. The firepit was part of an outdoor patio complex—far enough from the house for privacy, but close enough for security. Annalisa hadn't grown up in the country the way Eliana had. She was a town girl, and wide open spaces made her nervous.

The house's shadow stretched to the back fence and into the pasture, where some cows were moseying along to wherever it was that cows went at night. Recent rains had brought bursts of green to a landscape beginning to mellow into fall colors, while brightening the russets and pale yellows of the faded grasses. Away at the horizon, the elms along the creek showed a sprinkling of gold.

Dalia came out the back door with two fleecy blankets

in her arms and a black-and-white dog at her side. "In case you get chilly after the sun goes down," she said.

She seemed tolerantly amused, as she usually did by Eliana's schemes. The two sisters didn't look or act much alike, but once in a while Eliana showed a steely core that made Annalisa think of Dalia. Annalisa needed to develop a steely core of her own.

"Thanks," said Annalisa, taking the blanket Dalia held out to her.

The dog came over to Annalisa and gave a polite wag of his stub tail, as if he knew she needed encouragement. He was a pedigreed border collie, so he probably did. Annalisa scratched behind his ears and rubbed his soft white throat.

Dalia absently pulled Eliana's glass of sparkling grape juice away from the edge of the small side table to a safer spot near the center. Eliana was Annalisa's designated driver tonight, so no alcohol for her. She'd volunteered for the job, and it was a wise precaution to take. Annalisa was going to need a lot of liquid courage to get through this.

Dalia glanced into the box resting beside Annalisa's chair. "Are those the mementos?"

"Yes," said Annalisa, hoping Dalia wouldn't take too close a look. She felt a little sensitive about the contents of her box around capable, no-nonsense Dalia.

Dalia didn't pry. She pointed to the garden hose, capped by a spray nozzle, lying within easy reach. "The water's already turned on full blast. When you're done, remember to thoroughly hose down the embers. The burn ban's lifted, but you've got to be careful with fire."

"I know," said Eliana, sounding mildly offended that Dalia thought she needed to be told this.

"Well, I'll leave you to it, then," said Dalia. She looked at her dog. "Durango, stay here with them and keep them company."

Durango immediately settled down at Annalisa's feet.

"That dog is scary smart," said Eliana. "He understands human speech."

"Of course he does," said Dalia. And she went back to the house without another word.

As soon as the door shut behind her, Eliana turned to Annalisa with a businesslike air. "Okay. Let's get started. Take out Item Number One and tell me about it."

Annalisa took a deep breath, reached into the box and selected a crumpled paper.

"This is a rodeo program for the Seguin County Fair, my sophomore year," she said. "Javi had already graduated and started working with his dad by then. He was at the rodeo with his family, and I was there with mine. We didn't actually sit next to each other, but I was close enough to hear him talking and making wisecracks about the different riders. I can still remember exactly how he looked in his dark-washed jeans and cowboy boots and white T-shirt. I mean, he'd always been handsome, but he'd really bulked up since high school, and he just looked like such a *man*."

"He always did seem older than he was," said Eliana. "I guess that's because of what happened. He had to grow up fast."

"He did," said Annalisa. "It was rough on the whole family, of course, but somehow it seemed to hit Javi harder than his brothers."

He'd carried his burden of anger around with him for over twenty years now. Even when he was laughing and having a good time, like at the rodeo, it was still there. You could see it in the set of his shoulders and the fire in his eyes. But he'd never turned his anger on Annalisa. And she knew why it was there—as a hard protective shell around a core of pain.

"Now toss it," said Eliana.

Annalisa stared down at the worn and wrinkled paper. Javi had held another just like it in his own hand that night. He'd turned and looked at her once, just after the rodeo clown had made a particularly bad joke. She could still see the way he'd grinned and rolled his eyes.

Eliana's voice cut through the memory. "Annalisa Cavazos! Stop stalling and burn that program. You knew this was coming. You've made up your mind. Now toss it. Do it!"

Annalisa took a deep breath and dropped the worn program into the fire. The flames flared up, and in a few seconds the paper was gone.

"Yay! You did it!" said Eliana, raising her glass. Annalisa raised her own to meet it in a soft *clink*, then took a sip of blackberry mead. It was sweet and fruity and made a blossom of warmth in her throat and chest.

"Okay," said Eliana. "What's next?"

Annalisa picked up a small gold metallic bag. "Item Number Two. Party favor bag from Marisol Garza's quinceañera, my junior year. Javi was there. We didn't go together to that, either, but we saw each other and talked awhile. A band was playing. Javi didn't ask me to dance, but he did say my hair looked nice."

"I remember Marisol's quinceañera," said Eliana. "Your hair looked amazing. And as I recall, other boys did ask you to dance, but you turned them all down."

"I did. I wanted to stay available in case Javi asked me. I really thought he would. Why didn't he? It wasn't as if I didn't know how. He was the one who *taught* me to dance, that summer when I first started going to Gruene Hall on the weekends with the crowd, when I was fourteen and he was eighteen. I was pretty good, too."

"Of course you were good! You still are."

Annalisa ran a fingertip along a white crease that

marred the paper bag's shiny gold surface. Why hadn't Javi asked her to dance that night? They were old friends, after all. Maybe she'd made it too plain that she wanted him to, giving off a vibe of attraction that had pushed him away. She should have acted as if she didn't care. Danced with other boys. Maybe that would have gotten his attention. Maybe he'd have stalked onto the dance floor and cut in, and taken her in his arms, and looked down at her with those clear green eyes, and—

"Toss it," said Eliana.

Annalisa steeled herself and tossed the bag into the firepit. The shiny gold paper blackened and turned to ash.

Eliana cheered again, and Annalisa took another swallow of mead, a big one.

"What's next?" asked Eliana.

Annalisa reached into the box and took out a small wooden boomerang, just the right size for her hand. "Item Number Three. Carnival prize from the Persimmon Festival, summer before sixth grade. Javi won it for me at the ring toss booth."

"He won it for you?" Eliana asked, gently probing.

"Well, he won it, and then handed it to me to hold because I happened to be standing there, and he never asked for it back."

"You happened to be standing there?"

Annalisa squirmed. "Okay, I was watching him play and cheering him on. And I may have been following him around the festival before that." She shuddered. "Ugh, this is so embarrassing. I was such a silly little love-struck girl. What must he have thought of me then? What must he think of me now?"

Eliana gave a snort-laugh. "He must not be too repulsed, the way he keeps popping up in your life. The man is like a boomerang himself."

The V-shaped piece of wood turned blurry with tears. It was true. How many times had she waited and waited and *waited* to hear from Javi, and finally told herself, *That's it, he's gone for good this time*, only to have him show up again, usually with some thorny problem for her to help him sort out, acting as if he'd never been away? For a few days, or a few weeks, the two of them would be texting back and forth constantly, and then he'd vanish again, into the void.

"Sorry," Annalisa said as she wiped her eyes.

"Don't be sorry. Go ahead and get it all out there, and feel the way you feel. That's what tonight is for. Grief and closure. And then tomorrow…"

Annalisa sniffed. "I know. Tomorrow I move on."

"Exactly."

She closed her fingers around the lightweight balsa wood. The shape of it was familiar and comforting in her hand.

"Does it work?" asked Eliana. "As a boomerang, I mean. When you throw it, does it come back?"

"It does, when you throw it right. I got pretty good at it by the end of that summer. But mostly I kept it in the drawer of my nightstand."

She took one last look at the boomerang before tossing it into the flames. It didn't come back this time. The pale wood turned black around the edges, then all the way through, until there was nothing left of it but ash.

They proceeded through the box, with Annalisa explaining the significance of each item and its tenuous connection to Javi. There were a lot of wristbands from Gruene Hall, where they'd gone dancing as teenagers with a whole crowd of friends and Javi's brothers. A lot of ticket stubs from movies and concerts they'd attended, also as part of bigger groups. She and Javi always seemed to have a crowd around them whenever they were together in person. It was almost never just the two of them.

Sometimes Annalisa and Eliana took long breaks between items to talk and drink. The sky darkened and the moon rose, and still they'd only reached Item Number Ten, with a whole layer of stuff left in the box.

Whenever the flames started to die down, Eliana got up to stir the embers and lay more wood on the fire.

"Oh, look!" she said after picking up a fresh log from the pile. "An orb spider."

She held the log closer for Annalisa to see. Annalisa drew her legs closer to her chest and pulled her blanket tight. The spider was enormous, with a yellow-spotted black body and long spindly legs.

"Ugh! It's hideous! Make it go away!"

Eliana gave her a scornful look. "Don't be such a baby. Orb spiders won't hurt anybody. And they eat garden pests. They're our friends. Ooh, it has an egg sack."

Annalisa shuddered. "Is it about to burst into a swarm of a zillion little spider babies that will creepy-crawl all over us?"

"No, this is the wrong time of year for baby spiders to hatch. There aren't hardly any grasshoppers left for them to eat. I'll just move this log over here so we don't forget and burn it by mistake."

She laid the log gently against the fountain, crouched down beside it and started crooning to it. "There you go, little spider mama. Crawl into a nice crack in the wood and go to sleep, okay? Okay. Bye, now."

Annalisa burst out laughing.

"What's so funny?" Eliana asked as she came back to her chair by the fire.

"You. You're not drinking any alcohol, but you're acting like you are."

"I know. I feel like I'm drinking alcohol, too. It's the power of suggestion acting on my hypersensitive imagination and empathetic nature."

"Are you going to be okay to drive me home?"

Eliana waved a hand. "Oh, sure. I'll be fine once I get behind the wheel. I'm never empathetic then."

That made both of them laugh, for far longer than the joke warranted. Annalisa was definitely feeling the effects of the mead. Her limbs tingled, and her head felt light with a pleasantly swimmy sensation that blurred the edges of heartache.

By the time she reached the bottom of the box, the stars were out, and she and Eliana were both making full use of the fuzzy blankets. Durango hadn't moved from Annalisa's side.

Annalisa lifted a gray T-shirt out of the box and pressed it to her face with both hands. The soft cotton gave off a tropical, sunscreenish scent, flooding her with memories that had never lost their sweetness. It was for good reason that she'd saved the T-shirt for last.

"Item Number Seventeen," she said. "The summer after my freshman year of college. A group of us went tubing on the Comal River. You were there, Eliana."

"Yes," said Eliana. "I remember."

The fire crackled. Sparks rose into the dark sky and vanished. Annalisa shut her eyes and let the autumn night dissolve into a summer day, the sun warm on her skin, her feet trailing in cool spring-fed water, floating past a constantly changing shoreline of gentle slopes that led to fancy riverfront houses and high bluffs covered with trees.

"The river was really crowded that day," she said. "All these wild, noisy groups of college kids with their coolers of beer and their trays of Jell-O shots kept floating by. But none of that mattered. It was like Javi and I were in this perfect little bubble together and nothing could touch us. Whenever our tubes started to drift apart, he'd casually reach over and hold on to mine to keep us together. He'd taken his shirt off right away and laid it over the side of his tube. I had that red swimsuit on, the one with the ruffles, and I knew I looked good."

"Oh, I loved that swimsuit," said Eliana.

"We talked the entire three hours. He kept calling out the names of the different species of trees as we passed them—bald cypress, walnuts, cottonwoods. He knew all about trees from working with his dad. I learned a lot of tree names that day, and I've never forgotten them. When we reached the rapids, my tube flipped, and I went under. I got caught in an eddy between some big rocks with another tube over me and couldn't get free. Javi shoved the tube away and pulled me up. The water wasn't very deep there, but the rocks were slippery, and I sort of stumbled against him. He asked if I was okay. I couldn't say anything, couldn't breathe. He said, 'You poor thing. Your heart is racing.' He fished my bag out of the water, flipped my tube right side up and helped me in, and we went on our way."

She took a deep drink of mead. "After that he got more serious. He talked about how hard it was when his dad lost the business back when we were kids. And when we reached the end of the tubing route, he handed me his shirt and said, 'Hold on to this for me,' so I tucked it into my bag. He carried both our tubes to the shuttle, and we rode back to the parking lot together."

A log broke into pieces, sending a fresh shower of sparks into the sky.

"The rest of us were going out to eat in New Braunfels, but Javi had to go help his dad clear some land. He was always working. He had so little time to himself. So he walked me to my car, and when we got there he looked down at me with those beautiful green eyes, really *looked* at me, and I thought, *This is it. He's going to do it. He's finally going to ask me out.*"

Durango must have sensed how Annalisa was feeling, because he sat on his haunches, laid his head in her lap and gazed up at her with his ice-blue eyes. Annalisa stroked his silky-soft head and swallowed hard.

"But he didn't," she went on. "He just gave me a quick, light hug and said, 'Take care of yourself, Annalisa.' Then he walked away without even asking for his shirt back. And that was it."

She shook her head. "I held out hope for weeks. I'd been so sure, and I didn't see how I could have read him wrong. I told myself he must have lost his nerve at the last minute for some reason, and that any day now he'd call or text. But that was stupid. When has Javi's courage ever failed him? It must have been something else. The thing is, I *know* I didn't imagine the way he looked at me that day. I *know* he felt it, too, at least for a little while. So why didn't he act on it? I was old enough for him by then. I think—I think he must have taken another look at me and decided that, on second thought, I wasn't enough."

Eliana took another drink of sparkling grape juice and pointed at Annalisa while staring hard at her over the rim of her glass. "See, that's exactly why you have to give him up. You *are* enough, Annalisa. You're a beautiful, intelligent, accomplished woman. You could have been on a date with a man tonight instead of here with me burning old rodeo programs."

"I know."

"You've got to get over him. You've got to move on."

"I know!"

"All right, then. Act on it. Burn the shirt."

Annalisa's fingers tightened on the soft, sun-faded cotton. A thousand memories washed over her, swirling around her, pushing her under, like the eddy at the rapids in the Comal River. Javi smiling at her across a crowded room. Teaching her to dance at Gruene Hall. Holding her close after pulling her out of the water. Gazing down at her in that parking lot.

Then she saw herself, alone, all those miserable weeks while she'd waited to hear from him.

She drained her glass, set it down on the little table and threw Javi's shirt in the flames. The fragrance of coconut and pineapple rose up for half a moment and was gone. And in a few minutes, so was the shirt itself.

Annalisa leaned back in her chair with a sigh. "Well, that's it. That's the end of it."

Eliana tilted the box toward her. "Mmm, not quite. There's one more scrap of paper, or an old envelope or something, in here. Might just be a piece of trash that got in by mistake."

She handed it to Annalisa. It was an old envelope, all right, covered with Javi's big, loose, untidy scrawl. The words were clearly legible in the firelight's warm glow.

Wait for me.

A sob tore loose from her throat. "Seriously? This isn't fair."

"What?" asked Eliana. "What is it?"

Annalisa pulled herself together and held up the envelope.

"Item Number Eighteen. My senior year of high school. Yet another time when Javi and I went somewhere with a big group of people. We didn't have a clear plan, and part of the group got separated from the rest. Javi's phone died, so he couldn't text. He had to leave a physical note taped to my front door."

She traced the words with a fingertip. "It's funny. He and I have texted so much over the years, but this is the only handwritten note I have from him."

"Burn it," said Eliana.

Annalisa steeled herself, then tossed the envelope onto the fire. Eliana picked up the box, turned it upside down and shook it.

"That's it," she said. "Do you want to burn the box, too?"

"No. It's just an Amazon box. There's no special memory attached to it. And it's a pretty good box. I'll leave it here for Ignacio to play with."

"All right. Now take out your phone and remove Javi as a contact."

Annalisa slid her phone out of her sweater pocket, opened Contacts and tapped Javi's name—and there was his face, fixing her with that brooding green-eyed stare of his. Her heart gave a sickening lurch. Delete Javi? How could she? It would be like carving her own heart out of her chest.

She hit Edit and scrolled all the way down to the words Delete Contact in red letters. Her finger hovered over the screen for several agonizing seconds before giving a quick tap.

And just like that, he was gone. No second chance, no warning from her phone urging her to think it over and not do anything drastic. Just a list of alphabetical contacts without so much as an empty space where Javi's name should have been.

"I did it," she said.

"Now delete your text thread," said Eliana.

Annalisa groaned. Why was this such a long, hard, multistep process? Why did she have to keep burning and removing and deleting?

She opened the texting app. The thread was easy to locate, though it was now listed under Javi's phone number instead of his name. It was long, covering years of sporadic back-and-forth messages. She didn't open it. She didn't dare. She just selected it and hit Delete. The thread vanished without warning or fanfare.

"That's it," she said. "It's done."

The finality of it left her feeling blank and numb. She'd been deleting him all evening, and now, at long last, she was finished. She'd removed every trace of Javier Mendoza from her life.

"Good," said Eliana. "Now remember. If you're ever tempted to get in touch with him again, call or text me right away, and I'll help you get past it."

"Okay."

Annalisa got stiffly to her feet and stretched. They'd been sitting there for hours, and suddenly she wanted to go home and crawl into bed.

Eliana picked up the hose and started dousing the flames. Annalisa folded the blankets and put them inside the box, along with the mead jug and the sparkling grape juice bottle. She carried the box to the house with Durango following right behind her.

The house was quiet and dark except for a lamp in the living room and another light coming from the direction of the kitchen. Annalisa set the box on the floor next to the dining room table.

"All done?"

Annalisa gave a little jump as Dalia walked out of the kitchen.

"Sorry," said Dalia. "Didn't mean to startle you."

"That's okay. Yes, we're all done. Thanks for letting us use your firepit."

La Escarpa was a heritage ranch that had been in the

Ramirez family since before the Texas Revolution, but it was Dalia's home now. She and her husband, Tony, had been running the ranch together ever since Dalia's mother had retired from ranch work and moved to town.

"No problem," said Dalia. "You've got to do what you've got to do."

It was nice of her to say so, but Annalisa wondered if Dalia secretly thought the whole bonfire thing was ridiculous. The two of them were around the same age, but somehow they'd never been close. Dalia had always been an intimidating person, quiet and capable and serious. It was Eliana, five years younger, who'd become Annalisa's good friend in adulthood. They'd all played together as kids, whenever the Ramirez siblings would visit their grandparents in town. Eliana had been the cutest little girl, and Annalisa had loved taking care of her and dressing her up in her own outgrown princess gowns.

Now Eliana had an adoring husband and a pretty little house, while Annalisa was still renting and single. Which was fine. There was nothing wrong with that, no rule that said you had to be married and start a family by a certain age. But Annalisa wanted marriage and children, wanted them desperately. Wanted them with Javi.

These days, it seemed as if all Annalisa's friends were either planning weddings or expecting new babies. Even Dalia was four months pregnant. Annalisa could see the slight fullness in her untucked flannel shirt just below the waist. Tony and Dalia already had a three-year-old son, Ignacio, who had Tony's laughing eyes and springy black hair. Without meaning to, Annalisa imagined a toddler with Javi's lowering eyebrows and intense green eyes.

Well, she couldn't expect her feelings for him to vanish overnight. But they would fade, surely, now that she'd purged all physical reminders of him.

Eliana came inside. "You'll be happy to know that the fire is well and truly out," she told Dalia loftily.

"Good for you," said Dalia.

"But you're still going to go outside and check to make sure I did it right, aren't you?" asked Eliana.

"Of course."

"Oh, have you been waiting up for us, Dalia?" Annalisa asked. "I'm sorry."

Dalia waved a hand. "It's no problem. I'm a rancher. I'm tough. Anyway, it was for a good cause. I admire what you're doing, Annalisa."

Annalisa hadn't expected this. "You do?"

"Sure. I know how hard it can be to let go. Sometimes you have to take charge and do something proactive. A grand gesture can help with that." A faraway look came into her eyes. "You know, I actually did something similar myself, once upon a time."

"You did? Seriously?"

"Yeah, in college, when I broke up with Tony. I boxed up all the stuff he'd ever given me, all his letters and things, and mailed them to him."

"Without a word of explanation," added Eliana. "It was very dramatic."

Dalia shrugged. "I wasn't trying to be dramatic. I just wanted it done."

Annalisa admired her fortitude and matter-of-fact approach. But it wasn't really the same thing. Dalia and Tony had actually dated, so Dalia's mementos had real significance for both of them. If Javi received a package in the mail of all the items Annalisa had burned, it would just leave him confused, and maybe a little sad for her. And mailing them wasn't like casting them into the flames. Dalia had probably gotten all her mementos returned to her, years later when she and Tony got back together.

Still, it was nice of Dalia to tell her about it, and to say she admired her. Dalia wouldn't have said that if she hadn't meant it.

"All right, let's get you home," said Eliana. "Tomorrow's a big day for you. The first day of your new life."

The gravel driveway crunched beneath their shoes as they walked out to Eliana's car. Away from the cozy fire, there was a sharp chill in the night air. Annalisa pulled her sweater tightly around herself and folded her arms over her chest, the half-empty mead jug hanging from her fingers.

Once they were both in the car, Annalisa turned to face her friend.

"Thank you for doing this, Eliana," she said. "For listening to me rant about Javi, not just tonight, but day in and day out for the past I don't know how many years. And for helping me see what I needed to do, and for pushing me to do it. But most of all, thank you for drinking sparkling grape juice so you could drive me home tonight."

Eliana smiled. "No trouble at all. That juice was actually pretty good."

"Even so, I'm going to give you a bottle of that red wine you like for you and Luke to enjoy together. The two of you can toast my new Javi-free life."

Eliana's smile froze. "Um…actually…"

It was all she needed to say. "Oh, my gosh," said Annalisa. "You're pregnant, aren't you?"

"Yes," said Eliana, sounding happy and apologetic at the same time. "I'm sorry. I didn't want to tell you tonight."

Just for a moment, a wave of envy rose hot and choking in Annalisa's throat. With heroic effort, she pushed it down, leaned over and gave Eliana a hug. "Sorry? You don't have anything to be sorry for. Congratulations! You're going to make a wonderful mother. Oh, and Dalia's pregnant, too! You're going to have same-age cousins!"

"I know! Dalia's just a couple of months ahead of me."

Annalisa managed to ask all the right questions about due dates and baby names, and keep up her end of a light-hearted stream of pregnancy-related small talk, just as a good friend should. If Eliana suspected her enthusiasm was less than perfectly sincere, she didn't let on.

When they reached Annalisa's downtown apartment, Eliana gave her a big hug.

"I'm proud of you, Annalisa. Stay strong, and call or text me if you need me. I mean it. I'm here for you."

Annalisa blinked back tears. "I will. Thanks, Eliana."

She let herself in through the ground-level entrance of her building, climbed the staircase to the second floor and unlocked her front door. Stepping into the loft apartment was like wrapping herself in a favorite old quilt. She loved her little home, with its high ceilings, gorgeous old mill-work and fantastic views of downtown Limestone Springs. She'd been living here for four years now. It was within easy walking distance of the law office where she worked, and just the right size for a single woman.

She moved briskly around the kitchen, putting the mead jug away and loading the coffee maker for tomorrow morn-ing, leaving herself no time to stand around and think. Then she went to her desk, an oversize antique with beauti-fully turned legs and a leather top edged in gold scrollwork. She'd already arranged her notes and research materials in meticulous order. Everything was ready for her to start work on her new book.

Her old book, *Ghost Stories of the Texas Hill Country*, was lying on the corner of the desk, ostensibly because she might need it for reference, but really to remind herself that she'd actually done it, she'd already written a book once before, and she could do it again. *Ghost Stories* had been released seven years earlier. The publisher was a small press, and the book had gotten only local distribution, but Annalisa didn't care. She'd written it out of love for the subject matter and a desire to share the stories—and in the course of doing the research, she'd grown fascinated with Texas history. Now she wanted to explore deeper. The new book was tentatively titled *Seguin County in the Texas Revolution*.

She straightened some papers that didn't need straightening and laid a hand fondly on the front cover of her book. Then she headed to her room. She could barely keep her eyes open as she brushed her teeth and got dressed for bed.

She was just climbing under the covers when her phone dinged.

Ordinarily she turned off her phone sounds after eight, but this hadn't been an ordinary evening and she was off her routine. She picked up the phone and saw a text message from an unknown number.

Only he wasn't unknown. She may have deleted him as a contact, but that didn't mean she'd forgotten his number. Her heart gave a sudden painful throb in her chest as she saw those familiar digits, and the message below them.

Three words. The same three words she'd been waiting for him to say for the past two years.

I'm coming home.

CHAPTER TWO

JAVIER MENDOZA STOOD with his hands on his hips, surveying his apartment. He'd start packing tonight. No sense in messing around now that he'd made up his mind.

He'd been living in this apartment for well over a year now, and the place still felt huge to him. A big kitchen and living room, a big bedroom for him and another for his roommate, Diablo, with a private bathroom for each of them—it was the last word in luxury for someone who'd grown up sharing a room with his brothers in a house that would have been a tight fit for a family of four, much less a family of seven.

Without meaning to, he thought of the other house, the house they *should* have had, that had never been more than a set of blueprints and a bare slab of concrete. Right on cue, the familiar anger started churning in his stomach.

He stalked into his bedroom and pulled the suitcase out from under his bed. He had to take that angry energy and put it into action. That was the only way to cope, and it had gotten him where he was today.

He opened his top dresser drawer and started emptying it into the suitcase—underwear, socks, a couple of hunting knives and other miscellaneous items that he stored in there. Lefty followed him into the room and gave the suitcase a suspicious sniffing.

"We're moving away, Lefty," Javi said. "Leaving Midland and going home to Limestone Springs."

The dog raised his head, his big triangular ears standing up unevenly from his head, and looked Javi full in the face. With his thick, powerful build and speckled blue heeler coat, he was no beauty, and he didn't exactly have a winning personality, either, but he was Javi's dog and they suited each other fine. Javi had found him a couple of years back, crouching behind some mesquite brush near an isolated oil rig in the Permian Basin, covered with fresh wounds and old scars, and wary of human contact. It had taken Javi weeks to make friends with him, first by offering him bits of his lunch, and later by setting out bowls of water and dog food. But eventually Lefty had become a rig dog—keeping the men company on long shifts, napping in the shade under the rig floor, chasing jackrabbits and javelinas across the dusty expanse and riding home with Javi when the work was done.

"Limestone Springs is in the Hill Country," Javi went on. "They call it the Hill Country 'cause it's got hills. Lots of trees, too. Not like here. My whole family lives there. You're going to meet my parents and my brothers and—"

He stopped. Lefty didn't like new people. He didn't like anyone but Javi. He barely tolerated Diablo.

"It's a nice town, Limestone Springs," said Javi. "Lots of farmers and ranchers. Lots of small businesses. They're real big on community spirit and all that. Always celebrating something. The Persimmon Festival, the Fall Festival, the Firefighter Fundraiser—"

Lefty made a *whuff* sound in his throat, as if to remind Javi that he hated crowds.

"Yeah, well, you don't have to go to the festivals if you don't want to. Mostly it's gonna be just you and me. We'll be living rough at first in a small space. But later on, if all goes well, maybe we can buy us a little place in the country with room for you to run around. How would you like that?"

Lefty turned his back to Javi, walked over to his dog bed in the corner of the room and curled up with a sigh.

"Fine," said Javi. "Be that way."

He took out his phone and checked to see if Annalisa had replied to his text yet. She was the first person he'd told that he was moving home, and the only one so far. He always told Annalisa things, whenever he had anything to tell. Their text thread was mostly intense bursts of back-and-forth covering a period of a few days or weeks, followed by months of radio silence. Maya, Javi's most recent girlfriend, hadn't been too keen on his sporadic texting relationship with another woman. Javi had told Maya that there was nothing to be jealous of, that he and Annalisa were just friends. Maya had replied that in that case, Javi wouldn't mind not texting Annalisa anymore, to which Javi had replied that they'd never find out whether he'd mind it or not, because it wasn't going to happen. And at the end of the conversation, Maya wasn't Javi's girlfriend anymore.

Nope, no reply. Just his own words: I'm coming home.

Which, now that he thought about it, was a little ambiguous. He'd already come home a few times since moving west, for holidays and things, but he'd always returned to Midland afterward.

For good, he typed. Then he hit Send.

There, that ought to clear things up. She'd text him back soon, asking the sort of interested, encouraging questions that would allow him to tell the whole story a bit at a time. In the meantime, he'd get some more packing done.

The contents of his dresser filled the suitcase, leaving no space for his closet stuff. Javi stood a moment, frowning, before remembering that he had a good-sized Amazon box in the kitchen from his latest Subscribe & Save order of paper towels.

He went to the kitchen. It was pretty well stocked with pots and pans and things, purchased on a buying spree Javi had gone on some time back—a moderate, thoughtful buying spree, undertaken once he'd gotten past the initial heady thrill of freedom and big paychecks. His first few months working in the oil fields, he'd done a lot of wild living and overspending. But then he'd calmed down and started getting his life in order. Built up a healthy bank balance. Learned to cook. Got himself a nice apartment and furnished it entirely from Amazon. Turned out you could buy just about anything from Amazon, including the big stuff like sofas and beds. He'd even bought himself some throw pillows for the sofa. They really classed the place up.

Should he move the furniture back to Limestone Springs with him? There wasn't much space in the living quarters of the old horse trailer where he'd be bedding down, and it didn't make sense to pay to haul everything back home, much less store it for however many months or years it would take before he was ready for a bigger place. Probably be cheaper in the long run to buy new furniture once he had a place to put it. He'd leave the sofa and most of the kitchen stuff for Diablo.

He carried the box to his bedroom and started filling it with boots and shoes, taking care not to scuff his dancing boots. Man, he missed dancing at Gruene Hall. From high school on, he used to go there at least once a week in the summer months, along with most of his brothers and a group of friends that had sometimes included Annalisa. Javi had taught her to swing dance when she was fourteen and he was eighteen, back in the days when she'd had a crush on him. It had felt nice, having her like him, a smart, pretty girl like Annalisa, but of course she'd been way too young for him then. And later—well, there'd been other reasons for him to keep his distance from her. Eventually she'd moved on and dated other guys, and her crush had turned into a more sisterly feeling. It was all for the best.

He took his phone out again. Huh. Still nothing from Annalisa. Well, it was pretty late. Probably she'd gone to bed and hadn't seen his text yet. She'd surely get back to him first thing in the morning.

He stared awhile at the contact pic of her on his phone. He'd taken that pic himself, near the end of a summer afternoon when they'd gone tubing on the Comal River with a big group. That had been a good day. He kept the memory safe inside himself to think over whenever he needed comfort.

She was smiling in the picture, that strange, wonderful smile of hers that always seemed to have something behind it that he could never quite figure out. Her long black hair was pulled back in a ponytail, and the red straps of her swimsuit peeked out above a thin white cover-up. She had the most beautiful eyes he'd ever seen, huge and soulful in a face shaped like a valentine.

They'd talked a long time that day, floating down the river—well, mostly Javi had talked and Annalisa had listened. She'd always been a good listener, even as a kid. *Wise beyond her years*, was how Javi's mother used to describe her, and it was true. She was the oasis he could always come back to for refreshment.

As far as women went, Annalisa was in a category all by herself. Javi had put her there, and he kept her there, safe from the chaos and disappointment that was his dating life. He'd never pursued her romantically.

But he'd thought about it, that afternoon on the river, and later in the parking lot after they'd taken the shuttle back to their starting point. Just for a second, standing there by her blue Corolla, he'd thought maybe it would be okay, maybe it would be more than okay, maybe it would be the best thing that could possibly happen, for him to finally tell her about the feelings for her that he kept packed away in a back corner of his heart.

Instead, he'd given her a quick hug, said goodbye and walked away. There was a line here that he couldn't cross. This was the best relationship he'd ever had with any woman not related to him. He couldn't sacrifice that for a romance that he'd be sure to mess up.

Javi took his clothes out of the closet, hangers and all, and laid them across the tops of the boots in the box. Then he grabbed an armload of hats and gloves and things from a shelf and dumped them on top of the clothes.

Something shiny caught his eye from the back of the shelf—chrome, three-sided, jet-shaped. He picked it up, feeling the familiar sleek heft of it in his hand. It was a fender ornament from a 1959 Chevy Biscayne—the first car he'd ever seriously worked on with his dad, the one that was supposed to be his when he turned sixteen. Instead, the Biscayne was currently lying under a tarp, in the covered work area at the house where Javi had grown up. There'd been no time or money to finish the work, after what had happened.

Annalisa had been there the day they'd gotten the news. She'd been in and out of their house a lot back then. Small though it was, the Mendoza house had always been the gathering place for neighborhood kids. Both of Javi's parents were sociable, hospitable people, and one of the things they'd most looked forward to about the new house on the big lot at the edge of town was that it would provide more space for entertaining. But on that day, they'd learned that there would be no new house, and no classic car business, because his father's business partner, Carlos Reyes, had made off with the money, and there was no way to get it back.

Javi had been fourteen then, and Annalisa had been ten or eleven. He remembered her sympathy, that day in the cramped kitchen, with the sink full of breakfast dishes and the blueprints still spread over the table. She hadn't said much, which was good, because he couldn't have taken it if she had. Soft words would have undone him. She'd understood that. She understood everything.

His parents had never sold the land, though there were plenty of times over the years when the cash would have come in handy. They'd always held out hope that one day they'd get ahead enough to finish the house after all. Javi couldn't count the number of times when it had seemed as if the opportunity to get on with the construction was just around the corner, but something had always happened to prevent it.

He wrapped the fender ornament in a scarf and reached under the other stuff in the box to tuck it inside a dancing boot. He'd be needing that fender ornament soon, and not just as a reminder of how his family had been wronged. He was going to finish that car, and finish that house.

That had been his end game all along with the oil field work—to earn the money to make the classic car business happen and restore his family's fortunes. He'd never told anyone that, not even Annalisa, partly because his plan had been pretty vague at first, and partly because it was the sort of thing people said but didn't usually follow through on. Talk was cheap. What counted was action. Javi had to keep his energy focused, not spend it all on blabbing. When the time was right, he'd show everyone.

After that, once the weight was off his shoulders, maybe he'd see about getting some acreage of his own, enough to maybe raise a steer or two and not have neighbors right up against him all the time.

But he couldn't think about that right now. The main thing was to establish the classic car business and make it profitable, and get his family to a place of prosperity and security where people like that cheat Carlos Reyes could never hurt them again.

CHAPTER THREE

ANNALISA WALKED INTO Tito's Bar feeling fantastic. She was wearing new jeans, new boots and a new sweater in a particular shade of rich red that perfectly complemented her coloring, and she had her hair pinned up in an elegant twist. Looking good always boosted her mood, and the new clothes added to the sensation of overall newness in her life right now, not least of which was her new attitude toward Javi.

A full week had passed since the night of the bonfire, and Javi's text. Worst timing ever—or so she'd thought when she'd first seen the words lighting up her phone screen. The desire to text him back had almost overpowered her.

But she'd made a resolution, and she had to follow through. So she'd texted Eliana instead.

You'll never believe what just happened! J texted me and said he's coming home! What am I going to say to him?

Late as the hour was, Eliana had responded within seconds.

Nothing. There's no law that says you have to answer every text.

Annalisa had typed back:

It feels rude just to ignore him.

Eliana had replied:

Has Javi always responded promptly to every text of yours? Or at all?

Annalisa didn't have to think twice about that. No, he hadn't. Not even close.

Sitting there on the side of her bed with her phone in her hand, she had forced herself to be honest with herself. She'd gone to a lot of trouble to put her Javi infatuation behind her. So had Eliana, and Dalia and Tony, for that matter. She couldn't throw away all that effort the very first time she was tempted.

And the temptation probably wouldn't lead anywhere anyway. So he was coming home. So what? He'd just go away again like he always did.

She'd barely completed the thought when another message from Javi's number had popped onto her screen.

For good.

"Oh, come on," Annalisa had said aloud. "That's not fair."

But nobody ever said life was fair, or easy. It was time to put into practice the resolutions she'd made at her most rational. And maybe the timing wasn't so bad after all. Maybe it was exactly right.

So she'd deleted those two newest texts from Javi and taken her phone to the kitchen so she wouldn't be tempted to check it during the night.

In the morning, there'd been no additional texts from him, and she'd felt relieved and disappointed at the same time.

Now, a week later, what she mostly felt was proud of herself. It had been hard, but she'd stuck to her guns and thrown herself into work, both at the office and at home on her book, with the result that she had two milestones to celebrate.

Tito gave her a friendly smile as she took a seat at the bar. He was a very dapper guy, dressed in his usual white shirt, black vest and black trousers, with a neatly trimmed beard and dark eyes sparkling with intelligence and humor.

"Well, don't you look nice today," he said.

Tito was Javi's younger brother. He knew all about Annalisa's crush on Javi, and the bonfire, and Eliana's pledge to help her move on, and he thoroughly approved. His brother wasn't a bad guy, he'd once told Annalisa, but he could be awfully clueless at times.

"Thank you!" Annalisa said. "I'm treating myself to a day out. I finished my preliminary book research and my outline ahead of schedule. It's been one week today since I started work on it."

And kicked my Javi habit.

"Good for you! What'll you do on your day out?"

"I haven't decided. The weather's so beautiful, and I'm all caught up on laundry and bills. I'm sure I'll figure something out."

"I'm sure you will. What can I get for you? Blackberry mead?"

Annalisa rested her chin on her hand and scanned the liquor bottles on the shelves behind him. "Actually, I'm in the mood to try something new. Surprise me."

He chuckled. "All right, then. I will."

He picked up a double rocks glass and started muddling limes with sugar. Annalisa watched for a while, then stared at her own reflection in the antique bar mirror. With her hair twisted high on her head that way, she looked confident and in charge, like the sort of woman who would *not* ask her old crush's brother whether he'd heard anything about this coming-home-for-good thing. So she didn't ask.

Tito set the finished drink on the bar top. "There you are. A new drink for a new day."

She frowned. "It looks like a mojito."

"Ah, but it's not. Go ahead. Try it."

She took a sip. No, not a mojito. Similar, with that blend of sweet and tart, but…grassier, somehow.

"What is it?" she asked.

"A caipirinha. National cocktail of Brazil. Like a mojito, but with cachaça instead of rum."

She took another sip. Sharp and clean and sweet, like a fresh start.

"I like it," she said.

"Good!" said Tito. "So, anything new turn up in your research? Any big surprises lurking in those old documents?"

She smiled. "Not so far. But it's still fascinating. All those letters and diaries and military dispatches and land grants! It's remarkable that they've all been preserved as well as they have for a century and a half. I'm grateful to have access to them."

"No kidding," said Tito. "Man, I wish someone in *my* family would suddenly stumble across a pile of nineteenth-century documents written by our ancestors, but our people didn't cross the border until after the war. If my great-great-great-great-grandfathers did fight in the Texas Revolution, they fought on the other side."

She gave him a stern glance. "Well, it's the only bad thing I know about you, so I'll overlook it."

"Thanks."

He left then to serve a couple who'd just seated themselves at the other end of the bar. Annalisa swirled her drink, took another sip and smiled at her reflection. This was going to be a good day.

Then the smile froze. A man was standing behind her, just past her shoulder, and he was looking at her reflection, too.

"Annalisa?"

Her throat caught, because she knew that voice and that face, and this couldn't be happening, not right now, not today; she wasn't ready.

Ready or not, she turned around. And there was Javi, in the flesh.

Everything about him was solid and broad—forehead, cheekbones, shoulders, chest. Even the placement of his feet on the floor was broad, as if he dared anyone to try to knock him down. His eyes were a brilliant green with darker rims around the irises—eyes that had haunted her imagination for years. Something in the set of the eyebrows and the shape of the mouth made his face well suited to brooding, but he was smiling now.

The smile alone would have been enough to melt her, but then he said, "Hey!" And there was something wonderfully tender in his voice, something she'd never heard in it before. And then he hugged her—not just a light folding of his arms around her and a quick pat-pat on the back like he usually gave her, but a fierce hug that took her breath away. His canvas bomber jacket was rough against her face, and it gave off a strong odor of sulfur—or as oil workers called it, the smell of success.

Her hair came loose from its perfect tight twist and tumbled around her shoulders, and her hair clip clattered to the floor.

"Oh, sorry," said Javi. He released her, picked up her hair clip and handed it to her. It was gold, with little rhinestones set in it.

"That's okay," said Annalisa, clipping it to her purse strap. Her hands were shaking. So much for all the progress she'd thought she made this past week. She was as much in love with Javi as ever.

"Wh-what are you doing here?" she asked.

"I told you I was coming home," said Javi.

"You didn't say you were coming so soon."

"Well, you didn't text me back," he said, his voice playfully reproachful.

"Oh, right. Sorry."

Sorry? Why had she said that? What did she have to be sorry about? What was wrong with her?

"That's okay," he said, settling himself onto the bar stool next to hers. "I figured you must be really busy with the new book and all."

"Yeah, that's true, I have been," she said. "That and the day job."

He rested one arm on the bar top and turned to face her. "You still working for Claudia?"

"I am," she said as she sat back down beside him.

He nodded. "That'd be enough to keep anyone busy, I'm sure. I haven't seen Claudia in ages. How is she?"

"She's good. She's dating someone, and it actually looks serious this time."

Now, why had she said *that*? Why not talk about how busy Claudia was with her thriving law practice? Why did she have to bring romance into the conversation?

Javi's eyebrows shot up. "Really? Do I know the guy?"

"I don't think so. His name is Peter Longwood."

A shadow fell over Javi's face. "Longwood? That's Alex's wife's maiden name, isn't it?"

Alex Reyes was Tony's brother, and Dalia's brother-in-law. Lauren was Dalia's best friend from college. Annalisa had always felt a proprietary interest in Alex and

Lauren's romance, because her first book, *Ghost Stories of the Texas Hill Country*, had been instrumental in bringing them together.

"That's right. Peter is Lauren's father. He and Claudia met at Alex and Lauren's wedding. They hit it off right away, but he had his business up north, and of course, Claudia has her practice here. But they kept in touch over the years. And a couple of months ago, Peter moved down here from Pennsylvania, just in time for the new grandbaby to be born."

Javi nodded politely. He always had been a bit standoffish with Alex and his brother, Tony, Annalisa recalled. Apparently the feeling extended to Alex's father-in-law.

Tito came back from the other end of the bar. "*Javi?* What are you doing here?"

Javi spread his arms out. "Why does everyone keep asking me that? I told you I was coming home."

"Well, you didn't say when. Have you seen Mom and Dad yet?"

"No, not yet. This place was my first stop—no, second. No, third, if you count the Czech donut shop."

"Did they even know you were planning to arrive today?"

"I wasn't *planning* to arrive today. I just finished my packing and hit the road. It was too early in the morning to call them then, and after that I was busy driving."

Tito shook his head. "Mom's going to freak. She hasn't had a chance to cook all your favorite foods or even fix up a bedroom for you."

"She doesn't need to get a room ready for me. I won't be staying with Mom and Dad."

"You're renting a place?" Tito asked.

"Not exactly." Javi's chest visibly expanded. "But I am in the process of purchasing some real estate."

Tito's jaw dropped. "You're buying a *house*?"

"Not a house. The old building downtown. Dad's old building."

In the silence that followed, Tito looked as stunned as Annalisa felt. The building that Mr. Mendoza used to own, where he'd been planning to run his classic car business, had been vacant for months. Javi smiled smugly at them both, clearly pleased that he'd made such a sensation.

"How did you have time to buy it?" Tito asked. "It only just went on the market."

Javi shrugged. "What can I say? I'm a man of action."

All at once, in a quick intuitive flash, Annalisa understood.

"You're going to open the classic car business," she said. "That's why you went to work in the oil fields to begin with, to raise capital. That was your goal all along."

Javi smiled at her, a slow, deep smile that made her cheeks go warm. "You always did know me better than anyone," he said.

"You're opening the *business*?" said Tito. "Just like that?"

"Just like that," Javi said.

Tito made an exasperated sound. "But—but there must be a thousand things to consider."

"I've considered them," Javi said evenly. "I was actually planning to rent a building at first, save my money for equipment and merchandise, but then the property went on the market, and at a rock-bottom price, too. I already knew the place was perfect for what I wanted to do, and I also knew it wouldn't last long at that price. So I made my offer, and it was accepted. I close on Monday morning."

Another silence fell. Then, with an air of giving up on making sense of his brother, Tito asked, "Well, all right, then. Are you hungry? Can I get you something?"

"Thanks, but I filled up on tacos and *kolaches* at the donut shop. I wouldn't say no to a pint of Thirsty Goat, though."

"Coming right up," said Tito, and he went away to fill a glass with the red ale.

"Hey, where's Lefty?" Annalisa asked. "You brought him with you from West Texas, didn't you?"

"'Course I did. He's at the building. I dropped him off along with a load of stuff."

"I thought you said you hadn't closed on the property yet."

Javi smiled and held a finger to his lips. "Shh," he whispered. "Don't tell. Anyway, Lefty's not technically inside the building. There's a grassy area inside a privacy fence where he can rest and do his business."

"Will he be all right on his own in a strange place?"

"Sure. He's got food and water, sunshine and shade. The yard is about the same size as the one at my apartment, and he was always fine with that. Later I'll take him somewhere he can run around."

Tito set down Javi's beer, then left again to wait on a guy who'd just sat down at the bar. Javi frowned at the other customers.

"Getting kinda crowded here," he said. "Let's move to a table."

He picked up his beer and carried it to an empty spot at one of the long tables that ran in parallel lines down the room. He didn't check to see if she was following.

Annalisa watched him walk away with that confident stride of his. She could hear Eliana's voice in her head, saying, *Don't do it. Don't throw away all the progress you've made.*

Her hesitation lasted only a second. Then she took her

own glass in her hand, walked over and took a seat on the bench opposite him.

Javi swallowed some beer. "So, how's it going with the new book?"

"Really well. I've made my first perusal of the documents and sorted them into categories. Starting Monday, I'll read them more closely and take notes."

He shook his head. "You say that like it's fun."

"It is fun! Those documents are a treasure trove, and there are so *many* of them. Alejandro Ramirez was a diligent letter writer. Every time he was away from home, he wrote to his wife. And she saved all his letters and kept a diary that she wrote in every day. Plenty of historians would kill for primary sources like that."

Alejandro Ramirez was a Tejano rancher who'd fought and died in the Texas Revolution, and a beloved figure in the history of Limestone Springs. His primary property, La Escarpa, was the ranch where Dalia and Eliana had grown up and where Dalia still lived. Strangely enough, Tony and Alex Reyes were descended from Alejandro, as well, which meant that when Tony and Dalia had married, they'd reunited two distant branches of the family tree. Another of Alejandro's ranch properties, known simply as the Reyes place, was where Alex and Lauren now lived and worked.

"Have you found anything shocking?" Javi asked. "Any skeletons in the Ramirez closet?"

"No."

"Too bad. It'd be nice to see the sacred memory of Alejandro Ramirez taken down a peg or two."

She glanced at him. "I don't think that would be nice at all. Remember, I'm connected to that family, too. Tony and Alex are my cousins."

"Yeah, but on the Cavazos side, not the Ramirez side. You're not descended from the great Alejandro Ramirez."

Annalisa wondered, not for the first time, what Javi could possibly have against a respected ranchero who'd been dead for close to two hundred years. It was natural enough for him to hold a grudge against Alex and Tony's father, Carlos Reyes, after what Carlos had done to Javi's father. And while it wasn't fair to hold Carlos's sins against his sons, she at least understood the source of Javi's resentment. But blaming Alejandro for the actions of his great-great-great-grandson was taking things way too far.

She didn't say it, though. Doing so would only irritate Javi without changing his mind. Years of experience had taught her that.

"One of my Cavazos ancestors was at the Battle of Gonzales," she said, steering the conversation away from dangerous waters. "I saw his name in a dispatch."

"Nice," said Javi. "That's the battle where they made the cool flag with the picture of the cannon on it, right? The Come and Take It flag?"

"That's right. Gonzales was our Lexington, the first shot of the Texas Revolution. It happened in 1835, right after Santa Anna suspended the Mexican constitution. Santa Anna knew the Texians weren't going to roll over and let him trample their state constitution, as well, so a Mexican colonel, Castañeda, was sent to Gonzales to disarm the town. They all gathered at the Guadalupe River, Mexican troops on one side, Texians on the other."

"And the Texans said, 'If you want our cannon, come and take it,'" said Javi. "Which was a very Texan thing for them to do."

"Yes, it was."

She took a sip of her drink. "Something really interesting happened during the parley between Castañeda and the Texian commander, Colonel Moore. Castañeda said that he was a republican himself and that he didn't want to fight the Texians. And Colonel Moore actually tried to convince Castañeda to come over to the Texian side, along with his men. But Castañeda said no, he'd obey his orders. Wouldn't it have been something if Castañeda had taken Moore up on his offer?"

Javi frowned. "I guess. But that would make him a traitor, and a rebel."

"It's not a rebellion when you fight back against an illegitimate government. Governments draw their power from the consent of the governed. Once he suspended the constitution, Santa Anna was nothing but a tyrant."

She'd spoken more warmly than she'd intended. Javi stared at her a moment, his clear green eyes boring into her. Slowly his frown turned to a smile, then to a chuckle.

"What's so funny?" she asked, hearing the defensive tone in her voice. She didn't like being laughed at, even by Javi.

"Nothing," he said. "It's just so unexpected. You always look so sweet and gentle, and then you go and say something like that. You mean it, too."

"Of course I mean it. And I like to think that if I'd been around back then, I'd have done the right thing and fought for liberty."

"Oh, I know you would." Javi rested his arms on the table and leaned toward her. "I tell you one thing. If I ever found myself in the middle of a revolution, I'd want you to have my back."

He seemed very near all of a sudden. Annalisa realized that she was leaning forward herself, the way she always did whenever she started talking about some subject of deep interest to her. Javi's jaw and upper lip sported a few days' worth of stubble, and the straight fall of dark hair skimming his eyebrows was almost close enough to brush against her forehead.

She dropped her gaze. Long strands of muscle showed through the dark skin of his forearms, and his work-hardened hands were clasped on the table mere inches away from her own. It would be so easy to reach out and touch him—so easy, and so impossible.

She dimly felt that she ought to say something, but she seemed to have lost the thread of the conversation.

Javi broke the silence. "Sounds like you've got a lot going on, between your day job and your book research."

Annalisa drew back, away from danger, and seized the change of subject. "Yes. But I love it. There's so much to unravel in old handwritten documents. You can't just sit down and read them. You have to familiarize yourself with the person's handwriting, and deal with irregularities in spelling, and try to make out the words in places where the ink is faded or the writing is illegible. Romelia had beautiful handwriting—she was educated by Franciscan nuns—but Alejandro's handwriting is harder to make out, partly because he was usually writing under difficult conditions away from home. So I'm going to start with Romelia's diary and hope that what I learn there will provide some context for deciphering Alejandro's letters."

"Sounds like a good plan," said Javi.

"I hope it's enough. There's so much to decipher. A lot of passages are really cryptic. I want to figure out what they all mean, but I also don't want to get led down a bunch of rabbit trails."

Javi rubbed his chin thoughtfully. "Some of those rabbit trails might turn out to be important."

"They might. Or they might turn out to be really mundane."

"Aren't you curious, though?"

"Of course I am. But I do have a deadline. I can't let myself get bogged down in what could turn out to be a huge time suck, especially at this stage of my research. There's enough information in the documents I *can* read to keep me busy for a long time."

"Fair enough. I know I wouldn't want to sift through a bunch of old letters and things and try to make sense of them. But you'll do great at it and write a fantastic book that sells a zillion copies."

She smiled. "That's nice of you to say, but I'm not expecting the book to be a huge commercial success. I'm really writing it for my own satisfaction, to flesh out the part played in the Texas Revolution by the people of Seguin County. My friends and family will all buy copies, I know, but there's not a big market for this sort of thing. Most of my sales will probably come from other authors of local history books, and that historical reenactor group that Alex and Claudia belong to. It's a small audience."

Javi made an indignant sound. "What are you talking about? Of course your book will be a huge success. You're the best writer I know."

Annalisa's ego wasn't especially boosted by this. She was probably the *only* writer Javi knew, and he'd never been a big reader. But that only made his praise sweet in a different way, because it came from personal loyalty. That fierce light in his green eyes, that stubborn jut to his chin—he looked ready to fight anyone who said her writing was less than spectacular.

"Thank you," she said in a low voice.

She picked up her glass and swirled the ice cubes around. "So tell me about you, about the business. What's the plan?"

"Pretty basic, really. The first thing to do is to get the space in order. That's going to take a while because the last renters trashed it. Then I'll set up my equipment and start work on the Biscayne."

"You're not selling the Biscayne?" she asked. She loved that sixty-plus-year-old piece of non-running machinery almost as much as Javi did.

"No, no. It'll be a showpiece, so people can see what I can do—what *we* can do, me and my dad. Once it's finished, we'll move the other cars to the garage and get started on them, and sell them on spec. The Land Rover, the Impala, the Firebird..."

"The Caprice, the Camaro," Annalisa went on. She knew. She knew every old tarp-covered car Mr. Mendoza owned. He'd bought them all for pennies on the dollar, planning to do restomods on them and sell them to collectors. But after the loss of the money, he'd had to sell the building to pay his creditors and bring all the cars home, where they remained to this day. He'd worked on them periodically in the years since, and even managed to finish and sell a couple, but he was too busy making a living with his earth-moving business to devote the time the enterprise needed to make it really take off.

She shut her eyes, trying to visualize the building. "How big is the garage, anyway?"

"Fifteen thousand square feet. The footprint runs from the corner of Persimmon and Fannin to that little cell phone store, and all the way back to the alley between Persimmon and Pecan."

"That's plenty of space. Then there's that sort of overhang part right in the front corner."

"Yeah, that's left over from when it used to be a gas station back in the thirties. It's a nice big shaded area. I'd like to park something there for display, but I'm worried it might get vandalized."

"Does your dad still have that one really old pickup?"

"The Mercury? Yeah. But it doesn't run, and the body's not in great shape."

"Well, maybe park it under the overhang. It's old enough to fit your aesthetic, but not too precious to leave outside downtown."

"Yeah, that's a good idea," Javi said. "Then whenever we do decide to restore it, we can get another project car to park in that space."

"Perfect. Then the front of the building can be your showroom. It used to have big plate glass windows all the way across, didn't it?"

"Yeah. They're mostly boarded over now, and there's a weird partition on one side from when the former owners carved off some of the square footage to rent out as office space. All the garage bays open onto Fannin Street. Come over and I'll show you."

She opened her eyes. "What, now?"

"Sure, why not? There's no sense in us sitting here talking about what it looks like when it's right there, barely a block away. Come on over and see my place."

The offer was a tantalizing one. Just this second, there was nothing in the world that she wanted more than to take him up on it, even though she knew she shouldn't.

Before she could answer, the front door of the bar opened. Eliana walked in, breezy and confident, and came straight to her.

"Annalisa!" she said brightly. "Why haven't you been answering my texts? Have you forgotten? We have that thing to go to today."

For a moment Annalisa was mystified. She and Eliana didn't have plans together that day. Eliana had plans with her husband to shop for baby stuff.

Then she saw the fierce light in Eliana's eyes and the forceful cheeriness of her smile, and she understood. This was an intervention. Eliana was here to rescue her from falling under Javi's sway.

How did Eliana know? Annalisa stole a glance at Tito, who was standing behind the bar, looking blandly innocent and avoiding eye contact.

"Oh, right," she heard herself say. "That thing."

Disappointment settled in her stomach like a lead weight. This was why they'd made their agreement to begin with, so Eliana could save her from unexpected temptation, but she couldn't feel good about it.

"Well, hello, Javi," said Eliana, as if just now noticing him.

"Eliana," said Javi in a flat tone.

"I'd love to stay and catch up," Eliana went on, "but we really do have to hurry if we're going to make it in time."

She linked her arm through Annalisa's and pulled her to her feet.

"Yes, I guess we do," said Annalisa. "I'm sorry, Javi."

He shrugged. "Doesn't matter. Another time, maybe."

Then he stood, walked around to their side of the table and caught Annalisa up in another tight hug. She wanted to stay in his arms forever, but within seconds she found herself disentangled from his arms and hustled through the door and onto the sidewalk.

"Well!" said Eliana. "That *was* a close call. I saw the way he was looking at you before I walked over. He was turning on all the charm, wasn't he?"

"Yes," Annalisa said glumly. "He was."

Eliana had linked her arm through Annalisa's again, as if Annalisa might make a run for it if she let go. Annalisa had to walk fast to keep up with her. When they were still some distance away from the car, Eliana took out her key fob and clicked. The door locks chirped open.

"Good thing Tito texted me right away," she said.

"I guess so."

Those minutes spent in Javi's company had been so

sweet. But the good times with Javi had always been very good. It was the times afterward, when he disappeared again, that were so hard.

"Thanks for rescuing me," said Annalisa.

She didn't sound, or feel, especially grateful right now. But she knew she would later, once she'd had time to get her bearings.

"Of course! That's what friends are for."

Eliana opened the passenger door of her car and almost pushed Annalisa inside, then hurried around to the driver's side. Annalisa was surprised Eliana didn't lock her in.

Eliana started the engine and backed out of her parking space.

"Tell me all about it," she said. "What did he say? What did you say?"

Annalisa told her. She didn't leave out a thing—not the tight hug that had knocked her hair clip loose, or the tenderness in Javi's voice when he'd greeted her, or the way he'd looked at her with those clear green eyes, or how he'd invited her back to the building with him.

"Wow, I really did show up just in the nick of time," said Eliana. "Another few seconds and you'd have been a goner."

Annalisa sighed. "He seemed different this time," she said. "So warm and demonstrative, like he was finally seeing me as someone he wanted to be with. What if this was my one chance, and now I've missed it?"

The words sounded needy and weak even as she heard herself saying them. They certainly didn't faze Eliana.

"If he's really interested, he won't be put off by you being unavailable this one time," she said. "Javier Mendoza is a confident and determined man. If he wants you, he'll go after you. It won't hurt him to have to work a bit.

And if he doesn't want you…well, then, all the more reason to stand your ground."

She was right, of course. Annalisa stared out the side window, watching downtown buildings pass by.

"Wait, where are we going?" she asked.

"Back to my place. We'll pick up Luke and head out for a day of shopping and then have dinner out."

"What? No, no. You don't have to do that. This was supposed to be your day with Luke. I don't want to be a third wheel."

"It's no trouble. We'll have a nice time together. You can help us pick out baby furniture."

"I appreciate it, Eliana, I do. But I'll be okay now, honestly I will. I'll just go home and do some more book research."

Eliana frowned. "Your apartment isn't very far from Tito's Bar. I think you'd be safer in New Braunfels with Luke and me."

"That's really not necessary. I'll be fine now that Javi's not right there in front of me."

It took some doing, but she eventually persuaded Eliana to drive into the alley behind her apartment and drop her off there. Eliana kept the car parked until Annalisa had walked up the fire escape and gone through the back door, as if suspecting that Annalisa might otherwise sneak back around to Tito's.

The apartment seemed eerily quiet. Annalisa set her purse on the console table, unclasped her hair clip from her purse strap and twisted her hair high on her head. Then she shut the blinds on the beautiful fall weather and went to work.

CHAPTER FOUR

JAVI DRAINED HIS pint glass, went back to the bar and took the only remaining seat.

"Another beer?" Tito asked.

"Might as well."

He felt all prickly and irritated, as if he'd fallen into a cactus patch. What was this mysterious thing Annalisa had to do, anyway? What was so urgent about it that it couldn't be put off for a few hours?

Tito refilled the glass and set it down. "Something wrong?"

Javi took a drink. "No. Yes. I don't know. It's Annalisa. She's been weird lately."

Tito started wiping the bar top with one of the white cloths he always seemed to have nearby, and his face took on an attentive, concerned look. He was going into full-on sympathetic bartender mode, just like their uncle used to do when he'd owned the place. If Javi had been in a better mood, he'd have made a joke about it, but he didn't feel like laughing. Truth be told, he could use some wise bartenderly counsel right now.

"Weird how?" Tito asked.

"Like, standoffish. Not responding to texts. And running off with Eliana all of a sudden, just when we were having such a nice chat."

A sly smile quirked up the corners of Tito's mouth.

"That's it? That's your idea of weird? For her not to be at your beck and call twenty-four hours a day?"

"I don't expect her to be at my beck and call," said Javi. "It's just not like her to blow me off."

"Blow you off how? Did the two of you have plans together today?"

Javi glared at his brother. "You know we didn't. I just got here, and she didn't know I was coming, so we couldn't have made plans. What's your point?"

"Only that it isn't reasonable for you to be upset with her for having a previous engagement when you haven't made any claims on her time yourself. You can't expect her to be available whenever you decide you want her around. Annalisa has grown up, Javi. She's not that little girl who used to blindly worship you anymore. She's an accomplished woman with things to do and people to see. It was bound to happen eventually."

"Whoa, that's quite a speech," said Javi. "Sounds like you've really put some thought into this."

Tito shrugged and went on wiping the bar top. "Maybe I'm just smart."

Javi sighed. "Yeah, maybe."

He took another drink of his beer. Then Tito glanced past him, smiled and made a beckoning motion to someone Javi couldn't see. A few seconds later, a woman joined them at the bar. She was very pretty, with shiny blond hair and an angelic smile.

"Jenna," said Tito, "I'd like you to meet my brother Javi. Javi, this is Jenna Hamlin."

The pride and wonder in his voice were unmistakable. He might as well have said, *Isn't she great? Can you believe that a woman this fantastic is my girlfriend?*

Jenna's eyes widened as she held out a hand for Javi to

shake. "Oh, hi! I thought you looked familiar. I remember you from the birthday party, but that was just on a screen."

A few months earlier, Jenna had thrown Tito a surprise party at the bar for his birthday. Javi had always thought Tito didn't like parties, but apparently he liked them well enough when they were given in his honor by a beautiful woman he was in love with. From what Javi had seen and heard, it had been a very successful party. Half the town had turned out. Annalisa had arranged for Javi to join the festivities through FaceTime. Javi had given his brother a birthday toast, and afterward Annalisa had taken the phone around for him to say hello to other partygoers—his mom and dad, his older brothers, some old friends. He would never in a million years admit it out loud, but the whole thing had made him homesick. It had been part of what had pushed him into going ahead with the move back to Limestone Springs.

"Good to meet you, Jenna," said Javi, shaking her hand.

"Good to meet you, too. Are you here for a visit?"

"Nope. Home to stay."

"Oh, wow. Tito mentioned that you were thinking about moving back home, but I had no idea you were coming so soon."

Javi was getting tired of hearing people say that, but he replied, "Yeah, I'm going into business in Limestone Springs. Classic cars."

Jenna pulled up a stool and took a seat. "No kidding? That'll be brilliant! Exactly what the town needs. Are you a Chevrolet man, like Tito and your dad?"

"Pretty much, but if someone brought me a '64 Mustang to work on, I wouldn't say no."

She gave him a sly smile. "Don't you mean '64 and a half?"

Javi chuckled appreciatively at the familiar joke. Not many people knew that the original Mustang had been released halfway through the year, but those who did never missed an opportunity to laugh about it. Javi was beginning to understand why his father was always raving about Jenna. She knew a lot about cars, and she had spunk, in spite of her dainty good looks. And Tito was clearly smitten. He was staring at her now with a dopey smile and a glazed look in his eyes. Javi was happy for him in theory, but seeing the two of them together was making him feel something like envy.

Not over Jenna herself, of course. She was really great and all, and seemed like she'd make a fine sister-in-law, but she wasn't Javi's type. He'd always been partial to brunettes.

"I'd better get going," he said as soon as he'd finished his second beer. "Lots to do."

Back at the building, he parked in the small lot near the alley and let himself in through the gate of the fenced-in yard. Lefty was napping right by the back stoop, clearly unconcerned about his new surroundings. He raised his head and blinked sleepily as Javi dropped onto the stoop beside him and leaned his back against the door.

Javi let out a heavy sigh and scratched Lefty behind the ears. His mood was all snarled up. He was still annoyed at Tito for saying that he expected Annalisa to drop everything for him. That wasn't true—and he could prove it. If she didn't want to spend time with him, that was fine by him. It wasn't as if he was depending on her for anything. He was a big boy, and he had plenty on his plate. He'd get on with it, starting right now.

He took out his phone and made a call.

"Dad? Yeah, it's me. I've got a big surprise for you."

Juan Mendoza looked at his son across the clutter of empty oil cans and old air filters and said, "No."

Javi stared back at him. "What do you mean, no?"

"I mean no. I won't have you sacrificing your future to pay for my mistakes. I won't let you do it."

He kicked an old hubcap, startling Lefty, who had been slowly and cautiously making his way around the perimeter of the building. The hubcap clanged across the dirty concrete floor, then spun in a vibrating circle.

Javi didn't know what to say. He'd expected some pushback from his mom, some interrogation to make sure he had his ducks in a row, business-wise. But his dad? Never. Javi's dad was the most optimistic person Javi had ever met in his life. He always anticipated the best, even when he had absolutely no reason to. No matter what awful thing was happening, the man was always cheerful. Always looking on the bright side. He woke up at 4:30 a.m. every day with a smile on his face, and kept right on smiling through a grueling day's work clearing brush and moving dirt, week in and week out.

But he wasn't smiling now. It frightened Javi a little, as if his father's face had suddenly taken on the wrong shape, or the earth and the sky had switched places. Juan looked tired and discouraged, like an old man surveying the wreck of his hopes and dreams from another decade.

"Where is all this coming from?" Javi asked. "What are you so mad about?"

"I'm mad at myself. You want me to say it? I messed up. I was a fool to ever trust that rat Carlos Reyes. Your mother warned me at the time not to do it, but I thought he was my friend. I thought I knew best. Well, I was wrong— and my family suffered for my mistakes."

The hubcap had stopped spinning at last. Lefty crept

over to it and sniffed it, then shot a suspicious look at Juan, as if wondering what shocking thing he'd do next.

"Carlos stole from you," said Javi. "That sucked. But things are different now. We can start the business and make it a success. I've got the money."

"Yeah, yeah, you've got the money. You said you could make more in the oil fields than working for me, and you were right. Okay, great. Now, you take that money and you use it to make something of yourself."

Javi stretched his arms out wide. "What do you think I'm trying to do? Why do you think I went to work in the oil fields to begin with? This is what I wanted the money for—this, right here."

But Juan was already shaking his head again. "No," he said. "I won't let you tie yourself down to your old man, trying to fix the past. You invest in your future, son."

Javi swallowed over a lump of soreness that had suddenly formed in his throat. "This *is* my future, Dad. This is what I want to do, what I've always wanted to do. And I'm good at it."

Silence. Then Juan said in a different tone, "You are good at it. You'll get no argument from me there."

"I had a good teacher," said Javi.

Juan didn't answer.

"Remember the day we bought the Biscayne?" asked Javi. "You'd found the listing on OldRide. The ad said it needed a full restoration, but the price was right. So we got up before sunrise and drove four hours to get to that guy's house, out in… Where was it? Granbury?"

"Stephenville," said Juan.

He said it grudgingly, as if aware that Javi knew perfectly well that it had been Stephenville and was only trying to draw his father into the story by making him participate in telling it.

"Yeah, Stephenville," said Javi. "He had it out in that old dairy barn. The dust on the tarp must have been two inches thick. But when we pulled it back…"

"Man, that was a good-looking car," Juan said. "All those '59s were. A lot of people didn't like 'em when they first came out. Thought the styling was too radical. That rear-end design, those cat's-eye taillights…"

"It was a beauty, all right," said Javi. "And the body actually wasn't in too bad of shape. Remember how it was missing one of the fender ornaments? We were searching all over the dairy barn for it, you, me and the seller. I'd just about given up when I happened to check inside that rusted milk can, and there it was."

Juan gave an appreciative grunt.

"I had all my savings stuffed in an envelope," Javi went on. "Everything I'd earned that summer and the summer before, working for you, plus all the birthday and Christmas cash I'd saved over the years. You matched me, dollar for dollar. I felt like such a big man, handing the whole wad over to that guy, and watching him count it all out, and then shaking his hand. We aired up the tires and got the car loaded onto the flatbed."

"Stopped for lunch at Whataburger," Juan put in. "Made it home in time for dinner."

"But we didn't eat much, did we? We stayed up half the night removing the bumpers and big trim pieces. Some of the fasteners were so rusty, we had to heat them with the propane torch to get them to break loose. I remember you had the radio tuned to that classic rock station. To this day, I can't listen to Kansas or Supertramp without thinking of that night."

His dad was staring into space now. "We stripped that car down to every last nut, bolt and clip. Had over three hundred boxes of parts and I don't know how many different layout drawings by the time we were done."

The boxes were still in Juan's workshop, neatly labeled and stacked. A full restoration was a big, complicated job. Just about every piece had to be reconditioned or replaced, resulting in a car that was in as good a condition as when it first left the factory, or better.

But the Biscayne had never gotten further along than a reassembled frame. After Carlos had cleaned out the business account, the Mendozas had been too preoccupied with picking up the pieces of their shattered financial lives to spend any more time or money on it.

"That car should have been ready for you to drive when you turned sixteen," said Juan, a hard note of bitterness in his voice. "You ended up buying that old pickup instead."

Javi shrugged—as if it didn't matter much, as if the thought of Carlos's theft hadn't soured his stomach every single time he'd turned that pickup's ignition. "It's not like I could have actually used the Biscayne for a daily driver back then," he said. "The insurance alone would have put that out of reach. But I could swing the premiums now."

Juan rubbed a hand over his chin and jaw. "Would you do a full restomod? Modern brakes and suspension? Air conditioning?"

"You bet I would. I'm not sacrificing safety and comfort for the sake of authenticity."

"You could use the company that made the restomod parts for Tito's Eldorado and Eddie's Chevelle. They did good work, and they delivered on time."

Tito had bought his 1969 Cadillac Eldorado not long after inheriting the bar from his and Javi's uncle, also called Tito. Unlike his brothers, Tito had never been mechanically inclined, but he liked the look of old things. He'd bought the Cadillac and paid for the parts, and Juan had done the work. Eddie, the next older brother before Javi, had worked out a similar deal with his father for the 1967 Chevelle.

"Good to know," said Javi. "Give me their contact info, and I'll get in touch with them. I'll want them to get started right away. I need to send the body off for paint, too. And while all that's being done, you and I can get busy on the mechanical stuff."

Juan took a long look around the garage. "It would take a lot of work to get this building back in shape and ready to open its doors."

He was right about that. The most recent renters had really done a number on the place. They'd even smashed the old light fixtures.

"I know," said Javi. "But most of the work is needed in the other parts of the building. The garage area's still in decent shape. And the building is already zoned and set up as a garage, and on this big corner lot right in the heart of downtown. It's everything we could possibly want in a location."

"The past three businesses that have set up in here have all gone bust," said Juan.

"That's because they were all badly managed, or trying to compete with Manny, or both. This town can't support two full-service garages. That's not what we're going to do. We're going to be a specialty shop. People will be coming from Austin and San Antonio and even Dallas to visit our place."

Javi pointed through the glass door that opened onto Fannin Street. "That big overhang off the side entrance? We'll park the M47 there. It's a classic pickup, but we haven't put any work into it yet, so we won't have to worry too much about it being left outside overnight. Then this whole front area will be our showroom. We'll take out that partition and put plate glass back in all the windows. Everyone driving down Persimmon will be able to see all the gleaming classic cars inside."

He didn't mention that these had been Annalisa's ideas. What counted was that they were *good* ideas. He could see that his father thought so, too.

But Juan wasn't quite ready to admit it yet.

"I don't know, son. It was pretty rough when we lost the business the first time around. I don't think I can go through that again."

"You won't have to. You'll have me as your partner this time, not that scumbag Carlos. Come on, Dad. If you give up, if you let the dream die, you'll be letting Carlos win."

Juan waved this off. "I'm not really into vengeance or showing people up. I just want to take care of my family. The dirt work business is doing pretty well right now, with so much new construction in the area. It'd be a risk, setting that aside to start something new."

"You don't have to set anything aside. Getting this place up and running is going to be my full-time job—that, and working on the Biscayne. The Limestone Springs Sip-N-Stroll is scheduled for the first weekend in December. That's too soon for us to be fully operational, but it's enough time to get the place presentable—clean it up, install some good lighting, put up those windows along the front, get some epoxy on the floor. It'll take about six months to finish the Biscayne, but in two months I can have it far enough along to show off. You know what a big event the Sip-N-Stroll is. Half the town will be out and about that night, wandering in and out of all the downtown businesses. We could get Mom to make cookies and a batch of that hot chocolate of hers with the salted caramel topping for the hot chocolate contest."

Juan nodded. "It'd be a good way to get the word out,

all right. You know, there's a classic car club in Schraeder Lake. One of the mechanics they use is talking about retiring."

"Well, there you go!" said Javi. "The time is right. You've got fresh demand opening up in an established market."

Juan's gaze roamed slowly around the building once more, as if he was already getting glimpses of its future glory.

And then he smiled.

Javi let his breath out. Everything was okay now. The sky was overhead again and the earth was beneath his feet where it belonged.

"You know the first thing we ought to have?" asked Juan.

"A new set of lifts?"

Juan stretched out his arms. "A sign. A big one. My cousin Arnie has a sign shop, and he does nice work."

Javi nodded. "Yep. But before we have a sign, we need a logo. And before we get a logo, we need a name."

There was a brief silence. Then they both said at the same moment, "Mendoza Classic Cars."

They grinned at each other.

"We'll need business cards, too," said Javi.

"Stacy Vilicek at the print shop can take care of all that," said his dad. "She makes good logos."

Javi walked over to him and stuck out his hand. "So what do you say, partner? Do we have a deal?"

Juan gripped his hand and gave it a single brisk shake. "We have a deal."

CHAPTER FIVE

ANNALISA STOOD UNDER the shade of a live oak tree, with a soda in one hand and a paper plate in the other. Barely a day had passed since Javi had shown up in Limestone Springs, but his parents had still succeeded in pulling together a party, including a big chocolate sheet cake with Welcome Home, Javi spelled out in frosting letters. The square of cake on her plate contained the first half of Javi's name. *J* and *A* for Javi and Annalisa.

Her parents had taken it for granted that she would attend the party with them. The Mendozas were old friends and former neighbors, and Javi and Annalisa had always been close. Annalisa hadn't been able to think of a convincing excuse to stay away.

"It'll be okay," she'd told Eliana. "You know what the Mendozas' parties are like. There'll be a ton of people. Javi probably won't even notice I'm there."

"Hoping he doesn't notice you isn't much of a strategy," Eliana had replied. "You need to actively avoid him. I still think you should come down with a last-minute case of the flu and stay home."

"I can't get the flu on Sunday and then be perfectly fine Monday morning, and I can't play hooky from work right now. Claudia needs me. It'll be fine, really. I'll arrive late and leave early. And I won't talk to Javi at all."

So far, everything was going according to plan. Javi hadn't spoken or made eye contact with her. A few minutes more and she'd be able to thank Mrs. Mendoza for the party and slip away.

The Mendoza family home was located on a half-acre lot, with a big covered workshop filled with project cars and a house way too small for seven people. Somehow, Juan and Rose had managed not only to raise their five boys there, but also to practice extravagant hospitality at every possible opportunity.

Annalisa's text notification went off. The message was from Eliana.

Status report?

Annalisa smiled. She set her plate and drink down on a small table and typed:

Situation under control. No contact with the subject.

Avoiding Javi hadn't been difficult. Since the moment she'd arrived at the party, he'd been surrounded by a whole crowd of people, mostly girls he'd gone to high school with. As far as Annalisa could tell, he'd never even noticed she was there.

"Story of my life," she muttered.

Eliana replied:

Good. How's the party? Are you mingling or moping?

I mingled a little. I petted a cat, Annalisa typed.

That's not enough. Go find some people and talk to them. Giving up your Javi infatuation won't work unless you replace it with other things.

Annalisa sighed. She knew Eliana was right, but socializing took energy. Maybe she should just find that cat again.

"Annalisa?"

A pretty blonde was coming her way. Annalisa put on a smile.

"Jenna! Hi. How are you?"

"Couldn't be better. And yourself?"

She looked as if she really wanted to know, and Annalisa decided to level with her.

"Not great. But I'll be okay."

Jenna knew about Annalisa's hopeless crush on Javi, and about her decision to get over him. "Hang in there," she said.

Annalisa's gaze wandered to Javi. He had drifted away from the crowd and was standing alone, holding a beer in one hand. His feet were planted wide and his shoulders were squared, as if he expected someone to try to knock him down.

Then his eyes met hers, those clear green eyes beneath those brooding black eyebrows, and his face softened into a smile.

Her heart gave a quick, painful thud as she smiled back. "I'm trying," she said. "But it isn't easy."

Jenna glanced over her shoulder at Javi. "Do you know it was only a few months ago that you first spoke to me?" she asked. "Right here, at the Mendozas' Fourth of July party."

"Was it? It feels like longer. So much has changed since then."

Jenna had come to Limestone Springs a couple of years back, along with her niece Halley. The two of them had been pretty closed off at first—not surprisingly, since they'd had a big secret to protect. But that was all resolved now, and Jenna and Halley had fully embraced their new home.

Now Jenna kept up a stream of light chatter—about Annalisa's new book, and the horseback lessons Halley was taking from Susana Vrba, and even the new fall menu items coming to Lalo's Kitchen. Annalisa knew what Jenna was doing, and she was grateful for it. They passed a good twenty minutes in pleasant conversation, until Halley appeared and told Jenna that Juan was asking for her. He wanted Jenna to ride the mechanical bull that he kept in one of his outbuildings.

"Go ahead," Annalisa told Jenna. "I'm about to go home, anyway."

"All right," said Jenna. "Take care of yourself."

Annalisa took her empty plate and soda can to a trash barrel. She said goodbye to her parents and thanked Mrs. Mendoza for the party. As she turned to walk back to her car, she saw Javi standing right in her path, arms folded over his chest, staring at her.

She sucked in a quick breath. Why did he have to be so handsome? And why couldn't he have stayed away long enough for her to make her escape?

"Where do you think you're going?" he asked.

"Home," she said.

"But the party's barely started."

Annalisa smiled and shook her head. The party had been going strong for two hours already.

"I have to get up early to work on my book before going to my day job," she said. "That means I need an early bedtime."

He gave her an incredulous look. "It's barely five p.m.!"

"I've got stuff to do at my apartment."

"Like what?"

"Like loading the coffee maker, and pressing a blouse for tomorrow, and organizing my notes."

He studied her a long moment, probably thinking one of two things—that she was an incredibly boring person, or that she was bad at making excuses.

"I'll walk you to your car," he said at last.

As they went, she couldn't help thinking of another time he'd walked her to her car, after that afternoon on the Comal River, when he'd opened up to her and talked for hours, and she'd been so certain that he was going to make a move. Was he remembering it, too? Of course not. It didn't mean anything to him.

"I talked to your parents," Javi said. "I haven't seen them since they moved out of the old neighborhood. They're looking well."

"They are," said Annalisa. "Ever since they retired, they've gotten into bird-watching in a big way. I gave them a nice bird feeder as a housewarming present, and now I get weekly updates on all the birds that visit it. My group text thread with them is about eighty percent bird photos. They just about lost their minds when a pair of scissor-tailed flycatchers built a nest in the bur oak tree outside the dining room window."

Javi chuckled. "Did the birds lay eggs and everything?"

"Oh, yes, and raised a healthy family of four nestlings. I got ample photo documentation of the whole thing—in spite of the fact that I saw the nest in person every Sunday when I visited."

"Baby birds probably change a lot over a week's time. Your parents didn't want you to miss out."

"I guess."

"Well, I told them the old neighborhood's not the same without them."

"How would you know? You haven't lived here yourself in two and a half years."

"I just know. I always liked your house."

She gave him a sidewise look. "You hardly spent any time there. Your house was where all the neighborhood kids went to play."

"I know. But it made a big impression whenever I did come over. I remember the first time I saw your photo wall in the hallway. All the pictures were of you. Everywhere you looked, it was Annalisa this and Annalisa that. Annalisa in a baby dress. Annalisa taking her first steps. Annalisa playing in the sprinkler. Annalisa dressed up for a ballet recital."

The sound of his voice saying her name made her melt inside. But she only said, "That's how it is when you're an only child. Everything is about you. Until you move out, and then everything is about birds."

"It felt so big, too, your house," Javi went on. "Took me years to figure out it wasn't any bigger than my house. It just wasn't all crammed with stuff and people. You know, it was at your house that I first learned the concept of a guest room. A whole room with nobody living in it, with a full-size bed that nobody slept in except when someone came to visit, and a big old dresser with nothing in it. I know, because I opened the drawers and checked."

"Did you really? Snoop! I always liked *your* house. There was so much going on in it all the time. Your mom taught me to bake. I still think of her every time I make *conchas*."

"She loved having you here. She always said you were like the daughter she never had."

"It was good of her to take an interest in me. There weren't many girls in the neighborhood for me to play with, except when the Ramirez kids would visit their grandparents on weekends. Tito was always nice to me, but the rest of you boys didn't want me joining in your rough games."

"That was all coming from Enrique, not me," said Javi. "I always wanted you."

She didn't answer, and the words hung in the air, taking on a weighty significance that he surely hadn't intended.

"Have you found a place to stay?" she asked.

"Sure have. I'm going to be living in that old horse trailer on The Property. Got the last of my stuff moved in this morning."

The horse trailer was of '80s vintage, left over from Juan's rodeo days. For the past twenty-three years, it had been parked inside a metal barn on the acre of land that the Mendozas referred to as The Property. Most of that time it had sat empty, until Juan had rented it out to Roque Fidalgo, a newcomer to Limestone Springs who'd lived there for a little over a year before moving out about six months ago.

"How big are the living quarters in that thing?" asked Annalisa.

"About the size of a walk-in closet. But it's all right. It's got a bed, a minifridge, a microwave and a functioning bathroom. What more could a man need?"

"A lot of things, I would think. Why not just stay with your parents while you get things sorted out? I'm sure they wouldn't mind."

"They offered, but I can't, because of Lefty. He's not very friendly, and it takes him a long time to warm up to new people. I don't know how he'd do with a bunch of neighbor kids and cats and other dogs right next door, and I don't want to find out. It's less trouble for both of us to stay there. Anyway, The Property is right on the edge of town, so I won't have far to drive to get to the garage. I'll take Lefty to work with me during the day so he doesn't get lonely."

They'd reached her car. She clicked the key fob, and the door locks chirped open. Javi opened the driver's door for her.

"You weren't really going to leave without seeing me, were you?" he asked.

He sounded troubled. She supposed it did seem a little cold, ghosting him at his own party when they'd been friends for so long. She wondered what he would say if she told him the truth—that she was in love with him, and had been for years, and was trying desperately to get over him.

"I saw you," she said, keeping her tone light. "We made eye contact while I was talking to Jenna. Remember?"

She hadn't answered his question, and she prayed he wouldn't push.

He didn't. "Take care of yourself, Annalisa," he said.

"You, too," she replied. "And welcome home, Javi."

Monday morning Javi closed on his new property. Afterward he and his dad met at the bar for celebratory beers and burgers, then walked down the street to the print shop to talk about logos and business cards. Stacy said she'd have some designs ready to show them by the end of the week.

They parted ways. Juan headed back to his current earth-moving job, and Javi returned to the building that was now officially his property and got busy cleaning.

This part wasn't nearly as much fun as coming up with ideas for names and logos.

He needed to replace the busted light fixtures, but for now he used plug-in work lamps to light the space. He knew he would have to hire an electrician sooner or later, but not before talking to his cousin Zachary Diaz. Zac was a general contractor and the first call for any Mendoza who needed major construction work. Javi had already texted Zac twice but hadn't yet heard back.

It felt good to be making measurable progress toward his goal. But it would have felt a whole lot better not to have to do it all without any encouragement from Annalisa. He'd thought about texting her a time or two over the past few days, but something held him back. The way she'd acted at his welcome home party—it had almost been like she was blowing him off again. Things still felt weird between them, and he didn't know why.

He kept remembering what Tito had said, about how Javi expected Annalisa to be at his beck and call all the time. He was starting to think Tito was right. He'd never realized how much he depended on Annalisa until she wasn't there. He used to go a long time without checking in with her at all, but whenever he did call on her, she was always quick to answer and give him whatever he needed—sympathy, advice or just a listening ear.

Well, apparently that was over now. He didn't feel great about it, but he wasn't going to grovel. He had his pride. If she cared about him at all, if their yearslong friendship meant anything to her, she knew where to find him.

Lefty was having a great time sniffing and exploring the old building. Once in a while Javi heard scuffling sounds and squeaks. Apparently he had a rodent problem, but Lefty was on the job, so Javi left him to it.

At the end of his first full day of cleaning, the place looked worse than when he'd started. Three days later, on Thursday afternoon, he could see a clear improvement. Every time he hauled a bag of trash or a box of scrap metal out to his truck, it was like lifting a weight off his shoulders. Once in a while, he even forgot to resent Carlos Reyes.

But when he found the old sign that said Reyes Mendoza

Classic Cars, all his anger came back full force, burning his gut like battery acid. He stood there, hands balled into fists, staring down at the faded colors of the grime-covered words. His dad hadn't even gotten first billing on the name of the business that had been his idea to begin with!

He shut his eyes and took a few deep breaths. When the churning in his stomach had calmed down, he picked up the sign, took it outside and heaved it into the bed of his truck, where it fell with a satisfying smash.

There. It was gone now, and the new sign would soon be ready to hang outside, alerting all of Limestone Springs that the Mendoza family was back in the classic car business in a big way, this time with no Reyes partner to drag them down.

By midmorning on Friday, the place was clean enough for a contractor to start work, if Javi had had a contractor lined up. Unfortunately, Zac still hadn't called or texted him back. Javi sent his cousin yet another text and went to work on the big, heavy-duty plastic storage crate he'd found in the metal barn behind the horse trailer. Someone had written Friesenhahn Property on a strip of masking tape and taped it across the top.

The Friesenhahns, Javi knew, had come over from Germany at some point before the Texas Revolution and established a ranch in Seguin County. Over the decades following the revolution, their fortunes had declined, and they'd sold off their land piecemeal until they were down to one acre in what was by that time the edge of town. That was the acre the Mendozas had bought, where they'd planned to build the nice new house where Javi and his brothers wouldn't be tripping over each other all the time, and where his parents would finally have the space to entertain to their hearts' content.

Like everyone else in town, the Mendozas had referred

to that acre as the Friesenhahn property at first, but once the purchase had been made, this had been shortened to The Property.

Javi opened the box.

Spread across the top was a set of blueprints for the house that was never built. Javi lingered a moment over the blueprints. That room in the corner was supposed to be his, to share with Eddie and Tito, while Johnny and Enrique, the two oldest boys, shared the one across the hall. Then once Johnny was out of the house, Enrique would have his own room, and then Eddie after Enrique left home, until finally Javi and Tito were the only ones left, each with a room to himself. No more would Javi have to deal with all of Eddie's styling products or Tito's ever-expanding book and music collection.

Javi rolled up the blueprints and set them aside on the desk. Next came a manila envelope that held documents from the closing on the property. He set this aside, as well.

Everything else in the crate looked like a bunch of random junk, which wasn't far from the truth. There'd been a big trash heap on The Property when the Mendozas had bought the place. Most of it had ultimately been burned or taken to the dump. The rest—what Javi had thought of as "the good stuff"—had gone into this crate.

There were a whole lot of pieces of rusted iron, along with some hunks of limestone with fossils in them that his mother had wanted to use in landscaping. The iron pieces were fairly decorative, and Rose had planned to mount them on the back wall of the house.

But the house had never been built, and the pieces of metal that had seemed so interesting and ancient when Javi was a kid now looked like a bunch of junk. He could take all the metal to the scrap yard right now and get something for it. Yes, the pieces were old, but hardly museum-worthy. But they did belong to his parents, so that was for them to decide.

Tucked into one corner of the crate, snug against an old plowshare blade, was some sort of metal wad. Not iron. This was a softer, bluish-white metal that had crumpled into a misshapen ball, something like a gum wrapper with a piece of chewed gum balled up inside. The metal showed patches of tarnish but no rust. Tin, most likely. How had *this* ended up in the crate? It wasn't remotely decorative.

Javi picked it up and felt something shift inside. Apparently it was wadded up around some unknown object— probably why it hadn't been thrown away. He went and got some metal snips and cut the tin shell away.

The thing inside didn't look very promising at first. In fact, it looked like a ball of dirty rags.

Javi took a deep breath. The bundle smelled like… horses, somehow, or maybe a farm. He peeled back the tattered cloth covering, so dirty that he couldn't tell what color it was supposed to be, and revealed…

He frowned. What *was* this thing? It was covered in leather and looked something like a binocular case, but thicker and shorter. It had a slight curve to it, as if someone had taken a small shoebox and bent it just a bit. The leather was cracked and half-rotten, with glints of metal showing through, silvery white with a faintly bluish tint. More tin.

Javi drew back the leather flap that covered the top. Inside was a wooden block, encased in a tin shell within the leather covering. The wooden block had three staggered rows of holes, each a little less than an inch in diameter. The whole setup was something like a cartridge box, but made of wood instead of Styrofoam or plastic or cardboard. And instead of a full metal jacket, inside each hole was some sort of paper cylinder. Javi picked one up.

It disintegrated in his hand, revealing a black powder that gave off a whiff of sulfur.

The wooden block was sitting a little high in the metal case, as if swelled by moisture. Javi eased it out, careful not to dislodge the paper cartridges.

Beneath the wooden block was a shallow tray, also made of tin. And inside the tray was a flat packet of some sort, wrapped in a yellowish paper-like substance that gave off an oily odor. The wrapping cracked when Javi peeled it back. It had gone brittle.

Inside the wrapping were some stacks of folded papers. They looked like letters. The writing on the outside was faded, and the ink had an old-timey look to it.

Carefully, Javi unfolded the first letter.

The writing was in Spanish, which he knew well enough to get by, but not fluently. The faded ink was hard to read, but he could make out a few words, like *soldados*, and *artillería*, and *revolución*.

But what really jumped out at him was the date at the top.

2 octubre 1835

A tingle of excitement spread through him—not because he actually cared about a bunch of old letters from the time of the Texas Revolution, but because he knew someone who did. And it was only right to let her know what he'd found.

So he took out his phone and called her.

CHAPTER SIX

ANNALISA SAVED HER document and shut her laptop. She raised her arms over her head in a slow stretch, trying to ease the stiffness in her shoulders and neck. She'd been hard at work all morning, drawing up documents for a land sale. Another old family ranch was being carved up and sold off, and there were a million details to attend to—surveys, property lines, deed restrictions, easements, oil and gas and mineral rights.

Fortunately, Annalisa liked details. She liked huge, complex projects with innumerable interrelated components. She was good at them, too. As Claudia's paralegal, she was responsible for drafting documents, doing research—anything that made Claudia's life easier. Claudia depended on her to get things right, and she always, always delivered.

A muffled wave of laughter came through the wall from Claudia's office next door—Claudia's rich, throaty laugh, and the dry chuckle of the client who'd been in there for the past hour or so.

Annalisa's stomach growled. As usual whenever she came up for air after hours of work, she was suddenly ravenous, but she still had forty-five minutes to go until lunch.

A mug stood on her desk, emblazoned with the words Instant Paralegal—Just Add Coffee. It was a Christmas gift from her parents, and extremely appropriate. She picked it up and walked out of her office. Halfway down the hall, a welcome aroma washed over her, rich with undertones of cinnamon, vanilla and chocolate, as well as the promise of caffeine.

"It's almost ready," called a voice. "I just brewed a fresh pot."

Not everyone would brew a fresh pot of coffee at 11:15 a.m., but Claudia and Annalisa were both coffee fiends, and so were many of their clients. Annalisa had often heard it said that the Taste of San Antonio blend was the signature scent of the law office of Claudia Cisneros.

"Bless you, Mari," Annalisa called back. "The smell of it is already making me feel more alert."

She had no intention of making do with the smell alone, though. She took her mug to the minifridge in the waiting area, poured in a splash of milk and watched the dark liquid drip into the nearly full pot.

Claudia's law office was housed in a gracious old building located in the heart of downtown Limestone Springs, within easy walking distance of Tito's Bar and Lalo's Kitchen. Two big windows spanned the front, with a door in between neatly dividing the space in half. On one side was Mari's desk, backed by a deep blue accent wall covered with big brass letters that spelled out Claudia Cisneros, Attorney-at-Law. On the other side, two leather armchairs faced the Spanish colonial credenza where the coffee stuff was kept.

Mari was talking into her headset and typing something into the scheduling app on her computer. Mari was in her seventies, with decades of experience in office management, and perfectly comfortable with modern technology. She kept Claudia's busy practice running like a well-oiled machine.

The coffee maker gave a final gurgle and went silent.

Annalisa filled her mug, held it to her face and inhaled the fragrant steam.

The door to Claudia's office opened and a woman walked out. She was small and feisty-looking, with a toughness about her that made Annalisa suspect she came from ranching stock. Claudia—a striking woman in her fifties with strong features and beautifully cut clothing—followed her to the reception area. The two of them were chatting about people Annalisa didn't know. She heard a confusing jumble of names and some references to fourth cousins once removed. Claudia knew everyone in this town—in the whole county, probably—and could tell in an instant how any given individual was connected to any other.

"All righty then," the client said. "I'll leave you to it."

"Thank you, Constance. Mari will call you to make a follow-up appointment once the draft is ready for us to review."

Constance nodded to Mari and Annalisa and said, "Hi, how're y'all?"

It was a question that didn't really call for an answer. Annalisa and Mari smiled and made vague murmurs, and Constance went out the front door. Through the glass, Annalisa saw her heading not for the pickup parked right in front of the office, but for the battered Honda Civic next to it.

Claudia stood a moment, staring thoughtfully after Constance.

"Another old ranch getting sold to developers?" Annalisa asked.

"Not this time," said Claudia. "We're going to be working soon on a very interesting will. I'll tell you about it later, but first I have to tidy up my meeting notes."

The phone rang, and Mari answered it. Claudia went

back to her office and shut the door. It wouldn't take her long to put things in order. She was ruthlessly organized— smart and driven and forthright, with no nonsense about her. She was also one of the most sociable people Annalisa had ever met, with a motherly attitude toward the young people in the town, perhaps in part because she had no kids of her own. Annalisa knew, because Claudia had told her, that she had no regrets about that, or about staying single all her life.

Mari got off the phone. "That was the client who wants to set up the umbrella LLC for all those rental properties," she said. "I made his follow-up appointment for Wednesday afternoon. I put it on your calendar and Claudia's."

"Before or after the meeting about the property trust?" Annalisa asked.

"That got moved to Friday, right after that probate hearing."

The two of them were still going over the week's schedule when a delivery van from Hager's Flower Shop pulled up right outside the door, in the same space Constance's car had just vacated.

"Ooh, that looks promising," said Mari. "Do you know any young men who might be sending you flowers, Annalisa?"

"No, I do not," said Annalisa. "Could be from a grateful client."

They watched as the delivery woman took a big Styrofoam box from the van and brought it into the office.

"I've got a delivery for Claudia Cisneros," she said. She was wearing a name tag with Barbara printed on it.

Annalisa walked over to Claudia's door and knocked. "Oh, Claudia," she said in a lilting voice. "Someone sent you flowers."

"Or maybe a case of beer," said Mari, looking at the Styrofoam box.

Barbara smiled. "No, not beer. It's a luxury bouquet. The packing is to keep it from getting damaged in transport."

"Sounds expensive," said Mari.

"Oh, it is," said Barbara as she removed the lid off the box.

Claudia stepped out of her office just as Barbara finished unpacking the transport box.

The luxury bouquet turned out to be a stunning arrangement of orchids, anemones, calla lilies and roses. Claudia took the card from the holder and read it. Her lips edged up in a tender smile.

Not a grateful client, then.

"From Peter?" Annalisa asked.

Claudia nodded.

"Wow, the construction business must be doing really well," said Annalisa. Eliana's wedding had given her an education in the pricing of flowers, and she was pretty sure that she could buy herself two weeks' worth of groceries for what this arrangement cost.

"It is, actually," Claudia replied as she signed the tablet Barbara held out to her. "There's a huge building boom going on in this area, with all the newcomers moving to Texas. Almost every construction company I know of has all the business it can handle. Peter's still establishing himself here and making contacts, but he'll get there."

"I'm sure he will," Annalisa replied. "He has so much experience flipping houses in Pennsylvania. And he has such a comforting presence, just an air of decency and kindness about him, that people naturally like him and trust him."

Claudia's smile deepened. "That's true, isn't it?"

"Oh, yes. I liked him the instant I saw him at Alex and Lauren's wedding."

"So did I," said Claudia.

Barbara gathered her packing materials and left. Claudia bent her face to the gorgeous blooms and breathed in their scent.

"I'm very happy for you, Claudia," Annalisa said.

She meant it. She'd seen the two of them together, and she knew that Peter treated Claudia like a queen and that the usually coolheaded Claudia seemed positively smitten. But there must have been a hint of wistfulness in Annalisa's tone, because Claudia gave her a sharp glance and said, "Come with me to my office and help me decide where to put the flowers."

Annalisa followed Claudia to her front corner office with its dark wood and jewel-toned fabrics. "Shut the door," Claudia said, and Annalisa did.

Claudia set the floral arrangement on a console table and stepped back to study the effect. Without looking at Annalisa, she said, "I hear Javier Mendoza is back in town."

"That's right," Annalisa replied. "He bought the downtown building that his father used to own, and he's planning to open a classic car garage there."

She knew perfectly well that none of this was news to Claudia. Nothing happened in this town on the real estate front that Claudia wasn't aware of almost before it happened.

"Have you seen him?" Claudia asked, moving the arrangement to her desk.

"Only a couple of times, right after he got back."

"How long ago was that?"

"Almost a week."

It was hard, knowing Javi was right there in town, living and working within walking distance of her own home and office, and not going to see him. But she'd made up her mind and she wasn't backing down. Besides, friendship—let alone romance—was a two-way street. No one was stopping Javi from contacting her.

If he wants you, he'll go after you, Eliana had said, and she was right. Well, apparently he didn't want her, because he hadn't sought her out since that first weekend after he'd arrived. Even now, the memory of the unexpected meeting at Tito's Bar sent a shiver through her. She could still see the soft delight in Javi's eyes as he'd looked at her reflection in the bar mirror, still feel the way he'd held her in his arms for that long, tight hug. And at his welcome home party, he'd paid a few minutes' worth of flattering attention to her.

But then he'd faded out of her life again like he had a thousand times before. At least this time she'd kept her pride intact.

Claudia kept quiet, clearly waiting for more. Annalisa took a deep breath and said, "I've sort of given up on Javi."

"Sort of?" Claudia repeated.

"Well, my feelings for him haven't changed. But I'm not waiting around for him anymore."

"Good for you. Do the right thing, and the feelings will follow."

"That's what I'm counting on."

Claudia smiled at her. "It'll happen for you, *mija*. And it's worth waiting for the right one."

Annalisa sighed. She believed the second part of Claudia's statement. Trouble was, she couldn't shake the conviction that Javi *was* the right one, she just couldn't make him think so, too. And as for whether a loving, permanent relationship would ever come Annalisa's way, no one could know that for sure—not even Claudia, no matter how confident she sounded.

"I wish I could be as strong-minded as you are," Annalisa said.

"What's strong-mindedness have to do with it? I've always had all the male company I wanted—men who would take me to San Antonio or Austin, to musicals and operas and restaurants. We'd have a good time together, and at the end of the evening, they'd go home, and so would I. And I was fine with that. I wasn't staying single on principle. I just never met a man whose company I enjoyed more than my independence...until I did."

That sounded serious.

"Claudia? Are you engaged?"

"No. But we've talked about it. Peter knows better than to spring a proposal on me out of the blue."

"Oh, I hope he asks soon!" said Annalisa. "You would make a beautiful bride."

"Thank you, *mija*. But we were talking about you."

Annalisa collected her thoughts. "My situation is different. It's like you said—you were single by choice, not pining away for the one guy you couldn't have."

"That's true." Claudia tilted her head and studied Annalisa. "Maybe the trouble is that you don't have enough men to compare Javi to. You need to get out there and meet some other guys, and give them a chance. It might change your perspective."

"Maybe," Annalisa said.

After a brief silence, Claudia asked, "So how's it going with the research for the new book?"

"Really well," Annalisa replied, grateful for the change of subject. "I'm actually ahead of schedule. I've finished the overview of all the documents, and now I'm working my way through them individually in greater depth."

"Which one are you concentrating on now?"

"Romelia's diary. It's so fascinating. Did you know that Alejandro had a cousin his age who was serving in the Mexican army at the time of the revolution? They actually saw each other at the Battle of Gonzales—Alejandro on one side of the Guadalupe River, Gabriel on the other."

"I did not know that. Does Romelia mention it in her diary?"

"Yes. Alejandro was really broken up about it. He and Gabriel grew up together. They were like brothers. They had nicknames for each other—Gabriel was *Loco*, and Alejandro was *Cerebro*."

"Crazy and Brain?" Claudia chuckled. "That sounds like a fun pair."

"Doesn't it? Before the fighting started, Gabriel used to spend a lot of time at La Escarpa with Alejandro and Romelia. Now there they were, on opposite sides of a war."

"That must have happened in a lot of Tejano families. Farmers and ranchers with property to defend had to fight against brothers and cousins who'd joined the army as a career—not to mention all the poor conscripts who had no choice in the matter."

"It's sad, isn't it? Gabriel was an officer candidate, a *caballero cadete*, probably eager for promotion and just wanting to make his way in the world. I'd like to find out what happened to him, but I don't have much to go on— just a first name and a rank."

She took a sip of coffee. "Apparently Alejandro and Romelia were big on nicknames. There's another friend mentioned in the diary that Romelia refers to as *Guero*. I haven't been able to figure out who he was. *White guy* could apply to a lot of people."

Claudia pondered for a moment. "Interesting that the nickname is *Guero* and not *Gringo*. The word *gringo* is usually specific to a light-skinned American, but *guero* is more likely to refer to a fair-haired, light-complexioned person of any nationality."

"That's a good point," said Annalisa. "There were certainly plenty of first-generation immigrants from northern European nations in the area at the time, and probably plenty of fair-haired Spaniards, as well. I'll concentrate on them."

"Well, don't drive yourself too hard, *mija*. I know how you can be when you get going. You need to schedule time off for yourself and take it. Otherwise your thoughts get stale. It's one of the ironies of engrossing cognitive work. You have to step away from it once in a while to get a fresh perspective."

Annalisa knew that Claudia took her own advice. She worked hard and she played hard, maintaining a thriving law practice and an active social life. She was civic-minded, serving on boards and committees for various organizations and presiding at local events, as well as maintaining membership in the historical reenactor group. She even ran a small side business making and selling reproduction clothing from the mid-nineteenth century. Annalisa had no idea how she managed it all.

"So you've gone through Alejandro's letters and Romelia's diary," Claudia said. "What's up next on the research schedule?"

She knew all about the documents Annalisa was studying. She'd even helped get some of them to her. Being part of the historical reenactor group meant that she had a lot of contacts.

"Another diary," said Annalisa. "A local rancher found it in an old trunk when he was clearing out some of his grandparents' things and lent it to me. But I might have to reshuffle the schedule, because this one's in German. I looked it over during the initial survey, but I haven't yet taken the plunge. I wish it were in Spanish, or even French or Portuguese. You can get by in romance languages when you know the roots, but German is a whole other story."

"Oh, yes. You do not want to use Google Translate for that. But I know someone who could help you out."

Something in her voice made Annalisa look up. "Who?"

"Someone in my historical reenactor group. He's fluent in German, and of course he's familiar with the history of this area."

"And?" Annalisa prompted.

"And he's someone you should meet anyway. Handsome, intelligent, head on straight. And single."

"What's his name?"

"Grant Carstensen."

Annalisa laughed. "Really? Wow. Is he as hunky as he sounds?"

"More so."

Annalisa hesitated only for a moment before saying, "Okay."

Claudia's eyes widened. "Seriously?"

"Sure, why not? You're right. I need to put myself out there and meet some men. This is as good a way as any. Give me his contact info, and I'll get in touch with him."

"I can do you one better. This weekend is the Come and Take It Celebration in Gonzales. Our reenactor group will be there tomorrow. You could come and meet him there. That way you're not having to do a cold call."

"That actually sounds perfect. Text me the details."

"I will," said Claudia, looking pleased.

Annalisa took her coffee back to her office and opened her laptop. She had several loose ends to tie up before lunch. A pleasant thread of anticipation wove its way through the work, along with the name *Grant Carstensen*. She'd been on more than her share of blind dates in the past, and they had never gone well. It was too much pressure and felt unnatural, like a job interview for a potential mate. This would be different—a meeting at a neutral location, with an actual task for the two of them to work on together. If that led to something more, great. If it didn't—

if one of them clearly wasn't interested in the other, or if he had a weird vibe—then it was no problem.

But if Claudia spoke well of Grant, he probably didn't have a weird vibe. Claudia was an excellent judge of character, and she certainly knew an attractive man when she saw one.

Her phone rang—not the office phone, but her cell. She picked it up and let out a groan. There on the screen were the words Unknown Caller, followed by a familiar set of digits.

It was Javi. And he was calling, not texting, which meant it must be important.

Well, important to Javi, anyway. For all she knew, he could be calling for advice on what he should wear on a date with another woman.

She laid the phone face down on her desk. Typical. Just when she was allowing herself to get excited about meeting another man, here came Javi, stirring up hope again. Well, she wasn't going to give in. Anyway, she was at work. She couldn't take a personal call, even if it was only five minutes until her lunch hour. It wouldn't hurt Javi to leave a message for once.

The ringtone stopped. She went on typing, waiting for the chime that meant she had a new voicemail. It didn't come.

But the chime for a new text message did.

She sighed, then stared at the back of the phone for a full minute before picking it up and reading what Javi had to say.

Can you come over right away? There's something here you need to see.

CHAPTER SEVEN

JAVI STARED AT his phone screen, waiting for Annalisa to reply to his text. What was taking her so long?

He stuck the phone in his back pocket and forced himself to go on looking through stuff in the storage crate. Finally his text tone went off. He whipped the phone out.

Can't. I'm at work.

Javi let out an exasperated sound. What kind of response was that?

He typed his answer. You get a lunch break, don't you?

The instant after he'd hit Send, he wished he could take the message back. Seen on his screen, the words weren't playful and teasing, the way he'd heard them in his head, but surly and rude. It was hard to strike the right tone in a text message. He'd been told by certain people—women— that his texting tone left a lot to be desired. One of the nicest things about Annalisa was that she understood him. He didn't have to be on his guard all the time.

That was how it used to be, at least. But things were different now. Javi didn't know why, but they were.

Maybe she was looking at that message right now, thinking what a jerk Javi was. Maybe he should add a follow-up message or a laughing emoji to show that he was only joking. Or maybe that would only make matters worse.

Before he could make up his mind, Annalisa replied:

What is it that you want to show me?

Texas history stuff, Javi answered. I think it might be important.

Another long pause. Then, OK. I'll be there soon.

"Yesss!" Javi said, loudly enough to make Lefty turn and stare at him.

"What are you looking at?" he asked his dog. "I'm just happy to have some company for a change. I've been spending too much time alone lately."

Lefty cocked his head.

"Don't get your feelings hurt," said Javi. "You know I like having you here. But you've got to admit you're not the world's best conversationalist."

There was a taco truck parked just around the corner that had been supplying most of Javi's meals since he'd moved into the building. Javi grabbed his keys and hurried over there now. It should have taken him only a couple of minutes to get lunch for himself and Annalisa, but the taco truck ran out of foil wraps and couldn't find a new box right away. By the time Javi made it back to the garage, Annalisa was already standing at the locked door, glancing at her watch, cool and composed in a blindingly white top made of some smooth material and a short, straight, black skirt that made her legs go on forever. She had her hair twisted high on her head like it had been that day he'd seen her at the bar. It had come loose when he'd hugged her and tumbled over her shoulders, and his, in a cascade of dark silky waves.

Javi was suddenly conscious of his own grimy jeans and holey T-shirt.

"I'm on my lunch hour," Annalisa said. "I don't have much time."

The words took him aback. Not even a hello? That wasn't like her. Maybe she was upset because he'd made her wait. Or maybe she was just tired of him.

"Sorry," he said. "I was getting us some tacos for lunch. Barbacoa for me, chorizo and potato for you, with that green sauce you like."

"Oh," said Annalisa, her expression changing. "That's actually really thoughtful."

"Well, you don't have to sound so surprised about it," Javi said. "I can be thoughtful. What did you think I was going to do? It's only right to feed you when I invite you over during your lunch hour."

Annalisa held the taco bag while Javi fumbled with the keys. Why was he so clumsy all of a sudden?

He finally found the right one and managed to get the door unlocked. He opened the door wide and gestured for Annalisa to go in first.

She walked through the doorway, her heels making hollow clacks on the concrete floor. Javi followed, still feeling weirdly off balance. The familiar smell of metal and motor oil steadied him some. He'd get his bearings soon. She'd see everything he'd done, hear about all his plans and give him that wide-eyed, admiring smile that he missed so much.

She turned in a slow circle, taking it all in. The building suddenly seemed a lot shabbier and dirtier than he remembered. It looked much better now than when he'd started, but she had no way of knowing that.

"It's kind of a mess, I know," he said.

"Well, this is a big project you've taken on," she replied. "It's going to take a while to get things in shape."

"I'm not afraid of hard work."

"I know you aren't. Where's Lefty? Is he here today? I want to meet him."

"No, you don't. He's not a very friendly dog."

She gave him a look. "Of course I want to meet your dog. Lefty! Lefty!"

"He won't come," said Javi. "He doesn't come to anyone but me, and he's suspicious of strangers."

The words were barely out of his mouth when Lefty appeared from the dark corner he'd been holed up in and started heading their way.

Javi's stomach tightened. This was not good. Lefty had never bitten anyone that he knew of, but he'd growled and snapped at people who'd tried to make friends with him. And that was the last thing Javi needed to happen right now.

He should have thought this whole thing through better before inviting Annalisa over, should have taken the time to move Lefty to his yard before going to the taco truck. But he'd never expected his antisocial dog to come within twenty feet of Annalisa, much less walk straight to her and give her a thorough sniffing like he was doing now.

Annalisa stood perfectly still until Lefty had made a complete circuit around her. Then she lowered herself into a deep squat, looking impossibly graceful in that tightly fitted skirt and those high heels.

"Watch out," Javi warned. "I don't want him to hurt you."

Lefty stopped sniffing. He looked Annalisa full in the face, his big pointy ears doing that weird lopsided thing.

Then he sat on his haunches and nudged her hand with his nose.

Javi felt his jaw drop open. There was Annalisa, crouching on a dirty garage floor, looking like the most beautiful thing on the planet. And there was Javi's notoriously surly dog, sucking up to her like some goofy, sunny-natured golden retriever.

Annalisa reached out a hand and rubbed him under the chin. "Hi, there, Lefty. Are you a good boy? Yes, you are a very good boy, and handsome, too. Aw, you like having your throat scratched, don't you, buddy?"

Lefty shut his eyes and leaned into the petting. Then, with a contented sigh, he flopped onto his side and rolled over on his back, exposing his speckled belly.

Annalisa went on crooning to him. "Aw, do you like belly rubs? You do, don't you? What a good boy you are."

By now Lefty had all four legs splayed out and a dopey expression on his face that Javi had never seen before.

Annalisa glanced at Javi. "So this is your tough, dangerous dog, huh?"

"Yeah, well, he's not usually like that," Javi said lamely.

Annalisa gave Lefty a final pat and stood upright again. Lefty rolled back onto his side and lay there, panting and relaxed.

Annalisa looked at the work lamps, then up at the ceiling, where the light fixtures used to be.

"Looks like you need an electrician," she said.

"Yeah, the last renters really did a number on the place. What I really need is a general contractor. A lot of the work is stuff I could do myself, but there's just so *much* of it. I can't afford to spend time coordinating subcontractors, and I want to get the work done right and not have it take forever. I left a message with Zac, but he hasn't gotten back to me yet."

"He might not have time," said Annalisa. "All the builders are busy now, with half the state of California moving to Texas. You ought to give Peter Longwood a call. He's probably the only contractor in town with any room in his schedule, and that's only because he's new. He just moved here in mid-July."

Javi didn't answer right away. He did *not* want to give business to Alex's father-in-law. But if Claudia liked Peter, he must at least be good at his job. She was not one to suffer fools or incompetent workmen. And with the town's Sip-N-Stroll only two months away, Javi didn't have time to waste.

"Maybe I will," he said at last. "Do you have his contact info?"

"I can get it from Claudia. I'll text it to you if you want."

"Yeah, do that," said Javi. As an afterthought, he added, "Please."

"I will," said Annalisa.

She had a definite reason to get in touch with him now. If she forgot to send the info, he could send her a reminder text without coming off pushy. And once they got started texting, he'd find a way to keep the conversation going and get back to the easy give-and-take that they used to have.

She stole another glance at her watch. "You said you wanted to show me something?"

"Oh, yeah, right. But let's eat our lunch first."

Javi led the way to some plastic chairs and a battered coffee table in the old waiting area. They both sat down, and he reached into the taco bag and took out the warm, foil-wrapped packets, setting the ones marked *C&P* in front of Annalisa, along with the green salsa, and keeping the red salsa and the tacos marked *B* for himself. Lefty lay down on the floor in a sphinx pose. That was one thing about Lefty—he never begged for people food.

Annalisa unwrapped a taco, peeled back the tortilla partway and emptied one tub of salsa onto the filling.

"How are you enjoying living in the horse trailer?" she asked.

"It's a bit cramped, but big enough for Lefty and me. It feels weird, living on The Property. Remember that party we had out there, when my parents first closed on the place?"

She smiled. "How could I forget? You went spelunking down that old dried-up well. I was terrified that you were going to get hurt."

"There wasn't anything to be scared of. Just a hole in the ground."

The gathering had been small and simple for a Mendoza party—little more than a cookout. They'd expected it to be the first of many, but of course things hadn't worked out that way.

Javi was the first to finish his lunch. He wiped the grease off his hands and took a long drink from his water bottle. Annalisa took her last bite, wadded up the foil wrappers with the salsa tubs neatly inside and daintily pressed the paper napkin to her lips.

"Now, what was it that you wanted to show me?"

Javi had almost forgotten about the reason he'd called her to begin with. Now he walked over to the big plastic crate.

Annalisa followed him. "What is all this stuff?" she asked.

"It's from The Property," he said. "When we first bought the place there was this big trash heap right by that ramshackle old shed. It had cactus and dewberry vines growing all over it, but you could see all kinds of weird stuff poking through—broken tools, hunks of iron and pieces of furniture. My brothers and I wanted to scrounge through it so bad, but Mom wouldn't let us. She was convinced it was full of snakes."

Annalisa shuddered. "She was probably right."

Javi chuckled. "Yeah, she was. My dad eventually

scraped it all up with his dozer to get it out of the way before making the pad site for the house. We saw two big old
rattlers slithering out, and half a dozen rats."

Annalisa shuddered harder.

"Once the stuff was all spread out, Mom said it was all
right for us to root around in it, as long as we wore boots
and gloves and long sleeves and pants. I felt like an archae-
ologist digging up ancient artifacts. Probably most of the
things didn't go back any further than the 1950s, but they
seemed pretty cool to me."

"And these are the things? How'd they end up in this
crate?"

"Well, my mom thought it might be nice to display some
of them on the back exterior wall of the house. So anything
that looked even vaguely decorative got chucked into here
so it didn't get sent to the scrap metal yard by mistake. I
found it in the metal barn at The Property."

"Okay. So this is the stuff from the old trash heap." She
shot him a suspicious glance. "There aren't any snakes or
rats in here, are there?"

"If there were, they'd all be mummified by now. This
crate's been sealed up for years."

Annalisa shuddered a third time and backed away.

Javi picked up the leather-covered box and handed it to
her. "Here. This is what I wanted you to see. It's guaran-
teed rat-and snake-free."

Annalisa took it carefully in her hands, as if not quite
convinced that a rat wasn't about to jump out.

She inhaled deeply, just as Javi had done. The thing was
still giving off a whiff of that horsey or farm-like aroma.
Javi had put everything back the way he'd found it, with
the old letters folded inside their cracked, yellowish, paper-
like wrapping at the bottom of the container underneath the
wooden block with the holes in it. As she turned the box

over, another piece of the rotten leather exterior dropped off, showing the bluish-white metal beneath.

She opened the flap, and there was the wooden insert with the twists of paper sticking up from the little holes.

"This is a cartridge box," she said, her voice hushed with wonder.

He knelt beside her. "That's what I thought it looked like. But the holes are stuffed with these paper packets."

"That's how cartridges used to be made. Soldiers would put black powder and a musket ball on some paper, twist the paper to keep everything together, drop the packet down the barrel of a weapon and send it home with the ramrod. Brass cartridges weren't invented until around the middle of the nineteenth century. These paper cartridges might date back to the Texas Revolution, or earlier."

He liked the authoritative way she talked about things like that—the same way he'd have talked about the carburetors that had been used before fuel injection came along.

"So some Texian freedom fighter used to carry this pouch around during the revolution, huh?" Javi asked. He'd noticed how these Texas history buffs always said Texian instead of Texan whenever they talked about people from that time period.

Her eyes met his, huge and dark with excitement. "No," she said. "I think it might have belonged to a soldier in the Mexican Army."

She pointed. "See the curve? I think this was a ventral box. That means it was worn in front, along the soldier's belly. I'm pretty sure the gear used by the Texian troops was US Army surplus, and the Americans were using shoulder pouches for cartridges by that time." She frowned. "But I don't know, really. A lot of the Texian soldiers would have provided their own gear, especially in the early days, and there was probably a lot of variation among individuals. And some of the Tejano troops might have had old Spanish-style ventral boxes, too."

He grinned at her. "Either way, it's pretty cool, right?"

She grinned back. "Oh, it's very cool. Thank you for showing me."

"Well, of course," he said. "I can't come across some old artifact from the Texas Revolution and not show it to my favorite Texas history buff, can I?"

He'd meant that last bit to sound light and jocular, like something an old friend might say, but somehow it didn't come out that way. His voice had gone all soft and tender for some reason. What was wrong with him today?

Annalisa's cheeks flushed, and she looked away.

"Here, check this out," Javi said.

Still kneeling, he tugged the wooden block out of its tin case. It came free easier this time than when he'd removed it earlier. He set it on the floor, took out the packet of letters and handed it to her.

For a moment she just stared. Slowly she peeled back the crackled wrapping.

Then she stopped and set the packet back on her lap. "Do you happen to have any cotton gloves I could put on?" she asked.

"No," said Javi. "But I have some nitrile ones."

"Would you go get me a pair, please?"

"Sure."

He hurried out to the work area, grabbed a box of disposable nitrile gloves and brought them back to the office. Annalisa pulled on a pair. Slowly and carefully, she opened the packet and took out the first letter.

She unfolded the page and drew in a quick breath.

"Segunda de octubre," she read in a hushed voice. *"Dieciocho treinta y cinco."*

Javi felt a surge of triumph. "I saw that. That's when the Texas Revolution started."

She turned her gaze on him. "It's *exactly* when the revolution started. October second—that was the day of the Battle of Gonzales. And look at the salutation."

He leaned in close to her and squinted at the faded ink. *"Mi querido Loco,"* he read. "My dear Crazy? Who's that?"

She let out a breathy laugh. "I think it's Alejandro Ramirez's cousin Gabriel. Loco was Alejandro's nickname for him. They saw each other at the battle. Gabriel was a cadet in the Mexican army. I read about him in Romelia's diary." She skimmed the rest of the letter. "This has to be from Alejandro. I know his handwriting. And look at this!" She pointed to the signature line. "It's signed Cerebro! That was Gabriel's nickname for Alejandro. And see this flourish underneath the name? He put that in the signature line of all his letters to Romelia."

Javi studied the elaborate scroll with its multiple loops and twists. "Looks pretty distinctive, all right. I wonder how Alejandro managed to get the letter to his cousin. Seems like there wouldn't be a lot of mail being exchanged between two hostile forces."

"He must have found a way."

She studied the letter in silence for a minute or so.

"Well?" Javi asked at last. "What does he say?"

"I can't make out all of it," said Annalisa. "Some of the ink is faded, and Alejandro's handwriting is tricky to decipher at the best of times. But it looks as if he was trying to persuade his cousin to come over to the Texian side in the war. Just like Moore did with Castañeda. Javi!" She grabbed his arm. "What if Gabriel was there for the parley? What if he heard what Moore said to Castañeda, about tyranny and liberty and republican ideals, and decided that even if his commander wouldn't take Moore up on his offer, he would?"

Javi thought about it. "That would be something," he said.

"Yes. Yes, it would. Not as big a deal as if Castañeda had turned his coat and brought all his men over with him, but still a pretty big deal."

She seemed lit up with the idea, her eyes shining like stars. He was intensely aware of her hand on his arm, her heart-shaped face inches from his. She held his gaze, and his arm, a moment longer before drawing her hand away and looking back down at the letter. He wanted to take her hand in his and make her look at him again that way.

"Can I hold on to these?" she asked.

"Sure," Javi replied. "Keep them as long as you want. I'm sure my dad won't mind."

"I'll be careful with them, and I'll get them back to him. But I want to show the letters and the cartridge box to Claudia and some other people, and cross-reference them with Romelia's diary and Alejandro's letters."

She glanced at her watch. "And speaking of Claudia, I need to get back to work. Thanks again for showing this to me, Javi."

"You're welcome."

They both got to their feet. For a moment they stood there, facing each other and making awkward eye contact. Then Annalisa gave Javi a quick, light hug, the kind he used to give her—almost as if things were back to normal between them. But the way he felt with her in his arms, even for those few seconds, was anything but normal.

CHAPTER EIGHT

WATCHING THE SUN climb into a clear turquoise sky, Annalisa knew she was in for a scorcher of a day. The cold front that had blown through Central Texas the night of the bonfire at La Escarpa was only a memory. Now, here in downtown Gonzales on the first weekend in October, summer weather was back with a vengeance.

Of course, Gonzales was farther south than Limestone Springs, and closer to the coast, and at a lower elevation. She should have thought of that. She should have worn shorts, like most of the other people milling around— and she should have gotten an earlier start, so she could meet the handsome and erudite Grant Carstensen earlier in the day while she was still mentally sharp and looking her best.

But the letters Javi had found had been too tantalizing to resist. She'd stayed up way too late, going over them—and, if she was being honest with herself, thinking about Javi.

There'd been something different about him yesterday, when he'd shown her around his building. A certain eagerness, as if he'd wanted to impress her. A strange vulnerability that she'd never seen in him before.

She shook her head hard. She hadn't driven all the way from Seguin County to stand around mooning over Javi, wondering for the millionth time whether he was finally beginning to feel about her the way she felt about him. She'd come here for a purpose—to meet Grant and get him to translate the German diary for her. And if he was as attractive as Claudia said, maybe there would be a spark between them that would lead to something more than a work relationship.

She'd told Claudia not to introduce the two of them, not to talk her up to Grant beforehand or lay any groundwork with him whatsoever. Annalisa wanted to meet him for herself. No need to rely on other people to advance her love life for her. She was a strong, confident woman, and it was high time she started acting like one.

The city of Gonzales was doing itself proud for its annual Come and Take It Celebration. A *biergarten* tent stood on the town square just off Saint Joseph Street, opposite a food tent along Saint Paul. Booths for arts and crafts vendors clustered on the south side of the square near Saint Lawrence. Somewhere in between were a mechanical bull and a stage for live music. The Texas flag was in evidence everywhere she looked—the food tent canopy, shirts, shorts, coolers, coozies and actual flags—as well as the usual assortment of Texas-shaped things. There were plenty of American flags, too, and lots of red, white and blue in general. Carnival rides, a petting zoo and a snake exhibit were somewhere on the other side of Saint Joseph.

She lifted her heavy sheaf of hair off the back of her neck and wished for a breeze. She should have worn her hair up, but she knew it was one of her best features, and she'd wanted Grant to see it in all its glory.

Someone called her name. It was Lauren Reyes, pushing a baby stroller and wearing a calico dress straight out of the eighteen hundreds, with an expensive-looking camera hanging by a strap around her neck.

"Hey, there!" said Annalisa, giving Lauren a quick hug. "I love your dress. Is that one of Claudia's designs?"

The light cotton looked wonderfully cool, and Lauren's chestnut mane of hair was pinned sensibly up.

"Oh, yeah," Lauren said. "I get all my historical clothing from her. She made the kids' things, too."

Three-year-old Peri, sitting up straight in the front of the stroller and clutching a sippy cup, had on a pale pink calico dress, perfect with her fair skin and golden curls. Even little Emilio, stretched out in the compartment in the back of the stroller, wore a tiny linen shirt that came down past his knees.

"Your dress is so pretty, Peri," said Annalisa.

"Thank you," Peri said in an adorably prim tone. Then she craned around backward, patted Emilio's chubby leg and added, "This is my brother."

"I see," Annalisa said, crouching down to get a closer look at the baby. Emilio was fast asleep, with his arms stretched out and his hands in loose fists. A crest of thick black hair stood straight up from his head.

"He's so beautiful, Lauren! And he's grown so much since I first saw him. How old is he now?"

"Ten weeks. He's already outgrown his newborn clothes, but this outfit that Claudia made still fits him fine. Those nineteenth-century mothers had the right idea, dressing babies in blousy little gowns they can wear for months and months."

"I'm surprised Alex hasn't made you a period-appropriate baby stroller," said Annalisa.

Lauren chuckled. "Oh, he's mentioned it. But between the camera and the nose ring, I'm never going to look really authentic, anyway. I think he decided an up-to-date baby stroller was not the hill he wanted to die on."

"Speaking of which, what time is the battle reenactment?"

"Not until three. But the parade's about to start. Come watch it with us."

A crowd had already gathered along the side of Shiner Street, sitting in camp chairs or on the curb, some eating food from vendors, others munching on snacks from nearby coolers.

Annalisa followed Lauren to some wooden fold-out chairs set in a shady spot beneath a live oak tree.

"I wasn't expecting it to be so hot today," she said as she took a seat.

"It always is," Lauren said serenely. "It's tradition. We could be having an arctic blast the day before, but come the first weekend in October, the temperature shoots right back up into the nineties."

Lauren spoke with the familiarity of a lifelong Texan, though she'd lived only a few years in the area. She opened her cooler and took out a container of melon chunks for Peri.

"You really are dedicated, coming here with a toddler and a new baby," Annalisa said.

"Oh, I wouldn't miss it," Lauren replied. "I love these events. They're good for business, too. I've got my cousin Nathaniel here today, helping with my booth. I've already sold a couple of my landscape photos."

Peri delicately ate her melon chunks, and Lauren took two water bottles out of the cooler.

"I've never seen you at a reenactment before," Lauren said, handing one of them to Annalisa. "Which is funny now that I think about it, with you being such a Texas history buff."

Annalisa pressed the water bottle to her face for a moment, relishing its cool moisture, before opening the lid. "There's history, and then there's living history. I like my history in documents that I can study from the comfort of my own home."

"Fair enough."

Annalisa took a long drink, then said, "I did attend some reenactments the year my book was released. Got quite a few sales. But after that, I stayed home and let Claudia sell my books at her clothing booth."

"Dalia got her copy from the firefighter fundraiser," Lauren said with a smile.

Annalisa smiled back. She knew how Lauren had fallen asleep reading Dalia's copy of the ghost story book, and later seen Alex in his reenactor clothing and mistaken him for the ghost of Alejandro Ramirez. She was proud of having a hand, however unintentionally, in bringing Alex and Lauren together. Who knew? Maybe the new book would be the means of uniting another happy couple.

The parade was pure Texas. The color guard led off with rifles and three flags—American, Texan and a white flag emblazoned with a five-pointed star, a cannon and the words Come and Take It in black. A long line of trucks came next—county sheriff, county constable, Texas game warden, EMS and fire engines, political candidates. The high school and junior high bands were sensibly dressed in shorts and black T-shirts, and drill team girls wore short-skirted, fringe-trimmed uniforms with cowboy hats and boots. Then came another color guard, in reproductions of nineteenth-century Mexican infantry uniforms, white and navy blue trimmed with red and gold. Their long rifles were tipped with bayonets, and they carried a Mexican flag and the flag of Goliad—white, with a severed arm holding a curved sword dripping blood, all in red.

More reenactors followed, in various frontiersy outfits like those that would have been worn by the Texian defenders at Gonzales. Alex marched in front, carrying the Come and Take It flag tied to a big stick, and wearing the red jacket and knee breeches, black sash and hat, and high leather boots that he used whenever he portrayed Alejandro Ramirez in a battle. The *escopeta* carbine resting on his shoulder had been Alejandro's weapon in the war.

"Wave to Daddy," Lauren said to Peri, and Peri did. Alex darted a quick sidewise glance at them, and his mouth edged up in a smile.

"Alex looks so handsome," said Annalisa.

"He sure does," said Lauren, her eyes fixed on her husband. "There's a lot to be said for these nineteenth-century outfits for men."

Annalisa thought so, too. She wondered which of the other men was Grant Carstensen.

The marching reenactors were followed by horses and buggies and a covered wagon pulled by mules. Claudia rode in one of the buggies. She was wearing a gorgeous dress with an empire waist. She waved at them.

Then came floats carrying queens and courts in sparkling gowns and tiaras—Miss Gonzales, the Watermelon Thump Queen from Luling, the Persimmon Queen from Limestone Springs. Students from Victoria College rode a pirate ship float.

When the classic cars started driving by, Annalisa's thoughts inevitably turned to Javi. Maybe next year he'd be here, driving the Biscayne. She could just picture him, right hand on the wheel, left arm lifted outside the open window in a lazy wave…and herself beside him in the passenger seat.

She did her best to force the image away, but it wasn't easy. Burning her Javi mementos hadn't erased him from her mind.

Lots of people rode on horseback, including high school football players in jerseys with their sleeves rolled up to show off their muscles. One cowboy rode a longhorn. Peri giggled at the rodeo clown in a tiny clown car bringing up the rear.

A cheer rose up from the crowd and swelled into something like a roar. Annalisa swallowed over a lump of soreness in her throat and clapped until her hands hurt, filled with pride in this state of hers—this big, bold, brash place with its sweeping history, its rivers and lakes, hills and plains, deserts and forests and coastlines, and the men and women who thought it was worth fighting for.

And somehow it was all mixed up with Javi. He was *such* a Texan—hardworking and hard playing, quick to call out injustice, a little touchy in matters of honor, but generous and courageous to a fault. What was it he'd said to her that day at Tito's Bar, about wanting her to have his back if ever a revolution came? She'd want to have him on her side, too.

Beside her, Lauren was dabbing at the corners of her eyes. They looked at each other and smiled.

The parade-watching crowds dispersed as people went back to ambling around the town square. Annalisa walked with Lauren and the kids to the booth where prints of Lauren's photography were for sale. She bought one of a stormy sky over a Hill Country landscape that glowed eerily in the half-light.

"I'll hang it over my desk," she said. "It makes me feel like writing."

"Glad I could contribute to your artistic process," said Lauren.

Her cousin Nathaniel wrapped the print securely and put it in a bag.

"I guess I'll walk on over to Pioneer Village now," said Annalisa. "That's where the reenactors are set up, right?"

"Yes, but you'll have to drive. It's too far to walk."

Annalisa was not sorry to spend a few minutes in the air-conditioned comfort of her car. She parked near a big white clapboard building. Other structures—a weathered

clapboard house with people sitting on the porch, a log
cabin, a smokehouse and a covered well—were clustered
companionably around. The cream-colored tents of the historical reenactors were set up in a treed grassy area. She
saw Claudia's big tent with rows of reproduction clothing
for sale and Alex's tent where he demonstrated woodwork-
ing with hand tools. Reenactors in historical garb walked
around, along with visitors in modern clothing.

Alex smiled when she came into his tent. "Hey, *prima*!
Haven't seen you at one of these for a while. How's the
new book coming along?"

"Pretty well," Annalisa replied. "I made an interesting
discovery recently that I'd like to get your take on."

"Oh, yeah? What is it?"

"It's too much to get into right now. But I'll get in touch
with you later and tell you all about it."

"Okay, that's fine. I'll just lie awake at night tortured
by suspense."

She chuckled. "Sorry. I actually came here today to
meet someone who might be able to help me translate a
German diary."

"You must be looking for Grant Carstensen."

"That's right. Do you know him?"

"Sure. That's his booth right over there across from
Claudia's. See that guy binding a book? That's Grant."

Annalisa couldn't see much of him from this distance,
but what she did see was promising.

"Thanks," she said.

She started to walk away, then turned back. "What's
he like?"

"He's a good guy," said Alex. "Very smart, but not pre-
tentious."

Better and better.

She walked over and joined the small group of people

watching Grant work. His outfit had less of a rough and ready frontier vibe than what most of the reenactor men were wearing. He looked like a gentleman scholar, in his full-sleeved white linen shirt with its upstanding collar, cream-colored linen vest and black neck stock. A short coat in dark blue was draped over the back of his wooden chair. The wide brim of his white palm leaf hat screened his face from view, but the hands that were busily stacking sections of folded papers on a thin board were lean and strong, and the legs in their brown trousers were long enough to suggest considerable height.

He was giving a demonstration on bookbinding.

A few members of the crowd asked questions, which he answered clearly and patiently. He was a good speaker, knowledgeable but not pedantic, with steady blue-gray eyes, a calm smile and a quiet confidence that Annalisa found very appealing.

When the demonstration was finished, the rest of the crowd dispersed, leaving the two of them alone.

"Hello," she said. "Are you Grant Carstensen?"

"That's me."

"My name is Annalisa Cavazos," she began, but before she could get any further, his face lit up.

"Annalisa! It's good to meet you at last. Claudia's told me a lot about you."

"She has?" Annalisa asked. She'd told Claudia not to lay any matchmaking groundwork for her, and Claudia had agreed.

"Yes. I'm a big fan."

"Fan?" she repeated blankly.

"Of your book. I especially enjoyed your retelling of the White Lady of the Frio River."

Her annoyance at Claudia instantly evaporated. Grant Carstensen had read her book!

"Well, thank you!" she said. "That's nice to hear."

"I really like how you explore the cultural and psychological dimensions of ghost stories in general, and ghost stories of the Texas Hill Country in particular," he went on. "I bought extra copies of your book as gifts for relatives."

"How lovely of you! Did they like the book?"

"Loved it. I have a great-uncle who swears he saw the Ottine Swamp Monster when he was a boy."

"Are you from this area, then?" she asked.

"Born and raised in Bastrop County. Descended on both sides from early settlers—German, Dutch, Norwegian. Grew up hearing all about Texas history. Even heard some of the ghost stories in your book when I was a kid."

This was almost too good to be true. How was it possible that this handsome, scholarly, intelligent, Texas-loving man had grown up within a couple of counties of her and they'd never run into each other before now?

No sooner had she completed the thought than Grant said, "It seems strange that I've never met you before. I've read your book so many times that I feel as if I know you, but I bought all my copies from Claudia's booth. I couldn't even get them autographed!"

Annalisa laughed. "I'm sorry. I'd be happy to sign your copy for you if you'd like."

"Good. You should come to more of these events. Hold book signings. Meet your readers."

"I did a few years ago, when the book first came out," said Annalisa. "But I don't think we met then."

"No. That was when I was studying in Hamburg."

Grant stood and waved her into his booth. "Please have a seat," he said, indicating the wooden chair that he'd just vacated as he unfolded a small camp stool for himself.

They both sat. Grant took off his hat and fanned his face with it.

"Claudia tells me you're working on a new project," he said. "About Seguin County in the Texas Revolution."

"That's actually what I wanted to talk to you about. One of my primary sources is a diary written by an early settler in what eventually would become Limestone Springs. The diary is written in German. Claudia told me you'd be a good person to help me with that."

His eyes widened. "Two of my great loves, Texas history and the German language, united in one project? I'd be thrilled to translate it for you. Do you have it with you?"

"I do." She opened her purse and pulled out a bundle well wrapped in nonacidic paper and cotton padding inside a framework of lightweight outer boards.

Grant nodded approvingly as Annalisa handed it to him. "Looks like you know how to take care of old documents," he said.

"I do my best," she replied. "Before it came to me, this diary was stored inside an old quilt chest. It's actually pretty well preserved."

"I should probably wait until I get home to look at it," said Grant. "But I'm not going to."

He grabbed a pair of white cotton gloves from a drawer in the table at the front of his booth and put them on. Carefully he removed the wrappings, revealing a leather-bound volume, about four by six inches, with *Tagebuch*—German for *diary*—in ornate gilded letters on the front. Grant's eyes, alight with excitement, met hers across the book. Reverently, he opened it.

"It's written in German script," Annalisa said, though of course Grant could see that for himself. "I can't make out more than a few letters."

"I can manage it," Grant said serenely. "My PhD is in German studies."

"Oh! Claudia didn't mention that. Are you a professor?"

"Yes," he said without looking up from the diary. "I'm currently at UT Austin."

He turned one page, then another.

"How's it looking so far?" Annalisa asked. "Is it decipherable?"

"Oh, yes. This is an entry about the fencing the diarist put up in November of 1834. And this…" He turned another page. "This is a list of supplies purchased in town, along with how much he paid for them. And over here we have a record of everything he had to eat that week."

Annalisa gave a rueful chuckle. "I've been studying a different diary from the same period. That diarist kept track of everything that happened on the ranch—pasture rotation, which cows were bred to which bull, and what calves they all had, and when. It's interesting stuff, but not exactly what I'm hoping to focus on in the new book."

Grant turned another page. "This might be more like what you had in mind," he said. "It's an account of some drills the militia did."

He scanned the diary, examining it page by page until he reached the end. Annalisa kept quiet. When he'd finished, he shut the book, and his eyes met hers again.

"This diarist actually wrote a pretty fair hand," he said. "And the ink hasn't faded much. Based on the number of pages, and the legibility of the handwriting, I'm estimating I'll have the translation finished in three weeks."

This was better than Annalisa had hoped. "That soon?"

He smiled. "Oh, it's a conservative estimate. Once I get going, I doubt I'll be able to stop until I'm done. I'll probably stay up all night reading it."

"I did the same thing last night with some old letters!" Annalisa replied. "I knew I should stop. I told myself over and over that I'd quit after one more paragraph, one more page, one more letter—but I kept going right through to the very end."

"Did you find out anything interesting?"

"Kind of. But the letters weren't in pristine shape. There were entire passages that I couldn't make out. And the parts I was able to read raised more questions than they answered."

"Sounds intriguing. Where did the letters come from?"

"A friend found them while he was clearing out some old papers."

She didn't offer any details. She wasn't going to let Javi intrude on her conversation with another man.

"Have you visited the reading room at the Center for American History, on the UT campus?" Grant asked. "Plenty of old documents there, including the Archivo General de Mexico."

"I haven't gone yet," said Annalisa. "The reading room is open to the public only Monday through Friday, ten to five. I'll have to take the whole day off from work to make a trip worthwhile. By the time you drive all the way to Austin, you might as well make the most of it."

"I agree. Maybe we can meet for lunch while you're there."

"That sounds nice. I'll let you know when I schedule a day."

Grant rewrapped the diary in its protective coverings. "Shall we set a date to go over the translation? Say, three weeks from today?"

"Are you sure you want to set a date now? You might not be finished with the translation in time."

"I like to set deadlines for myself and attach events to them. It's a habit from my days working on my doctorate. When you're in charge of managing your own time, it helps to be as businesslike as possible about it."

"That's true."

They arranged to meet in San Marcos, roughly halfway between Austin and Limestone Springs, at a restaurant called Palmer's. Annalisa was surprised when Grant suggested it. She'd figured they'd get together at a coffee shop.

Things were moving fast. She'd only just met this guy and already they had a date at a nice restaurant.

Of course, it wasn't *that* kind of a date, she reminded herself. They were merely meeting to talk about old documents.

He handed the diary back to her. "You'd better hold on to this until after the battle reenactment," he said. "I don't have a safe place to keep it, and I don't think it would do well in my waistcoat pocket while I'm running around with a Kentucky rifle."

"Good idea," she said, putting it in her purse. "Have you taken part in many battle reenactments?"

"Well, I usually do this one, and Béxar. I've participated in Goliad a few times, but not on horseback. And I've done San Jacinto twice. And one year the group put on a reenactment of the Grass Fight, and I took part in that one, too."

"They did a reenactment of the Grass Fight? Really?"

He chuckled. "Yeah, it was fun. All those saddlebags loaded with grass."

The Grass Fight was part of the Siege of Béxar, the last engagement before the Texians made their final assault on the town. A rumor had been spreading among the Texians that some silver was being sent to San Antonio to pay the Mexican soldiers under siege there. When a Texian patrol saw a party of pack mules making its way toward the town, they figured this was the expected silver. A group under Jim Bowie attacked, and the Mexicans abandoned their mules and fled. The victorious Texians opened the saddlebags to find them stuffed not with silver but with grass. A group had gone out the night before to gather it as fodder for the horses in the town.

"Not one of the Republic's more glorious moments," said Grant. "But the reenactment was fun."

He was a very attractive man, and courteous, and intelligent. She ought to feel a strong attraction to him, instead of simply thinking what a nice guy he was. But they'd only just met. No need to put pressure on herself.

"I'd better go say hello to Claudia and look around some more," she said, getting to her feet. "I'll come back for the reenactment and hand off the diary to you."

He smiled at her. "Aren't you forgetting something?"

He opened a small wooden chest under his work table and took out a worn copy of *Ghost Stories of the Texas Hill Country*.

She sat down again. "Do you have a pen?"

Grant made a scoffing sound. "Do I have a pen?" He gestured to all the shaped quills on his tabletop.

"I've never written in quill before," said Annalisa. "I don't think my first attempt should be when I'm autographing your book."

"Then how about this?" He handed her a plain wooden shaft with a pointed metal nib. "An early fountain pen, filled with iron gall ink. I made the ink myself."

He showed her how to use the pen, and she practiced on a sheet of paper he had on his tabletop. Then she opened the book to the title page.

Grant tidied up his booth while Annalisa puzzled over what to write. She had some standard lines that she used when signing books. It was too much pressure to come up with something original on the spot, and she usually had to be quick about it. *Happy reading! Remember the Alamo!* But somehow those didn't seem appropriate.

She thought a moment, then wrote, *To Grant, in hopes of a successful collaboration.*

Then she signed her name with a flourish that would have made Alejandro Ramirez proud.

CHAPTER NINE

PETER LONGWOOD STOOD in the front room of Javi's building, slowly turning as he scanned the boarded-up windows, the clumsy partition and the cheap paneling peeling away from the walls.

He grinned. "This is going to be fun," he said. "When was this place built? The thirties?"

"Yeah," said Javi. "It started as a combination gas station and garage, but it hasn't been a gas station since the forties, I think."

"It's a gorgeous building. You said this part is going to be your showroom, right? That'll be eye-catching, all those plate glass windows across the front, right there along Persimmon Street."

"Yep," said Javi.

Peter kept scrutinizing everything around him, looking partly like a skilled workman sizing up a project, and partly like a kid in a candy store. He took a lot of measurements and wrote things down in a hardback notebook. Then he and Javi walked to the back where the garage bays would be.

"Looks like there's not a lot for me to do in here," Peter said. "Maybe a new coat of paint and a fresh coat of epoxy on the floor. Other than that, you'll just want some sturdy metal shelving and some good lifts. Are you going to do machining on-site or hire it out?"

"Probably hire it out initially," said Javi. "Then if business takes off, it might be worthwhile to invest in a CNC lathe and press."

He glanced at Peter over his shoulder. "Sounds like you know your way around a garage."

Peter chuckled. "Oh, you know how it is with guys who like tinkering with things. In my experience, they're rarely content to tinker with just one type of thing. I'm certainly not a real mechanic, but I've messed around with engines in a small way. And I taught Lauren to do routine maintenance on her van."

"Yeah, I've heard about Lauren's van," said Javi. "She used to live out of it back when she was traveling the continent. You and she did the work on the van yourselves, right?"

"We did. During the research phase of the project, we saw all kinds of things that people had converted into living quarters—old school buses, Volkswagen buses from the sixties. Lauren really wanted to go that route at first. She loved the aesthetics of the older vehicles, especially the Vee Dubs. But I didn't want her to be stranded somewhere hundreds of miles from a dealership and unable to get parts. In the end, she got the Ford Transit with the high roof so she could walk around in it without hunching over. It certainly isn't as flashy on the outside as the Vee Dub, but it was definitely more practical for the sort of travel she was doing. We saved our creative energy for the interior. We removed the seats and the interior paneling and—"

He broke off. "Well, I'd better stop there before I get carried away. I could talk all day about that project, but that's not what I'm here for."

Now that Javi had heard that much, he actually wanted to know all about the work on the van, but he knew Peter was right. He had a meeting at the bank after this and no time to waste.

They moved on, clockwise, through the garage bay area and back to the main room, now on the other side, where the office was.

Javi opened the office door. "This room isn't a high priority," he said as Peter took measurements. "It's not pretty, but it's functional enough as it is. I want to concentrate on getting the public areas ready for the Sip-N-Stroll in December."

"That's doable," Peter said with a quiet confidence that made Javi believe him.

"Good. Come see the bathroom."

It was a full bathroom, with a toilet, pedestal sink and cast-iron tub in a depressing shade of green, but judging from the dates on the old copies of the *Limestone Springs Clarion* littering the bottom of the tub, it hadn't been used since at least the late '90s.

Peter's face lit up.

"Check out these fixtures!" he said. "Art Deco sink, toilet and tub in Ming green porcelain, probably original to the building."

Next to the office was a small waiting area. Peter stared at the open space with its cheap plastic chairs, then swept his gaze around the room. A visionary light came into his eyes.

"Picture this," he said, pointing to the back corner at the other end of the showroom. "A bar over in that corner—some sort of vintage counter with a liquor cabinet behind it and a vintage fridge stocked with beer. Maybe an old Coke machine for sodas. And over here—" he turned back to the waiting room "—a sort of lounge area with some retro furniture, some classic car–themed decor, maybe a few issues of *Popular Mechanics*."

Javi considered. "The furniture and decor would be no problem," he said. "Ever since the town found out I was opening this place, people have been offering me all kinds of stuff for free. But a bar? That sounds like a lot of trouble and expense, especially when there's a real bar, my brother's place, barely a block away. I've got enough to do without worrying about a liquor license."

"I'm envisioning a BYOB situation. You wouldn't need a liquor license then."

"Why would people want to bring their own booze to my garage?"

"Because people who like classic cars also like talking about classic cars, and hanging out with other people who like classic cars. You're going to be catering to a clientele with some disposable income, people who've worked hard to get where they are and who want to sit back and enjoy themselves. You won't just be selling products or services, you'll be selling a whole experience. I could see your garage becoming a real gathering place for gearheads, once word gets out."

Javi rubbed his chin. "Yeah, maybe so. It's worth thinking about."

By now Peter had filled several pages in his notebook with measurements, scribbled notes and rough sketches. He and Javi sat down on the cheap plastic chairs and went over some specifics about the work Javi wanted done.

When they'd finished, Peter shut his notebook and stood.

"I'll get a bid worked up for you by the end of the week," he said. "If you have any questions or ideas before then, don't hesitate to contact me."

"How soon could you get started?" Javi asked.

"Right away. You'd be my first customer for a big job."

By now Javi was about 94 percent sure he was going to accept Peter's bid, and not only because Peter had been the first and so far only contractor, including Javi's own cousin, to return his texts. Peter was the kind of guy you couldn't help but like and trust once you met him.

"So how are you liking Texas so far?" asked Javi.

"I love it," said Peter. "Of course I'm thrilled to get to spend so much time with the grandkids and Lauren and Alex, and Claudia, too. But I also love Texas for its own sake. It's a place with a strong sense of itself, and a real pride in its history. It's like Pennsylvania in that way, but Texas is a whole other thing. Lauren and Alex are both very interested in what you're doing here. Just the other day, Lauren was raving about how fun it would be to photograph old cars. And you know Alex has that Chevy stepside pickup."

Javi had seen Alex's truck, a 1960 C10. Alex kept it in pristine shape, though Javi would have thought a horse and buggy would be more in his line. And the mention of Lauren's photography reminded him that he would need to get some promotional photos taken at some point, and also have someone put a website together for him. Come to think of it, Lauren did web design, too.

But all he said was, "Yeah." Just because he was probably going to hire Peter as his contractor didn't mean he suddenly had to have business and social relationships with the whole family. Alex was Carlos's son. No, Alex couldn't help that, and yes, it was irrational for Javi to hold Carlos's behavior against Alex. But that was how he felt.

Out on the sidewalk, Javi and Peter shook hands. "Thank you," Peter said. "I appreciate the opportunity to make a bid on this project."

The building seemed quiet and empty after Peter had gone. Javi took out his phone and brought up his most recent text conversation with Annalisa.

It hadn't been a very satisfactory conversation. Basically, he'd just told her that his parents were excited to learn about the letters inside the cartridge box and eager to learn what Annalisa uncovered in her research. She'd thanked him for letting her know. He'd asked how the research was going, and she'd said fine so far, but that she didn't have much to report yet because these things took time.

And that had been about it. The whole exchange had left him feeling hollow inside.

Well, maybe it was better this way. He needed to keep his head in the game. Big goals took time and energy to achieve. He had to stay focused and remember what Carlos had taken from his family. And do whatever it took to make his new business a success.

He'd heard someone say that success was the best revenge. He wasn't convinced that that was true. But it was the only revenge he was likely to get.

JAVI WAS TOSSING a roll of aluminum foil into his cart at H-E-B when he heard someone say his name.

He turned, and there was Annalisa, looking like a vision of fall in tall brown boots pulled up over her jeans, a sweater the color of golden oak leaves, and that long thick hair of hers pulled high into a bun. When had she gotten so grown-up and gorgeous? He'd been aware for some time now that she was a beautiful woman, but it had still sneaked up on him somehow. One day she was a skinny gawky kid, all arms and legs with eyes too big for her face, following him around. And the next day she was…this.

"Hey," he said. "What are you doing here?"

Stupid question, but she answered without saying so. "Getting my groceries for the week. That cold front's supposed to hit on Monday, and I want to be ready for it."

"Same," Javi replied. "Looks like fall's settled in for real."

"It's about time," said Annalisa. "October's almost over."

"Yep."

Javi tried desperately to think of something to say, something more interesting than what the weather was doing and what time of year it was.

"I see you grew a beard," said Annalisa.

"Yeah, sure did," said Javi.

"It looks good."

"Thanks."

An awkward silence fell. Then Annalisa said, "I heard you accepted Peter's bid on the renovation for your building."

Javi gladly seized the new subject. "Yeah, I did. He and his crew got the partition taken down, and the new windows should be ready to install soon. The plumber and the electrician have both come and gone, so I now have good lighting and running water. And last weekend my dad and I got the Biscayne moved to the garage so I could start working on it. The body's been sent out for fresh paint, and the restomod stuff has been ordered. Things should be in pretty decent shape by the time the Sip-N-Stroll rolls around."

"That's wonderful, Javi. I'm so glad to hear it."

"Thanks. How about you? How's your work on the book coming?"

"Slower than I'd like. I haven't actually started writing yet. I'm still in the research stage. Those letters you found opened up a whole new can of worms. I finished my transcription of them, and now I'm busy cross-referencing them to Romelia's diary and Alejandro's letters to Romelia."

"Have you figured out who wrote it? Was it Alejandro to his cousin?"

"It certainly looks that way. He was definitely an officer candidate in the Mexican army and an educated man

with republican ideals. But Alejandro only ever addresses
him as Loco—which was a wise precaution, because Gabriel would have been in big trouble if the letters were in-
tercepted and had his name on them."

Javi thought about this. "But how could Gabriel get in
trouble for what Alejandro said?"

"Because Alejandro's letters make it clear that Loco
was planning to switch sides in the war. Loco was taking
a risk in keeping the letters at all. But if they were discovered, he could always pretend he'd just found them."

"I guess so. Is that the last of the old documents you
have to go through?"

"Not quite. There's still the German diary that Dirk
Hager lent me. But someone's helping me with that."

"Who?"

"A professor at UT. He's fluent in German, and he
knows a lot about local history."

"Nice," said Javi, picturing an absent-minded, grand-
fatherly man in a worn tweed jacket with scraps of paper
sticking out of his pockets.

He glanced inside her grocery cart.

"What are all those little pumpkins and things for? Are
you planning to make some teeny-tiny pies?"

"Those are for decorations! I'll put them on my dining
table and on my windowsills and things."

"Hmm," he said. "Seems a little late in the season for
you to be getting started on your fall decor. I know how
you are about fall. I'd expect you to break out the sweaters
and start strewing pumpkins around by the end of September at the latest."

She looked embarrassed. "Well…okay, you're right. I
did. I got a whole load of squashes and pumpkins at the
pumpkin patch at La Escarpa during the firefighter fundraiser. But then I saw these in the display outside just now,

and I couldn't resist. I mean, *look* at them. Look at this one. Isn't it perfect? Look at its tiny curling stem. See this one over here? It's called a Cinderella pumpkin. Doesn't it look exactly like Cinderella's pumpkin coach? And this one is called a daisy gourd because of these light parts around the stem that look like petals. Look at this little green-and-white stripey one! And this one that's shaped like a bird, and this flat one with all the bumps. Aren't they beautiful?"

He wasn't paying much attention to the squashes. He was too busy watching Annalisa, the way her eyes shone with excitement, and the way her long slim fingers caressed the small vegetables as if they were diamonds or something.

She met his gaze. For a moment she looked almost shy. Then she said, "What have you got in *your* cart? Dog food and coffee, a case of ramen noodle packages…and a package of rib eyes? I thought the horse trailer didn't have a proper kitchen."

"It doesn't, but I bought me a grill. I set it up outside in that little fenced area. I'm even going to cook some vegetables in foil. Onions, potatoes, bell peppers, mushrooms."

Annalisa chuckled. "You've come a long way since your first pork rub. Remember the celery seeds?"

"Yeah, I remember," he said with a rueful chuckle. He'd been living in Midland then, just starting to learn to cook, and the recipe he was following had called for celery seed. He'd bought a package of fresh celery and then texted Annalisa to ask where on the plant the seeds were located. He could see the leaves, but he couldn't find any seeds.

"I had to go back to the grocery store just to get one little jar of celery seed spice," he recalled. "But that wasn't the only mistake I made, or the biggest one. I used tablespoons instead of teaspoons to measure the seasonings and ended up with three times as much spice mixture as I needed. I couldn't understand why I had so much rub left over—until you told me."

"And then you went back to the store *again*," said Annalisa, "and bought two more packages of pork shoulders, so the seasoning mix wouldn't go to waste."

Javi shook his head. He could have saved the seasoning mix for another time, but he'd been rubbing it all over the raw pork and figured he had to use it up or it would go bad. It hadn't occurred to him to put it in the freezer.

"I thought I was being so smart," said Javi. "I should have run the idea by you first."

Annalisa was laughing now. "You sent me a picture. Three hunks of pork meat, each one weighing a good four pounds, sitting there on your kitchen counter, beautifully coated with spice mixture and ready to cook. I told you to keep at least one of them back and cook it the next day..."

"But I was getting ready to work a long shift on the rig," Javi finished. "I wouldn't be around to cook it, because I had to leave first thing in the morning. And anyway, by that point I wanted the whole thing over and done with. So I had to go back to the store *again* and buy another Dutch oven because the meat wouldn't all fit in the one I had."

"Then you had to sear the meat and bake it for, what, five hours?"

"More like six. It took longer to cook than the recipe said because there was so much of it."

Another silence fell, but this one wasn't awkward. It was warm and comfortable and filled with years of shared history.

"The kitchen was a disaster area by the time I was done," said Javi. "I was up all night with that dang pork."

"So was I."

She said it without a hint of resentment. She even seemed to think it was a happy memory.

"Yeah, I guess you were," said Javi. "You encouraged me every step of the way and kept me entertained while I was waiting around for the meat to finish cooking. I sent you videos of me trying to pull the pork apart, and you kept telling me it wasn't ready and to put it back in the oven, until finally it was done. It didn't really occur to me at the time what a jerk I was being, dragging you into my problems and expecting you to stick with me until they were solved."

Annalisa shrugged. "Well, it wasn't as if I had no choice in the matter. I could have silenced my phone and gone to bed. You didn't make me stay up all night."

"Why did you?"

She considered the question. "I guess I was invested in the whole thing by then. I wanted to see how the pulled pork turned out. And there was something really admirable in the way you were determined to see things through. You could have thrown the meat away and called it a night."

"And waste perfectly good food?" He made a scoffing sound. "The thought never even occurred to me. I'm pretty sure my *abuelas* would have come back to haunt me if I'd done such a terrible thing."

"Well, you didn't. And judging from that last video you sent, the pork turned out fine."

"Better than fine. It was delicious. I took it with me on that long shift and shared it with all the guys."

"Sounds like a typical Mendoza party."

"Yeah, I guess it was. Everyone was eating it, even the higher-ups. It got me noticed by our driller. I never would have gotten promoted so soon if not for that pulled pork."

"I didn't know that," said Annalisa.

"I didn't tell you?"

"No. I didn't hear from you again for…oh, about a month after that."

"Really? Wow."

It seemed impossible that he could have been so thoughtless, but if Annalisa said so, it must be true. She'd seen him through his crisis, like she had so many times before, and as soon as it was over, he'd dropped her.

"You were always there for me."

The words were out before he knew he was going to say them. Her eyes met his, and something in her expression made his heart race, something more than the cool friendliness she'd been showing him ever since he'd come back to town, something he'd startled out of her. Whatever she'd felt for him when they were both teenagers—maybe it had never gone away. Maybe she'd just gotten better at hiding it. Maybe it was still there, waiting.

Or maybe Javi had a giant ego, believing a woman like this, beautiful and smart and tenderhearted, could carry a torch for him all these years.

What would she do if he told her how tired he was of living in a horse trailer with only his dog for company? Would she invite him to her apartment? He could see all her fall decorating, all the pumpkins and squashes and things, and tease her about them some more. Maybe she would take him to her parents' place for Sunday lunch. He could linger over coffee and pastries. See that bird feeder.

He had just opened his mouth to speak when Annalisa said, "I'd better finish my shopping. Good seeing you, Javi."

"Good seeing you, too," he said.

Then she was gone.

CHAPTER TEN

SITTING ACROSS THE polished wood table from Grant, Annalisa tried to muster up something more than friendly respect for him.

Unsure of the proper level of formality for what might turn out to be nothing more than an academic consultation, she'd gone with casual elegance—jeans and ankle boots with a scoop-necked top and a gold-flecked sweater coat that always got her compliments. Grant was looking good himself, in his well-cut sport coat, untucked button-down and admirably fitted jeans.

If only she'd felt even the slightest bit romantic about the man, everything would have been perfect.

Grant smiled. "So what have you been up to for the past three weeks?"

"Oh, the usual," said Annalisa. "Work and research. How about you?"

"The same. I've got my own research going on, my grad students to supervise, classes to teach and midterms coming up. And of course I've been translating the diary."

Annalisa stole a hopeful glance at the pressboard folder on the table beside him. It had about half an inch of pages between its covers. Resting on top of it was what looked like the German diary in its protective packaging.

"You finished the translation?" she asked.

"I did," he said, his smile warming.

Before she could pursue the subject, their server arrived. After a few moments' discussion, Grant ordered a bottle of red wine and an appetizer of roasted brussels sprouts. He had a pleasant way with the server, dignified and courteous.

"How's the research coming?" he asked when the server had gone. "What have you learned? Any surprises?"

"Actually, yes. You remember those letters I mentioned at Come and Take It? They indicate that a cadet in the Mexican army might have been planning to defect to the Texian side."

"Interesting. What's the provenance of the letters?"

"They were found at the bottom of an old cartridge pouch from the Mexican army, hidden under the block."

Grant set his wineglass down. "Really? Are you convinced they're authentic?"

"Yes. I've had them examined by an expert. Paper, ink and cultural phrasing are all in line with the time period. I even have corroborating evidence from another document. Romelia Ramirez's diary suggests that the cadet was Alejandro's cousin."

"What an amazing find! How did you say you'd come across them?"

"A friend gave them to me."

Why was her face heating up? She hadn't even said Javi's name. It wasn't fair for Javi to have this kind of power over her. He didn't belong here, on her date with Grant, who was handsome and well-dressed and polite and intelligent and had loads in common with her.

She took a swallow of wine and tried to recover some poise. "I'm pretty sure Alejandro wrote the letters," she said. "He didn't sign his name, but I recognized the flourish and the handwriting. He was trying to persuade the letters' recipient to switch sides in the war."

"I wonder if he had any luck."

"So do I. I'd like to find out, but I don't want to spend too much time on what could turn out to be a dead end."

Grant nodded. "Research is tricky that way. You come across a tantalizing side trail, but you don't know whether it'll turn out to be a startling new discovery or a huge time suck."

"Exactly." She glanced at the folder on the table. "How about you? Any startling new discoveries in the diary?"

He pushed the folder toward her. "I hate to disappoint you, but no. This diarist, whoever he was, was an obsessive record keeper. He kept track of every purchase he made and how much he paid for it, every fence post he set and every nail he drove, as well as which cows had what calves, how much milk they all gave, how much money his steers brought in at auction and what his housekeeper cooked for supper. He also recorded the weather every day, along with the phases of the moon."

By now Annalisa had the folder open and was skimming through the pages with their dry, factual content. "Isn't there *anything* about the revolution? Or other people?"

"Well, he talks about his housekeeper and her activities quite a bit. Laundry day, poultry husbandry, that sort of thing. The revolution gets a mention now and then. The area seemed to have received pretty frequent reports on nearby military action and movements of the Mexican army. But on the eighth of December, he spends a paragraph lamenting a pair of trousers and an old patched shirt that got lost in the wash, and one sentence on the Siege of Béxar."

She flipped through the pages of the translation and read the entry. "Wow. Some priorities."

Grant shrugged. "He wasn't necessarily indifferent to the war. This was his diary, for his own private use. If he wanted to keep records of how many eggs his chickens laid, that was his business. Maybe he just didn't feel the need to make political commentary in his own diary. He already knew what he believed. He didn't have to convince himself."

"Fair point," said Annalisa, still leafing through the pages. "Who's this Mrs. Guthrie that he keeps talking about?"

"That's the housekeeper. I made an index at the end of all the people he mentions, with notes about them and a list of all the dates and page numbers where they appear."

She turned to the end and scanned the alphabetized list. Baird, Owen, was the diarist's hired man. Casillas, Ruben, was a neighbor, and De Groot, Lars, was a storekeeper. There was the housekeeper—Guthrie, Agatha. All the way down to…

She leaned in to take a closer look. "Who is this *Zerebra*?"

Grant craned his head and glanced at the page. "Yeah, I'm not sure. That's why there's a question mark by it. I don't know if it's supposed to be a first or last name. I didn't get any hits when I googled it. But you know what spelling was like in the early nineteenth century. Maybe it's a misspelling of another name, like Zareba."

"It's a transliteration," said Annalisa. "Of *Cerebro*. Which might mean…"

Her gaze traveled back up to the middle of the page, where the *L*s were.

"There it is," she said in triumph. *"Loka."* Like Zerebra, it was followed by a question mark.

"I take it these names mean something to you," Grant said.

"They're nicknames for Alejandro and his cousin. Alejandro was Cerebro, and his cousin was Loco."

"Crazy and the Brain," said Grant. "They sound like cartoon characters."

Annalisa scanned the list again. "Does the diary mention anyone called Guero? I don't know how a German speaker would try to spell that."

"Guero, as in white guy? No, there's nothing like that. Why? Who's Guero?"

"I don't know. But the letter in the cartridge box was addressed to Loco and signed Cerebro. And Romelia's diary mentions both Loco and Guero."

"And the German diarist is aware of the other two nicknames, so maybe…" Grant's eyes narrowed. "Do you think the German diarist might be Guero?"

"I'm starting to," said Annalisa. "What does he say about the other two?"

"He only mentioned them once." He took the folder and flipped through the pages. "Here. The passage translates, 'Cerebro says that Loco is crossing the Guadalupe with his saddlebags full.'"

"Crossing the Guadalupe…" Annalisa snapped to attention. "That's it. Remember the Battle of Gonzales? Mexican troops and Texian defenders on opposite sides of the Guadalupe River? They saw each other there, Alejandro and Gabriel. Romelia's diary says so. Gabriel was there when the Texian commander urged the Mexican commander to switch sides. Castañeda said no, but Gabriel wanted to join the revolution. And he wasn't planning to come empty-handed. Remember the Grass Fight? How the Texians attacked the foraging party because they thought the mules were carrying silver in their saddlebags? Well, what if someone really was bringing Mexican silver to Texas, and it was Gabriel?"

EVERY WEEKDAY MORNING at 7:45, Claudia, Annalisa and Mari, along with Calvin, Claudia's associate, gathered in the front room, filled their mugs with freshly brewed cof-

fee and went over the day's schedule. Mari kept the calendar ruthlessly organized, so they all knew what they
were supposed to be doing and when they were supposed
to be doing it, but there were always last-minute briefings
and alterations to be made. If there was time afterward,
they'd chat about other things. Then when the hands on
the big clock pointed to one minute to eight, they all went
off to their desks.

It was a pleasant time of day. Annalisa always looked
forward to it, and never more so than on the Monday morning following her date with Grant.

The business portion of the meeting went by even more
briskly than usual. Then Mari and Claudia looked expectantly at Annalisa.

"All right," said Mari. "Spill."

"Okay," said Annalisa. "So I met with Grant Saturday night."

They nodded.

"And he got the diary translated," she went on. "He
printed an annotated copy for me, along with a transcription of the German text, complete with an index that keeps
track of all the cross-references. It was remarkably well
organized, really beautiful work. He even made a cover
page to slide into the sleeve in the front of the binder."

Mari's smile faltered a little, but Claudia said, "Okay.
So he's a conscientious man who pays attention to detail.
Sounds promising! Go on."

"Well, remember the documents Javi found in the cartridge pouch? How the letter was addressed to Loco and
signed Cerebro? And how Romelia's diary explains that
these were nicknames for Alejandro and his cousin Gabriel? Grant made an index of people mentioned in the
diary, and you'll never guess who was there."

"Where?" asked Mari, visibly confused.

"In the index! Two mysterious individuals known as Cerebro and Loco—only the German diarist spelled the names differently, because he was writing in German. Gabriel wasn't just planning to join the Texian army—he was bringing treasure for the Texian war chest."

They all looked blankly at her.

"Don't you see?" said Annalisa. "They're all connected—the German diary, Romelia's diary, Alejandro's letters and the cartridge box letters. And I'm almost positive that the German diarist will turn out to be the Guero that Alejandro mentions in his letter. Isn't that exciting?"

Claudia frowned thoughtfully. "You got the German diary from Dirk Hager, right?"

"Yes. He found it while clearing out some stuff from his grandparents' house."

"Hmm, yes," said Claudia. "You know, Dirk's grandmother was a Friesenhahn."

"What?" said Annalisa. "No, I did not know that. And the cartridge box was found on Friesenhahn land! I wonder if Dirk has any photos of his grandmother's ancestors, or records of when they settled here. We might be able to put a name to this guy!"

"But what about Grant?" Mari almost wailed. "Do you like him? Did you have a good time?"

"Oh! Yes. I had a lovely time. Grant is a lovely man."

Calvin chuckled. "Poor Grant," he said, and went to his office.

"Never mind him," said Mari. "Are you going to see Grant again?"

"Yes. He's coming to Limestone Springs this time."

"Ooh, good! Maybe I can get a look at him. When's he coming?"

"We haven't set a time yet. I have to coordinate with Javi."

"With Javi?" Claudia repeated. "Whatever for?"

"Well, he's the one who found the cartridge box letters. It's only right to bring him up to speed."

Mari and Claudia exchanged a glance and laughed.

"That'll be some get-together," said Mari. "Your old flame and your new love."

"It isn't like that! Grant isn't my new love. I barely know him."

"But you are attracted to him?" asked Mari.

Annalisa opened her mouth, but nothing came out.

"He's an attractive man with a lot of great qualities," she said at last.

But it wasn't enough. She knew that, and she could tell from their faces that Mari and Claudia knew it, too.

She'd never had to remind herself of *Javi's* good qualities or wonder whether she was attracted to him. She just knew. She couldn't *not* know. Her feelings for him were there all the time, whether or not she wanted them to be. Even now.

"Keep us posted," said Claudia, but she didn't sound very hopeful.

CHAPTER ELEVEN

JAVI SHOWED UP at Lalo's Kitchen a few minutes shy of ten o'clock Saturday morning, ahead of the time he and Annalisa had set for their meeting. He felt all fizzy inside, like a can of soda that had been shaken up. He'd been walking on air ever since receiving her text. He'd read it so many times he had it memorized.

The German professor finished translating the German diary. It turned up some very interesting stuff. Let's get together in person and go over it all.

Javi had dressed with more care than usual. He'd even gotten a haircut, and gone to his parents' house to iron a shirt. He hadn't been this nervous about meeting a woman in a long time.

Not that this was *that* kind of meeting, of course. But it was enough to be seeing her, and to know that she was the one who'd sought him out this time. There hadn't been any weirdness in her text. She'd seemed truly eager about this meeting. Things were back the way they should be.

Lalo's Kitchen was fairly empty at this time of the morning. Javi didn't see Annalisa, just some guy he didn't know wearing one of those fancy pullover sweaters with a neck collar and a button, sitting alone at a four-top table with a mug of coffee.

Javi went to the counter just as Luke stepped out of the kitchen.

"Javi! Hey! Good to see you, man."

"Hey, Luke. Good to see you, too."

Javi and Luke had worked together in West Texas a couple of years back. Luke had called Javi out of the blue one day and asked for Javi's help getting an oil field job—a request brought about partly by frustration with his job at Lalo's and partly by the fact that Eliana had just broken up with him. Javi had made some calls, and Luke had gotten the job. He'd spent several months in Midland before going back home and getting his old job back, along with more responsibility and better pay. He'd gotten Eliana back, as well.

"How's Lefty?" Luke asked.

"Surly and unsociable as ever. How's Porter? Is he here?"

Luke looked around. "He ought to be. I think he's just around the bar somewhere."

The lanky black-and-white dog had heard his name. He came out now from behind the corner of the bar to greet Javi like an old friend. Javi rubbed him behind the ears.

"I've hardly seen you since you got back into town," said Luke. "Hard at work at the garage?"

"You know it. There's so much to do, opening a business. So much paperwork, in addition to all the other kinds of work."

Luke lifted an eyebrow. "Enough to make you miss the oil fields?"

"Ha! Not hardly."

"I didn't think so. When will you be open to the public?"

"Soon, I hope. I'm planning a soft opening at the Sip-N-Stroll in December. Maybe that'll bring in some business."

"Sweet! I'll try to stop by. So what can I get for you?"

"Just coffee."

"Coming right up."

Luke grabbed a mug and went to fill it. While Javi was waiting, the guy in the fancy sweater joined him at the counter.

"You must be Javi," the guy said.

Javi was too surprised to say anything back. The guy put out a hand. "I'm Grant Carstensen," he said.

"Okay," said Javi, shaking hands automatically. Grant had said his name as if Javi ought to recognize it, but Javi had never heard of anyone called Grant Carstensen.

Just then, Annalisa walked through the door. "Oh, good," she said as she came to the counter. "You two have already met."

"Just barely," said Grant. "I knew he must be Javi when he walked in." To Javi he said, "Annalisa has told me a lot about you."

That's funny, because I haven't heard a thing about you. The words were right there on the tip of Javi's tongue, but he bit them back at the last second.

"Okay," he said again.

His confusion must have shown on his face, because Annalisa said, "You remember, Javi. I told you I'd been working with a German professor who agreed to translate the German diary for me. Well, here he is."

"Here I am," said Grant with a smile.

This was the professor? Javi had been imagining a much older man, sort of rumpled-looking and absent-minded. He felt annoyed, as if Annalisa had been dishonest with him somehow.

"Right, I remember," he managed to say. "I just didn't realize he'd be joining us today."

Annalisa frowned. "Didn't I tell you? I'm sure I did. I told you that Grant had uncovered some interesting things in the translation and that we should get together and talk about them."

Yes, she had said that, more or less. But Javi had thought she'd meant a different sort of *we*.

"My mistake," he said.

Luke brought Javi his coffee. Annalisa ordered one for herself.

As they walked to the table, Javi told himself that this Grant guy was just someone Annalisa had been working with, not like a—well, a boyfriend or anything. But he didn't like sharing her time and attention, or seeing that sweet smile of hers directed at a guy who wasn't him.

"So, have you found out anything about the cartridge box?" Javi asked.

"Not yet," said Annalisa. "I haven't had a chance to show it to Alex. He's the real expert on old firearms and ammunition. But I showed Grant the pictures I took of it, and he has thoughts."

Oh, I'll bet he does, Javi thought.

"It's certainly an interesting piece," said Grant. "It might very well be something a soldier in the Mexican army would have carried at the time of the revolution. During the Spanish colonial period, the Spanish army had a remarkably modern cartridge box, made of tin and covered with leather. It's possible that some Mexican soldiers were still carrying this type by the 1830s. Others might have had British-made cartridge boxes for their Brown Bess muskets, or locally made pouches or boxes with open compartments or wooden blocks."

"In other words, you don't know," Javi said.

Annalisa shot him a look. It wasn't an angry look, just surprised, and maybe a little disappointed. For a moment, Javi felt vaguely ashamed of himself. But it bothered him when people showed off that way, talking just to hear themselves talk. He didn't like it. And he didn't like Grant, not one bit.

Grant didn't get flustered or take offense. He gave a self-deprecating chuckle and said, "No, you're right, I don't know a thing about it. I'm just repeating what I read on the internet. I can't help it. That cartridge box is an exciting find."

Perfect. Now Grant came out looking like a great guy, and Javi just looked like a jerk. Score a point for Grant.

"It really is," Annalisa said. "No matter the provenance, it's clearly old. And those letters!"

"Yeah, what about those?" Javi asked.

"Well, it turns out they're connected to the German diary. Dirk Hager lent it to me. He didn't know who the diarist was at first, but Claudia mentioned that his grandmother was a Friesenhahn. I talked to Dirk, and he did some digging and found an ancestor on his grandmother's side, an Otto Friesenhahn, who once owned land in what's now downtown Limestone Springs. He even found a picture of the guy. Look."

She held out her phone. Javi peered at a digital image of an old photograph of a serious-faced young man with a rifle on his knees and white-blond hair.

"That's a *guero* if I ever saw one," said Javi.

"That's exactly what I said!" Annalisa replied.

"Which means," put in Grant, "that the property described in painstaking detail in the German diary is very likely the Friesenhahn property—which now belongs to your family, Javi."

Yeah, I figured that out, thanks, Javi thought but did not say.

"And besides his detailed property plans," Annalisa went on, "the German diarist—we might as well call him Otto—mentioned Cerebro and Loco. He knew about the plot for Loco to switch sides and bring some Royalist silver with him."

"Whoa!" said Javi. "Okay. So where's the silver?"

Annalisa and Grant exchanged glances. "That's what we can't figure out. The fact that no one's ever heard of a defecting Mexican cadet bringing a load of Mexican silver and giving it to the Texians might mean that it never happened. Something must have gone wrong. Maybe Gabriel changed his mind, or got caught, or died in battle before he could follow through."

"Or maybe," said Javi, "he did follow through, and Alejandro killed him and kept the silver for himself."

Annalisa sat back, her face stunned. "Why would you think that?"

Javi shrugged. "It would be a good opportunity. It's not like a lot of people knew the silver was coming. How much silver are we talking about here, anyway?"

"We haven't found any references to the specific amount," said Annalisa.

"No," Grant agreed. "But it wouldn't take a lot. Even a couple of saddlebags' worth of silver would have made a big difference in the war effort."

"And pose a big temptation to Alejandro," Javi added.

Annalisa shook her head. "That doesn't make sense. Alejandro was land rich but cash poor. If he'd had a sudden influx of cash, there'd be evidence of it."

"But he was killed in battle not long after, right?" Javi countered. "So maybe he just didn't have a chance. Maybe Romelia didn't know where he'd hidden it."

Grant and Annalisa looked at each other again.

"I mean, it's not out of the question," said Grant. "Alejandro could have stowed the silver somewhere and never gone back for it. So could Gabriel. So could Otto, for that matter."

"Maybe," said Annalisa, sounding unconvinced. "But in any event, what we ought to do now is go out to the Friesenhahn property, all three of us, and see if we can match the current layout to Otto's maps of his house and outbuildings. The fact that the cartridge box was found there is certainly suggestive."

"You mean the silver could be there, on The Property?" Javi asked. For some reason this hadn't occurred to him until now.

"It's possible," said Grant. "If it came over at all, it has to be somewhere."

"What would happen if it were found? Would the finder have to hand it over to a museum or the state or something?"

Annalisa shook her head. "Treasure trove is generally treated as lost property. Unless the true owner comes forth and makes a claim, lost property belongs to whoever finds it."

Javi downed the last of his coffee. "Well, then, what are we waiting for? Let's go treasure hunting."

THE PROPERTY LOOKED shabbier than usual, with Grant standing there in his fancy sweater and expensive-looking shoes, alternately scanning the place and glancing down at the map in his hands. It was a one-acre lot, all that was left now of the Friesenhahn ranch. Javi's horse trailer residence was hidden inside the big metal barn, which stood kitty-corner to the old bare slab of the house that had never been built. Weeds and brush, dry and leafless now, had grown up around the edges of the concrete. The whole thing was roughly fenced with a combination of T-posts and cedar posts, field fencing and barbed wire, with pieces of corrugated metal filling in gaps here and there.

The lot lay along Highway 281, with one-to ten-acre

lots to the south of them, and ranches and farms to the west, and downtown Limestone Springs to the northeast.

Grant had parked his Mercedes just inside the gate, next to Javi's truck. Annalisa's car wasn't there, because she had ridden with Grant. The Mercedes looked as out of place here as Grant himself.

Grant looked back and forth several times between the land and the map in his hand.

"So you said the old junk heap was over there, right?" he said, pointing to a stretch near the metal barn.

"That's right," said Javi. "My dad spread it over a big area for us to root through. He really had to dig to reach the bottom layer."

"Okay," said Grant, still glancing back and forth. "And the ramshackle building your father knocked down was... where, again?"

"Roughly where the metal barn is now."

Grant was silent for a while. Finally Annalisa said, "Are you having trouble getting your bearings?"

"Yeah," said Grant. "The problem is that there's nothing to give a frame of reference. The ramshackle building wasn't around during Otto Friesenhahn's time. And we don't know the locations of his house or barn, or even his smokehouse."

"There were definitely some signs of old construction when my parents first bought the place," said Javi. "Old sandstone stoops and things, I remember. But I don't know what was where."

"If only we had even one fixed point," said Grant. "Then we could extrapolate the rest. Do you happen to know where the old water well used to be before it was filled in?"

Javi pointed. "It's right there. And it never was filled

in. It has a concrete cover over the top, though. It's been dry since I don't know when."

Grant stared. "Where?"

"Right there, where those trees are grown up."

"Ohh, okay," said Grant. "So then that would mean…"

He walked slowly in the direction of the well, stepping carefully among all the thorny growth. "Yes," he said at last. "This is the site of Otto Friesenhahn's barn, right where the old junk pile used to be."

"I wonder what happened to his barn," said Annalisa. "It sounded really nice, with his fancy multicompartment feed bins lined with tin."

Javi looked at her. "The cartridge box was encased in tin," he said. "I don't mean the shell under the leather, I mean it had a whole outer layer of scrunched-up tin surrounding it. I had to cut through it with snips."

Annalisa's gaze snapped to his. "You didn't tell me that."

"Well, it was. And it was wrapped in some sort of fabric."

"Wool fabric?"

"Maybe. I don't know. It had mostly rotted away."

"What if it was a Mexican infantry uniform?" Annalisa asked. "What if Gabriel made it as far as Otto's place, and took off his uniform, and hid it and his cartridge box at the bottom of Otto's feed bin? It would be a good hiding place."

Her face lit up. "The cartridge box smelled like grain! The leather would have absorbed the odor of the grain in the feed bin. So would the uniform."

"But we're talking about almost two hundred years ago," Javi objected. "Doesn't that seem like a long time for some scraps of old leather to hold on to an odor?"

"Not necessarily. Not if the whole thing was encased in scrunched-up tin for however many decades. Tin resists corrosion. It would have offered some degree of protection from moisture. Then once it was unearthed, it was stored in a crate inside the metal barn, with enough airflow to keep it from getting moldy. It helps explain why the cartridge box was in as good of shape as it was. And the letters were tucked away between the wooden block and the tin tray and wrapped in paper treated with linseed oil."

"But why was the tin so scrunched up?" asked Grant.

"Because something happened to the feed bin. The roof collapsed, or a storm knocked down the barn, or something. And then the wreckage just sat there and slowly turned into a trash heap."

"Well, that would mean that no one ever knew the uniform was in there," said Javi. "Or at least that Gabriel never came back for it."

"That makes sense," said Grant. "Even if Otto never knew that Gabriel had reached his property, he would have known what to make of a Mexican infantry uniform wrapped around a Mexican cartridge box in the bottom of his feed bin, if he'd found it, because he knew Gabriel was planning on coming. But if the barn was destroyed before Otto could use up the grain and find what was hidden there, he might never have found out."

The three of them stood in silence a moment. Then Javi said, "But even if we're right, all that means is that Gabriel changed clothes at Otto's place. It doesn't tell us what happened to the silver, or whether Gabriel even had the silver at that point."

"What about the old well?" asked Grant. "Isn't that the obvious place to look?"

Javi shook his head. "I've been down that well before, and most of my brothers, too. If there was a bunch of silver hidden away in there, trust me, we'd have found it."

"But you weren't looking for it then," said Grant.

Javi made a scoffing sound. "I think I'd know it if I saw it, whether I was looking for it or not."

Grant didn't say anything, but Javi could tell he wasn't convinced.

"Maybe you'd like to check it out for yourself," said Javi. "You're welcome to go down there. See if there's anything I missed."

"Down the well?" Grant looked alarmed. "I don't think—I mean, you said it's covered by concrete, right?"

"A concrete slab. We could take it off."

Grant rubbed his chin and didn't say anything.

"There's nothing to worry about," Javi said. "Nothing down there but old leaves and dirt. Maybe a rattlesnake or two, but they'll probably slither up the sides of the well to get away from you."

Annalisa shuddered. "Nobody's going down the well," she said. "You said it yourself, Javi. If the silver had been down there, you'd have seen it."

"Probably," said Javi. "But like Grant said, I didn't know to look for it back then. We're here now. We might as well find out for sure. I'll go down myself and have a fresh look."

He headed over to the well. Annalisa followed him, protesting. Javi knew he was being a show-off, but he didn't care. He couldn't help it. Grant rubbed him the wrong way.

Javi threaded his way through the ring of young hackberries growing around the well casing. The cover made a hollow rasping sound as he heaved it off.

The well wasn't very deep, only twenty feet or so. It smelled of earth and stone.

"Do you have any rope?" Annalisa asked.

"Don't need any," said Javi. "Look how rough the surface is on the inside with all those rocks. I'll just brace my feet across the diameter of it and work my way down."

He did have second thoughts when he first started to lower himself down the casing. There really might be rattlesnakes down there, and rats, and probably some scorpions. Maybe a rabid skunk, or an armadillo with leprosy.

But he pushed the thought away, swung his legs into the well and got started.

Unlike Grant, he had on stout footwear—his all-occasion, ready-for-anything, black lace-up high-top work boots, equally good for hiking through underbrush and wearing to church on Sunday. The grippy soles found footholds among the rough stonework. He eased his way down, one step at a time.

"Be careful," Annalisa called.

"I will," said Javi.

Little by little, he descended into the earth. By the time he reached the bottom, the sunshine had faded into a grayish twilight.

He didn't see any snakes, or rats, or varmints of any sort. The well floor was covered with a shallow layer of dead leaves. They rustled when he drew his foot over them.

"There's nothing down here," he called, his voice bouncing off the limestone tunnel in hollow echoes. "No silver, no skeletal remains. Nothing but bedrock."

"Are you sure?" Grant called back. "Maybe someone hid the silver at the bottom and laid some cement over it."

Javi looked at the pale yellow layer of limestone with its fossils of shells and fish. "I've done a lot of dirt work over the years," he said. "I know what bedrock is."

He'd said the silver wouldn't be there, and he'd been right. Still, he couldn't help feeling let down. He wouldn't have minded being wrong if it had meant coming into a lot of money.

And that wasn't the only thing he felt let down about. He'd expected a lot out of this meeting, and now it was as if he was being pushed out of his own project. This was supposed to be his mystery to solve with Annalisa, and now here was this Grant guy taking over.

Annalisa has grown up. She's not that little girl who used to blindly worship you anymore. She's an accomplished woman with things to do and people to see. It was bound to happen eventually.

That was what Tito had said when Javi first arrived back in town, and what Javi couldn't get out of his head now. And it was true. Tito was right—Annalisa had grown up. More than that, she'd outgrown Javi.

"THE WHOLE THING was so awkward, Eliana. Javi had only just met Grant, but he clearly had it in for him. I could see it, and I know Grant could, too, because Javi was not being subtle."

Annalisa stared into the caffeinated depths of her coffee mug. Eliana sat beside her at the Mahan kitchen table, sipping some of Lauren's healthy pregnancy herbal tea.

"I believe it," said Eliana. "How did Grant react?"

"Oh, Grant was fine. He didn't take the bait. Which was commendable, because Javi was being kind of a jerk."

"Maybe Javi was always a jerk and you never noticed it before because you were so hung up on him and didn't have a guy like Grant to compare him to."

Annalisa shook her head. "I don't believe that."

"Of course you don't believe it. That's because you always see the best in people."

Annalisa lifted her head and looked her friend in the eye. "No. It's because it's true. I know Javi's touchy and prickly, but he's always ready to help anyone in need. Whenever someone's tire blows out or their car dies on the side of the road, he's the first one his friends call, and the first to pull over for a stranger."

"I hate to break this to you, but it's possible he just likes working on cars."

"No. It isn't only that. He's a good son and brother, a good friend, a good man. He's just got some baggage."

Eliana threw her hands into the air. "Well, so does everyone! That doesn't give people a license to be rude."

"You're right. But the way Javi was acting toward Grant…" She took a deep breath. "It's almost like he was jealous."

Silence. Then Eliana said, "Jealous as in envious, or jealous as in jealous?"

"Jealous as in jealous. Like it bothered him that I was with Grant." She gave Eliana a tiny smile. "Not going to lie. It was kind of fun."

She took a swallow of coffee. "I know what you're thinking. Maybe it isn't so much that Javi wants me for myself. Maybe he just doesn't like seeing me with another guy. I wondered that myself. But then I remembered all these things Javi has said and done since he got back in town. Each one is so tiny in itself, but when you put them together, they might just add up to something more. And they started before Grant was in the picture."

"But—"

Annalisa held up a hand. "I know! I made a decision to get over Javi and move on. I'm not abandoning my resolve just because Javi has dropped a few hints. If he does want me now, then it's on him to show me. I'm done waiting around."

"Good for you!" said Eliana. "So what about Grant? Are you going to see him again?"

"Yes, but not like that. I told him it's best if he and I are just friends."

She expected Eliana to protest, but Eliana simply said, "Are you sure?"

"I'm sure. I know I said I wanted to go out with other guys, but it isn't fair to use Grant as a sort of experiment to see if I can make myself be attracted to someone other than Javi."

"No, it isn't," Eliana agreed. "What did Grant say?"

"That he wasn't surprised. He thought Javi was an ex-boyfriend that I'd never gotten over. I told him the only romantic feelings in that relationship were coming from my end—at least, as far as I know."

Eliana swirled her tea in her mug. "Be careful, Annalisa. I don't want to see you get hurt. You've gotten your hopes up with Javi before."

"I know. I'm being careful. I'm keeping my expectations low."

It wasn't easy.

CHAPTER TWELVE

GRANT STARED UP at the three-foot orange sphere, topped with a green stem and mounted high on the front gable of the city planning building. "What is *that* supposed to be? A prize pumpkin? A giant heirloom tomato?"

Annalisa chuckled. "It's a ripe persimmon. Official town fruit of Limestone Springs."

"Huh! I would not have guessed that. Come to think of it, I don't know that I've ever seen a persimmon, much less tasted one."

"Oh, they're good. And they grow really well around here. A lot of people raise them commercially or just have them growing in their yards. And every summer we hold a festival to celebrate them. Carnival, parade, craft and food booths... You know the drill. It's a typical small Southern town food-based festival, and I love it."

"Do you elect a Persimmon Queen and a Persimmon Court?"

"Yes, and a Little Miss Persimmon. Oh, and Bill Darcy dresses up in a persimmon suit and goes around shaking hands and doing his persimmon dance and posing for pictures with people."

"Doesn't this Bill Darcy get hot, dressing up as a persimmon in the middle of summer?"

"Probably, but there's a frame inside supporting the suit to allow for a little airflow. He's not all filled up with stuffing. Anyway, Bill Darcy is always game to put on a

costume for a good cause, and he's committed to his craft.
At the fall festival and the firefighter fundraiser he's Scare-
crow Bill, and tonight he'll be in his Santa suit. Most of
the time he's a pretty low-key guy, but the second he steps
into his costume he turns into a total ham."

The evening's weather was perfect for the annual Sip-
N-Stroll—cold enough to feel Christmassy, but not cold
enough to keep people at home. The forecast had called for
rain and sleet, but they'd held off so far, leaving just enough
of a nip in the air to justify wearing sweaters and make
people glad to duck inside all the participating businesses
for a few minutes and sample the different hot chocolates
keeping warm in slow cookers and urns. Each business's
recipe was unique. Annalisa and Grant had been carrying
their mugs from one place to the next. At the end of the
evening, they would cast their votes for best hot chocolate in a papier-mâché ballot box shaped like a giant mug.

"I see a Darcy's Hardware across the street," Grant said.
"Is the hardware Darcy any relation to the guy that dresses
up as a persimmon?"

"One and the same. Let's go over and see him. Darcy's
Hardware always does a good hot chocolate, very rich and
creamy. And you can see Bill in his Santa getup."

They crossed the street. As they stepped onto the curb
together, she caught sight of their reflections in the big
front window of the hardware store. She had on jeans and
a sweater with a darling knit cap and her favorite knee-
high boots, and Grant was looking especially handsome in
twill chinos and a collarless flannel shirt with a pea jacket
and cashmere scarf. They looked good together. But she
didn't regret her decision to keep their relationship pla-
tonic. They'd met up several times for lunch in Austin on
days when she'd visited the university's reading room for

book research, and she enjoyed his company, but no more than she enjoyed being with Luke or Tito.

The center aisle of the hardware store now held a Santa throne in the form of a tooled leather chair surrounded by heaps of brightly colored presents, along with some tumbleweeds spray-painted green and hung with glimmer lights.

In addition to the usual red plush coat, Bill's version of Santa Claus wore a red cowboy hat trimmed with white fur. His neatly pressed dark-washed Wrangler jeans had a crease down the front as sharp as a knife's edge, and silver spurs jingled on his black cowboy boots. A lariat was strapped to his belt, which was cinched in place with an enormous prize buckle from some long-past rodeo. His chest-length beard had more red than white in it, and his ice-blue eyes didn't exactly twinkle, but the children crowding around him didn't seem to mind.

"Ho, ho, ho!" he bellowed as Annalisa and Grant came inside. "Merry Christmas!"

"Wow," said Grant in an undertone. "He's certainly robust."

"He does bring something new to the role," Annalisa replied. "Oh, look, Lauren and Alex brought the kids, and Tony and Dalia are here with Ignacio. We came just in time to see them sit on Santa's lap."

Little blonde, curly-haired Peri climbed right onto the cowboy Santa's knees, gently stroked his beard and smiled prettily for the camera. Emilio, in Santa's other arm, didn't seem to notice one way or the other. But when their three-year-old cousin, Ignacio, had his turn, he took one round-eyed look at the man in the strange red coat, let out a blood-curdling scream and ran away to hide behind Tony.

Tony chuckled as he bent down and picked up his son. Ignacio wrapped his arms and legs around his father like a koala clinging to a eucalyptus tree. Dalia and Tony smiled at each other over Ignacio's shock of thick black hair.

"It's okay, buddy," Tony said. "You don't have to if you don't want to. Let's go have some hot chocolate, huh? Would you like that?"

Ignacio drew a deep shuddery breath and asked, "And cookies?"

"You bet," said Dalia. "Cookies, too."

Annalisa and Grant followed Tony and Dalia to the hot chocolate table, where Bill's daughter-in-law filled all their mugs with the rich brew and topped them with dollops of whipped cream and chocolate shavings. She put Ignacio's in his sippy cup and handed him a sugar cookie with green sprinkles. Alex and Lauren were already at the hot chocolate table with Peri and Emilio.

Dalia's third-trimester shape was on full display in a waffle-weave sweater. She'd been barely showing when Annalisa had seen her the night of the bonfire at La Escarpa.

"Well, hey, there, Grant," said Alex. "Didn't expect to see you here tonight. It's a pretty long drive from Austin to Limestone Springs."

"Yes, but I can't be in the city all the time," Grant replied.

"Amen to that. You know Lauren and the kids. This is my brother, Tony, and his wife, Dalia, and that's Ignacio stuffing his face with cookies."

Tony shook hands with Grant. "Enjoying the Sip-N-Stroll?" he asked.

"Loving it," said Grant.

"Where all have you been so far?" asked Dalia.

"We started at Claudia's law office, worked our way down and then crossed the street to the hardware store."

"Be sure to hit up Bart's Gym," said Tony. "His decorations are on point. He even hung mistletoe on the pull-up bars. He's a shoo-in to win 'best keto hot chocolate made with almond milk and monk fruit.'"

"And don't forget the fabric store," Dalia added. "My mom went all out on their Christmas display for the front window."

While they were chatting and drinking their hot chocolate, Luke came in. He quickly scanned the store, looking troubled. When he saw Tony, he quietly called him over.

Annalisa couldn't hear what Luke said, but whatever it was, it didn't seem to be good news. Tony's megawatt smile faded away. He clapped Luke on the shoulder and said, "Thanks for letting me know."

After Luke left, Tony drew Alex aside. Annalisa didn't mean to listen, but she couldn't help overhearing.

"Dad's here," Tony said.

Alex looked as if he'd just been hit in the solar plexus. "Did you see him?" he asked quietly.

"No. Luke and Eliana saw him outside Hager's Flower Shop. Luke just told me."

"Was he drinking?"

"I don't know. Luke didn't say."

"Well, that's something, anyway," said Alex. "If he'd already been at the messy drunk stage, Luke probably would have said so. Maybe he won't be too hard to manage."

Annalisa kept her eyes averted. She couldn't imagine what it would be like to have a parent bring so much grief. She thought of her own cheerful, mild-mannered, hard-working parents, whom she and Grant had seen only a few minutes earlier.

"Hager's Flower Shop isn't too far from the Mendozas' garage," said Tony. "You don't think he'd have the nerve to show his face there, do you?"

"Yes," said Alex in a hard voice. "I do think that. I think

there's nothing he wouldn't have the nerve to do. We'd better go get him and ride herd on him for a while."

"No, you stay here," said Tony. "You know he listens to me more than he listens to you. I'll do better if I go alone."

Alex sighed. "Yeah, okay. Godspeed, brother."

Annalisa's eyes stung with tears of pity. It was awful to see cheerful, friendly Tony so sad, and solid, dependable Alex so beaten down. And the idea of Carlos visiting the very business he'd once gutted was too horrible to imagine. Surely he wouldn't. Surely he had some vestige of decency and shame. But his sons didn't think so, and they knew him better than she did.

In the weeks since she and Grant had gone to The Property with Javi, she'd run into Javi several times in town—at church, Tito's Bar and H-E-B. He'd had ample opportunity to make a move if he was so inclined, but he'd merely greeted her and then hurried away. She'd done her best not to get her hopes up, but it still hurt.

She'd heard through the grapevine that Mendoza Classic Cars was far enough along businesswise to open its doors to the public at this year's Sip-N-Stroll, just as he'd planned. He and his dad must be so excited. If Carlos showed up—well, he wouldn't exactly be spreading Christmas cheer.

After leaving the hardware store, Annalisa and Grant visited the feed store, which was serving peppermint hot chocolate with candy cane stir sticks. Some portable fencing had been set up in the parking lot, where Susana Vrba and Roque Fidalgo were giving pony rides and handing out flyers for Susana's equine center.

Saddle shop, newspaper office, lumberyard, antique store, real estate office, fire station, pharmacy—they all looked warm and welcoming, with bright lights and ornaments framing their doorways and Christmas displays nestled in their windows. Sew Many Things, the fabric store where Dalia's mother worked, had a Christmas village filled with miniature snow-covered houses and felted figures of mice and foxes, birds and frogs, all dressed in tiny sewn or crocheted vests and scarves and hats. Signs inside advertised classes on knitting, felting, quilting and spinning, and there was a big display of mohair yarn and roving from Tony and Dalia's Angora goats. The print shop had a gorgeous Hanukkah display in blue and white and silver, with a golden menorah front and center.

"Limestone Springs knows how to celebrate in style!" said Grant over a mug of rosewater white chocolate topped with cardamom whipped cream and candy sprinkles.

He was being so cheerful and attentive, so agreeable and fun to hang out with. He was going to make a great husband for some woman someday, and in the meantime, he was good company for Annalisa.

The Catholic church had a live nativity out front, the Presbyterians had a Bethlehem village, and the Baptists had a petting zoo. There were Christmas trees for sale in the H-E-B parking lot. At Manny's auto and tractor repair shop, someone had harnessed a John Deere tractor to a full complement of rustic reindeer made out of corrugated metal and twigs. The front windows of Tito's Bar and Lalo's Kitchen were crowded with glittering ornaments hanging at different heights. Directly upstairs from the bar, the front window of Tito's apartment was hung with a lighted wreath, and Tito's black-and-white cat lay on the windowsill, looking down at the town. A few buildings over, Annalisa could see her own apartment window, with a rosemary topiary surrounded by oversize ornaments.

Hager's Flower Shop was brilliantly decorated with a luxuriant botanical display that combined blooms and greenery indigenous to Texas with exotic plants that Annalisa couldn't even identify.

"I'm about to pop from all this hot chocolate," Annalisa said as she swirled the spicy-scented mixture in her mug, topped with a soft blob of whipped cream and a single pod of star anise.

"I think I'm good for a few more," said Grant. "Isn't that your friend Javi's garage over there?"

It was. Annalisa had been deeply aware of it all evening—the shining plate glass windows of the showroom, the greenery-trimmed overhang, the old Mercury pickup parked outside with a wreath on the grille and a Christmas tree in the back. Parking the Mercury there had been her idea. She wondered if Javi remembered that.

"Should we go say hi?" Grant asked.

Annalisa put on a smile. "Sure," she said.

CHAPTER THIRTEEN

JAVI WATCHED IN amusement as a shabbily dressed man around his own age walked slowly through the showroom, wearing the same glassy expression Javi had seen on the faces of all the visitors who'd come by Mendoza Classic Cars tonight. A Christmas mug dangled loosely from the guy's hand, looking as if it might fall at any moment.

"Hey, Curt!" Javi said. "Good to see you. Come have some hot chocolate and cookies."

Curt greeted Javi absent-mindedly, still gazing around him. Javi led him to the back corner, where a semicircular bar fashioned from old beadboard held platters of Christmas cookies and a big silver urn. Behind the bar, a cast-iron sink stood between a retro refrigerator in bright aqua and a vintage Coke machine.

The showroom's floor gleamed with its fresh coat of epoxy. Overhead, Art Deco light fixtures hung from the high ceiling with its pressed tin panels. Next to the office, visitors lounged on the low-backed sofa and chairs—mid-century modern, according to Peter—and leafed through car magazines that were fanned out on a three-legged kidney-shaped coffee table. Shiplap walls sported all kinds of car memorabilia—hubcaps, old metal signs, vintage magazine ads. A grille from a '63 Thunderbird was mounted on the wall above the sofa, complete with headlights that actually lit up.

Up front, given pride of place in the showroom before

the sparkling plate glass windows, was Tito's Cadillac Eldorado, long and lean, with light chasing along its smooth
red paint, articulating all its gorgeous lines. Juan's beautifully restored '65 El Camino was in the showroom, too,
along with Eddie's '67 Chevelle. A Christmas tree stood
near the center of the room, hung with tiny car models
and topped with a star-shaped Chrysler hood ornament.

Javi took Curt's mug and filled it with hot chocolate.
Curt thanked him and finally looked him in the eye.

"You've done a fantastic job with this place," Curt said.
"You've respected the building's heritage while bringing
it into the twenty-first century and turning it into a fun
place where people will enjoy hanging out."

Javi glanced over at Peter, who was standing near the
side entrance, handing out business cards as fast as he
could. "Most of the credit for that goes to my builder. He
was the one with the vision and the architectural know-
how. Every other day he came to me with a new idea for
something he wanted to do with the place. Eventually I
told him to do whatever he wanted and send me the bill. I
couldn't be happier with the result."

They talked awhile as Curt sipped his hot chocolate.
Then Curt asked, "Have you ever worked on British cars?"

"No, but my dad has," Javi replied. "Way before I was
born, he and my grandfather did a full restoration on an old
Bentley for a family in town. My dad still talks about it."

"Well, I've got my eye on a 1955 Rolls-Royce Silver
Cloud. A client of mine is thinking of selling it, and I might
just buy it myself. I don't know how much work it would
need, but it's been in a barn since the Carter administra-
tion, so probably a lot. I like to hire local whenever I can.
Do you think your dad would be interested in the job?"

"Are you kidding? He'd think he'd died and gone
to heaven."

"Good! I'll go talk to him."

Curt headed over to the front entrance, where Juan, wearing mechanic overalls and a Santa hat, was chatting with a small group and having the time of his life. Juan had made Javi wear a Santa hat, too, but Javi had forgone the overalls in favor of jeans and a button-down.

If Javi had judged Curt by his clothing, he'd have seriously doubted whether the man could have afforded a Rolls-Royce in any condition, but Javi knew better. He'd first met Curt at Tito's Bar, and Tito had filled him in. Curt dressed like a flood victim most of the time, in torn jeans and T-shirts stained with grime, but according to Tito, he was a rich man, with a nationwide business that made alternative housing, whatever that was, for rich clients.

Javi poured himself a fresh mug of hot chocolate and surveyed his domain. He'd witnessed the months-long restoration firsthand, but he could never get enough of looking at it. All the major work was done; the only room left to fix up was the office. The bathroom was back to its 1930s glory, and the green color of the fixtures had grown on Javi, once all the grime was cleaned off and the white subway tile had gone up on the walls.

Curt must have told Juan about the Silver Cloud. Juan was talking vigorously, waving his arms around, his eyes bright with excitement. Juan was in his element tonight. He loved parties, holidays, people and cars, so the Sip-N-Stroll was pretty near a perfect combination for him.

It wasn't only classic car owners or aficionados who'd stopped by tonight. A lot of people were curious about the building. Parents of young children came to let their kids ride around in the tiny toy tractor outside under the overhang. Someone had given it to Javi, and it had turned out to be quite a draw. Others came to sample Rose's sugar cookies and hot chocolate with salted caramel topping. She'd managed to get a hold of a ton of cookie cutters shaped like cars—VW bugs, race cars, jeeps, the works. She and Halley, Jenna's niece, had worked for two days, baking and decorating sheet after sheet of car cookies. Javi had protested at the sheer volume of cookies, but they were flying off the platters.

Whatever drew them to the building, once people were there, they stayed awhile. Gearheads gravitated to the garage bay in the back to see the Biscayne, which was now well along, with the freshly painted body once again united to the power train. People debated good-naturedly about different manufacturers, and talked about the lack of imagination in modern automotive styling, and waxed poetic over the elegance of earlier designs. They reminisced about cars their parents or grandparents had owned in bygone decades, or that they themselves had owned as teenagers and failed to properly appreciate at the time. Some of these had last been seen deserted in pastures, or draped with dusty tarps in old barns or garages. Speculation was rife as to whether or not these vehicles could be made to run again, with Juan and Javi both quick to offer assurances that, yes, they could.

After Curt left, Juan joined Javi at the bar.

"Curt has a lead on an old Rolls-Royce," he said, sounding dazed. "He wants us to do the work."

"He told me," said Javi. "Pretty cool, huh?"

"Oh, yeah. And he's not the only one who's talking about sending work our way. You know Kevin Fox? That guy with all the old cars and tractors parked on his land, rusting away? He wants to make a deal. We get all the junk cleared off of his place, and anything we find that's worth keeping is ours."

"Seriously? Whoa. I'm pretty sure I've seen a decent-looking first-generation Thunderbird hardtop coupe out there."

"Me, too! We could fix it up on spec. Wait for the right buyer to come along."

"Judging from the amount of interest we've seen to-night, we might not have very long to wait."

Juan reached for a cookie and took a bite. "You might as well go ahead and say it."

"Say what?"

"That you told me so."

The words warmed Javi through. "Oh, well, I don't think that's necessary. But I did tell you so."

Overall, the evening was going far better than Javi had dared to hope. Standing there with his father, gazing out at a fledgling business that was well poised to succeed, he felt almost giddy, like a little kid at Christmas. He hadn't felt this good in a long time—years, maybe.

Then the front door opened, and Carlos Reyes walked in.

It had been well over a decade since Javi had laid eyes on the man, but he would have known Carlos anywhere. That cocky walk, that crooked grin—he was the same old Carlos. He walked in breezily, like a man sure of his welcome, a man who never doubted himself.

Before he knew what he was doing, Javi had stepped out from behind the bar and started to cross the floor, moved by an instinctive desire to meet Carlos halfway, as if Carlos were something that had to be stopped.

At the sight of him, Carlos put some extra oomph into his smile. "Javi! Look at you, all grown up. Good to see you."

His voice was as warm and gooey as fudge sauce, as if he were speaking to the son of an old friend whom he hadn't robbed and betrayed. There was a touch of condescension in it, as well. It was a voice that could persuade just about anyone of just about anything—or it used to be. Now it made Javi sick.

Carlos actually held out his hand for Javi to shake. Javi didn't take it. He stood there, his feet planted wide, without moving a muscle, like a gunfighter about to draw.

He didn't speak. He didn't trust himself to. Opening his mouth now would be like opening a floodgate. Once he got started, he wouldn't be able to keep a lid on his temper. And he didn't need trouble now—not when things were going so well.

Carlos kept his hand out a few seconds, his expression puzzled and faintly hurt. Then his gaze wandered past Javi, and his smile perked up again.

"Juan!" he called. "Hey, there, buddy! How've you been?"

"Carlos," said Juan. "What are you doing here?"

"Oh, you know. Just revisiting some of my old stomping grounds. It's been a minute since I've walked the streets of good old Limestone Springs."

He said the town's name with a hick twang in his voice, the way he always did, like the place was countrified and backward and not good enough for him.

Anger boiled up inside Javi. He wanted to punch the grin right off that arrogant face. But he stood still as Carlos walked past him to the bar and picked up one of Rose's cookies.

Carlos chuckled. "I see you're getting some gray in that mustache," he said to Juan. "Do you have any hair left at all, or are you as bald as a cue ball underneath that Santa hat?"

Carlos's own hair stood up as thick and black as ever, but as he munched a cookie, Javi saw that his dashing good looks were starting to slip a little. His jawline wasn't as clean as it had been, and he was getting paunchy. Juan had aged better.

"I see you got the garage up and running," Carlos said, looking around and nodding in an approving sort of way. "Good for you. How's Rose?"

"Get out," said Javi.

Carlos turned to him. "What'd you say?"

Javi walked over. "You heard me. Get out. You're a liar and a thief, and you're not welcome here."

The crowd had gone quiet. Of the people in the building, maybe half knew about Carlos's history with the Mendoza family, and the rest had surely figured out that something was terribly wrong.

"You know, Javier," said Carlos, "anger is like acid. It does more harm to the vessel it's stored in than to anything it's poured on. Mark Twain said that."

He reached for another cookie. Javi slapped his hand away.

Just for a second, Carlos's mask of charm slipped, and Javi saw a flash of anger in his eyes. But before anything else could happen, the side door opened, and Tony came hurrying in.

"Dad! Hey! What're you doing here? You didn't tell me you were going to be in town tonight."

Somehow Tony managed to keep his tone friendly and casual. He had a smile on his face as wide as his father's, but the quick glance he shot at Javi was like an apology.

Javi could see the wheels turning in Carlos's mind as he weighed his options. Go along with Tony's little game and escape with his face intact, or stay and fight it out?

"Well, hey, there, son. How've you been? How's the family? Is my grandson here?"

"He's with Dalia. We took him to see Santa at Darcy's Hardware. You should come say hello."

Carlos flashed a dazzling grin at Juan and Javi. "Take care, you two," he said, and let Tony lead him away.

After the door shut behind them, there was a sound like a sigh, as if everyone in the building had let out a breath at the same time.

"Can you believe that guy?" Javi muttered. Now that Carlos was gone, he was shaking, his body full of angry energy that had nowhere to go. "Who does he think he is, coming in here, talking to us that way? Asking about Mom, as if he has any right to speak her name, as if he's just some old friend and not a backstabbing swindler."

"Let it go, Javier," said Juan. "He isn't worth it. Anyway, he's gone now, and he won't be back. Tony will see to that. Come on. Have another cookie."

But Javi didn't want another cookie. He knew he ought to be grateful that Tony had taken Carlos away before things had escalated, but he couldn't feel anything but mad.

Visitors continued to come by the garage. Javi greeted them, answered their questions, showed them around, accepted their compliments, laughed at their jokes. But it was all an act. He couldn't get back the joy he'd felt earlier in the evening before Carlos had shown up. All the jollity and noise were fraying his nerves.

He slipped away to an alcove near the lounge area, leaned his back against the wall and shut his eyes. Only a few more hours of this, and then everyone would go away. Then he could lock the doors and go back to his horse trailer and climb into his bunk, with Lefty curled up on the cushion on the floor.

A voice called his name in a soft singsong. "Javi. Wake up."

He opened his eyes. Annalisa was there, jaw-droppingly beautiful in a softly clinging sweater and a hat that came down low on her forehead, setting off her cheekbones and making her eyes look huger than ever. Her hair was down, tumbling over her shoulders in long black waves. The sight of her was like a long cool drink of water to a man dying of thirst.

"Annalisa," he said. "Hey."

Then he took her in his arms without thinking about whether it was a good idea, without thinking at all. He ached to hold her, and he did, pressing her tight against him. She smelled so sweet. His ugly mood lifted like a cloud of smoke blown away by a fresh wind.

She hugged him back, then gently pulled away. He fought the urge to hold on.

"How are things going?" she asked. "Are you having a good night?"

He shrugged. "For the most part. Better now."

"Well, the place looks awesome. I'm so happy for you, Javi. You did it. You did what you said you were going to do."

"Yeah, I did, didn't I? But I'm only partway there. I've got a lot more work to do before I can call it done."

She looked around, a frown creasing her face. "Hey, where's Lefty? Did you shut him up in the office? You didn't leave him out in his yard with all these people walking around, did you?"

He smiled. It was just like her to be worried about his dog.

"Are you kidding? No way. He'd be barking his head off. I left him at The Property so he wouldn't be bothered by the crowds. I can't have my surly dog snapping at potential clients."

"He isn't surly, he's a sweetie pie. He was fine that day with me."

"I guess you're just special."

She smiled. "That's nice to hear."

An awkward silence passed.

"I like your hat," Javi said at last.

"Thanks. I like yours, too."

He swept off the Santa hat. "I forgot I had it on. My dad made me wear it."

She chuckled. "Your hair's standing up all over your head now."

She lifted her hand. Just for a second, he thought she was going to smooth down his hair, and he felt as if a piece of his heart went out to meet her partway. All the tension and weirdness that had been between them since he'd come home didn't matter anymore. She was meant for him, and he was meant for her. Part of him had known it all along, but he hadn't been ready—until now.

Before her fingers could reach him, someone rounded the corner.

"Hello, there, Javi. Good to see you again."

It was Grant.

Annalisa redirected her upraised hand to the back of her neck.

Grant held out his own hand for Javi to shake, just like Carlos had done, only this time Javi couldn't ignore it. He shook Grant's hand and with superhuman effort managed to keep the force of his grip to a normal level.

"Grant," he said. "Good to see you, too."

The lie tasted bitter in his mouth. It wasn't good at all to see Grant. What would have been good would be for Grant to be miles away from here.

"Are you two enjoying the Sip-N-Stroll?" he heard himself ask.

The question was addressed to both of them, but Annalisa was the one he was looking at, while her own gaze wandered around the room, down at her feet, or at something behind Javi's shoulder—anywhere but at him.

"Oh, yes," said Grant. "We saw Cowboy Santa, and drank about a gallon each of hot chocolate, and ate lots of cookies, and visited with people. This is a terrific little celebration. It was smart of the city to organize it. Gives people a reason to get better acquainted with the business owners in the downtown area. They're more likely to shop local if they know what's here. Limestone Springs is a charming place with a lot of community spirit. I like small rural towns that haven't forgotten their roots."

"Glad you approve," said Javi. His tone was level, but inside he was roiling with rage. Grant sounded just like Carlos, condescending and superior.

Annalisa did meet his gaze then, and there was something in her eyes that went right through him. Not anger. Disappointment and hurt.

For a moment no one spoke. Then, without taking her eyes off Javi's, Annalisa said, "I'm ready to go if you are, Grant."

"Sure," said Grant. "Whatever you want. See you, Javi."

Annalisa didn't even say goodbye. She just turned and walked away, Grant at her side. Javi watched them go, crushing the Santa hat in his fists.

They got as far as the front door. Then Annalisa stopped and said something to Grant. He went outside and waited there, while she turned and came straight back to Javi.

"You've been making snide remarks to Grant ever since you first met him," she said. "Why is that?"

Her voice was calm, but Javi quailed inside. He'd never seen her like this before, so cold and calm. He didn't know what to say. He couldn't tell her the truth—that he was eaten up with jealousy because he wanted her for himself.

She was waiting for an answer, and Grant was waiting for her.

Javi pulled his thoughts together. In a low voice he said, "You can't be serious about that guy."

She folded her arms across her chest. "Oh? Why is that?"

Javi felt trapped. Desperately he searched for something, anything to say to get himself out of this mess.

"He's a snob," he said at last, keeping his voice low. "All that stuff about charming small towns. That's just the sort of thing some guy from Austin would say."

"Grant isn't some guy from Austin. He grew up in Bastrop, on a farm. His family lost land and livestock in the Bastrop fires."

Javi dropped his gaze to the Santa hat. "He doesn't seem like your type."

"Really? What is my type, Javi? Tell me, since you know so much about it."

He couldn't answer, couldn't look at her. Seconds dragged by like years.

"You know what I think?" Annalisa asked at last. "I think you're just mad that I'm not hanging around waiting for you to notice me again, always available to stroke your ego."

He lifted his head. *What* did she just say?

She pressed her lips together. "I thought better of you than this, Javi. I never believed you were intentionally stringing me along all those years, no matter what anyone else said. But maybe that was because you knew you didn't need to. You knew all you had to do was lift a finger and I'd come running. Now you've lost that and you're trying to get it back—not because you want me for yourself, but because you don't want me to have someone else. And I'm done. I don't have time for this anymore."

She turned and walked away. This time she didn't look back.

CHAPTER FOURTEEN

"EVERYTHING ALL RIGHT?" Grant asked.

Annalisa wanted to say yes, that everything was fine, and say it with the breezy confidence of a strong, independent woman who had made her peace with the past and fully gotten over her childhood crush on a man who wasn't interested in her and never had been. But she couldn't, because it would be a lie. She couldn't say anything at all. She needed every bit of concentration and energy she possessed just to keep from crying.

Grant didn't push. He let her be quiet and walked beside her, shielding her from the crowd when necessary. He really was a great guy.

She caught a glimpse of Luke and Eliana once, just for a moment when the crowd parted enough for her to see across the street. They were standing beneath a streetlight. Eliana was talking animatedly about something, and Luke was listening, with a tender smile on his face. He dropped a kiss onto the top of her head just as a group of people walked past, obscuring them from Annalisa's view.

"Look at this red jingle bell garland hanging over this doorway," Annalisa said. "It looks like holly berries. Isn't it pretty?"

Her voice sounded almost normal. Grant accepted the change of subject, and before long they were chatting in a way that would have fooled almost anybody.

The evening was winding down. It was getting late,

and Grant had a long drive ahead of him. Annalisa walked him to his car.

"Thanks for inviting me to this," he said as he took his key fob from his pocket. "I had a good time."

"So did I," she replied. It was mostly true.

He clicked the fob, and his car door locks chirped. "Hang in there," he said. "And if you have any more questions about the German diary, or anything else I can help you with, don't hesitate to ask. Okay?"

She smiled at him. "Okay. Thanks."

She gave him a quick hug, and he got into his car and drove away.

The wind was starting to pick up, driving icy prickles against her cheeks. She shivered and started walking, leaving the festive sounds of the Sip-N-Stroll behind.

Grant had parked in the alley behind Claudia's law office, not far from Annalisa's apartment building. As she turned the corner, she saw someone standing in front of the downstairs entrance.

It was Javi.

Her heart seized up in a spasm of pain. She walked to the overhang, her legs feeling heavy as lead.

"I'm sorry," Javi said. "You were right. I was a jerk. Carlos came by the garage earlier and was his usual arrogant, obnoxious, narcissistic self. It made me mad, and I took it out on Grant. He didn't deserve that. But the thing is—"

He stuffed his hands in his pockets. "The thing is, Annalisa, you're special to me. You always have been. You're like the sister I never had. And I guess no guy is ever going to seem good enough for you in my eyes. But you seem to think pretty highly of Grant, and you're a pretty good judge of character. Anyway, you're all grown up now, and you can choose for yourself, and it's really none of my business either way. So—well, that's it. I, uh, I'm happy for you."

She couldn't speak. Her throat felt all hot and choked, and her eyes swam with tears.

Javi stepped closer. With his hands still in his pockets, he leaned close and kissed her on the forehead. He smelled of chocolate and automotive chemicals.

"Good night," he said. "Merry Christmas."

As he turned to go, sleet began to fall in slanting sheets. He didn't pick up his pace, just kept walking.

THE BREAKFAST AROMAS of coffee, bacon and eggs washed over Javi in a fragrant wave as he walked into Lalo's Kitchen. He hadn't slept well the night before, and he could probably use some coffee right now, but he cut across the room to the pass-through that divided the space from Tito's Bar next door. The accordion-style door that folded into the wall was mostly stretched out across the pass-through, leaving just enough space for employees to pass back and forth between the two businesses. Javi squeezed through.

No traces remained from last night's Sip-N-Stroll. The bar was meticulously clean, with the benches still upended on top of the tables that ran the length of the room, leaving the hardwood floors bare. The bar stools were upside down on the bar top, except for the one where Tito sat, doing something on his laptop. He looked at Javi over the top of his old-timey gold-rimmed spectacles.

Javi went straight to the bar, took another stool down and sat on it. "Whiskey, neat," he said.

"It's ten o'clock in the morning," said Tito. "I'm not even open for business yet."

"I'm your brother," Javi replied. "Your favorite brother. I taught you how to tie your shoes, and believe me, that was no easy task. You can make an exception."

Tito took off his specs, folded them and laid them beside his laptop. Then he went behind the bar and picked up a glass. Javi stared at the wood grain in the countertop.

Tito set down the glass in front of Javi. It was filled to the brim with a red liquid.

"This doesn't look like whiskey," said Javi.

"That's because it's pomegranate juice. High in anti-oxidants and vitamin C. Drink it, and tell me what's bothering you."

"What makes you think something's bothering me?"

Tito raised an eyebrow at him. "Call it my keen percep-tion of human nature. So? What's up?"

Javi took a suspicious sip of the red stuff. It wasn't bad. Then he said in a rush, "Annalisa is dating some guy, and I can't stand him."

"You're talking about Grant? He seems all right to me."

"I didn't say he was a bad guy. I said I can't stand him. There's just something about him. He isn't right for her."

Tito set another glass on the bar top and filled it with pomegranate juice. "If he wasn't dating Annalisa, if he didn't even know her and you met him in some other way unconnected to her, would you still dislike him?"

"I don't know. Maybe not."

"Then the real question is, why? Why don't you like that Annalisa is seeing Grant? Is it out of concern for their compatibility and her future happiness? Or could there be another reason?"

Javi planted his elbows on the bar and gripped his head between his hands, trying to contain and make sense of all the thoughts tumbling through his mind. "Well, you know what she's like. She's special. Smart and sweet and—and beautiful. Those eyes of hers just look right into you, right into the heart of you, the parts that you don't share with anybody else. She sees it all, and somehow she still cares and believes the best about you. And it makes you want to be a better man."

Tito took a drink of his own juice. "Sounds like the reason you don't like Grant is because you don't like having competition for Annalisa's time and attention. The truth is, you're jealous."

"I guess so. I—she—"

"What?"

"I love her," said Javi.

He let out his breath in a rush and hung his head, drained. "I love her. She's my best friend. She knows me like no one else does, and she's never turned away from me. And if I mess that up, then it's gone, and I won't be able to get it back. And I can't risk that. But I can't keep on the way I'm going."

"No," Tito agreed. "You can't."

He leaned forward. "Here's an idea. Instead of giving the whole thing up because you're not good enough for her, try being the guy she needs, the guy she deserves."

"What good will that do? None of it matters, anyway, because she's with Professor Perfect now. She might have had a crush on me at one time, but she's over me. She's outgrown me."

"Has Professor Perfect put a ring on her finger?"

"No. I don't think so. I don't think they've been going out for more than a couple of months."

"Well, then, maybe it's not too late."

Javi frowned. "Isn't that kind of a jerk move, though? Going after her when she's with someone else?"

Tito didn't answer right away. Javi raised his head and saw his brother staring into the middle distance.

"What?" Javi asked. "What are you not saying?"

Finally Tito spoke. "I admit that the timing is not great. But maybe seeing her with another guy is what it took to wake you up to how much she means to you. I think you ought to tell her how you feel. You can't go back in time and do it earlier, but you can do it now, before you're a day older. Tell her, and let her decide what to do about it."

"She might tell me to get lost," said Javi.

"She might."

They stared at each other a long moment.

"All right," said Javi. "I'm going to do it. Right now. I'm going to go to her apartment and tell her how I feel."

He knocked back the remainder of his pomegranate juice and set the glass down.

Tito put his spectacles back on. "Let me know how it goes," he said.

Last night's sleet had melted, leaving the streets and sidewalks shiny. A south wind ruffled Javi's hair as he strode down the sidewalk to Annalisa's apartment. He'd never actually been inside the place before. She'd moved in around the time he'd gone to West Texas, and he hadn't had the time or energy, then, to spend on her. He'd been focused on earning as much money as he could and socking it away. He couldn't let himself be distracted by anything that might make him soft. He'd gotten used to the idea that she'd always be there, waiting. He shouldn't have taken that for granted.

But Tito was right. Regret wouldn't help him now. It was time to make his move.

Along the way, he passed the flower shop. Should he stop and buy her a bouquet? No. That would just make it weird. Besides, he didn't have an instant to lose. She might be on the phone with Grant right now.

He opened the ground floor door and climbed the stairs, his footsteps making hollow thuds. She had a pretty doormat laid out and a wreath hanging on the front door. The door itself was painted red and had one of those big old-fashioned brass knockers that looked like a lion's head, right in the center of the wreath.

Javi stretched out his hand and steeled himself. Then he seized the knocker and banged it against the door.

As the echoes bounced off the walls, Javi suddenly felt sick to his stomach. What would she say to him? How would she look at him? What if she wasn't even home? What if she was with Grant? They might be having brunch at some fancy place in Austin right now. Or—he sucked in a breath at the thought—Grant might be here! That would be hideous.

He listened. Were those voices he heard? Maybe he should run away while he still had a chance.

The voices abruptly stopped. Somewhere on the other side of the door, something rustled, and soft footsteps came toward him. Javi planted his feet wide on Annalisa's door-mat and waited.

ANNALISA SAT ON her sofa, curled up under the fluffy comforter her grandmother had made her when she was eight years old. Decades of washing had faded the floral print to a mellow pastel palette and worn the fabric's nap smooth. It had been years since she had used it on her bed, but she kept it in a chest in her living room, ready for when she was sick or exhausted or otherwise in need of comfort.

That's why it's called a comforter, she always told herself whenever she brought it out.

She hadn't done a lick of work on her book today. Her notes were spread out on her desk, staring at her accusingly from across the room. If she were better and stronger, she would be over there right now, finishing that tricky chapter that had been giving her so much trouble. Or getting ready for a date with some guy other than Javi, washing her hair, planning her outfit. She might have been doing a lot of things, instead of sitting alone in her apartment, wearing her oldest sweats, with her hair a tangled mess, watching *Casablanca* and eating kettle chips straight from the bag.

She'd known all along that it would be hard to give up her hopeless crush on Javi, but she'd never dreamed there would be so much active temptation. His move back to Limestone Springs, the extra attention he'd suddenly started paying her, the animosity toward Grant that had seemed like jealousy, only to turn out to be nothing more than brotherly concern—they'd strained her resistance to the limit. She was worn out.

A knock at the door made her jump. It was a brisk knock, as if the person on the other side meant business. The kind of knock that you expected to be followed by a voice saying, "Police! Open up!"

But there was no voice. Annalisa sighed, brushed the crumbs from her hands and paused the movie. Then she got up and walked over to the door.

She looked through the peephole and saw a man.

She would have recognized him by his posture alone—feet braced, head set, shoulders squared. It was the posture of a man who expected the worst and was ready to meet it. But she could see his face, too—the jutting chin, the clear green eyes, green as the Guadalupe River.

Her hands were shaking so hard that she could barely work the chain and the dead bolt, but she managed it at last and opened the door. And there he was, Javi, in the flesh.

Ordinarily she would have taken some time with her appearance before a Javi encounter, but not this time. She didn't have a speck of makeup on her face. She hadn't even put in her contacts this morning. She was wearing her oldest pair of glasses, the ones with the cracked frame that she'd mended with packing tape.

Javi's presence made her react the way it always had. The rush of heat to her face, that gone feeling in her stomach as if the floor had suddenly dropped away from her feet—she might have been thirteen years old again.

"What do you want?" she asked. She was in no mood to be polite. She was tired. She wanted to get this over with so she could crawl back under her comforter and try to forget.

"Are you alone?" asked Javi.

Was she *alone*? What sort of question was that?

"Yes," she said. "Yes, I'm alone." *As per usual.*

"Good. I, uh, I need to talk to you."

She let out a groan and leaned her shoulder against the doorjamb. "Look, Javi, please don't mess with me. I can't go through all this again."

"I'm not here to mess with you. I'm here to tell you—"

He broke off, swallowed, shuffled his feet. He actually looked nervous.

A tiny bubble of hope rose in her chest, even though she was telling herself not to get ahead of herself, not to set herself up for disappointment.

"I wasn't completely honest with you last night," he said at last. "The truth is, I don't think of you as the sister I never had. Maybe at one time I did, but not anymore. I think of you in the, uh…" He swallowed again. "The romance category."

She waited, but nothing else came. He appeared to have shot his bolt. She had never seen him so tongue-tied, so awkward.

"Since when?" she heard herself ask.

"I don't know. Maybe a while now. But I didn't do anything about it, didn't let myself think about it, because I didn't want to mess things up. You're too important for me to lose you. And now—well, you're with Grant. And maybe I'm too late. But I thought I should tell you anyway, just in case you—well, just in case."

The bubble of hope blossomed into a cataract. He wasn't stringing her along. He meant it. Those signs she had seen, and wondered about, and doubted, weren't imaginary. They were real.

"I'm not with Grant," she said. "I never was."

It was wonderful to see the wild surge of joy light up his face. "You're not? You weren't?"

"No. It wouldn't have been fair to him when I was— when I cared about someone else."

"Cool," he said. "Wait, that's me, right?"

She laughed, a trembly laugh that might dissolve into tears at any moment. "Of course it's you. It's always been you."

He grinned harder than she had ever seen him grin in her life. "Wow," he said. "That's great. Um—would you like to go to dinner with me?"

"Yes," she said.

"Tonight?"

"Tonight."

"Okay. I'll text you."

"Okay."

He was backing away now. "Well, I guess I'll see you tonight, then. Bye, Annalisa."

"Bye, Javi. See you soon."

And he was gone, down the staircase, taking the steps three at a time. She heard the ground floor door open and shut. Then she shut her own door, pressed her back against it and sank down to the floor. She could hear her breath going in and out fast and shallow, almost hyperventilating. She was shaking all over.

It wasn't until then that it occurred to her that the entire conversation had been conducted at her front door. She hadn't even invited him in, and he hadn't seemed to expect her to. But it was just as well. Having him inside her apartment, all to herself, would have been too much. She needed space and time to process her happiness. Otherwise she might burst.

CHAPTER FIFTEEN

AFTER TEXTING BACK and forth for a bit, they agreed that Javi would pick Annalisa up at three o' clock. Javi had suggested they drive to San Antonio for dinner, and Annalisa agreed at once. She didn't want this first date to be conducted in full view of people who'd known both of them all their lives. Maybe Javi didn't, either.

Javi showed up so precisely on the dot that Annalisa wondered if he'd actually arrived early and then kept an eye on his watch in order to knock on her door right at the stroke of three. She was ready.

"You look beautiful," he said when she opened the door.

It didn't matter that it was a stereotypical thing to say. She could see that he meant it. And it felt good to have some validation after hours spent selecting an outfit— a sleek sweater dress in midnight blue—and doing her makeup and hair.

"Thanks," she said. "So do you."

He flushed to the tips of his ears. He had on a green button-down, black pants and his usual black lace-up boots, along with a black bomber jacket.

"Would you like to come in?" she asked.

"Sure."

It felt strange to see him walking around her apartment, checking out the furniture, her work desk, the books on the shelves. "Nice place," he said. "It looks like you."

Then he took out his phone. "Okay, so, I've got some

ideas for what we're going to do tonight. I'll tell you all the options, and then you can pick."

"All right. Let's hear them."

He tapped his phone screen. "There's a concert at the Aztec Theatre and a musical at the Tobin. They're both pretty full, but I can still get us some balcony seats. For dinner, I thought we could eat somewhere on the River Walk—at Domingo's, or Bonahan's, or Biga on the Banks. The Spanish Governor's Palace is open until five, so we could go see it if you want. I've never seen it, but it's supposed to be pretty cool. Then there are some tours available for all the old missions—the Alamo, the San Juan Capistrano, the Espada, and I forget the names of the rest. We could drive the tour route ourselves, but that sounds like a pain because of the parking. But there's a rideshare option. We could get Lyft Lux, and ride in a Bentley, or a Maserati, or a BMW, or a Porsche, or any car you want." He paused. "What? What are you smiling at?"

She was smiling because he'd obviously been so diligent to choose activities rich in culture and history—things he thought she would like—while still squeezing in a ride in a luxury vehicle for him.

"Nothing," she said. "Let's just go to the River Walk and eat at Domingo's and then walk around. The River Walk is so beautiful this time of year, all decorated for Christmas."

The relief on his face made it plain that he liked that idea. "Okay. Maybe we can take the mission tour another time. There's a hiking trail you can take that hits all the missions. It's eight miles, but we could use a rideshare for part of it if you didn't want to walk the whole way. It might be a fun thing to do in the spring."

"That sounds perfect," said Annalisa, thrilled by his expectation that they would still be together then.

She opened her entry closet and took out a dressy shawl.

He draped it over her shoulders, lifting her hair out of the way. He was being scrupulously formal and respectful, as if she were a stranger he wanted to impress.

He had parked his green Silverado on the street. It was shiny clean and dripping. He had always kept his vehicles spotless. When he opened the passenger door for her, the scent of Armor All wafted out.

Conversation on the drive to the city was a little stilted. He asked about her research and writing; she filled him in on her progress. She asked about the garage, and he outlined his business plan and recent expenditures in concise but thorough detail, almost as if he wanted to demonstrate that he was a good marital prospect.

When they got to San Antonio, he effortlessly backed his truck into a fairly tight space in a parking garage, and they walked down a stone stairway to the river level.

"Are you hungry yet?" he asked. "We could get a table now and have something to drink, or walk around for a while."

"Let's walk first."

The leaves of the live oak trees were as lush and dark green as ever, but the elms had their bright gold December color, and the feathery foliage of the cypresses was turning orange brown. Javi walked at her side, close but not too close, and didn't take her hand. Except for helping her in and out of the truck and with her shawl, he hadn't touched her yet, and she was starting to wonder why. He'd touched her enough during their only-friends years, with hello hugs and goodbye hugs and plenty of casual contact in between.

"Did you tell anyone we were going out tonight?" he asked.

"I told Eliana and my mom."

"What did your mom say?"

"She played it pretty close to the vest, but I think she

was pleased. She wants to have us both over for Sunday lunch sometime after she and Dad get back from visiting my aunt."

"Cool. I can see that bird feeder."

"And take a peek inside the dresser drawers in the guest room. Spoiler alert—they're still empty. How about you? Did you tell anyone?"

"Just Tito. Actually, he was the one who convinced me to do it."

She gave him a sidewise look. "You needed convincing?"

Javi shrugged. "I thought I'd missed my chance, because of Grant. But Tito thought I still had a shot."

Annalisa mentally blessed Tito for that.

It wasn't quite five o'clock when they went to Domingo's. They sat on the terrace, close to a heater. Annalisa ordered a Mexican candied *paloma*, and Javi ordered a Modelo Especial, with some skillet cornbread as an appetizer.

"I'm not going to be able to help you with that cornbread," said Annalisa. "Not unless I want to take half my entrée home in a carton."

"That's all right. I'm pretty hungry. I haven't eaten since…well, I guess I haven't eaten at all today."

"Why not?"

"I forgot to." He flashed her a quick grin. "I had a lot on my mind. I did have a glass of pomegranate juice at Tito's Bar."

"Well, that's not very filling. You should have said something before. I wouldn't have minded eating earlier."

"I know you wouldn't. But in the past, our relationship has been all about me. You've always been there for me, supporting me, advising me. I took you for granted, like oxygen, or gravity. I want tonight to be all about you."

The words, the way he looked at her when he said them—this whole day was like a dream come true, and it felt even better than she'd imagined.

Javi made quick work of the cornbread. Just before their entrées arrived, he got a text.

"Oh, nice," he said. "The new dashboard and instrument clusters are ready for the Biscayne. That's sooner than I expected."

"Good! How soon will the Biscayne be up and running?"

"I think by April. I'm going to take you for a lot of drives then."

"I would love that. We should take it to that drive-in theater in New Braunfels. Sometimes they show classic movies there. Wouldn't it be something if they showed something from 1959, the same year the Biscayne came out?"

He chuckled. "I love that you know what year the Biscayne is. I love that you know so much about cars in general."

She gave him a sly smile. "You know why, don't you?"

"No. Why?"

"Because *you* love cars. And I—"

She stopped herself just in time before saying, "I love *you*," changing it at the last second to, "I wanted to know about everything that was important to you. So I learned. And somewhere along the way, I realized that cars are actually pretty interesting."

"What a woman I've got!" said Javi.

While they ate, the sun set. The lights in the trees came on, brightening as the gentle blue-gray twilight gave way to darkness. After dinner, they walked some more, taking their time, going nowhere in particular, since everywhere they went there was some fresh beauty to see.

At one point they crossed a bridge, pausing at the top to see the moonlight sparkling on the water. When Annalisa shivered, Javi opened up his jacket and put his arm around her, bringing her inside the jacket with him, which made her shiver more than ever in spite of the warmth.

He pressed his face against her hair and murmured, "Am I going to have to wait until our third date to kiss you?"

"Don't you dare," she replied.

And then he was kissing her, right there on the bridge, holding her close to him with one arm around her shoulders and his other hand cupping her cheek. She slid her arm deeper into his jacket, around his back, relishing the solid strength of him. It was all so new, and at the same time so familiar, so exciting and yet so easy, and she knew at once that he was hers, he'd always been hers, as she'd always been his.

For the walk back to the truck, he took off his jacket and put it on her. Her heart was filled to bursting. If only her younger self could see her now, wearing Javi Mendoza's leather jacket, walking hand in hand with him on the River Walk.

The bald cypress trees that grew along the river were dropping their spiky round cones. One of the little spheres had fallen on the stone railing of the staircase that led back up to the street level. Annalisa picked it up and tucked it into Javi's jacket pocket—a new memento for a new memory. But with or without a memento, this was one night she would never forget.

"It's still pretty early," Annalisa said as they drove back to Limestone Springs.

Javi glanced over at her. "Yeah? You want to go someplace else?"

She smiled at him. "I have an idea, but you might think it's a little silly."

"Go ahead. Lay it on me."

"Well, how would you feel about going back to the shop and sitting in the front seat of the Biscayne together?"

He thought about that. "It's in the garage, you know. Lots of tools and lifts and oil cans around."

"I know. I just want to be there with you."

He didn't answer right away. He couldn't. His heart was too full.

"You think I'm silly," Annalisa said.

"No," said Javi. "I think you're amazing."

They stopped at The Property to pick up Lefty, then drove on to the garage. Javi parked the Silverado near the back entrance, where the garage bays were, and opened the gate to Lefty's yard. Lefty got down from the back seat of the truck cab, stretched and sauntered over, wagging his tail and sniffing the grass.

While Javi searched for the back door key, Annalisa crouched down beside Lefty and scratched his ears and throat. "Hello, Lefty. Are you a good boy? Yes, you're a very good boy."

Lefty flopped down to the ground with a grunt. He lay on his side with his legs stuck straight out as Annalisa rubbed his belly.

Javi unlocked the door, and Lefty followed them inside. Javi flipped on the lights, bolted the door and hung his keys on their hook. And there was the Biscayne in all its sleek-lined glory, its Highland Green paint shining in the LED overhead lights.

"Make yourself at home," he said as he headed to the refrigerator in the bar area. "I'm going to have a beer. You want one?"

"Sure. Hey, why'd you name him Lefty, anyway? Is he left-pawed?"

Javi took two bottles of beer out of the fridge. "The day he showed up on the rig, one of the guys was playing some Willie Nelson. That song came on, the one he sings with Merle Haggard, 'Pancho and Lefty.' I took one look at that dog with his left ear sticking straight up and his right ear out to the side, and the name just seemed to fit."

She chuckled. "Can't argue with that."

She was still wearing his jacket, with her shawl wrapped around her neck like a scarf. She took the jacket off now, folded it over her arm and ran her hand over the leather.

Javi reached for it. "Here, I'll take that," he said.

"Just a minute," Annalisa said. "I left something in one of the pockets."

She reached inside and took a small object out. Javi draped the jacket over the back of a chair, then opened the passenger door of the Biscayne. Annalisa slid onto the leather bench seat.

"Oh, look at Lefty," she said.

Lefty was standing with his head cocked, looking longingly into the car.

"Can he come in?" Annalisa asked. "There's plenty of room on the floorboard with the seat so far back."

"I don't see why not. It's not like he'll tear up the seats. He's not much of a jumping dog. Go on, Lefty. Get in."

Lefty clambered through the door, turned around twice and lay down on the passenger floorboard.

Javi handed Annalisa the beers, then walked around to the driver's side and got in. Annalisa scooted over next to him and drew her legs onto the seat. He twisted the lids off the beers and handed Annalisa's back to her. They clinked the bottles together. Then Javi laid his arm across the seat back, and Annalisa snuggled against his side.

"What's that spiky thing resting on the dashboard?" Javi asked. "It looks like a bald cypress cone."

"It is a bald cypress cone," she replied. "I picked it up on the River Walk."

"What for?"

She shrugged. He couldn't see her face. "I like to have mementos of important events."

"What kind of mementos?" he asked. "What kind of events?"

"You'll laugh at me," she said.

"No, I won't. Tell me. What kind of things do you keep?"

"Let's see. A rodeo program from the year your family sat near mine. Ticket stubs for movies we saw together. A little boomerang you won at the Persimmon Festival. And a T-shirt you wore to the Comal River once when a bunch of us went tubing together."

He turned and looked her in the face. "Are you serious? You saved all those things? Why?"

"Because they were connected to you, at least a little. Because they reminded me of times you'd paid attention to me—or had just been close by, without realizing how much that meant to me."

Javi was floored. "But you're talking about years' worth of stuff."

"That's right."

He was quiet a moment. Then he said, "Hold on. Was the T-shirt gray?"

"Yes. You took it off as soon as we got in the water. And when we finished the route and got into the shuttle, you carried our tubes and asked me to hold on to the shirt for you."

"I remember that shirt! I always wondered what happened to it."

"Well, now you know."

He fell silent again.

"I had no idea," he said at last. "I always knew you had a little crush on me when I was in high school, but I never realized it was anything like this. Where do you even keep all this stuff?"

"I *did* keep it in a chest at the foot of my bed. Until three months ago, when I burned it."

"Burned it?" Javi repeated. "*Burned* it? Why?"

"Because I thought you were never going to feel about me the way I felt about you. I needed to move on."

"But *burning* it? Isn't that a little extreme?"

"My feelings for you were extreme. I needed a ceremony, for closure. That was what Eliana said, anyway."

"Oh, Eliana. So it was her idea? That makes sense. She's never liked me."

There was a pause. Then Annalisa said, "Well, in fairness, you've never really liked her—or Dalia, or their brother, Marcos."

"That's true. All those Ramirez kids were stuck-up. Born into ranching royalty, descendants of the great Alejandro Ramirez."

"They're not like that, though. They're very down-to-earth. And it isn't fair to blame people for who their ancestors are."

"You're talking about Alex and Tony now, aren't you?"

She shrugged. "They're good guys, Javi. And they can't help who their father is."

Javi was silent a moment. "We used to see them at church a lot. Their mother brought them. And we saw them socially because our fathers were friends, even though they were both younger than me. I remember the Sunday after Carlos took the money, Tony and Alex both had on new boots. And that summer Tony went to a pricey football camp. He was only nine years old! Why does anyone need to go to football camp at that age? When I think about all the stupid stuff Carlos must have bought for them, frittering away the money he stole from my family—"

He broke off. His chest was getting tight.

"Let's talk about something else," he said.

"All right," said Annalisa.

For a long time they didn't say anything at all. It was enough to be together, kicking back with a couple of beers with a good dog at their feet.

Then Javi said, "I can't believe you burned my gray T-shirt. It was so soft."

That sent Annalisa into a giggling fit. "I'll buy you a new T-shirt."

"It better be soft," he said.

"It will be."

She sighed. "This is a dream come true for me, sitting here in this car with you."

He squeezed her shoulder and kissed the top of her head. "Just wait until I get it running. I'll take you driving all over the county."

It felt so good and natural, having her by his side.

"Can I see you tomorrow?" he asked. "I thought maybe we could go to Tito's Bar and Lalo's Kitchen. Eat, drink, hang out."

"You know half the town will be there."

"I know. I don't mind. I want them to see us together. I want the whole town to know that you're my girl now."

She turned and looked at him. "Am I your girl now?"

"Well…yeah. Aren't you?"

"That depends. Are you my guy?"

"Of course I am. I'm all in, baby."

The smile that lit her face was a flash of pure joy. It blew his mind to think she really cared that much about him, that she'd been carrying a torch for that many years. He didn't deserve devotion like that, from a woman like her. He felt humble and thankful, and a little scared.

He kissed her.

CHAPTER SIXTEEN

JAVI AND ANNALISA'S presence together at Tito's Bar on Sunday afternoon caused all the stir she had imagined it would. Everyone saw them together, and everyone had something to say about it.

A lot of the remarks people made were variations on the words "It's about time."

And Javi would look at Annalisa and say, "It sure is."

It was almost too much. He treated her with scrupulous care, as if she were incomparably precious. It was like she'd always imagined, but better, because it was real.

And at the same time, amidst all the excitement and wonder, there was something very comfortable and familiar about being with Javi. They'd known each other for all of Annalisa's life. Everything was the same, and everything was different.

They sat at one of the long tables in the bar, which made it easy for people to drop by. Javi's parents were there, and all of his brothers—Johnny with his wife and kids, Eddie and Enrique with groups of friends. Tito was there by virtue of being the bar's owner, and Jenna was one of the managers at Lalo's Kitchen. They both sat down with Javi and Annalisa for a while and chatted over burgers and beers, cheese curds and blackberry mead.

It didn't seem very long ago that Annalisa had been helping Jenna pull together a last-minute outfit for her first

date with Tito, and now here was Jenna, giving Annalisa
a conspiratorial grin across the table.

"So this is pretty cool," said Jenna, glancing from Annalisa to Javi and back again as Javi and Tito compared
notes about the Sip-N-Stroll.

"Yeah, it is," said Annalisa.

"Are you going to the Mendozas' Christmas party? Rose
is already making the decorations."

"I don't understand how she does it. She just got through
baking about a million dozen cookies for the Sip-N-Stroll."

"I know. And after Christmas it'll be time to get ready
for the New Year's party, and then Juan's birthday, and
on and on throughout the year. Cinco de Mayo, Fourth of
July. And in between she's making casseroles for people
who've just had surgeries, and volunteering at church, and
I don't know what all."

"She and Juan are very generous people," said Annalisa.

Somehow that made the thing that Carlos had done to
them seem worse. After the business account had been
cleaned out, leaving the Mendozas' finances in ruins, everyone had said what a horrible thing it was to happen to
such nice people.

"Yeah," said Jenna. "So how's it going with the new
book? Any breakthroughs on the missing silver?"

"Unfortunately, no. I've thoroughly cross-referenced the
Friesenhahn diary with Romelia's diary and Alejandro's
letters. At this point, all I'm certain of is that at some point,
Gabriel intended to come over to the Texian side and bring
the silver with him. Whether he actually followed through,
or even attempted to follow through, I don't know."

"Boy, wouldn't it be something if that silver turned up
after all these years?" said Javi, who had caught the tail
end of what Annalisa had said.

"It sure would," said Annalisa. "It would be a whole

new episode in the Texas Revolution, and I'd be the first one writing about it."

"Well, yeah, there is that aspect of it," Javi agreed. "But I was thinking more about the money. I wouldn't mind finding a big old stash of silver. I'd buy me a high-end engine lathe so I could machine my own parts in the shop."

"I'd definitely spring for that new Kate Spade handbag with the laptop compartment that I've had my eye on," said Annalisa. "And maybe a nice Spanish colonial armoire. But I don't own any real estate for the silver to be found on, so my chances aren't very good."

"If I find the money, I'll get you the handbag *and* the armoire," said Javi. "I'll take you out to dinner, too."

"Aw, thank you."

Tito got to his feet. "In the absence of revolutionary-era treasure, I've still got to work for a living. I'd better get back to it."

"Me, too," said Jenna. "See you later, Javi, Annalisa. Enjoy your evening."

After they'd gone, Javi said, "I like her. She's good for Tito. She's got his back."

"I like her, too," said Annalisa. "Have you heard the way she sasses your dad?"

"Yeah, I have. He loves it."

He downed the last of his beer and stood. "I'm going to get another. You want some more mead?"

"I'm fine, thanks."

While he was gone, Alex came over and sat down on the bench beside Annalisa.

"Hey, there, *prima*!" said Alex, giving her a quick side hug. "How've you been? How's the book coming? You find the silver yet?"

"Everyone keeps asking me if I've found the silver," she said, hugging him back. "And I keep having to say no. Most likely the silver never even made it over from Mexico."

"Maybe it'll turn up. There's no telling what's squirreled away on some of these old ranches. Did you ever hear about the old Brown Bess musket found at La Escarpa about twenty years ago?"

"No."

"Yeah, Marcos found it when he was a kid. He found some old arrowheads, too, and some musket balls. And there's a site on my place, not far from the creek, where the vaqueros used to sleep under the stars when the cows were calving. There's a sort of pit nearby, a sinkhole, that they used as a trash dump. I used to find stuff there—nothing as good as a two-hundred-year-old musket, but still pretty cool. Cooking equipment for an open fire, broken spurs, bits of old tack, rusty knives. I even found a 1932 penny once."

Just then, Tony came over and dropped onto the bench on the other side of the table, next to the spot Javi had vacated. He leaned across the table, his eyes wide, and asked, "Annalisa, are you here with Javi?"

"Yes," she said.

Alex turned and looked at her. "I thought you were dating Grant."

"No. Grant and I are just friends."

At that moment, Javi came back with his beer. He looked at Tony, then at Alex, and took his seat.

"Hello, Javi," said Alex.

"Hey," said Javi.

There was a definite coolness in the atmosphere. Tony looked as if he'd like to say something friendly and jovial about the fact that Annalisa and Javi were dating but knew it wouldn't be well received.

As if on cue, Tony and Alex both got to their feet.

"Good seeing you both," said Tony. "Take care."

When they were gone, Javi took a swallow of his beer. "They've got a lot of nerve coming over here, after the scene their father made at the shop two nights ago. You should have seen the way he strolled in with that smarmy grin on his face, as if he was the most popular guy in the world and we'd all be thrilled to see him."

"That wasn't their fault," said Annalisa. "I'm sure they were embarrassed by it."

"Maybe. But I don't like Tony. That smile, and the way he acts with people, all charming and friendly—he's just like his father."

"I don't think Tony is anything like Carlos. They look alike, and yes, Tony is very friendly and outgoing, but in his case it's sincere. He really cares about people."

Javi shrugged. "Maybe. But I don't have to be friends with him, or Alex."

"No, you don't. But…"

He glanced across at her. "But what?"

"Nothing," she said. She'd been on the verge of saying that he didn't have to be rude to them, either. But she'd only been dating the man for two days. This hardly seemed the time to start nagging him about his social skills. And it wasn't as if he'd verbally abused them. He'd just kept his mouth shut. From his point of view, it probably seemed that he'd shown a great deal of restraint.

A silence passed. Then Javi asked, "When can I see you again?"

The warm urgency in his voice made her melt inside. "I have a client meeting with Claudia Monday evening," she said. "And after work on Tuesday I need to go to my parents' house. They'll be back in town by then, and I said I'd help them set up their new doorbell camera. I'm off on Wednesday, but I need to work on the book all day. Are you free Wednesday evening? Maybe you could come over then. I could make dinner, and we could watch a movie."

"That sounds perfect."

"Good. Bring Lefty."

CHAPTER SEVENTEEN

ANNALISA AWOKE WEDNESDAY morning to the rich aroma of American roast coffee burbling away in the drip coffee maker. She pulled on her favorite writing-at-home clothes—soft yoga pants and a tunic sweater—and went to the kitchen.

Through the filmy gauze of her living room curtain, the lights on the pecan trees in the square cast a soft glow. She poured herself a steaming mug of coffee and took it over to the window, where she switched on the glimmer lights on her rosemary topiary. The fragrant little shrub was hung with tiny gold balls and crystal snowflakes.

She stood awhile, looking down at the town and feeling happy. For the past several months she'd been waking up at five to allow herself an hour's writing time before getting ready for work, a schedule that had enabled her to make slow but steady progress. Now she had a whole day ahead of her with nothing to do but write, and dinner with Javi to look forward to this evening.

Everything she'd done and thought over the past two days had been tinted with the consciousness of Javi—the way he looked at her, the things he said. After all these years it had finally happened, and it was glorious. *You're my girl*, he'd told her. *I'm all in, baby*.

She went to her desk in a haze of pleasure and contentment. The spiky little globe from the River Walk cypress tree rested on the corner, one more reminder that it was all real.

A few minutes later, she was fathoms deep in the nineteenth century, swimming in a sea of military dispatches, family records, oral tradition, and dates and names from tombstones in old cemeteries, trying to discern the signal from the noise and figure out what it all meant.

She'd had plenty to write about before coming across the clues about the Mexican cadet and the Royalist silver—stories of local ranchers and farmers, shopkeepers and adventurers, Tejanos and Anglos and Irish and Germans and Dutch, who'd come together to fight for independence against a tyrannical government. Settlers had poured in from the United States, some carefully vetted by Stephen Austin, others immigrating with cheerful disregard of the law, drawn by stories of prosperity and opportunity in the vast new land, and many of them had ended up in what was now Seguin County. Annalisa had been excited to tell their stories.

But today she kept coming up against reminders of the lost silver. Sam Houston's frustration over trying to make a regular army out of his undisciplined band of volunteers took on new meaning when she thought about what he could have done with a fresh infusion of cash. He could have bought equipment and offered good pay to competent officers. A note written by one of Juan Seguín's men in October spoke of the artillery that they planned to buy after the silver came—but the silver never did come. Houston's quartermaster general, the confusingly named Almanzon Huston, wrote to a fellow officer of being stuck in Louisiana, awaiting funds from the provisional government to purchase supplies for the ragtag army. The delay lasted a full month, and it wasn't until early March that Huston was back in Texas, supplying the volunteers—too late to save the defenders of Goliad and the Alamo from slaughter.

By the time Annalisa finished her first cup of coffee, she was feeling as frustrated as General Houston and Colonel Huston combined. She felt as if she were trapped in a maze, constantly retracing her steps to try a fresh route, only to hit another dead end.

She stretched at her desk chair, then stood and took her mug back to the kitchen. While she was there, she checked her phone, which she kept on silent mode in a little drawer whenever she wrote.

She had two unread texts. One was from Javi.

Good morning, beautiful. Hope you have a great day and get pages and pages of writing done. Can't wait until I see you tonight.

She smiled, letting herself linger over the words.

The other message was from Grant, and it was a long one.

Hey, hope you're well. I was talking to a colleague in the history department and she told me about some new acquisitions to the archives. I think you're going to want to see them.

She kept reading. A few lines in, she set down her coffee mug. She scanned quickly through the end of the message, then scrolled back up and slowly reread the whole thing.

Half an hour later, she was dressed in very different clothes with hair and makeup done, driving to Austin.

JAVI STOOD IN front of the tiny mirror in the horse trailer's cramped bathroom, working gel into his damp hair. He was showered and groomed, with his beard neatly trimmed, wearing his best jeans and a nice V-neck sweater—an appropriate look for an evening in with his girlfriend, or at least he hoped so. Annalisa used to give him advice about what to wear on dates, but this time he was on his own.

His stomach rumbled. Annalisa had told him she was making chicken piccata and pasta. After dinner they were going to watch some old movie that she loved, and Javi was going to keep an open mind about it.

Stepping out of the bathroom, he saw Lefty standing there, eyeballing him warily, clearly sensing that something was up.

"Don't worry," said Javi. "You're coming, too. You're invited. We're going to Annalisa's place. You like her, remember? So be a good dog and don't tear up any of her nice things."

Lefty made a scoffing sound, as if to remind Javi that he never tore things up.

"I know," Javi said. "It's just—I really like this girl."

He leaned his shoulder against the doorjamb and stared into space. "I never knew it could be like this, you know? That a woman could know me, really know me the way she does, with all my moods and grudges and faults, and still want me."

Even now it didn't seem possible. He kept thinking it was all a dream, and any second now he would wake up and it would be over—or Annalisa would come to her senses and realize that Javi wasn't such a prize after all and that she'd been foolish to have a crush on him all those years. But it hadn't happened so far, and she'd known him too long to have any illusions about him. It gave him hope, that he could be more than he was, that he had it in him somehow. Annalisa thought he did, and she was the smartest person he knew.

"I don't want to let her down," he said. "I can't let her down."

Lefty sat on his haunches and cocked his head, his ears sticking up unevenly.

Javi glanced at the clock. "We'd better hit it. We've got a couple of stops to make along the way. Let's go find your leash."

Lefty turned his gaze to his leash, hanging from its hook by the door. Javi took it down and crouched in front of his dog.

"I love her," he said—quietly, as if someone might overhear. "But it's too soon to tell her that, right? We've only been together for a few days. We've known each other all our lives, though—but as friends, not romantically. I mean, the smart thing to do would be to take things slow, right? Slow and steady. Give it time."

Lefty nuzzled the hand that held the leash and gave a muffled woof.

"Yeah, you're right," said Javi. "We need to get going."

He clipped the leash to Lefty's collar, and they headed out.

Their first stop was Tito's Bar. Javi walked straight to the back, where his brother was executing a perfect pour of craft beer into a pint glass.

"Have you got it?" Javi asked.

Tito didn't even look up. "Hello to you, too. Hold on a second. I'm in the middle of something."

Javi glanced at his watch. Lefty sat close to him, his rear resting on Javi's boot, and cast a suspicious eye over the room.

Tito served the beer, reached under the bar and took out a bottle of wine. "Here you are. A nice full-bodied rosé. Should pair perfectly with chicken piccata."

"Thanks," said Javi. "I owe you one."

"Yeah, you do owe me one. Will that be cash or credit?"

Javi took out his wallet and paid.

"You should bring her flowers, too," Tito said.

"Bouquet's ready and waiting at Hager's Flower Shop," Javi replied. "I'll pick it up on the way."

Tito's eyebrows lifted. "All right, then. I guess you'd better get to it."

A few minutes later, bouquet in one hand, Lefty's leash in the other, with the bottle of wine tucked under his arm, Javi climbed the steps to Annalisa's apartment and banged the lion's head knocker.

"Come in! It's unlocked."

Javi opened the door. Something sizzled in the kitchen, giving off an aroma that made him breathe deep. Lefty sniffed it, too.

Annalisa stood at the stove, turning some golden-brown chicken pieces with a fork. She was dressed for the office, in black pants and a sleek sweater, with her hair twisted high on her head.

"You look very paralegalish," he said. "I thought Claudia gave you the day off."

"She did, but I ended up going to Austin. I just got back a little while ago."

She poured some liquid from a measuring cup into the pan, covered it, turned down the heat and set the timer. Then she hurried over and gave Javi a quick kiss and Lefty an even quicker scratch behind the ears.

"I'll change clothes while it's simmering," she said. "Be right back."

While she was away, Javi set the wine bottle on the counter, unhooked Lefty's leash and wandered slowly around, still holding the flowers. A salad in a glass bowl stood on the kitchen bar, looking freshly tossed, glistening with dressing and flecked with pepper and Parmesan cheese. The table was set with gold-rimmed china, wineglasses and cloth napkins. Both the dining and living rooms had lots of dark wood and lush fabrics—formal, but at the same time very comfortable-looking.

Lefty took his own route around the room, sniffing along the baseboards.

The door opened and Annalisa came out, now wearing a long scoop-necked sweater and dark stretchy pants that made her legs go on forever. Her hair was down, tumbling over her shoulders in deep waves.

She came back to Javi and gave him a longer kiss. He plunged his hand into that thick mass of hair and held the back of her head in his palm. Their lips had just parted when the kitchen timer went off.

They laughed. Annalisa took the flowers and headed to the kitchen.

"Want me to do anything?" Javi asked.

"You can pour the wine," she answered. "I'll just put these in water and whisk some more butter into the sauce."

Within a few minutes, food and flowers were on the table, and they were seated.

The food was so good. Javi could have wolfed it down in about three minutes flat, but he made himself go slowly, savoring every bite.

"Why'd you go to Austin today?" he asked.

"To look at some documents. The university has that reading room at the Center for American History. They just got some new papers added to the archives. Grant told me about them this morning."

"Oh, yeah? Nice of him to let you know."

"Yes. He knew I would be interested. He has a friend in the history department who's aware of my research and thought the new document would be relevant."

"Is it?"

"Very much so. It's an eyewitness account, written in 1868 by a woman who'd lived through the Texas Revolution."

"What made her do that, thirty years after the fact?"

"Well, the Civil War had ended just a few years earlier, and evidently she suddenly realized that she'd lived through two wars and wasn't getting any younger and ought to get all her recollections on paper before she was gone."

Annalisa set down her fork, clasped her hands and rested her chin on them. "Her name was Clara Monroe. She lived in this area at the time of the revolution but later moved to North Texas. Her memory of places was a little fuzzy in spots, but good enough for me to consider her a reliable source."

"So what exactly did Clara Monroe have to say for herself?"

"Plenty. But the thing that interested me the most was that she claimed she saw a Spanish-speaking man shot for desertion, executed by firing squad, by a Mexican infantry detachment, in the barnyard of her family's ranch."

"Whoa! Did she know who the guy was?"

"She said she'd never seen him before. He was dressed in a plain linen shirt and trousers that didn't fit him well, so if he *was* in the army, he'd ditched his uniform somewhere. The Mexican lieutenant that led the detachment had somehow tracked him to the Monroe farm and found him hiding in a smokehouse. The lieutenant tied the man to a post with his back to a stone wall, lined up five soldiers all aiming at his heart and ordered them to fire."

"Dang. That would do it."

"You would think, but the man survived, at least for a little while. He was horribly wounded, of course. The merciful thing to do would be to finish him off with a point-blank shot to the head. But the lieutenant left him to suffer and bleed out. He and his men made off with most of the Monroes' poultry and one of their steers and rode away. Clara tried to help the guy. He was a young man, she said, with the look of a gentleman. He actually lingered for almost an hour."

"Any last words?"

"Yes. He kept raving about his cousin—*mi primo Cerebro*."

"Seriously?"

"That's what Clara said. He also begged her to tell his cousin that the silver was in the soldiers' pit."

Javi frowned. "What does that mean? What soldiers' pit?"

"I don't know. Clara didn't know, either, but she never forgot what he said. Oh, and there's more. I cross-referenced Clara's account with some records from the Archivo General de Mexico that's kept at UT. Turns out there was a report of a young Mexican cadet who secretly broke away from a relief column headed to Béxar. He took three mules with him. The report said he was eventually tracked to somewhere north of Cibolo Creek and shot for desertion on December 12. Somewhere north of Cibolo Creek could admittedly be a lot of places, but present-day Seguin County is one of them."

"Did it say the cadet's name?"

She smiled triumphantly. "Gabriel Antonio Ramirez."

"Well, that's got to be him, right? Alejandro's cousin?"

"It certainly looks that way. He took the silver to Texas, just like he said he would."

"Then where is the silver now?"

She shook her head. "I don't know. The relief column was on its way to Béxar. Maybe he hid the silver in a pit near one of the places where they camped?"

"But in that case, why leave the relief column at all?" asked Javi. "And why take the mules?"

"I don't know. It doesn't make sense. Unless… Javi, what if he hid the silver in a trash pit near a *Texian* soldiers' camp? Not a camp they were currently using, but an old camp?"

"Yeah, that might make sense, if he knew he was being tracked and didn't think he could escape being captured. Were the mules with him when he was taken?"

"No."

"Then maybe he temporarily ditched the silver and the mules so he could travel quicker on horseback and find a good place to hide."

"Only he got captured anyway. But he didn't give up the goods. Of course, the lieutenant who was chasing him wouldn't have known about the silver. From his point of view, it would have looked like he just made off with some food or supplies."

"But an old camp," said Javi. "That could be anywhere. It's not like there are historical markers that say, 'Soldiers camped here once and disposed of their trash in this pit.' He didn't give any other clues?"

"No. And we have to remember that Clara Monroe was remembering something from thirty years ago. She could have gotten the details wrong."

"Maybe. But if a runaway soldier showed up on my land and got shot by firing squad, I think the details would stay pretty clear in my mind."

"Yeah, me, too. Oh, this is maddening! Gabriel got the silver out of Mexico all right, but I'm no closer to learning where he hid it, or where it is now, than when I started. Alejandro never knew, because he was already dead at the Battle of Béxar. Romelia never knew, either, because Clara couldn't tell her, because Gabriel didn't say his cousin's name. Gabriel was the only one who knew, and he can't tell us."

He reached his hand across the table, and she took it.

"Well, you've got a lot more to go on than you did. Heck, a few months back you didn't know anything about Gabriel or the lost silver. Now you've got tons of information. I can't even begin to tell you how proud I am of you. A lot of people can get an idea for a book, or talk about writing a book, but hardly any of them follow through. You did the research and the work, and when you're finished you'll put it all out there for the whole world to see. It takes a lot of guts."

She smiled and squeezed his hand. "Thank you. I think the same thing about entrepreneurs like you. Hanging out your shingle, putting your name above the door, investing in equipment, jumping through hoops of permits and regulation—it's all a giant leap into the unknown, with no guarantee for success. It's incredibly brave."

"I guess you're right," he said. "I guess we're both pretty brave. And I have a feeling we're both going to make it."

They finished their dinner, and Javi helped clean up, and then they settled onto the sofa together and watched the old movie, which turned out to be surprisingly good. But even as he chuckled at the witty dialogue and softly stroked Annalisa's long black hair, part of his mind was worrying over a problem.

What Annalisa had said about the risk involved in starting a business hadn't been wrong. He'd always said he wasn't afraid of hard work, but he'd never known just how much administrative stuff would be involved, how many hoops he'd have to jump through and how bad the consequences could be if he got something wrong. If he had, he might not have had the courage to begin. Even at this stage, there was enough bookkeeping and clerical work to keep someone busy for a good twenty hours a week, and that would only increase once the garage had actual customers—assuming they made it to that stage. Javi had given serious thought to hiring a part-time administrative assistant, someone with the skills and experience to do the job right, to free him up to work on cars. But he couldn't justify spending the money. His savings from his work in the oil fields had seemed plenty sufficient four months ago, but they were quickly evaporating, and at some point he was going to have to pay back his small business loan.

Even if he did hire someone to do the office work, it might not be enough. He was on track with the restoration of the Biscayne, but he couldn't afford to spend six months or more on one car. It would help if his dad could work at the garage full-time, but Juan had bills to pay. All the new construction in the area meant plenty of demand for dirt work, and he wasn't ready to walk away from his excavation business in favor of something as speculative as a classic car garage. They might be on the verge of success, or the whole thing might crash and burn.

You had to have money to make money. Javi knew that, and he'd thought he'd had enough to start. Now he wasn't so sure. It would be too awful to come this far and raise everyone's hopes only to fail in the end—especially now, when dreams of marriage and a family were just beginning to raise their hopeful heads.

CHAPTER EIGHTEEN

As ANNALISA WORKED on the first draft of a client's last will and testament Thursday morning, the memory of last night's date with Javi warmed her more effectively than the heat coming through the floor vents in her office.

So much had happened yesterday that it seemed like too much to fit in one day. But then that had been true of a lot of days in her life recently. Not even a full week had passed since Javi had shown up at her door unannounced and told her that he thought of her "in the romance category." Since then, they'd had their first, second and third dates, and made another date for church and Sunday lunch with her parents. It felt as if weeks had gone by instead of days.

She'd lost a day of writing yesterday, but gained so much more from her hours spent in the reading room— an actual declaration of where the silver was hidden, and a confirmation of Gabriel's identity.

But what did it all mean? *The silver is hidden in the soldiers' pit.* Couldn't he have been a little more specific? Probably not. Massive blood loss and imminent death didn't tend to make people especially lucid.

She turned her attention back to the description of the property in the client's will. The property was bounded by Gander Slough Road on the north and by the Serenidad Creek on the south.

She stared for a while at the paragraph on her screen, lingering over the words *Serenidad Creek*. Then she spun her chair around to face the bookcase behind her desk and took out a slender paperback volume—her own book, *Ghost Stories of the Texas Hill Country.*

She opened to the story of Alejandro and Romelia, which had been told to her by Tony and Alex's grandfather, her great-uncle Miguel, who'd heard it from his grandfather, Antonio, who'd heard it from his grandmother, Romelia herself. By now she was deeply familiar with the tale. Alejandro had gone away to fight at the Siege of Béxar, leaving pregnant Romelia behind, and told her he'd be back in time to lay a sprig of esperanza blossoms in the cradle of their unborn child. Alejandro never came home again—at least not as a living man. He was killed at Béxar and buried in a hasty grave far from home. But years later Romelia claimed that he did return, in spirit form, to help fight a fire that threatened to destroy La Escarpa.

The part of the story that held her attention now, though, was the part that told about Alejandro's departure—how he'd left the house and ridden east, toward a bend in the Serenidad, to join the group of Tejano freedom fighters who'd gathered there from their ranchos in the west the evening before. From there they would follow the creek to the river and come at last to San Antonio, where they would join Captain Seguín at the Siege of Béxar.

Annalisa had always assumed that Alejandro had departed from La Escarpa. But now that she thought about it, something about the leave-taking description didn't seem quite right.

She left her office and went out to the long hallway, where filing cabinets lined the wall opposite the office doors. Google Earth was a great tool, but sometimes you needed a physical map. She found the plat for La Escarpa, took it back to her office, spread it out on her desk and studied the aerial view of the ranch where Eliana had grown up.

It took Annalisa a minute to orient herself. The plat was from several years earlier, before the renovations that had increased the footprint of the house. But when she saw the well house and the big barn, everything fell into place. The firepit wasn't on there, of course, but she saw the spot where it would later be built. It was there, just a few months earlier, that she had drunk half a jug of blackberry mead and burned her Javi mementos. She could still see the panoramic display of the ranch. To her left, the sun setting brilliantly behind the horse pasture. To her right, the tree line that marked the Serenidad Creek.

It was as she'd thought. The creek ran north to south at this part of its course, cutting through La Escarpa. The description from Romelia's story of Alejandro's leave-taking didn't fit.

But La Escarpa wasn't the only property Alejandro had owned.

She went back to the file cabinets and took out another plat—the one for the Reyes place, now run by Alex and Lauren.

This ranch was northwest of La Escarpa—and, coincidentally, not far from the property described in the will she'd been drafting. Here, the Serenidad ran northwest to southeast, a suitable course for rancheros traveling from the west to follow.

The Reyes house was on the south side of the creek, roughly 3,000 feet west of a bend in its course. She scanned the space between the house and the creek. If the rancheros had come the evening before, and departed early in the morning with Alejandro, they would have had to make camp somewhere overnight.

She picked up her phone and called Alex.

"Hey, *primo*. Remember what you were telling me the other night at Tito's, about that old vaquero campsite at your place with all the interesting stuff in it? Well, I've been thinking…"

THE NEW TAILLIGHT lenses Javi had ordered for the Biscayne arrived Thursday just before lunch. He took them out of their package and held them in his hands, staring down at the red plastic lenses with their cat's-eye shape, eager as a little kid with a new toy. He wanted to install them right away in their chrome bezels, but decided to wait until the new exterior trim strips arrived so he could put everything on at once and get the full effect. The original door handles and interior knobs hadn't been in too bad of shape, so he'd removed the pitting and flaking, stripped them down and sent them out to be re-chromed. Once the door panels came back from the upholsterer, he'd have everything he needed to finish the interior.

Barring unforeseen disaster, the project should be complete within a few more months, just as he'd planned.

Come spring, he'd take Annalisa out in the Biscayne for rides in the country. Maybe they'd drive it to the city, to San Antonio or Austin, for some fancy high culture event like the symphony or the opera, if he could be sure of a secure parking garage. It was going to be sweet, having the Biscayne up and running at last, more than two decades after he'd first bought it and Carlos had derailed his dreams of fixing it up, along with a whole lot of other dreams. Cruising the open road in his classic Chevrolet, his girl at his side, with everything that had been wrong in the world now made right.

Of course, all this was assuming he was still in business by that time.

The black fog of worry came back, clouding his joy.

He had to hold it together and work his hardest to make his plans into reality. But what if he couldn't? What if his best wasn't enough?

This must be how his father had felt, back when he'd tried to start the business years earlier—hopeful and fearful at the same time. And then that rat Carlos had stepped in and smashed the dream to smithereens.

The familiar surge of anger flooded Javi's face and chest like a wave of suffocating heat. All that money, gone forever. It wasn't right. It wasn't fair.

He stood there a moment, staring down at the new lenses in his hands. Then he laid them on a metal shelf in the garage and went back to work on the Biscayne's alternator, because there wasn't anything else for him to do.

A few minutes later, he heard the newly installed door entry chime give its cheerful little chirp. Someone had just walked into the shop.

"Javi? Are you back there?"

He wiped his hands off on a rag and walked into the front room. Annalisa was there holding a grease-stained paper bag and a cup caddy with two drinks in it.

"Hey, there, beautiful," he said. "Do I smell tacos?"

She held up the bag. "Barbacoa for you, chorizo and potato for me, plus a Dr Pepper and an iced tea."

"Thank you," he said, taking the cup caddy from her. "I didn't even realize I was hungry before, and now I'm drooling. Let's eat in the lounge area."

He set the drinks on the kidney-shaped coffee table and took a seat on the sofa while she took out the foil-wrapped tacos and distributed them. She kicked off her high heels and sat down beside Javi on the sofa.

"Where are Peter and his crew?" she asked. "I thought he was supposed to start work on the office today."

"He was, but his supplies got delayed. He's hoping to be able to get back to it on Monday."

Annalisa unwrapped her first taco and poured green salsa on it. "That's too bad."

"Yeah, I wouldn't have moved everything out of the office if I'd known."

He pointed to the makeshift arrangement of desk and file cabinets, piled with a laptop, a printer and stacks of paper—glaring reminders of the administrative work that he was already behind on. Just looking at it raised his blood pressure.

He was tired of being surrounded by ongoing construction all day, and going home to his cramped living quarters at night. More and more over the past few days, he found himself daydreaming about buying himself a little place in the country. Not too far out, and not too much acreage. Just a bit of land for him to spread out on, with a big garage and workshop, and space for Lefty to run. And maybe, just maybe, room for another person, or two, or three.

It was too soon to think like that. He wouldn't be in a position to buy any more real estate until the business was turning a good steady profit. And even if he'd been flush with cash, it was way too early in his relationship with Annalisa to start talking about their future. But he couldn't help it. He'd been on his own long enough. He wanted a home, a wife, a family—wanted them desperately. At times he could almost believe they were within reach, but maybe he was fooling himself. He was balancing on a knife's edge, trying to keep from falling.

They chewed and swallowed for a while. Then Javi asked, "Any breakthroughs with the lost silver yet?"

"Maybe," said Annalisa, and she took a drink of tea.

"Seriously? Tell me."

"Remember Sunday evening, when we saw Tony and Alex at Tito's Bar?" she asked.

"Yeah," said Javi, trying not to show the prickle of irritation he felt at the mention of the names of Carlos Reyes's sons.

She turned and faced him on the sofa. "Well, Alex was telling me about this spot on his ranch where the vaqueros used to camp overnight during calving season. There's a pit nearby that they used as a trash dump. He's found some interesting stuff there—knives and spurs, cooking equipment, a 1932 penny. And I got to thinking. If it was a good camping spot during the 1930s, it was probably a good camping spot during the 1830s, too. The land hasn't changed all that much in the past two hundred years. It's been in the same family all that time, and they've always used it for ranching. I took a fresh look at Romelia's account of the day Alejandro left to join the Siege of Béxar, and it sounds as if he left from the Reyes place and not La Escarpa. Some other Tejanos had come over the night before from ranchos in the west, and it seems reasonable that they would have camped somewhere on Alejandro's property. What if they camped in or around that same spot? It would have been October when they made their camp. There might well have been traces left when Gabriel came with the silver two months later. It makes sense that he would want to hide the silver on land that belonged to his cousin. So I thought…maybe…"

The smile that had been on her face when she'd started talking had faded by now, along with the excitement in her voice, until the words trailed away and stopped. Javi couldn't see his own face, but he could feel the stiff set of his jaw and the sharp stab of anger that always pierced him at the mere thought of any of the Reyes family.

"So the silver's on Reyes land," he said. "Lucky them."

Annalisa folded her foil packet around the remains of her taco. "Are you mad?"

"No. Not at you. It just—it doesn't seem fair, that's all."

"Fair how?"

He twitched a shoulder in a half shrug. "The rich getting richer, while the poor keep slogging along trying to keep their heads above water."

"Javi, Tony and Alex are not rich. And you're not exactly poor. You own a very desirable downtown property, and a business that's just about to take off."

"Yeah, that I bought with money I earned, working long hard hours under the hot sun."

And that could still fail.

"Alex and Tony work hard, too! Ranching is a very demanding occupation. So is construction."

"Well, nobody starts with nothing. And they started out with money their crook of a father stole from my family."

"Okay, now *that's* not fair, and you know it. Alex and Tony suffered as much as anybody in this town from their father's scheming ways. Maybe more."

"More than my family?"

"It's not a contest!"

"My experience has taught me otherwise."

She stared at him. "Javi, listen to yourself. You sound like a bitter, angry man. Have you been so warped by what happened that you can't see things properly anymore? Your mom and dad wouldn't be like this. They'd be happy for Tony and Alex."

"Yeah, you're right. I'm not as good as they are. I'm not as good as *you*, or as good as Grant."

Her mouth opened in a silent O. "That's a low blow. You're being ridiculous, Javi. I have stood by you, I have sympathized, I have been more than patient. But this is too much. If your grudge against Carlos and everyone connected to him means more to you than I do…then it's a good thing I'm finding it out now."

He sat up straight. "Wait. Are you breaking up with me?"

Her chin trembled. "I don't know. But I think I'd better go now. If you want me, I'll be at the Reyes place. I'm taking the afternoon off to help my cousins."

She sat up and slipped her high-heeled shoes back on. She had her head bent so he couldn't see her face.

"Annalisa," he said.

His voice sounded strange in his own ears, shaky and hollow. She paused for a moment, long enough to give Lefty a pat on the shoulder, before standing and walking out the door.

JAVI SAT WHERE she'd left him with the taco wrappers and the paper bag and the drinks. At his feet, Lefty lay on his stomach with his front legs out like a sphinx, staring after her with his head cocked and his ears sticking out unevenly.

Well, she'd done it. She'd gotten up and walked out. Not half an hour earlier he'd been wondering how long he needed to wait to ask her to marry him, and now it was all over. He should have known. He was an idiot to ever think it could work between the two of them—sweet, high-minded, idealistic Annalisa and, well, him.

He should go after her, or call her. Tell her she was right and he was wrong. That he wasn't going to be bitter anymore. But could he say it and mean it? He'd been carrying this grudge for a long time. It had put a fire in his belly, pushing him to keep working and not give up. If he didn't have that, then he didn't know who he was anymore.

He gathered up the remains of their lunch and threw

them in the trash. Then he went back to the garage and started working on the alternator again.

He'd only been at it five minutes or so when the front door gave another cheerful chirp. For an instant Javi's heart leaped with the wild hope that Annalisa had come back. Then he heard the big booming voice calling out from the front room.

"Hey, *mijo*! You in there?"

"Back here, Dad."

His father's footsteps thumped back to the garage. Juan appeared, holding a box. "I picked up the mirrors and door handles from the place that does the chrome plating."

"Thanks. You can set them on that shelf back there."

Juan put the box on the shelf. "Don't forget the Christmas party next week. You're going to be there, right? You and Annalisa?"

"I don't know."

"What do you mean you don't know?"

"I mean I don't know. I think she might have just broken up with me."

He hadn't meant to say that. It just came out.

Juan turned and looked at his son, his usual grin gone. "What did you do?"

Javi bristled. "What makes you so sure it was my fault?"

His father made a scoffing noise. "Oh, come on. Tell me what happened. Here, come sit down."

Javi let himself be led to a chair. He felt very tired all of a sudden.

"Well, you know that thing she's been working on, the new book about Seguin County in the Texas Revolution? She's been researching all these old diaries and things, and she found out about a cadet in the Mexican army who was plotting to switch sides and bring over a load of silver. But she didn't know whether the guy actually did it, and if so, what ever happened to the silver. Yesterday she saw some different old documents that show that the cadet did bring the silver to this area and that he hid it somewhere, but he died before he could make it clear where the hiding place was. Now she thinks she's figured out where the lost silver is. She thinks it's on the old Reyes place."

Juan let out a low whistle. "Wow. What if it is? What happens then? Do they get to keep it or sell it or whatever?"

"Yes. That's the law on treasure in the state of Texas."

"Well, how 'bout that? I never knew they had laws about treasure ownership, but I guess lawmakers have to cover all their bases. But what does this have to do with you and your girl?"

Javi let out an impatient sigh. "If the silver is on the Reyes land, Tony and Alex are going to get a lot of money."

"So?"

"It doesn't bother you?"

"Why should it? It's no skin off my nose."

"But it's wrong. They have so much already. And it *was* a lot of skin off your nose, and my nose, too, when that cheat Carlos—"

"Hold on," said Juan. "Is this about Tony and Alex, or is it about Carlos? Is Carlos going to get the money? Because I don't think he can. His father cut him out of the will and left the ranch directly to the boys."

"But—"

"But nothing. I know Carlos stole from us, but that's not Alex and Tony's fault. Those boys never did me a bit of harm. I like them. If they get themselves a nice little windfall, that doesn't take anything away from me. I've got my own blessings, a lot of them."

"Of course you wouldn't understand," said Javi. "It's always been so easy for you to be happy all the time."

"Easy?" The sharp tone in Juan's voice took Javi by

surprise. "*Easy?* That was the worst day in my life, when Carlos cleaned out our business account. But there was nothing I could do about it, and being angry didn't change anything. I had a lot to be thankful for. I had your mother. She never said a word of blame to me, never said I told you so, although she could have, because she did tell me so. I had you boys. I had my health, and a roof over my head, and tools and skills that I could use to earn a living. I was better off than most of the people in this world."

Javi didn't answer.

"You know what your problem is?" his father asked.

"I'm sure you're going to tell me."

"You're a fighter. I knew you were a fighter from the moment you were born. You let out a squall like one of those screaming goats and you didn't stop for two hours. You came into this world with a chip on your shoulder, and ever since then you've been daring people to knock it off. It's not always bad, being a fighter. It's actually one of the things I like best about you. You always stick up for your family, and you work your tail off to take care of people. But sometimes you get in your own way. Everything isn't a fight, Javier. Everything isn't a competition. And there are some things more important than winning."

Still Javi didn't speak. He sat with his head bowed, elbows resting on his thighs, hands clenched tightly together. His throat felt funny and his eyes were hot.

After a long time he raised his head, sniffed and blinked rapidly. Juan pretended not to notice.

"Hey, Dad," he said. "Do you still have that goofy-looking metal detector?"

His father narrowed his eyes. "Goofy-looking? I'll have you know that's the most powerful metal detector money can buy. I've found all kinds of stuff with that thing on job sites. It can detect large objects to a depth of one and a half meters, and it's waterproof and fully submersible."

"I don't want to submerge it. I just want to borrow it for the afternoon. Can I?"

Juan grinned. "Only if I get to come along."

Javi stuck out his hand. "Deal."

CHAPTER NINETEEN

"LET'S SEE," mused Tony. "If I were a bunch of Royalist silver, where would I be?"

"The real question is, if I were a nineteenth-century Mexican turncoat with a load of silver to hide, where would I hide it?" Alex replied.

"It comes down to the same thing," said Tony.

They were standing on a flat, dry, treeless space, conveniently close to the creek, with room for tents and campfires, and elevated enough to offer visibility.

Annalisa had gone home from Javi's shop and changed into jeans, a sweatshirt and boots before coming here. She'd switched out her jeweled hair clip for a more rugged and practical one. She was ready to help. She wished they could start digging right away, but Tony and Alex favored a more methodical approach that didn't waste effort.

The pit wasn't as pit-like as she'd expected. It was shallow, like a bowl.

"I've been using my magnetic nail sweeper out here," Alex told her. "That's good for any ferrous metals—iron, nickel, cobalt and some types of steel. Not so good for silver."

"Do you think the guy would have dug a hole and buried it?" Tony asked. "It's not like he'd be carrying a big spade around with him. Maybe he just put it in a low spot on the ground, covered it with a rock and called it good."

They flipped over several large rocks and dug at the ground underneath for a bit. No luck.

"What we need is a really good metal detector," said Alex. "It's no use digging random holes. We need to locate the silver first, then dig. Once we know where it is, we'll know what equipment to bring. Depending on how deep it is, we might want to use a tractor attachment to dig. We might have to cut through tree roots."

All this was assuming the silver was out here at all.

It has to be here, Annalisa thought. It would be too awful if that whole stupid fight with Javi turned out to be for nothing.

On the other hand, if she wasn't worth more to him than a pointless old grudge, it was better to find out now than further down the road.

It was cold comfort. She was already in deep. This wasn't some brand-new romantic attraction. It wasn't light or momentary. It was one of the facts of her life. And she couldn't give it up just by willing herself to do so. The past several months had taught her that.

This was worse, far worse, than all those years of loving Javi with no return. She'd come so close, only to watch it slip away. He cared about her, but not enough.

Alex was watching her. "You're awfully quiet," he said.

She shrugged. "I don't have anything to contribute."

She didn't even know what she was doing here. She wasn't any use. She'd tried to dig, poking the cutting edge of the spade into the stony ground, balancing both feet on the shoulders of the blade and then sort of hopping up and down on it, but the blade hadn't budged, and Tony had kindly taken the spade away from her and done the digging himself. If there was digging to be done, her brawny cousins were more than capable of handling it without her.

But she'd wanted to be here, if only to avoid being alone with her thoughts.

Tony's phone went off. He answered with, "This is Tony."

He listened a moment, then rattled off four digits that Annalisa recognized as the gate code.

"Yeah, drive on toward the house and turn left just past the big cactus clump," he said. "Then follow that roadbed toward the creek. You can't miss us… All right, see you in a bit. Thanks for coming out."

"Who was that?" Alex asked as Tony returned his phone to his back pocket.

"Mr. Mendoza," Tony replied. "He's coming to help look for the silver."

"Oh, good," said Alex.

Annalisa's heart gave a great painful throb. It would have been natural enough for the Reyes brothers to ask for Mr. Mendoza's help, and just as natural for Mr. Mendoza to accept. His years of experience in dirt work would be a definite plus, as would his earth-moving equipment, and he was always eager to lend a hand in any outdoor project, the stranger the better.

But it didn't sound as if they had asked him. It sounded more like he had just shown up. How had he even found out that the lost silver might be here, and that a search was underway right now? Annalisa hadn't told him. But she had told his son.

Don't get your hopes up, she told herself—just as she'd been telling herself day after day since she was old enough to notice Javi, and to wish he'd notice her.

Here came the truck, rolling down the caliche roadbed, raising clouds of white dust.

"That doesn't look like Mr. M's truck," said Tony.

"Yeah, you're right," said Alex. "Who do we know that drives a green Silverado?"

"Javi," Annalisa said. "That's Javi's truck."

As HE HEADED down the packed gravel roadbed at the Reyes ranch, Javi looked around with interest. He'd never actually been here before. Tony and Alex hadn't lived here as kids, though he knew they'd spent a lot of time here with their grandparents. They'd lived in town, not far from the house where Javi had grown up. They were younger than he was, around Annalisa's age, but they weren't bad little kids, and he'd tolerated their presence in neighborhood games, at least until the year that had changed everything.

He thought about that horrible time after the loss of the money—his parents' shock and disbelief, their desperation to find some way to recover what had been taken from them, and the gradual grim realization that there was nothing to be done, no law that could help them, that the business was not going to happen and neither was the new house. But he'd had the same thought so many times that it was like a rut in his mind, spinning his wheels, going nowhere.

So he thought instead of what it must have been like for Tony and Alex, knowing their dad was a gambler and a swindler and a thief. As rough as things had been at times for Javi, some things had stayed solid and dependable. His father would still get up every morning before dawn with a smile on his face and put in a full day's manual labor to support them all. His mother would still cook and bake in the tiny kitchen, for her own family and anyone else who might be in need of comfort or aid, and make decorations for party after party. After all, they did have a lot to celebrate.

He saw the Reyes brothers now, walking around with

their hands on their hips, kicking at tufts of grass. Apparently the search for the lost silver wasn't going well.

And there was Annalisa, standing a little apart from them, watching his truck as it drew near.

His mouth went dry as he remembered the last words they'd exchanged. What would she say, how would she act, now that he was here, hat in hand? He wanted things between them to be good again—not like in the old days, when she was stuck on him and he was too dense to do anything about it, but like they had been this past week, when he wasn't some out-of-reach crush, but a real live man, sometimes clueless and rash, but willing to do better.

He parked the truck and turned off the ignition. Juan, who had been uncharacteristically silent during the drive here, now turned to Javi and put a rough hand on his shoulder.

"It's gonna be okay," his father said.

Then Juan opened the passenger door and stepped out.

By now Tony and Alex had walked over to meet them. Annalisa held back, a few yards off. Javi took a deep breath and got out of his truck.

"The cavalry has arrived," Juan bellowed with all his usual bluster. "Stand aside and let the pro handle this. That treasure will be found in no time."

Tony laughed. "Thanks for coming, Mr. M. Hey, Javi. Thanks for coming."

"Yeah, thanks," said Alex. "We need all the help we can get."

If they were at all surprised to see him there, they didn't let on. They acted as if it were perfectly natural for Javi to show up and lend a hand. Memories crowded Javi's mind, of every time he'd been cold to them, thinking himself the offended party, as if he had a right to be standoffish.

"No problem," he said. He glanced at Annalisa and

added, "I've got to help my girl with her research. She's breaking new ground in Texas history."

Annalisa's face blossomed into a smile, and her eyes filled with tears.

"Breaking ground is my specialty," said Juan as he lifted his metal detector from the truck bed. "Feast your eyes on the Minelab Equinox 800. This bad boy has led me to lost keys, lost earrings, old coins, old chains, plow-shares and more nails than I can count. Its Multi-IQ simultaneous multifrequency engine operates across the full spectrum all at once for maximum results. It can sense ferrous and nonferrous metals, including gold and silver, and it can detect to a depth of one and a half meters. It even has Bluetooth."

Javi walked over to Annalisa. "I'm sorry," he said. "I was wrong."

Her only response was to put her arms around him and hold him tight. It was the only response he needed or wanted.

An hour later, they had nothing to show for their efforts but a chipped enamel coffeepot, a belt buckle and two battered horseshoes. Even Juan's optimism was starting to wear thin. He tried everywhere, including a massive sprawling mesquite tree with a fold in its trunk that looked as if it might have offered a decent hiding place for the silver at one time and then grown around it in the century since. No luck.

"You want to sit down?" Javi asked.

"Sure," Annalisa replied.

They found a big sandstone that made a pretty good bench. Since Javi's arrival, they hadn't had much opportunity to be alone together. He took her hand and laced their fingers together.

She let out a sigh. "Well, looks like my big idea was a bust. I feel terrible for getting everyone's hopes up."

"Alex and Tony don't seem too disappointed," said Javi. "They're really good guys. I missed out by not being friends with them before."

She smiled at him. "You're a terrific boyfriend, you know that?"

"I'm glad you think so."

Her smile faded. "I guess it was always a shot in the dark, thinking the silver was here. It's not like I had a lot to go on. But I wanted to believe that it was real and we could find it. And when I read that account from Clara, I put it together with what Alex said about the pit at the campsite, and it seemed to fit. But maybe that was just because I wanted it to."

"What was it that Gabriel told Clara Monroe, again?"

"*La plata está en el foso de los guerros.* Clara wasn't a native Spanish speaker, but she knew a few words, and she said she never forgot what Gabriel said. I guess it would make a pretty big impression, seeing someone executed by firing squad and then witnessing his dying words."

"And she didn't do anything about it? Like try to find the silver for herself?"

"Well, to be fair, she had a lot of other things going on at the time, with a war being fought close to home and a dead stranger to bury. And she had no reason to think he was talking about silver bars. She actually seemed to think he was talking about silverware. He might have been, for all I know. Or she might have misheard him completely. He might have said *flauta en posta* and been talking about a flute in a post chaise. At this point, who knows?"

"Silver bars? I didn't realize they were bars. I was envisioning coins."

"It might have been coins. But bars would be easier to transport."

"Yeah, I guess that's true."

He thought about that. "So *guerros* means soldiers, huh? I didn't know that. Of course, my grasp of the Spanish language probably isn't that much better than Clara's."

"The meaning of *guerros* is closer to *warriors*," Annalisa said. "*Guerra* means *war*, so you can see the connection."

"In Alejandro's letter, though, he used the word *soldados*."

"Yes, he did. That does seem like a more natural word choice."

"What about this word *foso*? What does that mean?"

"Like a hole in the ground, or a ditch, or a pit. Pretty vague, I know. I guess my mind just made an association between Gabriel's *foso* and the sinkhole by the campsite that Alex mentioned. It's interesting all the shades of meaning there are with words. *Hoyo* means a pit, too, or a pockmark, or a grave. And *pozo* can mean a pit, a cesspool, or a well."

Javi let the words, their sounds and meanings, wander around his mind. *Foso* sounded a lot like *pozo*. And *guerro* sounded a lot like...

Suddenly everything came together in a thought so wonderful, so perfect, and yet so improbable, that for a moment he couldn't breathe.

"I need to go to town," he said. "There's something I need to check."

She turned and looked at him. "Right now?"

"Right now."

"Okay. Do you want me to come with you? I don't think my ongoing presence here is going to make or break the search for the silver."

He stared back at her. He didn't want to tell her yet. He could be wrong. He probably was wrong. The whole thing was too outrageous to be true. But more outrageous things had happened, like Annalisa caring about him.

"I do," he said at last. "I want you to come. But will you do something for me? Don't ask me any questions about where we're going or why. I have an idea, but I don't want to say it out loud, because I might be wrong."

A slow smile spread across her face. "Sounds intriguing. All right, I'm in."

The others barely took note of their leaving. Javi simply told them he and Annalisa were going to make a trip to town. Juan didn't notice at all. He had his headphones on and was operating his metal detector in the creek bed.

They drove in silence. Annalisa didn't say anything, not when Javi parked the truck at The Property, or when he led her to the old well and took the cover off, or even when he lowered himself down with his feet braced against the rough stones inside the shaft. They'd done all this before, that day with Grant. But Javi hadn't known then what he was looking for.

He reached the bottom. The dry leaf litter crunched beneath his boots.

"Be careful," Annalisa's voice called from overhead, echoing off the stones. "Watch out for snakes."

Javi didn't look up. His eyes were fixed on the stones that made up the interior of the well. Mostly limestone, from the looks of them, oblong in shape, a lot like russet potatoes, only bigger. But right about at Javi's eye level were several that were more regular, and of similar size to each other—roughly brick-sized, but with rounded corners. They weren't all in a clump together, but spread around in an attempt to look random. Like the other stones, they were whitish, but with more of a grayish cast than the pale gold limestone, almost as if they'd been smeared with mortar.

Javi took his knife out of his pocket and opened the blade. Carefully he pulled the blade across the surface of one of the brick-sized stones.

The coarse gray coating came off in a flake, revealing a whitish gleam underneath.

Javi's whoop careened off the stone walls.

"I DON'T UNDERSTAND," said Mr. Mendoza. "I thought you said the silver was in the soldiers' pit."

He'd come to The Property right away, along with Tony and Alex, in Alex's truck. Now he looked dazed, like a small child just waking up from a nap.

"That's what I thought," Annalisa said. "*La plata está en el foso de los guerros.* Those are the words Clara thought he said. But what he must have actually said is *La plata está en el poso del guero*—in the white guy's well. *Guero* was a code name or nickname for Otto Friesenhahn. He knew about the plan for Gabriel to defect and bring the silver, and Gabriel would have reached his farm on his way to Alejandro's, after he broke away from the supply train. So Gabriel stopped there—but Otto Friesenhahn wasn't home, and Gabriel didn't know who else he could trust. A man in a Mexican infantry uniform would be pretty conspicuous, and he must have assumed that his disappearance had been noticed by now and that he was being tracked. So he took some clothing off the line, wrapped his uniform around his cartridge box and stowed the bundle at the bottom of Otto's feed bin. Then he took the saddlebags off the mules, turned the mules loose and took the saddlebags down the well with him. The well must have still been under construction, with stones and mortar down the shaft ready to use. So he just worked the silver bars into the masonry and covered them with mortar."

"That couldn't have been easy," added Tony, who'd been busily scrolling his phone screen. "It says here that a silver ingot weighs sixty-two and a half pounds."

"That's almost twice the weight of my dog," said Javi.

"But it was a great hiding place," Annalisa went on. "No one ever suspected a thing, not even the well-digger—until Javi figured it out."

"How many ingots did you say were down there?" asked Alex.

"Six that I could see," said Javi.

"That sounds about right," said Annalisa. "Two per mule, one in each saddlebag."

"Whoa," said Tony, still reading from his phone screen. "I don't know the exact current value of silver, Mr. M, but you're looking at six figures, easy."

Alex clapped a hand onto Mr. Mendoza's shoulder. "Congratulations, Mr. Mendoza. It couldn't have happened to a nicer guy."

"You hear that, Dad?" asked Javi. "You're a rich man. What are you going to do with the money?"

The dazed expression faded from Mr. Mendoza's face, replaced by a wide grin. "I'm going to throw a party," he said.

CHAPTER TWENTY

WAY BACK WHEN the Mendozas had first bought The Property, they'd held a cookout there to celebrate. Twenty-three years later, the Mendozas' party in celebration of finding the lost treasure was a bit more elaborate, with food provided by Lalo's Kitchen, beer provided by Tito's Bar and outdoor furniture borrowed from the fire department, but it had the same casual, cozy, impromptu feel as the earlier party. Tito had made an upbeat playlist for the occasion and set up speakers on the old concrete slab.

The unbuilt house wasn't going to remain unbuilt for much longer. Peter Longwood had already come out to view the property and taken lots of notes. Construction would start as soon as the details were squared away.

The weather was a little nippy today, but the food was hot, and there were portable heaters set up inside the metal barn.

"This is all on you, you know," Annalisa said to Javi. "You're the one who figured out where the silver was."

The two of them were walking around The Property, leading Lefty on a leash. The spotted blue dog wasn't thrilled about being around so many people, but he was getting better. Javi had decided it was high time his dog was socialized.

"That was just a lucky guess," Javi replied. "You're the one who did all the work that showed that there was any silver to find."

"I didn't know what it all meant, though. And you never would have been around to make the lucky guess if you hadn't shown up at the Reyes place to help look for the treasure."

Javi shrugged. "I don't deserve praise for being a decent human being. I only wish it hadn't taken me so long to bury the hatchet."

He felt as if he'd been carrying a heavy weight around for most of his life, and now it had come off and rolled away, and he was standing up with his back straight, looking up at the sky.

"Was it just my imagination," he asked, "or is Claudia suddenly wearing a diamond on her left hand?"

Annalisa smiled. "It's not your imagination. She and Peter are engaged."

"Good for them. Did Peter do one of those fancy event-type proposals, like Luke did with Eliana?"

"He just asked, and she said yes. They're both pretty down-to-earth people, and I think they just wanted it settled so they could move on to the wedding."

He nodded, filing the information away. He wished he knew what her own preference was. Did she want a fancy proposal full of photo ops, like Eliana? Or a no-frills, let's-just-get-it-settled proposal like Claudia? He could ask her, but that would be like asking whether she wanted a surprise party for her birthday, or a regular party that she knew about all along. He'd find out her preference all right, but the surprise, if that was what she wanted, would be pretty hard to pull off after that.

Knowing her, though, even if he did plan some elaborate surprise without asking her first if she wanted one, she'd probably figure it out anyway.

But he was getting ahead of himself. He hadn't even told her he loved her yet.

He stopped in his tracks. Lefty stopped, too, and sat down. Annalisa turned to face Javi.

"I love you," he said.

The smile on her face made his heart swell up until it felt too tight for his chest.

"Oh, Javi," she said. "I love you, too. I always have."

"Come here and kiss me, then," he said.

She stepped close to him and laid her hands against his chest. He put his arms around her, drew her to him and lowered his face to hers. Her lips were warm and soft against his, and she smelled sweet.

The kiss ended, but he didn't let her go. "I've been wanting to say that for a long time."

She chuckled. "How long? We've only been together since Saturday."

"Since Saturday, then. I've loved you for longer than that, but it took me a while to figure it out."

"I'm glad you did."

"Me, too."

They resumed their walk, slower now. After a while Javi said, "Dad's turning over the dirt work business to Johnny. He's going to come to the garage and work with me full-time."

"I hoped he would do that. I guess all this cash means he can invest in more equipment and build up some inventory."

"We've already got some inventory coming our way. You know that deal Dad made with Kevin Fox, where Dad and I clear away all the junkers from Kevin's land and get to keep anything valuable that we find? Turns out Kevin's got a '57 Thunderbird convertible with a hardtop sitting there, and it's not in quite as terrible of shape as you would think, though it's going to need a lot of work, of course."

"Of course. But the work is half the fun, isn't it? What

a great find. The '57 was the last year of the first-generation T-Birds, wasn't it? Maybe this one will turn out to be one of the supercharged 312s with the McCulloch-Paxton blower."

"Maybe, but there were only 212 of those ever made, less than one percent of the '57 production run. It would be something else if one of them turned out to be rusting away in an overgrown field at Kevin Fox's house."

"Stranger things have happened," said Annalisa.

It was true. Stranger things had definitely happened.

They completed their circuit of The Property and walked into the big metal barn, where the horse trailer was parked. Roque Fidalgo was there, describing the trailer's shoebox-sized living quarters to some people Javi didn't know.

"I lived in there for a whole year," Roque said in his New Jersey accent. "Never suspected there was a small fortune in silver stowed away not a hundred yards from where I was laying my head at night."

"How do you think I feel?" Juan called out.

Javi chuckled.

"You look happy," Annalisa said to Javi.

"I am," he said.

He was still discovering the truth of what his father had said that day at the garage, about how blessed he was—not just with the silver, but with his family, his friends, his community and the woman beside him. He didn't deserve any of it. Being thankful was the least he could do. He only wished it hadn't taken him so long to realize it.

He knew he couldn't actually propose right now. He needed to give Annalisa more time. But his heart was set on her, and that wasn't going to change. She was the one for him. He knew that now. He'd always known, but he'd kept the knowledge pushed back in a corner of his mind until he was ready to be the man she needed and deserved.

He wasn't there yet, not by a long shot. But he was going to try.

"I'm happy, too," said Annalisa. "I don't remember ever being this happy. My new book is finally coming together. I've got a great family and friends. And I finally got my guy."

"Will you marry me?" Javi asked.

She let go of him and looked him in the face. "What did you say?"

"Sorry," he said. "I didn't mean to say that."

Her brow furrowed. "You didn't?"

"I mean, I did, but not yet. It just slipped out. I guess I'm tired of waiting."

A slow smile spread across her face, blossoming into radiance. "So am I," she said. "Yes, I'll marry you."

EPILOGUE

On a cool crisp day in early October, Javi took Annalisa for a drive in the fully restored Biscayne, with a picnic basket in the trunk and Lefty in the back seat.

He drove down long stretches of country road, turning now and then. Annalisa studied his profile. He had his right hand on the wheel and his left arm resting in the rolled-down window's space, right where she could see his titanium wedding band. Like lots of guys who worked with their hands, he also had a silicone wedding band, safe to wear around machinery. His green eyes stared straight ahead with confident purpose, as if he knew exactly where he was going. He still had that brooding look, but he was smiling a little.

Seat belts hadn't been part of the original Biscayne package, but Javi had added them in the restomod, not forgetting one in the middle of the bench seat, in case the passenger wanted to sit close to the driver. More often than not, the passenger did.

She laid her head against his shoulder and breathed in the autumnal scents of burning brush and gently decaying foliage coming through the open windows.

"This is my favorite time of year," she said.

He took the wheel in his left hand and put his arm around her. "I know," he said.

"And this is a beautiful area. Look at that farmhouse! I just love perfect little tidy farmhouses, with kitty-corner garages and old metal barns and nice green pastures with just a few good trees to give shade to the cows. I wouldn't want to do the work of a farm or ranch, but I do like looking at a well-run farm or ranch owned by other people."

"It's the best of both worlds," Javi agreed. "I like some space around me. I got used to it in West Texas. But I wouldn't want to be a farmer or a rancher."

"Oh, look at that pretty gate! It looks like a headboard from an old iron bed. I just love that."

"Yeah?" Javi pulled into the entrance and put the car in Park. "It does look pretty nice. Let's see what's on the other side."

She pulled back and stared at him. "We can't just drive onto private property. Besides, the gate will be locked."

"Nope. It's just got a chain looped around holding it to the post. See?"

Before she could protest further, he'd gotten out of the car. He unwrapped the chain, swung the gate open and used the chain to secure it to another post alongside the driveway. Then he got back in the car and put it in Drive again.

Annalisa looked around nervously. "Are you sure about this? You don't know what might be back here. The driveway's probably crowded with thorny mesquite trees that'll scratch up your paint job."

"It'll be okay," said Javi, driving through.

She craned her head around to look behind them. "You're not going to leave that gate open, are you? Country people get really mad if you open their gates and don't close them again."

"It'll be fine," Javi said.

By now she could see a house ahead, a dear little farmhouse with a wide front porch liberally decorated with pumpkins and softly twinkling lights. An old-fashioned wrought-iron table stood on the porch, flanked by two matching chairs, with a flickering candle on top.

"Javi," she said. "Did you buy this house?"

He threw his head back and laughed. "You are impossible to surprise, you know that? You are always one step ahead of me, with your uncanny intuition. But in this case you're wrong. I did not buy this house. It is for sale, though."

"And you brought me out here to see it? Because you want to buy it?"

Her voice was high with excitement. He gave her a tender smile as he parked the car in front of the detached garage and turned off the ignition.

"Bingo. I read all the specs online and talked to a Realtor, and I think it would be a good house for us. But we don't have to get it."

"I love it already," said Annalisa. "The porch looks amazing, with the pumpkins and the lights. Did you do that yourself?"

"Heck, no. I got Eliana to do it for me. I figured since you didn't get a fancy proposal, you might enjoy an element of surprise in the house-shopping process. I should have known you'd figure it out."

"Oh, but it's wonderful! Thank you for doing this, Javi."

"You're welcome. But we've hardly gotten started yet. We've still got our picnic."

He took the basket out of the trunk and carried it up the porch steps to the table, with Annalisa holding his hand and Lefty following behind. While Javi unpacked the basket at the table, Annalisa peeked through the front windows of the house. It was too dark to see much. She wanted to wander around the whole house and maybe find an unlocked door, but she made herself sit down at the table.

Lefty sniffed around the front porch a bit before settling down under a front window with his back against the wall.

"The Realtor can show it to us tomorrow if you want," Javi said as he poured the wine.

"I do want. As early as possible."

He smiled. "Done."

The picnic repast was a light one, of the cheese and crackers variety, but it tasted heavenly, and there was plenty to talk about.

After turning the earth-moving business over to Johnny, Juan had started working at the garage full-time. He was currently up to his eyeballs dismantling Curt's Rolls-Royce and loving every minute. Javi had several other restoration jobs lined up with contacts he'd made at the Sip-N-Stroll, as well as maintenance work to do on classic cars in the area. He was also in the process of moving the Thunderbird from Kevin Fox's place to the garage. The infusion of cash from the lost silver had allowed him to buy some new equipment and to hire an administrative assistant. If business continued to thrive, he and Juan might even bring on another mechanic.

Annalisa's book had turned out to be a lot more successful than she'd anticipated. The discovery of Gabriel's sad story and of the lost treasure had brought the past to life. She'd been keeping busy with signings and speaking engagements, and was thinking about future areas of research. Maybe she could focus on the Mexican Revolution next, or the Mexican–American War, or track down Alejandro and Gabriel's ancestors in Mexico and Spain. Maybe she'd just start doing some casual research and see if anything popped.

It was wonderful to sit here with her husband, and count their blessings, and dream about the future.

"The view from this porch is spectacular," she said.

"I agree," said Javi, but he was looking at her.

She squealed and pointed. "Look! Horses, two of them. Aren't they gorgeous?"

Javi turned. "Yes, they are. And they're my favorite kind of horses."

"What kind is that?"

"The kind that belong to someone else."

"That's my favorite kind, too. We get all the fun of looking at them without the bother of taking care of them."

He put a slice of cheese on a cracker. "I can't believe you thought I'd make a major real estate purchase without consulting you."

"You did once," Annalisa retorted.

"Well, yeah. But you weren't my wife then. The place really is okay, though. It needs some work, but Peter can handle it. Now that he's finished one Mendoza house, he's ready to start another."

"How many acres?"

"Five. The rest of the land's been sold off. We'd have just enough space to spread out without all the hassle of a big place. We might get us a ruminant or two just to keep the grass and brush under control."

"Not cattle, though. Cattle are big and scary."

"How about goats?"

"Pygmy goats. Small enough that I could take them in a fight if it came to that."

He nodded. "Perfect."

"Does it have a big old barn?"

"Sure does. Fully wired. It'll make a great garage for me."

"You've already got a pretty great garage in town," she said.

"Yeah, but that's my work garage. I need a home garage, too, that I can tinker around in."

"How many bedrooms?"

"Four. One of them could be turned into a writing room for you. It's even got a window seat."

Annalisa sighed with pleasure. Casually she said, "We'll need another one for a nursery."

He frowned. "Like for plants and stuff? That doesn't seem practical. I'll build you a greenhouse if you want to garden."

"I mean the other kind of nursery."

He froze with a cracker halfway to his mouth, and the cheese slice fell off onto the plate. It seemed like a long time before he spoke again.

"You mean, like, for a baby? A human baby? Are you saying...?"

She laughed. "Yes, a human baby. Our baby. I'm pregnant, Javi."

His eyes were wide now, a little stunned, but he was smiling. "Wow," he said. "You hear that, Lefty? I'm going to be a father."

Lefty thumped his tail against the porch without raising his head.

Javi dropped the cracker and reached across the table. He took Annalisa's hands in his and gripped them tight.

"I'm so happy," he said, his voice shaking. "I didn't think it was possible for anyone to be this happy. Oh, Annalisa, I love you so much."

Annalisa swallowed over a lump of soreness in her throat. "I love you, too, Javi," she whispered.

Javi's eyes were shining. "I feel like I've been waiting for something all my life, and now I finally have it, and it's even better than I dreamed it would be."

"So do I," Annalisa said.

It was worth the wait.

* * * * *

WESTERN

Rugged men looking for love...

Available Next Month

That Maverick Of Mine Kathy Douglass
Courting The Cowgirl Cheryl Harper

....

Fortune's Faux Engagement Carrie Nichols
The Rodeo Cowboy's Return Cathy McDavid

....

LOVE INSPIRED

A K-9 Christmas Reunion Lisa Carter
Bonding With The Cowboy's Daughter Lisa Jordan

Keep reading for an excerpt of a new title
from the Special Edition series,
A FAIRY-TAIL ENDING by Catherine Mann

Prologue

Cocoa the Caring Canine

Did you know that dogs can sense magic? Well, it's true.

Enchantment releases a distinctive sugary smell in the air that only our canine olfactory nerves can detect. That aroma is even more enticing than the barbecue in progress next door.

If I'm having an off day with my Labrador nose, luckily real-life fairy tales also release a hum into the air. And I'm guessing you know all about our enhanced hearing since we can detect that doorbell ring even in a deep slumber...

On the second floor...

Burrowed underneath three layers of covers.

Compared to alerting about a ringing doorbell or smoking grill, sensing the musicality and perfume of magic is easy-peasy.

For those of you who are tuning in to my blog for the first time, my name is Cocoa, and I'm all about watching for magic everywhere I go. Somebody has to make sure that not even one note or a single whiff slips by unnoticed.

Unutilized.

Making the most of every magical opportunity is especially important to me because I'm a service dog. A chocolate Labrador retriever, mobility assistance dog to be exact. My whole life is dedicated to the job. Now, don't worry for even a minute about my day being devoted to tasks, because I love to work. I mean really, really love it.

The best day of my entire existence came when the facility where I trained for two years—yes, two whole years—matched me with a forever person to help. Lottie. She's only six, and she uses a wheelchair because she was born with something humans call spina bifida. I can't explain it like a doctor. I just know there's a place in her spine that didn't close up right when she was inside her mom.

So I help Lottie. I go to school with her and pick things up, like her pencils, when she drops them. I push elevator buttons with my paws—I like putting extra oomph into that cue. I lay over her lap and press if she's having nerve pain—or if she's sad. Don't we all need a hug every now and then? I can even pull the covers up for her with my mouth.

How cool is that?

When Lottie's asleep, sometimes I help her mama—Isobel—when she is sad. Usually when she curls up in her reading chair, those tears start leaking. I'm not sure if it's because she's tired or worried about Lottie or sad that Lottie's dad doesn't live with them. The reason doesn't matter to me. I'm all about the solution that I offer best. More of those special hugs that are designed to press just right.

But lately, I'm worried I may not have enough cues up my sleeve to give this family. The last time I went with Lottie to the doctor, things got a lot more complicated. She needs all the magic I can sniff out. The doctor says she needs a new kidney.

My sniffer also tells me she needs it sooner than they think.

Chapter One

Who wouldn't be charmed by a man who dressed up as a swashbuckler for a child's sixth birthday party? And as a single mom, Isobel Dalton certainly wasn't immune.

Besides, she figured she was due a bit of covert drooling over the firefighter wearing an eye patch and red head scarf while folding himself into a tiny chair for a tea party. Her friend had gone above and beyond today.

Cash Warner, aka charming pirate guy, lifted his little pink cup in a toast. "Ahoy, matey!"

"Yo-ho-ho!" her daughter Lottie echoed, dark pigtails sticking out from under her paper pirate hat.

The rest of the children at the other tables followed with a jumbled chorus of "Surrender the booty" and "Shiver me timbers!"

Isobel pressed a hand to her mouth to hold back a laugh, thankful for the happy distraction from the upcoming reading of her grandmother's will. Gran. Her rock. Gone for one month.

But Gran would have been the first to insist this birthday be celebrated. Lottie had requested a pirate tea party, and somehow the plan had come together. The logistics had been a challenge, because this celebration wasn't hosted at a park or in a family backyard. This kiddie get-together was being held in the activity room of a physical therapy rehabilitation clinic where her daughter received both physical and occupational therapy for the effects of spina bifida.

Lottie had invited children she'd bonded with over the years at the center. Like her best friend Jasper, who carried a different superhero lunchbox each week. A premature delivery had left him with cerebral palsy. And newcomer Isla, who'd lost a leg in a car accident, but given how quickly she was adapting to the prosthetic, she was spending less time inside these four walls.

Isobel adjusted the pirate scarf around her head, easing her ponytail back over her shoulder. She and Lottie had spent endless hours a week here since her daughter was born with the condition that affected her spinal cord. Some of them were painful hours. Others more uplifting and liberating. She would never gain full use of her legs, but thanks to her service dog Cocoa and the staff here, Lottie increased her independence daily.

Medical equipment beeped and shooshed lowly in the background. Undisturbed, the chocolate lab rested beside the wheelchair with her head on her paws, immobile but ever ready for a task. Staff were positioned throughout the commons area, albeit wearing party hats to match the children's. Chicken nuggets were labeled "cannonballs," and fruit skewers were held together by miniature plastic swords. Placemats resembled treasure maps for a hunt that would take place at the end. The sheet cake was decorated like an ocean and sported a chocolate ship on top. A treasure chest overflowed with party favors...

And no matter how much Isobel looked around the room, her gaze continued to land on the muscular firefighter giving Captain Jack Sparrow a run for his money.

"What did the ocean say to the pirate?" he asked, a parrot puppet on his hand.

Lottie's arm shot up. "Nothing. It just waved."

"That's absolutely right, matey." He passed a mesh bag of candy doubloons into her eager hands.

Cash had come to the rehab center about six months ago after being injured on the job battling a housefire. He'd rescued five of the six family members before a falling beam had shattered a leg and an arm. His journey to recovery had been difficult. And not only from the broken bones and the painful skin grafts over his burns. She could tell the memories still haunted him, even if he refused to speak about that time in more than cursory statements.

Although no one would guess at the moment. "How much does it cost for a pirate to get his ears pierced? A buck an ear."

Silence met that joke. The pun seemed to have flown right over their heads.

"Get it?" he explained, tugging each ear that sported a clip-on gold hoop. "A buck...an...ear. 'Buccaneer' is another name for 'pirate.'"

Realization spread over each little face until giggles

erupted, mixed with exaggerated boos from Jasper at the corny joke.

Lottie waggled her fingers again, looking too cute for words in her costume—a vest and sash with loose black-and-white striped pants. "I got one. Wanna hear?"

Cash tipped a salute in her direction. "Go for it."

"Where does a pirate put his trash?" She only paused for a minute as if rushing to make sure no one else got to say the punchline she'd been practicing all morning. "In a garrrrrbage bag."

At the laughs from the rest of the children at the clinic, Lottie beamed, rocking from side to side in her chair until her napkin slithered to the floor.

Cocoa promptly plucked it up, the paper trailing like a checkered flag from her mouth, and dropped it back onto Lottie's lap. Lottie plucked a dog treat from the pouch clipped to her waist.

With an all-in drive for her job, Cocoa thrived on picking up everything from a dropped pencil to a favorite doll. Cocoa could even tug on socks. Sure, Isobel could help with these tasks. She was Lottie's mom, after all. But her daughter battled for every bit of independence, so much already having been taken from her. Cocoa's aid gave Lottie that freedom.

A priceless gift.

On her best days, her daughter could maneuver with the assistance of a walker and leg braces. Others? Lottie needed her wheelchair. And always by her side, good and bad days, her service dog Cocoa.

Who also happened to be the "voice" of Isobel's newest blog. Her freelance writing allowed her flexibility to be present for all the appointments, a benefit she did not take for granted. Especially since her ex-husband spent so much time on the road as a truck driver. And they desperately needed his insurance.

Since her divorce and reclaiming her maiden name, her life in Montana has been filled with work and her daughter Lottie—until a surprise friendship developed between her and Cash over lunch in the cafeteria. He'd sat next to her one afternoon when the place had been packed, then the next day even though there had been empty seats available. A pattern began.

A pattern she would miss deeply now that his recovery was drawing to a close. She was glad for him. Truly.

He certainly looked fit and ready to return to work.

Her shoulder was jostled by Jasper's mom as she angled nearer to whisper, "Cash is yummy, don't you agree?"

Isobel glanced over quickly. Could the woman be interested? Isobel's stomach flipped, then settled as she remembered that the young mother was happily married to an art teacher who'd given Lottie an assortment of the drawing supplies, along with the promise of lessons.

"Of course I agree," Isobel said. There was no denying the obvious.

"Then what's stopping you from making a move?" Anna elbowed her. "You're single. He's single... I think?"

From the other side, another mom, Evelyn, an executive who always brought a full briefcase, added, "He most certainly is. I did a deep dive on his social media, and he's single." She winked. "I was only checking for my niece, of course."

The full-time father across from her laughed. "Make sure you get his number before these ladies scoop him up for their single relatives."

Heat crawled over Isobel's cheeks, but she knew insisting she had no room for a relationship would make no difference to determined, well-meaning matchmakers. So she settled for a more benign answer. "Thanks, but we're just friends."

Good friends.

Friends who spent weekends hanging out together.

Evelyn snorted. "What kind of magic do you wield that makes a *friend* dress up for a kids' birthday party? Because I would pay good money to get my husband in that getup. And not for a kiddie party, if you know what I mean."

Isobel shrugged. How could she explain the simple truth? "He's a great guy, no question."

Cash's friendship had been a godsend to her over the past six months. She looked forward to their dinners together after rehab sessions. Movie outings. Having a plus-one for a big rodeo fundraiser for the clinic. And now he was restored to health. He would be moving on with his life, and she wanted that for him even as nerves made her ill with impending dread of the first time she would pull up in the parking lot knowing that he wasn't inside.

She knew their relationship would never be more than friendship. Her bruised heart couldn't handle more. But she was lonely. Her marriage had been lonely. Life after her divorce wasn't any different.

Her ex-husband loved Lottie and tried his best to spend time with her. Except he traveled for work so very much, and his job as a truck driver brought in decent money. And with Lottie's medical bills they definitely needed every extra penny. Her career as a blogger was taking off, particularly her "Cocoa the Caring Canine" writings, keeping her all the busier. Which didn't leave much time for a social life.

Cash's friendship these past months had been a sanity saver.

A friendship she could no longer afford to even fantasize about taking further, as Cash would soon be moving to another fire station far from her. Today, she needed to focus on her child and getting through the Zoom call with the attorney about her grandmother's will. An impending conversation that made her eyes sting already.

But she would face that as she faced every day now. Strong and alone.

For the past six months, Cash Warner had counted down the days until he could say goodbye to this rehab clinic, put the pain behind him and reclaim his old life.

Except, now that the time approached, his gut knotted with something he couldn't name. Something that insisted he wasn't ready to put this place in his rearview mirror and reenter the work world. But there wasn't a choice. He was finished here and would return to his job in three weeks, relocating to a new department on the other side of the state.

He would say goodbye not only to this place but to Isobel and Lottie…and of course Cocoa. The knot in his gut twisted tighter.

In the clinic courtyard, Cash shoved aside the unease. He'd offered to keep Lottie and Cocoa occupied while Isobel cleaned away the party mayhem.

He scooped up the tennis ball and tossed it for the chocolate Labrador retriever. Cocoa sprinted ahead, past a fountain, leapt and snagged the ball out of the air on its first bounce. The leggy canine trotted over to Lottie in her wheelchair under the concrete water fountain.

Giggling, the little girl plucked the toy from her lab. "Good, Cocoa. Now go get it."

Lottie tossed the ball into a bush, and the dog sprang into action again, pouncing and foraging. They could keep this up all day serving the dual purpose of exercising her service dog and increasing Lottie's arm strength. Cash had learned that every task here at the clinic had a purpose, pushing toward independence.

Man, he was going to miss this little girl and her mom.

At least he'd gotten to help with the party today, a small thanks for the way their friendship had saved his sanity as he'd recovered from the injuries in the five-alarm fire. His wounds were minor compared to what his fellow firefighter, his best friend Elijah, had suffered. Elijah had lingered for five days before dying from the burns that covered eighty percent of his body.

Even thinking about it filled Cash's senses with that awful scent of smoke…and his friend.

He swept his bandana off his head and stuffed it into his back pocket. "Did you get everything you wanted for your birthday, kiddo?"

"Everything. And a lot more." Pitch. Wait. Beyond the low brick wall, cars rumbled in and out of the parking lot. "It was the best party ever. Thanks bunches and bunches for all the new toys for Cocoa. And I really like the matching collar and T-shirt you got for Cocoa and me. But most of all, thanks for being a pirate. That made Mommy really happy too."

"My pleasure, kiddo." He shot a quick glance over to the picture window showcasing the moms and dads helping Isobel clean up and load gifts. Isobel bustled at the speed of light, her trim legs in yoga pants and an overlong T-shirt with a pirate dog image. She had a scarf tied around her head, swashbuckler style, big hoop earrings glinted, and her thick ponytail trailed over her shoulder stopping just shy of her—

Nope. Not going there. He tore his gaze away. He'd offered to help, and she'd asked him to keep Lottie entertained for just a few minutes—easy enough. "Glad I was still around to attend."

Pitch. Wait. "Will we get to see you now that you're better?"

"Of course, but when I go back to work, they're sending me to a new fire station in a new city."

Lottie chewed her bottom lip. "Oh, right. Mommy told me. I kinda hoped she was wrong. We got firemen here too, you know. But I guess now that you can run and stuff, you'll want to do things with your old friends."

"Hey," he knelt in front of her. "I love playing ball with you and Cocoa. But I also have to pay my bills, which means going where the job sends me."

For as long as he could remember, he'd wanted to be a firefighter. Every Halloween growing up, he wore variations of the same theme. His family hadn't had much money, so the costumes had been homemade from clothes around the house. A two-liter soda bottle had been repurposed into an oxygen tank on his back. Another year he'd carried a big red cardboard fire hydrant, and his dad wore a paper bag house with crimson tissue paper flames. Another year he'd made a fire engine out of an old box. He'd colored every inch of it in great detail for weeks leading up to October 31. He'd been crushed when it started raining and the box fell apart.

But as much as he yearned to be back on the job making a difference, he would miss Isobel, Lottie and Cocoa. The counselor—mandatory after an accident like the one he'd suffered on the job—had asked if they represented the security of the rehab facility.

He'd bristled then, still did. He wasn't *afraid* to go back to work. In fact, he owed it to his partner, who had died in that accident, who hadn't gotten a second chance like him. But Cash hadn't been ready to delve into the reasons why he wasn't ready to leave the rehab center—not for the counselor and not even for himself.

Lottie dropped the tennis ball beside her footrests. Cocoa huffed and flopped onto the ground beside it, drawing Cash's gaze over to Lottie's furrowed face. "Aw, kiddo, no need to look so sad. Is there something else wrong? Are you not feeling good? Maybe too much cake?"

She shook her head. "*I'm* okay."

"Are you sure?" He dragged a lounge chair over and sat in front of her, searching her wide blue eyes. "You look sad, way too sad for a birthday girl."

She picked at the loose black-and-white striped pants. "I'm just worried about my mommy."

"Your mom?" Concern nipped at him. He thought about Isobel setting up the party, now cleaning up, on top of all the time she spent writing. She looked tired. Overworked maybe? People assumed she had it easy working from home as a blogger, but he knew the long hours she put in to make a success of her "Cocoa the Caring Canine" brand. "What's going on?"

Spring sun beaming down around her, Lottie leaned closer and whispered, "She was crying this morning. She tried to pretend like she wasn't, but I saw her wipe her eyes and her nose with a tissue."

Crying? Now that wasn't like Isobel at all, and it tore him up to hear as much. As far as he'd seen, she was the eternal optimist. "You're a sweet kid to care about your mom. Hopefully it wasn't anything big." He made a mental note to let her know her kid was concerned while, at the same time, trying to keep Lottie's worries at bay until her mother could address them. "My mom cries at the drop of a hat."

Her eyebrows pinched together. "What does that mean? Drop of a hat?"

Lottie conversed with adults so easily, sometimes he forgot to speak in simpler terms. "It means that she cries easily. Like as easily and fast as a hat falling to the floor."

"That's a silly thing to say." Lottie scrunched her nose. "Why not say she cries as easily as I forget to brush my teeth?"

"That a really good question." And a really good way of phrasing things. Maybe the kid was destined to be a writer like her mother.

"Besides, my mommy doesn't cry when a hat falls or when I forget to brush my teeth." She tugged the end of one of her braids, a self-soothing habit of hers he'd noticed. "I overheard her tell my daddy she has to be strong 'cause of all my doctor visits. That made me sad."

His heart squeezed in his chest. This kid sure got to him. "I'm sorry you overheard something like that."

"So when I saw my mommy crying this morning, I knew it had to be very bad. Can you help her?"

He wanted to. Very much. But he didn't have a clue where to start. "I think you need to talk to your mom about it. It's not good to keep your feelings bottled up... Uhm, by bottled up, I mean keep them all inside."

"Oh. Do you let yours out?"

Was the kid listening in on his counseling session? Because her admonition sure sounded like Dr. Thomas 101. "I thought we were talking about your mom?"

"Can you help her?"

"I intend to try." When had he been able to say no to this cute kid? That's what landed him in a pirate costume at a tea party. He grinned, imagining the grief he would get over those photos if Elijah saw—

His chest went tight and a roar started in his ears. When would he stop looking for his friend around every corner?

Cash cleared his throat. "What do you say we get some water for Cocoa?"

Lottie nodded. "And while she's drinking, I can wipe the slobber off the tennis ball. Yuck."

She wiped her palms on her pants.

The dark cloud over his mood edged away a bit. Lottie had that knack. Great kid. But children weren't in the cards for him. Since his breakup, he was committed only to his career. Dangers on the job had put too much stress on his relationship. His girlfriend had left. She hadn't even issued an ultimatum. She'd vowed she loved him too much to ask him to give up the profession he lived for. He'd offered to give it up anyway. She'd insisted he would resent her. And she left. That was it. No tears or shouting. Just complete silence.

His gaze darted back to the picture window view of Isobel, her hair swishing as she loaded gifts into a wagon. Her face was tipped to the other parents, and she smiled at something. Even from a distance, he knew instantly how her bluish-green eyes would sparkle and that a husky laugh would follow.

He remembered well the first time he noticed both. She was reading a romance novel, amused by one thing or another. He never knew what, only that he couldn't look away from her. He stared for so long that she looked up over the top of her page and her gaze held his. Just as he started to apologize, her smile went wider and she'd plucked another book from her bag and offered it to him. Unable to resist, he'd taken it, read it from cover to cover, trading it for another the next time he'd seen her.

Everything about Isobel then and now was full of light. Yes, he enjoyed basking in the glow she brought, even to the simplest tasks like adding sprinkles to a milkshake or watching a sunset. But he had a wealth of darkness in him, not just from the divorce. The accident haunted him.

And he refused to add one more weight to Isobel's already complicated life.

 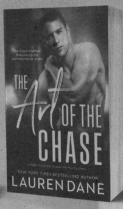